Praise for *A Traitorous Heart*

"Queer French princesses who kiss girls in the garden? A bi for bi romance with a swoony king and a ferocious lady-in-waiting? A widowed Queen obsessed with dark magic and the dangerous secret society trying to stop her? Some of the best banter and romance scenes I've ever read? Yes, please! Lushly written and brilliantly researched, this dazzling fantasy romance pulls you into a galloping story of power and the very real people behind it. *A Traitorous Heart* has it all and will leave readers eager for Erin Cotter's next brilliant book!"

—JAMIE PACTON,
author of *The Vermilion Emporium*, *Lucky Girl*, and *The Life and (Medieval) Times of Kit Sweetly*

Praise for *By Any Other Name*

"A well-balanced, well-researched dramedy, Cotter's quippy, heart-wrenching debut is ideal for fans of Mackenzi Lee and F. T. Lukens. To read or not to read? There's really no question: pick this one up."
—*Kirkus Reviews*

"A delight from start to finish—highly recommended."
—JENN BENNETT,
critically acclaimed author of *Alex, Approximately*

A Traitorous Heart

ALSO BY ERIN COTTER

By Any Other Name

A Traitorous Heart

ERIN COTTER

SIMON & SCHUSTER BFYR

NEW YORK AMSTERDAM/ANTWERP LONDON
TORONTO SYDNEY NEW DELHI

SIMON & SCHUSTER BFYR

An imprint of Simon & Schuster Children's Publishing Division
1230 Avenue of the Americas, New York, New York 10020

This book is a work of fiction. Any references to historical events, real people,
or real places are used fictitiously. Other names, characters, places, and events
are products of the author's imagination, and any resemblance to actual events or
places or persons, living or dead, is entirely coincidental.

Text © 2025 by Erin Cotter
Jacket illustration © 2025 by Mona Finden
Jacket design by Krista Vossen

SIMON & SCHUSTER BOOKS FOR YOUNG READERS
and related marks are trademarks of Simon & Schuster, LLC.
For information about special discounts for bulk purchases, please contact
Simon & Schuster Special Sales at 1-866-506-1949 or business@simonandschuster.com.
The Simon & Schuster Speakers Bureau can bring authors to your live event.
For more information or to book an event, contact the Simon & Schuster Speakers Bureau
at 1-866-248-3049 or visit our website at www.simonspeakers.com.
Interior design by Hilary Zarycky
The text for this book was set in Sabon.
Manufactured in the United States of America
First Edition
2 4 6 8 10 9 7 5 3 1
CIP data for this book is available from the Library of Congress.
ISBN 9781665960809
ISBN 9781665961219 (ebook)

To all the girls who were told they wanted too much—
keep asking for more

And to Jess, my first reader, my oldest friend

A Traitorous Heart

June 1572

JUST OUTSIDE PARIS

CHAPTER ONE

I T IS A truth universally acknowledged that a gentleman creeping about a ball uninvited is up to no good.

The château is ablaze, light knifing through the forest's dark heart beyond. One can almost spy the walls of Paris just north for all the tallow and oil burning away the shadows. Tables groan on bronzed legs beneath soaring ceilings, their glistening meats and cakes barely touched. Thrice I've counted the servants heaving out fresh great wine barrels from the kitchens, their faces pink and damp, expressions teetering someplace between exhaustion and despair. It is well beyond midnight and the court dances on, toes bloody and blistered in their gilded slippers. Still the young king roars for more.

This ball is one of so many, they all run together like a long, boring illness. One demanded we dress like animals, another as pagan gods. At the latest, the king and his princely brothers snarled and galloped on all fours to see who could frighten the most ladies. Oncle reminded me five times that kicking the king of France was still a crime no matter how much he deserved it. The king only stopped when his mother suggested it would be more fun to shoot songbirds from her rosebushes.

Such is the way of the French court, a place run by boys

and their egos and women and their wits. Everyone knows the Queen Mother, Catherine de' Medici, truly wears the crown, but we must pretend that is not the case by satisfying King Charles's whims whenever he shouts them into the sky.

Truth be told, this unknown gentleman is the most interesting thing that's happened to me for weeks.

Is this sad? Yes. Perhaps even a little bit pathetic? Also yes. But a girl must find her fun somewhere.

I watch him prowl through the seething ballroom. His clothes are finely made, if a season or two out of fashion. It's his shoes that betray his true rank—ever so slightly scuffed, the leather water-stained.

I sit up straighter, suddenly wide-awake.

I wonder which royal guard he paid off, which one he blackmailed or conned into looking the other direction so he could slip in unseen?

I caress the familiar pins in my hair, fighting the itch to slide them free. I should find Oncle. This is what he says to do. With a winning smile, he'll slip away from whomever he's charming to dirty his hands. Later in our family's private apartments, I'll cajole him into telling me how he caught the man, how he saved the night from disaster.

He doesn't like to tell me these stories. He says they give me ideas. And God forbid a lady has ideas.

The man pauses at the unguarded corridor at the back of the ballroom. I lean forward, no one at my empty table to notice my interest. He disappears inside after a single glance over his shoulder.

My eyes slice to the empty seat beside King Charles, my chest clenching. Sneaking into a busy ballroom is one thing, but trespassing into the quiet gardens is quite another. It's time to find Oncle. But a quick sweep of the room reveals he's gone, vanished without a word. *Even though he promised you he wouldn't leave.*

A sharp breath pulls through my teeth. I shove the thought away, trying not to let it bother me.

Oncle wouldn't want me to do this. But if he's gone, then I've no choice but to trail the man myself.

Sometimes being useful feels like being wanted, and I'm the only person left sitting alone.

The ball's animal heat disappears in the stone corridor. A breeze sighs past, damp and redolent of roses from the garden beyond. Most of the torches have already sputtered out. The man makes no effort to hide himself, so I don't either.

"No one would ever see you and see a threat," Oncle said when he first slid the pins with their hidden blades into my hair. Our eyes met in the mirror and his mouth quirked. "But they should."

I loosen one of my pins now and follow the man into the greenery.

The garden is a riot of shadows: blue, violet, and grey all smudged together. There's no music save for the soft rustle of the forest beyond, the gentle lapping of the moat against the stone wall fencing us in.

Then, a barely there sigh.

The man whips his head toward the noise. His hand twitches—

I'm on him before he touches his weapon.

I strike his temple with my still-sheathed blade. He slithers to the ground with a soft gasp. Before he can get a good look at me, the loose ribbon from my gown pocket is around his eyes. Then I tie his wrists with another ribbon and his legs with a third.

I dearly do love a gown with pockets. So useful!

Now if only I could convince Oncle to let me carry rope instead.

"Godless—royal—scum!" the man wheezes.

I cup his cheek and smile, all of Oncle's rules and warnings forgotten. "*Mon cher*, you must be more vulgar than that to shock me."

I grab his bound legs and drag him to the wall. It is difficult work—he's got at least several dozen pounds on me and the rose briars are rather thick and prickly—but eventually I get him up the wall that separates the gardens from the moat.

The moat glitters, deadly and deep. Wind shakes the forest just beyond, low branches twisting across the surface as if to grab the prisoner. The scent of the stagnant water cuts through the sweet roses. He starts crying softly.

"Don't be afraid," I say. "Can't say you'll love where I'm sending you, but there are worse places."

"There are places for people like you with us." His words are so quick and low, I nearly miss them. "The Valois family must be stopped! Their reign is a wolf feasting on the French people! We'd take you, even though you're a woman!"

There's a pang under my ribs. I ignore it and lift the man

higher. "Tell your master the princess sends her regards, but regretfully, she is occupied at the moment."

His mouth drops open—shocked that I know his target—but before he can ask me more questions, I cut the bindings on his legs and shove him over the wall.

At the enormous splash, a torch flares brighter in the chatelet guarding the drawbridge. Then there's the distant murmur of male voices and the whoosh of more torches sputtering to life.

I disappear before their light catches me. The would-be assassin won't drown—as long as he can swim, which he should have considered carefully before infiltrating the Château de Fontainebleau and its fearsome moat—but he won't be escaping with his bound hands anytime soon either. The royal guards will catch and question him, and that shall be that. If he's a decent liar, he might even walk away with all his bits.

I sheathe my blade and tuck the pin back into my hair. It's time to find Margot. If an intruder figured out the best place to find her would be in the gardens, then it won't be long before the court does as well.

I walk until I see a tremendous boxwood cut into the likeness of a lion trembling. Pausing beside it, I clear my throat.

The boxwood goes still. And then a frosty voice demands, "Who disturbs us?"

"Only me, madame. May I have a word?"

The bushes tremble, and out steps Marguerite de Valois, Princess of France, with a pretty girl shielded behind her skirts. Upon seeing me, the princess sighs and heaves her eyes heavenward.

I curtsy to her—more for the girl's sake than for the princess's. It's been years since Margot has allowed me to pay her any sort of royal deference. "But it's the proper greeting for a princess!" I protested when she demanded I stop curtsying. She had yanked me up wearing that mischievous smirk I've grown to know all too well. "Yes, but it's no way to greet your dearest friend."

"Jac, you scared me half to death!" Margot says.

"Someone is snooping around the gardens. Perhaps it's time to return to the ball? You've been busy for quite a while," I say, pushing on the final word just a little.

Margot pouts. "You're no fun at all, but I see your point. Make me presentable?"

I straighten her hair and dab carmine on her mouth from the tiny pot she keeps close for occasions such as these. Satisfied, she turns back to the girl. The two share a final kiss and whispered conversation that ends with a giggle. The girl gets up and leaves. I swallow, keeping my gaze politely on my feet, not wanting to know whom Margot has beguiled tonight.

Margot stares after her longingly, freshly painted lips pressed together. "*Mon dieu*, I love the countryside. Can't find girls like that in Paris."

I force a laugh and pat her shoulder consolingly. "You aren't looking in the right places in Paris then."

Her face darkens. "It's difficult to find someone to kiss in the city when your mother never lets you leave her sights."

She tilts her face toward the moon, a delicate crescent nestled against the blue-black clouds. A cool breeze rustles the treetops beyond the walls, caressing the nape of my neck and its loose curls. It beckons like a crooked finger. An invitation to explore the world on the other side, a promise of more.

Margot heaves an unladylike sigh, and I know she feels it too.

"Let's get on with it, then." She offers me her arm and we return to the brilliant ballroom. With our dark hair swept up with golden pins, only the clinking sapphires sewn on her bodice readily distinguish Marguerite, Princess of France, from me, her loyal lady-in-waiting.

I watch the heads turn as we arrive, see how Margot's presence ripples through the crowd like a body tossed in a lake. The suitors swarm her in their peacock-bright doublets, with hungry smiles and eager hands. So close, I can almost pretend they're there for me. When I'm beside Margot, the entire world feels at my fingertips, the shine of Catherine de' Medici's gorgeous youngest daughter spilling over me just by being near.

"We could be sisters," Margot had said today as we beheld ourselves in the grand mirrors before the ball began.

We could be. Were it not for the, oh, let's say, about a hundred ranks of nobility separating her royal Valois titles from my own lowborn birth. I bite my lip and push back the old urge to tell Margot more. How I not only spotted the assassin but apprehended him myself.

"Secrets stay among family," Oncle said in a sharp voice the one and only time I had asked if I might show Margot how to hurl my knives. He gripped my arm so hard, it bruised. "Don't you *ever* forget that."

One of Margot's suitors stops us with an elaborate bow, just a hairbreadth above what would be appropriate for her brother, His Royal Highness King Charles IX. "Madame, would you do me the honor of a dance?" He extends one leather-gloved hand to her.

Margot considers the hand for a long, long moment. The man's fingers tremble with nerves. I bite back a laugh and turn it into a polite cough. Margot catches my eye and winks wickedly before yanking me closer.

"That depends. What could you possibly offer me that my dear Jacqueline cannot?"

The man's throat bobs, searching for words. Another gentleman steps smoothly in front of him, his hand slipping about Margot's without asking. He brings her knuckles to his lips.

"Dance with me instead and find out," he promises against her skin.

Margot breaks into a delighted laugh and allows herself to be swept away, leaving the dejected suitor behind with nothing but an air kiss. The young man's cheeks flush bright red and he flees the room without even inventing an excuse.

He never stood a chance. But he doesn't know that the suitor with Margot in his arms doesn't stand a chance either. Even still, watching them waltz makes my vision spot. Once, Margot and I were the lovers in the garden. It's for the best our romance is behind us, but seeing her in the arms of this unworthy man still fills me with a sour, sulky feeling.

I'm glad Margot is enjoying herself—and has been, for hours—but I'm not, and now that the thrill of the would-be assassin is over, all I want to do is flop on my bed, but I can't. Not until King Charles decides the night is over.

I turn away, ready to spend the rest of the night alone, when a long, horrible scream pierces the noise.

The entire ballroom pivots toward the throne. A woman sobs inconsolably, half in the king's lap. The music screeches to a halt. The crowd surges, confused and alarmed. I search the room for Margot, hairpin already in hand. My mind races through the potential threats.

I caught one would-be assassin tonight, but what if there was another? One I missed?

I move to unsheathe my blade, but someone catches my wrist, stopping me. Oncle stares down, his mouth a serious slash.

"The queen is dead. We must leave."

CHAPTER TWO

TELL ME AGAIN why the death of the queen of Navarre—a kingdom smaller than a garden—makes us rush back to Paris?"

Vicomte Gabriel d'Argenson-Aunis stops sharpening his dagger and gives me a pointed stare that would stop the heart of a lesser person. I meet his stare head-on and slouch, propping up my stockinged feet on his velvet carriage bench. His look turns to my feet, to the muddy boots discarded on the floor below, and his mouth pulls into a disagreeable expression.

I wiggle my toes just to irritate him. "Well?"

"Queen Jeanne of Navarre was an important French ally. The peace she brokered with the Valois royal family, fragile as it was, helped stave off the bloodshed between the Huguenots and the Catholics at the border. Now that she's dead, I don't think it'll hold."

France has been at war with itself as long as I've lived. A German preacher's fierce words caught fire and spread, saying there were better ways to worship God. Thousands, if not millions, of people agreed with him. France is not a place that embraces change, and the Valois kings resented the challenge to the Catholic church—the font from which they'd drawn their royal power for centuries. People began to whisper that perhaps God did not pick kings. Perhaps a man's actions mattered more than his royal blood. Maybe the Catholic kings did not deserve to be kings at all. The slaughter since has been like a sow turning on her young, France itself wounded and bleeding in a dozen places because of it.

He rubs his furrowed brow. "Navarre may be the size of a thistle, but it is a Huguenot thistle stuck squarely betwixt Catholic Spain and France. The new king of Navarre is only nineteen—too young, I fear, to handle the situation he's inheriting. I must go to Paris to make sure nothing turns violent."

I sit up straighter, heart beating faster. "So you're going to Paris to nanny a fledgling king."

He flashes a razor-thin smile. "I'm making sure no one pushes him from his nest before he can fly."

Rumor says that Gabriel d'Argenson-Aunis is the most dangerous man in France. They say he sleeps with a poisoned knife beneath his pillows. That he has dogs to sniff out the racing hearts of liars and traitors. That he could, without looking for more than a second, transcribe hidden ciphers in no less than seven languages. That he knows twenty ways to kill a man, each more excruciating than the last.

To the French court, the vicomte is the Valois spymaster. Their weaving spider whose webs ensnare their enemies before they can endanger the royal family's power. People believe his skills were honed on the brutal fronts of religious wars, where the lives of an entire battalion depend on a note sliding into the palm of the right person, where a single messenger hawk escaping the burst of bullets could turn the tides of power.

But I know the truth; Gabriel's prowess is not battle trained so much as sired by shadows.

He answers not only to the Valois kings and queens of France but to a higher power, a court of intrigue whose influence spreads beyond borders and digs deeper than the blood-soaked French soil. He answers to the anonymous men that would see the world hale and whole and not torn asunder by struggles for power: the Societas Solis.

Let the Valois court whisper that Gabriel d'Argenson-Aunis is the most dangerous man in France.

It's true.

I know because my oncle's taught me all his tricks.

I push my feet under his thigh, determined to goad him into telling me more. "Are you worried about assassins? Or something else?"

He scowls and pulls away. "Jac, your feet are ice."

"And if *someone* had let me fetch my furs before we left, then *someone* would not have to be my personal warming stone for this journey."

His mouth twitches. Anyone else would assume the movement means he's cross, but I know he's trying hard not to smile. "Is that so, dear Niece?" Margot moans about long carriage rides with her family, but I love them. It's one of the only times I have Oncle all to myself.

"You're avoiding my question."

Oncle inspects the edge on his blade, not meeting my eyes. "Assassins would be simple to handle. The ego of a young man is less manageable. And that goes double if he's king." He sets the blade aside and rubs his brow again. I note the fine lines around his eyes, the spreading silver at his temples. Oncle has spent most of my life away. Away in wars, away working for the royal family, away with the Societas Solis. The queen of Navarre's death means more sleepless nights, more work needed to keep the Valois family happy while keeping the Societas Solis's schemes secret.

A spark ignites in my chest, so bright, it's blinding.

"Let me help, then." I mean for it to sound commanding but instead it's a breathless rush. "Please. We both know I can be useful. Think of what I did last night."

This is what I've been waiting for. A chance to influence the politics always slithering beneath the court's soirées. A chance to prove I'm capable of more than looking lovely at a party. I won't be left behind as Oncle stalks the shadows for secrets or bite my tongue when Margot asks one too many questions about my childhood.

The spark leaps from my control, the brightness racing through my limbs, making me fidget. I can imagine it so clearly, 'tis as though I've already lived the scene. Me creeping through the Palais du Louvre after dark, lighter than ever in breeches instead of skirts, quick fingers picking the locked strongboxes and flipping through illicit letters, sniffing out secrets just like the hounds I trained back at our ancestral estate.

Me, a member of the Societas Solis. Just like Oncle.

He stills. The air catches in my chest, and I hold it back, letting the pressure build until there's a roaring in my ears.

"The man in the moat was a clever bit of work, I'll give you that. He was alive, which let us question him. His assassination attempt was clumsy and unlikely to succeed, but he did show us a more concerning problem: a royal guard was bribed to let him inside, which means one of the guardsmen has turned traitor."

I lean closer. "What I did was helpful, then?"

Oncle sits back, frowning. "At the very least, you prevented a public scandal."

I hate the way my pulse stutters at his frown. His praise, his approving nod, means so much to me. "Which is a good thing, is it not?"

Oncle draws out a filthy length of something from his pocket and twines it about his hands. I recognize the ribbon I used to bind the would-be assassin. The delicate pink is stained algae green alongside a darker blush, like blood.

"The assassin talked a lot. And no one would have believed that a woman had bested him were it not for this." The ribbon coils around Oncle's hands, a serpent ready to strike. "This ribbon is silk, which is not remarkable on its own, but there are also silver roses embroidered on its length." He lifts a brow, both of us remembering how I had demanded the ornamentation be added on when the dressmaker came for my summer wardrobe fitting.

His voice grows darker, the dirty silk twisting faster. "Only the wealthiest tailors import silk like this, and few can embroider a delicate pattern with this skill. Which means the ribbon could have come from one of two shops in Paris where *only* ladies of the royal court buy their wardrobes. Consequently, not only did it seem entirely possible that the assassin wasn't lying about a woman besting him, but one could see that this mysterious woman was undoubtedly a noble."

He snaps the ribbon taut, and I flinch. A savage smile settles onto his mouth. "You almost revealed your identity. If you belonged to Societas Solis, this could be enough to kill you."

The snapping sound stings like a switch. All at once I'm sitting up straight, fists clenched. "You weren't there! I had no choice but to intervene. You send me into these balls armed with nothing but the pins in my hair. How do you expect me to be useful with nothing?"

Oncle settles back onto his carriage bench and crosses his ankle over his knee. "I don't expect you to be useful. I expect you to defend yourself if needed, and that is all. If anyone ever suspects you are more than you seem, they will begin to suspect me, and all I've worked for could be lost."

I fall back with a thump. The velvet cushion is too soft for the tension in my shoulders. We've had this same argument for years, ever since Oncle was named royal spymaster and we left sun-dappled Aunis for Paris, France's royal heart. In our tiny ancestral estate it was impossible for me to not notice the strange men who came to our doors at all hours, who lingered so late at our fire that they and my oncle became nothing but bowed silhouettes, their whispers just out of reach from where I hid behind the armchairs, yearning to be included.

And I was, in some ways. Unable to bear my crying each time he left for weeks, Oncle taught me all that he knew with blades and chains, with picking locks and picking hearts to reveal the secrets people kept close. I can walk soundlessly in boots or bare feet; I can launch a dagger through the darkness with nothing but a breath guiding my blade. I can do everything my oncle can do, and I can also do it in a gown and with a smile on my face, because Jacqueline d'Argenson-Aunis, the pretty and occasionally charming seventeen-year-old niece of the aloof and mysterious vicomte, is who the court expects me to be. No one save Margot has ever tried to scratch beneath the surface. No one suspects I am more than what they can see.

Oncle still will not share with me the true origins and purpose of the Societas Solis because I'm not a member. But I've learned enough to know that they do not seek sumptuous riches or golden crowns. They seek to stanch the sluggish bleed of violence in France.

My voice is all edges. "You refuse to let me join because of the blood we share!"

Oncle winces, cut. "I made a promise. You know that." He drags a hand through his hair and looks at me with such despair that I know he's picturing her. His sister, my mother. Who used her dying breath to push her newborn daughter into the arms of her seventeen-year-old brother after wrenching out his word that he would keep me safe, no matter what. Her portrait hangs in our hall, and I know we share the same dark brows and serious mouth. Sometimes I catch Oncle watching me when it's only us, a rare softness on his face, and I know he's seeing her, too.

I resent how I look like her, how it's a constant reminder to my oncle of the promise he's made to a woman near eighteen years gone. A woman who is a stranger to me despite the fact that I bear her name. If my mother had cared for me—if she had truly cared for any child she would bring into the world—she would not have thrown away her noble birthright to marry a peasant farmer who fled his marriage vows the moment she grew cold and let her only daughter grow up in the shadow of scandal.

A woman's reputation is all she has to stand on, and mine is already cracked by the circumstances of my birth. A single too-heavy step is all it would take to shatter it completely.

"My mother doesn't know the person you shaped me to become." I reach out and take his hand imploringly. The ring on his thumb, bearing the likeness of a sun, pinches my skin. "You can't know what she would've wanted for me."

"She would've wanted you to be happy." Oncle pulls away. "And the path you want to follow doesn't lead to happiness."

My empty hands fist. My ribs squeeze tightly, the bones scraping the softest parts of me. "You insult me by pretending you know my heart better than I do!"

Oncle sighs and rubs his face, refusing to meet me in anger. Suddenly he seems far older than his thirty-four years. "As your guardian, it's my duty to look out for your welfare, not your heart."

I tuck my chin, hiding the hurt behind a hardened jaw. "You can't protect me forever. I'm not a child anymore."

Oncle suddenly straightens. He is so tall that, even seated, his head brushes the carriage ceiling. The exhaustion and another emotion I can't name slip from his face until he's safe underneath his mask: the bland expression he wears as both royal spymaster and member of the Societas Solis. The one I despise because nothing I ever say or do can break through to him.

"Gérard de Montbéliard has asked my permission to court you."

I frown, thrown by the strange pivot in our conversation. I remember the boy—the only noble child within an hour ride of our estate. We were forced to spend many stultifying afternoons together as children until I accidentally poisoned him with a buttered snail and he was an absolute baby about it, claiming I had tried to kill him, and that was the end of the dreadful visits.

A snort escapes me. I slap a hand over my mouth to hold in the laughter. "I bullied Gérard as a child. He hates me."

"Well, you're not children anymore. You are of the proper age—"

"Oh yes, the horror of turning eighteen! Better act now before I become a shriveled old raisin—"

"—and of the proper birth—"

"I thought I wasn't marriable?" Confusion and something that feels horribly like fear threads through me. I hide them behind brittle words and blazing eyes.

Oncle's jaw tenses. We both know I'm a worthless bride. Oncle himself is the one who explained to me, gently, of course, when I asked him as a girl when my chevalier was coming to rescue me from my lonely days and lonelier nights. Oncle had laid his hand consolingly over mine, his gloves still dusty from his journey, his smile lopsided and not quite reaching his eyes. "You'll save yourself, Jac, just like me."

No one wants to sully their noble titles by marrying the likes of me—a peasant's daughter—Oncle's protection or not.

"Gérard is willing to overlook your father's background with a large enough dowry. No, do not scoff! His noble connections could do a lot for you. You'd finally have a name of your own in court, Niece."

I flinch. "I'd rather have yours. I don't care if people think less of me."

Oncle's mouth pulls, a flicker of feeling breaking through his façade. "You think that now, but you might change your mind later on."

His calm, the way he talks to me as if I'm a petulant child, splits something in me. *"I won't change my mind!"* My fist slams against the carriage wall. The pain is a sweet release, the rending of skin and welling of blood. Outside there's a murmur from the outriders and the carriage slows, then stops. There's a rap at the window.

"Vicomte, is all well?" asks the driver.

Oncle's expression is all scorn and disappointment. "All is well. Please do continue." He reaches into the pocket of his doublet and offers me an embroidered handkerchief. I notice with a stab of fury that it has the same embroidery pattern as the ribbon I used to bind the assassin. When I make no move to take it, Oncle sighs and flings it on my lap.

The silence stretches. I imagine it looping about my neck, holding me back like the too-small dogs the courtiers keep on jeweled chains. I finally bundle up my bloodied knuckles. Oncle looks everywhere but at me. The knife he was cleaning has clattered to the floor. I pick it up and heft the weight, imagining how it would feel flying from my fingers.

I'm certain Gérard would not think knife throwing a suitable pastime for his wife.

"I saved Margot's life. You said yourself it was helpful. Does that mean nothing?" My words are soft, but inside me something thrashes like a wounded bird. I feel the awful, angry burn of tears. This makes no sense. Noblegirls aren't taught to throw knives or pick locks. Why would Oncle teach me all he knew just to send me away? Why bother mentoring me if he planned to deliver me to some strange man like a beautifully wrapped parcel? "I don't want to marry Gérard."

I want to stay with you. The words are there at the tip of my tongue, but I can't say them. They skirt too close to the fear I keep locked and hidden.

Perhaps Oncle is tired of having me around. Perhaps he regrets the promise he made to his dying sister and has looked forward to the day I shall no longer be in his care. Were I to marry, I would become my husband's burden. One less problem for him to worry about.

He squares his jaw and stares at the curtained window. "I don't need your help. I need you to be safe. It's what your mother would've wanted."

The mention of my mother stokes the embers of my anger. "Why are you so convinced me being safe means being with a man?"

And why can't it be you?

Oncle gives me a dark, withering look. "I'll give you a garrote as a betrothal gift. Please don't use it on your husband."

The rest of the ride to Paris is as silent as a funeral procession.

CHAPTER THREE

WHEN THE ROYAL family arrives in Paris two days later, I invite myself into Margot's chambers before the horses are unhitched from their carriages.

She catches a single glimpse of my face and demands, "What's amiss?"

The princess stands in the center of the room flanked by golden mirrors, a royal ransom's worth of jewels heaped on every surface. Her attendants unlace the sleeves and stays of her traveler's clothes and lace her into a dazzling court dress. Though none of them pay me any attention, I know they are listening. I choose my words carefully.

"There is . . . a situation."

She cocks an eyebrow. "The bad kind and not the fun kind, I'm assuming?"

I let out a laugh that's just a breath of air. Oncle and I have not spoken for days. When I find him in our burgundy parlor, I go to my bedchamber. When we pass each other, I press myself against the wainscoted wall, gaze fixed to the ceiling. More than once I spy him from the corner of my eye reaching out— as if he wants to catch my hand, to say something. But then the shuttered look comes over his face once more and he leaves me alone. Each time he fails to say something, the anger smoldering in my belly grows hotter. I ignore the painful ache that also grows, hiding it behind haughty glares and pointed silences.

Oncle will not listen to me. Which means I shall have to move him with action, not words.

And Margot is the only person powerful enough to help me.

When life at court feels too much like a dream—a vicious dream where your wings are cut and you're plummeting to the earth with no means to save yourself—Margot catches me, carries me back to myself.

"Don't get too attached. She won't be here forever," Oncle warned the first time he found Margot in our apartments. "Princesses marry and leave their families." I pretended I didn't hear him. In these château walls my disreputable birth ranks me somewhere beneath the princess's lapdogs and above the scuttling mice. With Margot I can always be Jac, jagged edges and all. She saw what I was when she found me breaking the little finger of a boy who was being cruel to the hunting hounds my first week in Paris. A boy who turned out to be her odious royal cousin.

"We shall be great friends," she had announced when I stammered my apologies, filled with dread that Oncle and I would be ordered to leave before our trunks had even been unpacked.

I move a necklace with sapphires the size of sparrow's eggs and ease myself into a plush chair. Margot flicks her wrist toward the door and smiles. "Could we have a moment alone, please?"

With choruses "of course" and "anything that pleases you, madame," the servants leave. If Margot decreed she wished to move by litter for a week, her feet never touching the ground, I've no doubt that straws would be drawn for the honor of carrying her. All of France is in love with the king's youngest sister, the most perfect jewel in the Valois family crown. Even now, half dressed, black hair tangled and face dirtied with travel, she blinds like sunlight glancing off gold. Margot's machinating mother keeps her close, dangling her slender hand just out of reach from the French nobles who believe their loyalty to the crown might bring them close enough to slip a ring on the princess's finger.

Margot drops into the chair beside mine and pillows her chin on her fist. Her other hand catches my wrist. She presses soothing circles into my skin. "Tell me everything."

So I do, ending with the letter I saw Oncle send away with our footman, Jehan. The one addressed to Gérard de Montbéliard that says he is welcome to come court me—which I know from the way Jehan stammered when I demanded to know what the letter said.

The princess wrinkles her nose. "You, abandoning me for *marriage*? Horrible!"

I exhale softly, the tightness in my shoulders easing. Her support puts to bed a secret fear. If Oncle thinks me old enough to marry, then perhaps Margot and I have outgrown the days of running around with muddy skirts and biting our thumbs at the boys who thought that taunting defenseless animals made them men.

"Tell me what you need me to do and I shall do it," she says.

"I need you to write a letter for me. If—if you're willing." The last phrase catches in my throat. I've never asked for a royal favor from the princess before. While Margot can pretend all she'd like that the distance betwixt our stations is nothing, it's not something I can ever forget. I hate how powerless it makes me feel, knowing I must always rely on Margot or Oncle to get what I want.

A delightfully familiar, wicked smirk lights up Margot's face, and she kisses my cheek. "Don't be daft, darling. I would do anything for you."

I nod, my throat closing up, and lace my fingers through hers. If Margot thinks I can escape this trap, then I can slip free. If she believes in me, I can do anything.

The princess is pressing the wax seal with her royal monogram when there's a knock at the door. Her head whips up. "I do believe I called for privacy!"

The herald ducks his scarlet face. "'Tis your mother, madame. Catherine de' Medici. She was"—his throat bobs—"*most* insistent to speak with you."

I suck in a breath. The Queen Mother doesn't exactly think highly of me, and I imagine she'd think even less of me if she knew what sorts of letters I was begging her royal daughter to write. I move to escape through the servants' door, but Margot is already there, pushing me onto her canopied bed and dragging the curtains closed.

Right as the most terrifying woman in France breezes inside.

Catherine de' Medici is always in black. Black skirts, black sleeves, and black bodices so plush and matte, they seem to suck all the light from every room she enters. Today is no exception. The only thing more severe than her appearance is the frown she levels at Margot.

Catherine's husband, King Henry II, was killed in an accident years ago, and she has donned her mourning clothes for him ever since. Her insignia is the broken lance that pierced her husband's skull. The inscription *lacrimae hinc, hinc dolor* scrolls beneath it.

Tears from this, from this sorrow.

More unsettling than her appearance is her ongoing interest in the occult. She surrounds herself with sorcerers who observe the movements of the planets and whisper dire predictions in her ears. Rumor has it, there is an entire chamber of her private apartments filled with saints' bones and dusty tomes bound in human skin—a library preaching the practice of the dark arts. More than one frightened courtier has whispered that she has seen Queen Catherine's eyes roll back as a vision of the future grips her. And more than one person has whispered that whatever dark things Catherine saw came true.

Through a sliver in the draperies, I watch Margot curtsy, still only half dressed. "Mother. What a delightful surprise."

Catherine de' Medici snatches her daughter's hand. She bends the fingers carelessly despite Margot's pained hiss, scoffing at the ink stains. "You better not be writing to the merchants about funding that scandalous school of yours again."

Margot's biggest want is this: a school where commoners and nobles, girls and boys alike, can learn whatever they wish.

Margot snatches her hand back. "Who cares if I am? What's the point of having the most printing presses in Europe if less than half the kingdom can read?"

Catherine de' Medici prowls closer, each click of her shoes like the scrape of a dagger along stone. I slink farther back into Margot's endless pillows, trying not to squash the little dogs already nesting there.

"Women and the poor have no use for reading. You will never oversee that school as long as you live here," Catherine says.

A ruthless smirk splits Margot's face. "We'll see about that."

The Queen Mother's frown, impossibly, grows even darker. Her eyes fall to the letter on Margot's table. My only chance at escape. I tense, itching to snag it from her sight before she can rip it to pieces.

When she finally looks away, I close my eyes and release a shaky breath.

"The king of Navarre is coming to court this week," Catherine says. "I need you to beguile him for your brother's sake. Cosimo Ruggeri has made you a potion to help."

Catherine snaps her fingers, and the herald brings over a golden cup. Margot's nose scrunches at the contents. I shudder along with her.

No good comes from the name Cosimo Ruggeri.

The man is Oncle's greatest enemy on the Valois privy council. He's Catherine de' Medici's advisor publicly and sorcerer privately. Margot says he is a charlatan, a con man from her mother's native Florence who seeks to fleece her of coin and patronage in exchange for his lies and false cures for King Charles's illnesses. The Louvre's priest even banned Ruggeri from mass, saying his false spells and heretical lies make a mockery of God, but still, Catherine keeps him close.

Margot doesn't move. "I won't touch anything that man makes."

It happens so fast, I miss it.

A *slap*, then Margot reeling sideways.

Still hidden, I leap to the edge of the bed, heart pounding, but Margot's dark eyes catch mine, one of her hands over her reddened cheek. She shakes her head once.

But her dogs miss the message. They pour out from under the bed curtains, barking madly. Catherine de' Medici scowls and kicks at one. "By God, you'll drink this, or I shall make sure one of your little dogs finds its way into the Seine!"

Margot gasps with outrage, face paling around the red handprint. With a savage gesture, she takes the cup and downs it in one go. "Happy now, Mother?"

I flinch as the cup hits the floor. The sound rouses all the dogs again.

Catherine looks at the pack with disgust, like she might just make sure they all find their way into the river. "Insolent girl! One day you'll see a woman's place is beneath her husband. If your father were still alive—"

Margot laughs cruelly. She presses a cold sapphire necklace to her flushed cheek. "I'm glad he's not. Father was unfaithful to you for your entire marriage. He doesn't deserve your respect, and he won't get it from me!"

I wince, bracing myself for another slap, another sickening guilt-filled moment of hiding there and doing nothing.

Instead there's a slow, hair-raising chuckle, a knowing smile on Catherine de' Medici's face that fills me with ice.

Margot flinches when her mother's shadow falls over her, but all Catherine does is cup her uninjured cheek.

"Tomorrow you will charm the king of Navarre or I will drown your dogs. Do we understand each other?"

Margot's eyes drop to the floor. Only I see how her jaw clenches. "Of course, Mother."

CHAPTER FOUR

THE KING OF Navarre's arrival to France feels like a feast day without a feast. Even though the gates of the Palais du Louvre are thrown wide, and gold banners hang from the windows, all anyone can focus on is the sound of King Charles's snores. The exquisitely dressed nobles assembled in the courtyard might gamely pretend their monarch is not hungover, but 'tis no help. All the splendor in the world cannot hide the fact that our king has shown up for this important political meeting with less care and respect than he'd bring to a brothel. "He means to destroy this alliance before they even shake hands on it." Oncle tears his gaze from the snoozing king. "And what are you smiling about?"

I drop down from my tiptoes. "Oh, nothing. Just imagining what Margot will say later on."

In truth, I was staring at Gérard's royal standard, the swallow-tailed flag that bears his family's coat of arms. Each noble house's flag is held aloft by a footman and the place beneath the Montbéliard standard is, blessedly, empty. My would-be suitor's family should be here.

Which means today is the day I'll find out whether or not my scheme worked.

The sound of drums and trumpets grows louder as the Navarrese entourage draws closer, but the Montbéliards are still nowhere to be seen. My heart starts beating faster. My fingernails press half-moons into my palms when the first Navarrese outriders appear. A delighted cheer surges from me when King Henry enters the courtyard—

And I break off with a choking gasp when a horribly familiar dark head scuttles beneath the Montbéliard standard.

Oncle laughs softly. "Does the king displease you, Jac?"

I tear my eyes away from the back of Gérard's head. King Henry is a handsome boy done up in leather and rough-spun wools from his mountain kingdom. He rides on horseback like one of his own chevaliers but has the face of a squire. He looks . . . young. And unprepared, and completely, utterly out of his depth. King Charles half rises from his throne, eyes flashing, a slumbering dog roused by the scent of fresh meat.

I feel bad for him, I really do. But I feel worse for myself.

"I think the French court is going to eat King Henry alive," I answer truthfully.

Oncle sighs. I can't tell if it's coming from a place of agreement or disappointment.

The tiniest movement from Gérard's direction catches my attention. I turn only to catch Gérard turning away, a burgundy flush darkening the tawny skin of his neck.

I smile at the sight of blood.

The expression stays on my face all through the too-long greeting ceremony between the kings, the endless welcome feast, and straight to the late-afternoon meeting Oncle has arranged for me and my beloved-to-be in our private apartments.

"Mademoiselle d'Argenson-Aunis! We've been most excited to meet you again," the Baron de Montbéliard says more to my childbearing hips than to my face.

I hide a wicked grin behind a curtsy. "Oh, I can assure you. The pleasure is all mine today."

Gérard stiffens and stares at the floor like it might bite him.

His mother, the Baronne de Montbéliard, smiles approvingly at the rubies on my throat. "Tell me, darling Jac—I can call you Jac, right? Of course, we're practically family already—tell me about your accomplishments these days."

"Embroidery and needlework." My grin grows so big, my cheeks ache. "I excel at all activities that involve pointed objects, madame."

A low keen escapes Gérard. I beam even more brightly at him.

"*Mon petit chou*, is everything well?" his mother whispers. "Do you need more of your tonic?"

A muscle flexes in Oncle's jaw. His eyes snag on mine, and I keep my own wide and guileless. "That is enough talk about sharp objects," he demands in a frosty voice. "Jacqueline has many talents. She is an accomplished horse mistress and speaks five languages. She often joins Princess Marguerite's salon discussions on the ancient philosophers, don't you, dear Niece?"

Baronne de Montbéliard gasps, a hand fluttering to her bejeweled throat. "Why, you have connections to the royal family! Oh, isn't that just marvelous."

"Well dowered and royally connected," the baron says approvingly as if I am not there at all. "Well, well, that's something, isn't it, Gérard?"

He elbows his son, and Gérard nearly falls. His face has grown pale at Margot's name. He takes one step back, and then another. "I—I wish to rescind my offer of courtship!"

A shocked silence falls. I want to celebrate its arrival with a cheer.

"This is not what we discussed!" the baron gasps, reaching for his son like he's an escaped cat to be scruffed and stuffed back into his tasseled basket.

But Gérard is already gone, leaving nothing but an anguished cry in his wake.

Oncle is still speechless, taking in the scene like he's just found all the Valois family murdered. Gérard has made such a massive breach of propriety that Baronne de Montbéliard begins crying and hides her face in her hands. The baron turns to Oncle with open-mouthed horror. He holds up his hands as if he fears he may be stabbed. "My Vicomte d'Argenson-Aunis, I—I can assure the boy means no disrespect—"

"I think it best if my niece and I had a moment alone," Oncle says.

The baron and baronne take one look at his stony expression and flee. I clasp my hands and meet his stare head-on. The quiet in our parlor feels like that of the gallows: not the moment after, when the air is filled with death and bloodthirsty cheers, but the moment before, when the tension is as tight as a knotted rope.

Oncle cracks first.

"*You*," he finally pushes out between clenched teeth. "This is *your* doing somehow."

I laugh recklessly. "And where is your evidence?"

Oncle's mouth falls open. His gaze ransacks my face, the sideboard, as though I've left out a piece of paper documenting my schemes. *Where is your evidence?* is what he'd always say to me as a child when I would accuse him of hiding my toys or lying about the whereabouts of promised sweets. It was how he trained me to lay a trap so cleanly and neatly that no one could ever trace it back to me, even if the wronged party *knew* I was behind it.

Now I've taken our childish game and turned it into something savage. Something that proves he taught me so well that not even he, the most dangerous man in France, can best me. I can see the understanding forming in his eyes, when the unwelcome realization lands that I've won and he's lost as they frost over like a winter pond.

He'll never know about the letter I asked Margot to write—much less ever find it.

Gérard de Montbéliard,

If you marry my dear friend Jacqueline d'Argenson-Aunis, know that I shall personally make sure every snail in this kingdom is pressed into service to hasten your untimely demise.

Her Royal Highness, Marguerite de Valois
Princess of France

My fingers lace together so Oncle cannot see how they shake. "Give me a chance in the Societas Solis, and I'll show you just how much more I can do." It's an effort to keep my voice steady. To rein in the part of me that wants to demand why he's silent, why he won't give me the same opportunity he'd give any man who had bested him. All I need is one chance to prove myself. Is that so much?

His jaw clicks shut. He scrapes his scalp and laughs mirthlessly. "You think this is a game." He takes in the armor of my best gown and gems, the slight tremble of my hands. He smiles, the expression cruel and taunting. "And that winning this little game somehow means you . . . *deserve* something."

I shudder at his scorn. A hot itchy feeling blooms under my skin, the cringing anxiety that I've misjudged him and the situation growing bigger and bigger until it's all I can feel. I hate the picture he's painted of me. A bored, bejeweled girl, too young and feckless to know what's best for her.

Oncle's voice glitters. "Do you know what makes you a liability, Niece? You think you know what you're doing, but you know nothing of how the world works. Training you was clearly a mistake."

A hole punches straight through my chest, and I'm suddenly seven years old again, screaming in my nurse's arms as Oncle's shape got smaller and smaller on the road, not believing her for a second that he's going to come back this time. "Send me to the convent then, if you think I'm so useless!"

Oncle lifts my chin with a finger. His eyes are colder than winter. "If the convent is what you want instead of a husband, then so be it. You will never, ever join me, Jac. The sooner you get over this childish fantasy, the better."

The words cut me to the bone, piercing through skin and sinew and muscle. They confirm my very worst fear.

Oncle truly doesn't want me around anymore.

Perhaps he never did. After all, what seventeen-year-old lord would've been excited to be saddled with an infant? Oncle was my entire world, but I was just one small part of his. Like a soft-eared puppy, I amused him when he taught me his tricks as a little girl. Then I grew up and the tricks became a nuisance.

There is no space for me at his side anymore.

He has told me, over and over again, with words and actions, that I'm neither needed nor wanted, and I refused to listen. Didn't *want* to listen.

I always thought he expected more of me. I believed he raised me differently for a reason.

Worse, I believed the strangeness we shared made us special. That we were just as close or closer than parent and child because our family was something we'd chosen, not something we'd made.

But he only kept me because my mother asked him to.

His face grows blurry. I swallow back the humiliating tears. "Why did you keep me around at all if you never wanted me?"

Something in his stormy expression breaks, like waves cresting into the giant felled trees on the cold beaches we visited when I was young and clinging to his hand. "Jac. I—I cannot do this right now. Please leave."

I gather up the splinters of my dignity and rush past him

without a word, sailing straight through the heart of the clamoring Palais du Louvre into the courtyard beyond. Only when I'm alone do I sink to my knees behind a rose hedge and let angry sobs claw out of my chest.

Only when I'm alone can I acknowledge that I was wrong.

I might've chosen Oncle, but he never chose me at all.

CHAPTER FIVE

FLEE TO THE stables.

Unlike people, animals cannot lie. They're not asked to pretend to be something they're not. They can't be anything other than themselves, and I love their stubborn honesty. Perhaps I'm even jealous of it, how honesty is something to be praised in a horse but never a girl.

The horses move and shift in their stalls, a moment of quiet just outside the grand machinations that take place beneath the Louvre's soaring ceilings. Their warm breaths and bodies lift my spirits at once. I take in a deep lungful of musk and straw and will my pulse to slow its rabbit-race. Making each step as slow and measured as possible, I walk to the white-and-grey marbled head hanging over the edge of a crescent door. My mare, Anémone. I cradle her face in my arms and press my damp cheek against her long muzzle. She blows warm, comforting gusts against me.

Perhaps having Margot threaten Gérard de Montbéliard was a step too far. I can understand why Oncle is angry.

But I cannot think of another way to get him to *listen*. Not when he so adamantly insists that he knows me better than I know myself.

Forcing me into an unwelcome marriage would be taking a wild horse and forcing her into the yoke of a plow. It would bow my back so deeply, I would forget how to look up. Marrying Gérard would take all the wide-open edges of my horizon and place them behind leaded windows. Close enough to see but too far to reach. I have traced the edge of the breathless place where the sky meets the land far too often to have it snatched from my grasp.

"Pardon me, mademoiselle, but are you well?"

The voice jolts me from my thoughts. I knuckle away the dampness beneath my eyes and turn.

A stable boy stands watching me. More of a stable man, I suppose, given that he looks about Margot's age, which is two years older than me. He leans against the neighboring stall with his arms crossed, a muddy bootheel casually balanced against the beam. Golden hair falls in roguish waves to his sharp cheekbones. He fills every inch of the narrow frame like a too-pushy tomcat, one you know you'll have to step over the entire day because there's no hope of moving him. His stare is dark, curious, water sliding down my skin. Something about it feels almost inappropriate.

I hide my embarrassment behind straightened shoulders and a lifted chin. "I'm fine, thank you. I want to go for a ride, if you would be so kind."

His eyebrows rise. Half his mouth hooks in a smile. "Would you, now?"

I rock backward, shocked by his rudeness. He must be a new stable hand, perhaps brought in by the king of Navarre.

Someone too new to know how things work and too stupid to know he shouldn't flirt with nobles.

The stable hand's insolent smile has grown the entire time I've been quiet, and now it takes up his entire face. It's a handsome smile, teetering on the edge of mocking. He's come to gawk at me, and I'm already annoyed by the story he'll tell the other boys over dice. *Poor noblegirl, alone and crying, covered in jewels.*

"I would like it very much indeed." I gesture to Anémone. "Is readying my horse a task you're hired to complete, or shall I do it myself?"

My eyes bore into his and I fill them with all the ice I can muster. I shouldn't treat servants this way; I've been taught better. But then again, servants don't treat me like this either. As if my requests are *suggestions*. On the heels of my disastrous failed conversation with Oncle, the instinct to fight, to bend someone to my will, is too strong to contain, and this stable hand rankles me.

He looks away first. The sound of Anémone's stall finally unlatching fills me with fierce glee.

"Has anyone ever told you you've got a look that could turn a man to stone?"

I peek at his muscled back from under my lashes, surprised by the reference to the Medusa, my favorite Greek monster. It's always seemed tremendously helpful to turn one's enemies to stone.

"Who says it hasn't?"

His soft laugh races down my spine. He leads Anémone

out. Our eyes meet again over her dappled grey shoulders as if neither of us can help ourselves.

This time I look away.

I want to say something devastatingly clever, but snark abandons me just when I need it most.

He begins dressing my mare for me. "What can I call you?"

I bite my lip, considering. If I were Margot—if I had even a thimble of her boldness—I'd crook my fingers and lead this rude stable hand with his frank interest and his generous mouth into a shadowy corner and kiss him to rid myself of this unwelcome spark. But I'm nothing like her, and letting this boy have something from me that I can't take back feels like too much.

"'Mademoiselle' would be most proper."

He snorts, the sound something between a scoff and a laugh. "All right, mademoiselle. Do you have an improper name as well? Perhaps one your friends call you?"

My teeth catch the inside of my cheek. "We're not friends so I see no reason to share that with you."

He slips the saddle on my horse and our eyes meet again. This time, the water is a drenching torrent. His mouth hooks into that half smile again, and I have the awful suspicion he *knows* I'm flustered. All at once I'm assailed by the urge to mount Anémone and gallop through the gardens as fast as possible, saddle or no saddle.

Men! They're bad enough when they think they're good-looking and even worse when they know it. Their arrogance is one reason I prefer women far more than I prefer men. Some man, somewhere, could pass my exacting standards, but it certainly won't be this cheeky lad.

"My friends call me Rye," he offers as he cinches the final buckle.

"*Enchantée.* Are we done here yet?"

He laughs, the sound grating and unkind. "Are you always this charming?"

I bat my eyelashes. "Only to people who stand betwixt me and what I wish to do."

He leads Anémone outside. Before us spreads the Tuileries Garden, a snarl of unkempt roses and ivy hedges. The garden was supposed to be a verdant bridge betwixt the Palais du Louvre and the Queen Mother's Italian dream of the château, the Tuileries. But when her kingly husband died, Catherine de' Medici gave up her grand palace schemes. Now the garden for the unbuilt château is the only place where I can ride unattended, the only place in Paris where I can be truly alone without a servant or guard lurking just out of earshot. The mere sight of the greenery and the unbroken blue expanse behind it allow me to take the first full breath I've taken since my fight with Oncle. Tonight I'll let my emotions gallop until they run themselves ragged. Tomorrow I'll concoct a new plan with a cooler, more cunning head. It'll take more than marriage for Oncle to get rid of me.

I move toward the mounting blocks but Rye swings Anémone around, blocking them from view. The low evening sun snags on the gold of his hair and spins it into fire. He's tall—taller than I expected. I resent that I must look up at him to unleash the full force of my glare.

In the sunlight his eyes are not brown, as I'd assumed, but a blue so deep they look cut from the patches of night betwixt the stars. I freeze, blinking like a sunbeam has glanced off a dazzling surface to blind me.

Christ, since when have the stable boys *looked* like this?

Rye moves first, and I flinch. But all he does is cup his hands into a stirrup.

I stare at his hands, scoffing. "I'd rather use the block."

He smiles again. This time I know he's mocking me, and I'm certain he's very well aware of his pretty stare. He probably loves using it to fluster his betters. Probably practices winking at himself each morning in the water trough. "It seems like you would rather escape my company as soon as possible."

I grit my teeth, annoyed he's not only described exactly how I feel but also had the gall to say it aloud.

He's right. The sooner I get on Anémone, the sooner I can leave and decide if his impertinent behavior is worth reporting, or if I'll be admonished for somehow bringing this unwelcome masculine advance onto myself. All I wanted to do was go for a ride alone, for God's sake!

I roll my eyes and slam my heeled boot into Rye's waiting hands. His fingers catch my ankle, strong and firm around the delicate bones. I half expect him to do something crass: make a lewd comment, slip a hand up my stockinged calf, but instead he helps me into the saddle as perfectly as a French gentleman.

He bows, his expression all feigned innocence. As though our entire interaction has been completely ordinary, and he hasn't broken at least a score of rules about how we ought to interact. "Is there any other way I can assist you, mademoiselle? It has been a *delight* so far."

I feel the push of his words like a push in the skin, and I hiss, a cat teased too far into unsheathing her claws. "Don't insult me by lying! I imagine you say that to all the girls you harass."

He laughs softly. "No, I only say it to the ones I find crying." He peers up at me with those midnight eyes, not a trace of mockery to be found. As if he means it.

As if perhaps this entire encounter was just a ruse to stop my tears.

I want to deny that he caught me crying, but the lie gets stuck. I didn't come here to be seen. I came here to disappear, and he won't let me go.

"Your improper behavior could get you dismissed," I say coldly. "*I* could get you dismissed."

His look grows more intense. His eyelashes are a dark fringe that don't match his golden hair. "You could," he agrees pleasantly. "But you're not going to, are you?" His fingers skim across Anémone's bridle, down her neck, to my hands in their dainty lace gloves holding the reins.

He lifts one and presses his lips to my knuckles.

His hand is rough with callouses, but his *lips*—I tear away from the thought before it can finish, gasping like a drowning person.

A stable hand kissing a noble—even a proper courtier's kiss such as this one—is a breach of propriety so extreme, it would be grounds to get him dismissed at once or worse. My skin feels nettle-stung where he's touched it. I run a finger over the spot, half expecting an angry red mark. He notes the movement with his too-blue stare, dragging it up to my face. There's no chagrin in his expression, no sign he regrets what he's done. Only that frank curiosity, as if I'm a riddle he wants to solve. His insolence should make me angry. It ought to offend. But instead, the mystery of it makes my skin flush, robs me of my thoughts.

There's a clatter of metal and male voices. Armed men. Without thinking I nudge Anémone between me and the stable hand. My fingers go to the tiny knife hidden in my riding boot.

Four men in a noble livery I don't recognize spill into the yard.

"Sire, *mon dieu*, we were looking all over for you!" the oldest of them exclaims.

"Sire" is the proper address for a king. I search around me for a flash of gold brocade, a spray of diamonds, but there's nothing.

Nothing save for *him*.

Rye the stable hand in his rough-spun clothes.

My body boils from inside out. My skin breaks out in burgundy patches, and I choke back something that could either be a scream or a laugh.

Henry de Bourbon, king of Navarre, has saddled my horse.

And I had not the slightest inkling of it.

I should've recognized him. He all but told me with his sly looks and impertinent words, and I didn't notice. Humiliation fills my chest with an choking pressure.

He steps forward with the ease of someone who's belonged

in every space he's ever inhabited. "As you can see, I'm quite well, gentlemen. Thank you for your concern."

Rye—King Henry, I correct quickly—turns over his shoulder back to me, a laugh on his lips, as though I have been in on his little jest and not the subject of it.

I curtsy as best as I can in the saddle, which is not dignified in the slightest. "You should have told me, Your Highness." I force out the words through clenched teeth, addressing the ground instead of his face.

He laughs again, the sound all swaggering confidence. "But this was so much more fun, mademoiselle, don't you agree?" He blinds me with that obnoxious smile. "You can make up for any offense you feel you've caused me by letting me accompany you. A beautiful girl should never ride alone." Before I can respond, he's addressing his men. "If you could be so kind as to fetch the stable hand—"

My mouth falls open. Did he think . . . he was *charming* me with his act?

My humiliation overflows into rage, all of it concentrating in the intense desire to strike the laughing look from his face, to humiliate him the way he's humiliated me.

Which, of course, would not be an appropriate way to treat a king. Even the king of a kingdom so small I can scarcely make it out on Oncle's map.

Instead of striking him, I do the next best thing.

I kick Anémone's sides and shoot like an arrow into the wild gardens before he can finish his sentence, leaving him alone and flustered amid his men.

CHAPTER SIX

IMAGINE THERE ARE battles less gruesome than the one being waged in our apartments in the Palais du Louvre. Each day Oncle and I eat across from each other at opposite ends of the great carved table in a silence so complete I can hear the noise from the neighboring apartments. Each sip of wine a declaration of war; each stab of the fork a pike thrust.

I wish I could tell Margot everything. But even if I could tell her about the Societas Solis, she wouldn't be there to listen. Entertaining King Henry and his entourage fills all her days and all her nights. Not even Margot's royal blood is enough to keep me at her side right now. While the princess's favor elevates me among her many ladies-in-waiting, I'm still the lowest born among them, and her mother, Catherine de' Medici, is only letting the wealthiest, bluest-blooded ladies be seen with her daughter as long as King Henry is here.

Fear not, my mother can't keep us apart forever!
Everyone is a hopeless bore, but there is one lady
whose spirited conversation I am most *enjoying.*

M

I reread Margot's latest note with bitterness, the paper crumpling in my fist. She's found another paramour—*of course* she has—but it's an unwelcome reminder of the vast distance between us. Though Margot is my closest friend, she has dozens of other people in her life.

Just like Oncle.

A scream scrambles up my throat. There is no place for me in court. There is no place for me with the Societas Solis. There is no place for me anywhere at all.

Why must I be both not enough and too much for the life I wish to live?

The injustice of it all makes me want to destroy things. To tear down the useless ball gowns in my wardrobe and rip out the jewels hanging from my ears.

I settle for laying out the items I would take with me if I ran away. Just to imagine what else I would need. The helpful things go on my bed and the useless things go on the floor. Every drawer is yanked open and rifled through until all the bare surfaces on my vanity are cluttered. I tell Jehan when he knocks at my door to inform my oncle that I shall not be joining him for dinner. Later, when the sky to the west is a burgundy blush, I hear the door ease open.

I grit my teeth and whip around. "I said I was not to be—"

My words vanish at the sight of Oncle.

"Is there a reason you refuse to join me tonight?" He sounds . . . wounded, of all things. As if another night of stony silence and doing violence with the cutlery is something he truly enjoys.

You know what the reason is! I want to shout. Instead I shove my rage down into a hard knot.

"I felt like rearranging my wardrobe. Is that a crime?"

His eyes track the clothes slumped haphazardly on the bed and then leap to the open traveler's chest beyond. I catch my bottom lip betwixt my teeth and fight the urge to block his view of it.

Our housekeeper, Madame Dupont, would never reorganize my things this sloppily. Which means—

"Are you going somewhere?" he asks.

I cross my arms and pitch myself taller. "That entirely depends on you. Am I going somewhere? Have you found another man who'll stoop to marry me? A convent for obstinate orphans, perhaps?"

He examines the clothing again, noting how it's my fighting breeches and practical dresses. Not the fine things the niece of a vicomte would be expected to wear. A wardrobe for running.

Oncle sighs. The sound seems to undo all the tension in his shoulders, and suddenly it's my oncle before me, the man who led the halter of my first pony as we galloped around the orchards under a russet autumn sky, no trace of the royal spymaster nor the cunning agent of the Societas Solis.

"In fact, we are going somewhere. Have Madame Dupont dress you for riding. Leave all these other things here."

My heart slips into my throat. "Where are we going?"

"I have need of your talents."

I can barely force out my words, the hope so huge, it chokes me. "The Societas Solis?"

He smiles, the expression not quite reaching his eyes. "Yes."

. . .

We ride through the crooked streets of Paris. Tucked at the edge of the Seine River, the city is a bright ruby, its white plaster walls crowned with red clay roofs. In the dawn light from my bedchamber, the city looks like it's on fire. Beneath the bright roofs are the twisting alleys and shops. Each bend in the streets is likely to bring you to a flower stall overflowing with freshly cut roses or a stone building so old and grey, it looks built by Charlemagne himself.

Even though I'm far from the only woman riding, my presence causes the crowds to grow quiet, whispers trailing after me like the hem of my heaviest gown.

"The likes of them aren't welcome here—"

"Up behind those walls eating cake whilst the rest of us starve—"

"A noblewoman, here? I'll show her what our men are like—"

I grip the reins tighter, wishing Oncle had let me ride astride like a man instead of sidesaddle so I'd draw less attention. One man makes a rude gesture at me. My eyes slide over him like rain down glass, even though my gut coils angrily. If I want to succeed in Oncle's world, I must learn to ignore offenses like these.

King Charles and his father taxed Paris dearly, taking both gold and spirit from their people until Parisians had little left of either. After years of endless wars and hardship, resentment floods the streets like gutter filth. I can hardly fault the people for their anger. Each night the Palais du Louvre glitters, like coins falling thoughtlessly from a banker's too-full pockets. The Huguenot belief that perhaps the right to rule should be earned, and not granted by God, grows ever more popular as support for King Charles's reign plummets.

When we reach an apothecary near the city's easternmost wall, my insides are in such snarls, I can barely breathe. Seeing where Oncle disappears to now, after wondering for years, doesn't feel real. I fight the urge to race closer before the vision vanishes.

But it won't. The Societas Solis needs me.

The reminder sends a thrilling shiver down my back.

Oncle secures our horses in a stable and goes to the building's back door. He presses his hand against the door—his sun signet ring catches the dying light, momentarily blinding me—and the door swings open.

The scent of blood fills my nose.

A woman stands at a table, elbow deep in the chest of a fresh corpse.

"Monsieur Gabriel!" She wipes her hands on a rag. Blood still freckles her fair skin. Her quick, dark eyes study me curiously. "I didn't expect you to bring a guest."

Oncle's hand lands on my shoulder. "Louise, this is my niece, Jac. She knows the princess."

Louise gives a delighted caper that sends all the ruffles on her apron fluttering. The action is so unexpected I take a step back. "What MARVELOUS news!"

I swallow and point unsteadily at the corpse.

"Right, him. How much do you want her to know, Gabriel?"

"As little as possible," Oncle growls, drawing a length of canvas over the body.

But not before I see the scarlet crater in the chest.

Louise rolls her eyes good-naturedly. "Yes, yes, I know, *veritas loquitur*, and all that." She turns to me and whispers loudly, "Tell me, is Gabriel as much of a bore at home as he is here? Never mind. I'm certain he is. Someone is defiling corpses in the graveyard, and I'm . . . seeing what parts are missing."

A hand claps over my mouth, too late to hold in a shocked gasp. I know what happens when graveyards and bodies are disturbed. People want to blame someone.

Someone with less power to fight back.

Someone different from themselves.

"I've already warned the non-Catholics in Paris. All the Huguenot, Jewish, and Muslim families we know about," Louise says quickly, seeing how my face pales. "But I fear the situation is . . . different from what we expected. Perhaps even worse."

"Worse?" Oncle throws down his riding gloves with a smack. "What can be worse than neighbors turning on one another?"

Louise lifts her hands against Oncle's impatience. "There are rumors the grave-robbing is supernatural. That perhaps the Navarrese delegation . . . brought something with them."

Cold slivers down my backbone. I think of the story of "Bisclavret," and how whispers of bloodthirsty *loups-garous* tearing through the countryside still make rounds in the gossip pamphlets. The court rolls their eyes but eagerly devours every word, especially when the villages decide to burn the accused. A rumor can be far more dangerous than the truth.

Oncle rubs his sun signet ring, scoffing. "Fools will believe anything. Louise, you must figure out who is behind the grave-robbing as soon as possible so they can be punished. *Publicly.*"

Louise nods.

I clasp my hands tightly. "Is this what I'm helping with?" Stalking the streets of Paris, searching for a criminal? It's something plucked straight from my most daring daydreams, the ones I fall into whenever Catherine de' Medici sends a priest to read the Bible to Margot's ladies-in-waiting whilst I waste the afternoons embroidering crooked flowers. It's something useful, something I know I can do. It's something that can make a difference.

Oncle dashes my hopes with a bark of laughter. "Don't be ridiculous."

He beckons me up a worn staircase and down a long hallway. Beneath the floorboards there's the murmur of voices and clink of vials of the storefront below. Behind another locked door is an armory. Weapons of all kinds hang on the walls. There are provisions wrapped and neatly labeled on shelves. Men's clothes for all weather and of all sizes hang in an open wardrobe. There's even a bedroll.

"So there are women in the Societas Solis. You told me there weren't." It was hard to miss the shimmer on Louise's bodice—a tiny sun pendant swinging from a chain, a miniature of the one on Oncle's ring.

"I said there were no *noblewomen* in the Societas Solis." Oncle gestures for me to sit and begins browsing through a stack of letters.

A sudden bout of nervousness comes over me. Not the wrong kind of nerves, but the good kind, the ones I got as a child when Oncle would decide it was time to raise the fences my pony would jump over. My entire life has led to this moment—me joining Oncle just as I always wanted.

"So what now?" I ask when the silence grows too much. "Do I finally get to select my own garrote?"

He purses his lips and glances at the weapons wall. "I suppose you might as well while we're here."

I nod slowly, hardly daring to believe it. "And my sun signet. When do I get that?"

He stills, back going stiff. "Only full members may bear the sun signet. And you, dear Niece, are a mere acolyte."

Oncle pulls out a letter and pushes it across the scratched tabletop. I tilt the parchment in the dim light streaming in from the single, dingy window. The wax seal, which might have once held a stamp of the sender's insignia, is long gone. A gasp escapes me when I see the letter is addressed to Catherine de' Medici. "You *stole* from the Queen Mother?"

Oncle smiles, the expression razor sharp. "Go on and read it."

The letter discusses the death of the queen of Navarre. How her loss has stirred up the French Huguenot city of La Rochelle, how the queen's passing invalidates a promise she made on behalf of her son, Henry of Navarre. A *marriage* promise.

I get to the bride's name—Marguerite de Valois—and stop reading.

A ringing fills my ears. "Margot is betrothed to Henry of Navarre?"

"She *was* betrothed to him," Oncle corrects.

King Henry of Navarre, that rude, self-confident brigand, was *engaged* to my best friend?

And she did not tell me?

The paper trembles ever so slightly in my hands. "Did she know about this?"

Because last I spoke with her, Margot was decidedly and definitively not engaged to be married. She would have told me. It would have been all we talked about. Like me, the princess never imagined she would marry. She's too valuable to her family to be offered to a husband like a stuffed swan on a gilded platter.

"Catherine de' Medici is telling the princess today." Oncle paces across the floor, hands clasped behind his back, his cloak a dark, billowing storm cloud. "Navarre may be Henry's kingdom, but to the Huguenots of France, he is also *their* king. The monarch who practices the one true faith."

He stops and pivots to me, his stare piercing. "This betrothal was the Societas Solis's plan for peace. I convinced Catherine de' Medici that the kingdom's love for Marguerite might translate into tolerance for her Huguenot husband and his followers. Uniting the most powerful Huguenot and Catholic families in marriage could end the civil wars.

"But now, this foolish boy-king is tired of being told what

to do and doesn't need to listen to anyone but himself. He has threatened to pull out of the betrothal unless Marguerite and the French court convince him to honor it. It's why he's here."

The future knits itself together. The Huguenots—oppressed in France due to the lack of tolerance for their faith—would see the Huguenot king's rejection of his Valois bride as a rejection of the peace. It would be seen as a signal to reject their own Catholic lords and laws.

It would become an act of war.

And God knows wars have been waged over lesser issues than this.

I swallow back a wave of unease, but beneath it there's cold betrayal. Oncle knew my only friend was engaged and didn't tell me. He knows what Margot means to me and decided that didn't matter while the fate of France hangs in the balance.

That's precisely why he didn't tell you, a vicious voice whispers.

After all, what is one woman's life and happiness compared to a kingdom's?

"Why shouldn't Henry get Margot's consent? She has a right to choose for herself."

Oncle gives me a narrow-eyed look, as if I'm being childish. "Not when there are millions of lives on the line." The words hang there, ominous and dark. "The princess is strong willed, as we both know, and the Queen Mother did not imagine she would take kindly to the news. Henry was not supposed to be in Paris yet, and him coming here early has made things worse. There was going to be a portrait of him."

"A portrait?" I repeat, edging forward on my chair. "What on earth does a portrait have to do with anything?"

He swallows again, his expression growing uncomfortable. "As you have doubtless noticed, Henry is handsome. It was hoped that by . . . persuading the princess first with his beauty, she could be warmed to the idea of marrying him in advance of the wedding."

"But Margot doesn't even prefer men!" I burst out. "A handsome man will never win her over. You, of all people, should understand that."

Oncle is pink cheeked and making very determined eye contact. As if he'd rather be looking anywhere else and doesn't want me to know it. His preference for men isn't a secret he keeps from me, but it's not something he likes to talk about either. "Precisely. Which is why I've let the Societas Solis give you this mission. You must persuade the princess to marry the king."

My stomach rolls as if there's something rotten in it. "You can't be serious."

His stare doesn't waver. "People like us have married before. Attraction and marriage have nothing in common. Help the princess find a reason to marry the king."

The rotten feeling fills my mouth. Matchmaking for my best friend and the most arrogant man I've had the misfortune to meet?

This is the mission the Societas Solis imagines I'm fit for?

It's nothing like the daring heists and careful assassinations I dreamed of. This mission would have me use none of the skills Oncle has taught me.

Instead, it asks me to manipulate my closest friend into doing something she doesn't want to do. It asks me to use our sacred friendship to push Margot around like a pawn on a chessboard.

"I can't do this. Margot would never listen to me."

Oncle looms over me. "This is the work the Societas Solis needs done. You are the only person we know who could get the princess to listen to reason."

I shift away from him "This isn't reason! This is a trick, plain and simple! We have entertained Margot in our apartments! You know she would never wish to marry a king and become a cooking pot for his heirs."

"Marguerite de Valois is a princess of the blood. It's her duty to do what's best for France." His words are a low, dangerous growl. I ought to back down, but injustice rages through me like an unchecked fire, Oncle's words about duty adding to the heat. Why must soldiers and women always think of duty whereas powerful men do not?

"The mission won't work!" I say. "You know it. I know it. The Societas Solis ought to know it as well. Give me another task."

Oncle goes completely still. The sight is a knife to my neck. I'm suddenly anchored to my chair, all the words stuck in my mouth. He only goes still when his feelings are coursing so strongly that he must throttle them all down before he does or says something he regrets. He slowly sinks into the chair across from me.

I swallow, bracing myself as he finally cracks.

"I heard from Gérard's family today. Despite your appalling behavior, they're willing to go forward with the courtship."

I flinch. After I tried everything I could to get Gérard and his family to dislike me, they're still interested?

"I told them the princess's letter was a jape. A mean trick you're ready to apologize for next time you see Gérard," Oncle says.

My stomach sinks. "What else did you tell them?" I demand brusquely. He may have discovered my trick, but he won't discover my dread.

"Nothing more yet." Oncle leans forward, his expression tight. "You've asked me to listen to you, and I've tried. I know you don't believe me about the dangers the Societas Solis would put you in, but they're very real. It's either this mission or marriage, and I won't choose for you, but *mon dieu*, don't tell me I didn't do everything in my power to give you the choice!"

His voice rises and rises and now the dust motes quiver in the abrupt silence. I'm hunched over the table as if I've been caught in a sudden storm. Choice has always felt like something close to freedom, but nothing about this choice feels like freedom. It feels like deciding which of my legs I'd like to have snapped. Both options leave me broken.

Oncle closes his eyes and lets out a shuddering sigh. "If you accept this mission, lying to Margot is only the beginning. The Societas Solis might demand you to turn on your other principles as well. They will ask you to place your loyalty to the cause above country, kings, and even kin. Not everyone has it in them to do what must be done." His expression softens. "Jac. You're still young and have experienced so very little of the world. Let your heart stay open. Marriage might make you happy if you give it a chance."

I wince, the words tearing through me like an assassin's arrow, the pain all the sharper for the surprise. I flex my hands and observe how my skin pebbles, how the tendons press white against my knuckles.

Not everyone has it in them to work for the Societas Solis.

Even after all this time, even after everything he's taught me, he doesn't think I have the mettle to make it.

No, it's worse than that.

He hopes that I'll settle for less. Something more befitting a girl of my lowly station.

The whisper of Paris settling down for the night presses through the now-dark window. I imagine Louise in the apothecary below, listening to every creak in the floorboards overhead; the black-cloaked boys of the Societas Solis drawing closer to the city, the secrets to make and unmake kingdoms held fast to their beating hearts. I straighten and feel how furiously my blood rushes through my body. I meet Oncle's pleading look, my expression smooth, emotionless.

I have my doubts, yes.

But he's not the only one who can put on a mask.

I won't live a life where settling is praised as success.

"I'll do it," I say.

Oncle bows his head and sighs. "Jac—"

"The choice is mine to make, is it not?" I say coldly, throwing his own words back at him.

Oncle's mouth twists, as if he's resigning himself to my decision even though every part of him rebels against it. "Let us pray you do not live to regret it."

CHAPTER SEVEN

THE PRINCESS OF France's parlor is bigger than our entire apartment suite.

When Margot's mother was sent from the Tuscan hills to marry the future king of France, she brought her Italian tastes with her and remade the royal apartments with a fortune's worth of beauty. Margot's ceilings soar a score of feet above us. Vivid frescoes depicting plump cherubs and all the good, chaste heroines of the Bible stare down at us benevolently. We ladies-in-waiting circle Margot like spring flowers, each of us more splendidly arranged than the last. I'm wearing one of my least favorite dresses: an enormous blush gown accented with so many beads, my feet have gone numb beneath it. I feel like the wilting peony at my elbow, so large it can no longer support itself. I shall have to send for Jehan to carry me home.

Another somber hour tolls out from the bells of Sainte-Chapelle. I silently mourn the loss of another hour from my precious life. We have been here all afternoon and there is no sign we shall be dismissed anytime soon.

Margot's mother has gathered us to view Henry of Navarre's portrait and to paint portraits ourselves. The Queen Mother is the only person in the room who does not look like a dying blossom. She is in her customary black, greying dark hair pulled back so severely, her skin stretches. She stalks around our half crescent of extremely amateur paintings like a wolf among sheep, the sheep all too frightened to cry out or run away. Her beetle-black eyes catch my stare. I look away quickly and wipe my brush with a cloth.

Perhaps we should all just be grateful that Catherine de' Medici hasn't summoned Cosimo Ruggeri to help us force-feed Margot a love potion brewed with Henry's toenails.

"*Mon dieu*, is that really what you see when you see the princess?" Hélène de Châlons, the lady-in-waiting seated beside me, leans over to peek at my portrait and frowns.

I glance at my canvas. Painting is not one of my finer skills. Margot's likeness looks as if a plague victim has made passionate love with my horse. I dab my brush in a pink color and add spots to her too-long face to complete the illusion.

"Is this a fairer likeness, my dear comtesse?" I say.

Hélène stammers helplessly. On my other side, Margot's lips curve into a barely there smile. I add another few pockmarks just to keep her smiling, anything to keep her mood from souring. Margot has reacted to her mother's and king-brother's decision to marry her off like a cat fated to be bathed: badly, with claw marks on anyone who tries to persuade her differently. All afternoon we have given furtive glances to the portrait of Henry of Navarre as if it were an uninvited guest, no one quite sure how or if they should be welcoming given Margot's foul mood.

Someone had dared comment that Henry's portrait was handsome when we first arrived, and Margot silenced her with a glare so poisonous, I half expected the girl's heart to stop beating.

The taste of metal floods my mouth. How am I supposed to begin to carry out the Societas Solis's work when Margot hisses at Henry's name? Would she turn on me as suddenly as she tore into the other girl? If I lose Margot's favor, I won't be useful anymore. The Societas Solis would have no further need of me.

"You're a genius, Jac!" Margot peers closer at my canvas. "I rather think painting is your best talent." She dips her brush in a lurid yellow-green color, mouth hooked into a fierce smirk. "In fact, you've given me an excellent idea for how to improve my own work."

She flicks her wrist.

The paint plinks onto the portrait of Henry of Navarre. It lands just beneath his nose and begins to ooze. The slow slide is mesmerizing, utterly obscene. A chorus of gasps goes around the room.

The king of Navarre's official portrait—commissioned from a Florentine master, lugged through the mountains by a dozen men—now has an enormous, glistening booger.

Catherine de' Medici's face goes white. *"Margot!"* The word is filled with enough reproach and disappointment to make a grown man quail. I've seen her cow the king of France by whisper-hissing his name the exact same way.

Margot mock gasps. "Oh dear. How careless of me." She

lifts the corner of her painting smock and wipes the paint glob. It smears over Henry's face, giving it a sickly, jaundiced hue. She looks at her work and sighs prettily. "Alas, I'm so clumsy! I've made him worse and not better."

"Enough!"

Catherine de Medici's chair falls backward with a *bang* that sends the other girls cringing and the canvases trembling. Henry of Navarre's portrait wobbles once, twice.

And then the portrait plummets paint-first onto the floor.

"You will be marrying him whether you want to or not," Catherine says, her eyes all fire. I half expect smoke to billow from her ears. "Do you understand?"

Margot glares from beneath her eyelashes, nostrils flaring. "Not if I can help it. Henry has said if I don't give him my hand willingly then he shall not take it at all." She grins suddenly. "*And* I've found a place to hide my dogs from you, so don't try to threaten them anymore either. You've got nothing on me, Mother." Her gaze cuts to mine, a flicker of triumph. Hiding the dogs was my idea.

My chest squeezes so tightly, I fear a cracked rib. This is the Margot I love, all wild and insolent. But this is also the princess I cannot reason with, the one so stubbornly set in her own ideas that no one can reach her. For once, as much as it fills me with so much guilt I can barely sleep at night, her mother and I are on the same page.

I've got to get her to say yes to Henry. To charm him, the opposite of what she's threatening. Otherwise I'll be married away. Otherwise France might be torn apart by war.

"Do you want the peace shattered because you care more about yourself than the rest of France?" Catherine bears down on her daughter, a thunderhead blotting out the summer sky. "Do you care at all for anyone other than yourself?"

Margot leaps to her slippered feet, a vision in Valois blue. "There are other ways to create peace! You could stop levying taxes to build your useless palaces and let people buy food instead. You could build my school so the people can learn and decide for themselves if my brother is the king they deserve!"

A soft gasp goes up among the ladies-in-waiting. Resisting one's mother is bad enough, but criticizing the policies of the king and Queen Mother of France is an entirely different rebellion. One that would be rightfully called treason were it uttered from anyone else's lips. Only Margot, royal herself, could get away with this unpunished.

I swallow back a burst of panic. This afternoon is over. I must defuse their anger before it boils over and scalds everyone.

While Margot and her mother argue, I oh-so-carefully ease from my painter's stool on cramped, stiff legs and seize Henry of Navarre's portrait. I turn it upright.

There is now a not-insignificant amount of dog fur stuck to his jaundiced cheeks.

Carefully, lest the portrait suffer another indignity, I slide it back on its easel. Despite the fur, yellow skin, and the booger, it is a handsome likeness of the king. The painter managed to capture the arrogant bend of his full lips, the comeliness of his distinct cheekbones. His imperious stare dares the viewer to look away. The only detail amiss is the blue of his eyes. They lack a certain darkness, perhaps a violet or the green of a forest's shadow, to do the color justice. My thumb slowly swipes the yellow from the blue paint, lingering on his too-black lashes. My chest trips at the sight. God, if only his personality matched his looks!

Catherine de' Medici finally takes note of me scuttling beneath her feet—how could she not, with my skirts the size of a frigate's sails—and her dark eyes widen with fury. I hasten back to my stool before she can yell. Except her eyes keep widening. Until they roll toward the back of her head. Until all I can see is the whites flecked with blood.

Until she collapses across my feet.

Screams burst out.

"She's having a vision!" someone cries. "The second sight possess the queen!"

Slippers stampede, half of the women rushing to the Queen Mother's side, half rushing from the room shouting for help. Paint splatters the fine walls and floors. I pull Catherine's head in my lap as she convulses, and a wall of people press toward me, all too terrified to do anything else but watch.

At my touch, her eyes fly open.

"*The Valois line will end!*" She screams in a voice nothing like her own. Gasping, I drop her head back into my skirts.

She screams again, her clutching fingers and quill-sharp nails digging into my arms. "*The Valois line will end when the Seine runs red!*" Her huge unseeing eyes latch on to me like a person drowning, unknowingly dragging me down with them, suffocating us both. Pulse rioting, I try to pull away, but she only pulls me closer, her nails breaking my skin.

All at once, she goes as limp as a corpse. I scoot backward on all fours. Her head makes a hideous thump on the rug. A frightened cry wrenches from my throat.

Men burst into the room. With much shouting and stamping of boots, they push me aside and take the Queen Mother away. The other ladies swarm after them like a flock of rooks, screaming and sobbing. The uproar grows dimmer as the horde disappears, but I don't follow them. I stay rooted to the spot like a fox hiding from the hounds, panting hard, even as the candles slump into puddles and flies swarm over the sweating half-eaten sweetmeats. I flinch when I look up.

The portrait of Henry of Navarre stares at me with his cruel mocking smile.

I pull in a steadying breath and look to the frescoed ceiling. Oncle's words come back to me, his words suddenly more awful than the ones spewed from the Queen Mother's lips: *The Societas Solis will ask you to place your loyalty to the cause above country, kings, and even kin.*

What terrible future did Catherine de' Medici see that conceals itself from me?

And does my promise to the Societas Solis play a part in that terror?

CHAPTER EIGHT

THE SUMMONS FROM Margot arrives mere minutes before the ball begins. The wax seal is still warm when I split it open with a fingernail.

Disaster. Come now.

A tiny, petulant *please* was scrawled in the lower corner. My painted lips twist. I can imagine Margot at her mess of a desk—no, if she has proclaimed this a disaster, then she certainly wrote this from her canopied bed—making this begrudging concession to politeness even though we both know that according to courtly etiquette, I must answer her summons whether I wish to or not.

I release a long, slow breath.

It's never good when Margot is late.

As soon as the doors open, Margot's thrown herself into my arms, sobbing.

"She is *leaving*, Jac! Sent away to her husband's house. I shall never see her again!"

She crushes her snotty, damp face into the crook of my neck, heedless of the pearls grinding into her skin and mine. I pat her back and make soothing sounds even as foreboding chills my skin.

"Is this the girl from the Fontainebleau gardens?" It takes a moment, but I remember the girl behind Margot's skirts, right after I tossed her would-be assassin into the moat.

Margot sniffles miserably, squeezing a damp wad of paper so tightly, I can spot rips in the paper. "No, this is the sultan's granddaughter, newly married to the Marquis de Marseille. Honestly, how could you forget? I wrote you about her *several* times."

I grimace and give her a few more awkward pats. The anxiety of the maids whom Margot dismissed—the ones who gave me desperate looks as I slipped past them—presses against the closed door like a silent siege. If the maids cannot ready the princess to be at the ball soon, it shall be their livelihoods on the line when Catherine de' Medici grows vexed enough to investigate the delay herself. Tonight's ball is especially important. It shall celebrate all things Navarrese as a gesture of welcome to King Henry from his bride's royal family. If Margot forsakes the event, it would be the greatest insult to the foreign king. It would give him one more reason to call off their engagement and abandon all plans of peacemaking.

It would also be an utter failure on my part. I can nearly picture Oncle's relieved smile at the news, how he would ask—with nauseating sincerity—if I imagined myself more as a summer bride or an autumn bride.

I must get Margot to this ball as fast as possible.

Fortunately, this isn't the first time the princess has been heartsick. Margot falls in and out of love as predictably as the tides. Her heart is as capricious as the sea. I have guided her through those storms before, and I'm certain I can do it again.

I unfist her snotty hand and read the note myself.

"Why, she's not leaving you. She says right here that if you should ever find yourself in Marseille to call upon her."

Margot laughs darkly. She snatches the paper and sends it sailing into the fire. She watches the edges curl and blacken, her jaw set stubbornly.

"And we both know I shall never go there because Mother won't let me. Princesses of the blood aren't allowed to do anything on their own."

Henry might let you go as his wife. I swallow the words back, knowing it would be deadly to give them breath. "Then we shall find someone else for you tonight. Did you not say that Lady Charlotte has a maid who was besotted watching you read the other night?"

Margot's dark eyes snap to me, narrow slashes. I drop my gaze, skin prickling as I remember the last time Margot gave me a look that singed my soul.

She kissed me first, in this very chamber.

I kissed her back, and we kissed again and again that glittering winter night. The taste of frangipane still brings me back to that heady moment. Until I felt her lips on mine, I did not have words for how our friendship felt different, or for how when I brushed my hair after the grand court fetes, I imagined it was her fall of black silk hair in my hands. Margot preferred women to men, and that night, I learned a part of me did as well.

For a glorious month, we spent every single second together. But then I remembered all the girls who had come before me.

Couldn't stop thinking of all the girls who would come after. My heart clenched like a fist, and I knew—even though I hated it—I would have to end things.

My heart is not generous like Margot's, vast enough to contain countless shores. Mine is a rushing river, stuck in its narrow bed, strong enough to punch through stone. There was no space in me to share Margot with anyone else, and I knew she would never settle. I alone could never be enough for her.

So I ended things with her before she could end them with me.

And the very next day, I saw her slip out into the winter garden hand in hand with another girl.

Margot sighs and leans beside the fireplace. Orange light glows through the edges of her peignoir, her lovely shape made shadow beneath the silk. "I grow weary of loving people who do not love me back."

I reach for her fire-limned silhouette and stop. I want to tell her she's wrong. That no other person in the entire kingdom is as beloved as her, but how can I? When even I, her closest friend, the person who still remembers what she tastes like, must lie to her for my own gain?

While I've hidden the Societas Solis from Margot for years, it never felt like a lie. Whatever I'm doing now feels deliberate and poisonous. It slowly tears my soul in two.

Margot laughs unkindly. "Fine. Don't say anything. You would never understand. You've never let your heart be cap-tured by anyone, not even me."

I swallow back the lump. "Margot—"

She suddenly seizes my hand. "You *must* help me escape

this engagement. I helped you escape yours, did I not?"

I shudder, the guilt an iron fist around my neck. "I don't know how—"

Her hand grips tighter, nails breaking my skin. "Your oncle is a royal advisor, and my mother listens to him. Convince him to end this."

The guilt chokes me. This is a hundred, a million times worse than I could've imagined. "He doesn't listen to me. He thinks of the religious conflict, war—"

"Ruin me, then. Let us get caught, and they can send us away."

Her mouth is on mine. She still tastes of marzipan though there is no gâteau in sight. Almond and sugar, rich butter, and cutting like a knife through it all, the salt of tears. I let myself kiss her back just once before I gently, oh so gently, push her away. It feels like breaking my own heart.

"We both know that shall not work." My voice is guarded even though a torrent of feeling rages beneath my skin: desire, surprise, and growing larger by the second like a vast creature rising from the hidden depths, frustration.

Nothing will soften Margot toward King Henry of Navarre. She meets all my words and suggestions with anger and surliness. And not only me, but her other ladies-in-waiting as well, who share stricken looks with one another before one of them bravely offers a kind observation about the Navarrese king, which Margot ignores. I even found his befouled portrait stashed amid the tasseled pillows where her little dogs sleep.

And I get it, to an extent—I truly do—but to have her ask

me to throw away my future along with hers when she has made it clear she can't love me the way I want her to is cruel and selfish.

"Have you considered marrying King Henry for convenience?" I ask.

Margot rocks back, blinking like she's never seen me before. "You think it convenient for me to marry him? Have you not been listening?"

I bite my lip, panic a high keening wail in my head. I've thought of the best way to bring this up for days, but now I have no choice, no subtle grace to dress it up in. "I only suggest a convenient match since love between you and Henry is impossible. Perhaps he could offer you something you can't get on your own. Funding for your school? Imagine how sour it would make your mother!"

Margot stumbles away as though shoved. Her chest heaves, her red-rimmed eyes blacker than the new moon night. "*You* think I ought to marry him? Even you, Jac?" Her voice breaks on my name.

A copper taste rises in the back of my throat. I would give anything to banish the betrayal from her face. But I don't know how. Perhaps the happiness of one person *is* a fair trade for peace. My mother pursued her happiness without regard for anyone else, and seventeen years later, I still pay the price for her recklessness. I've scrapped for my entire life for a place in court, a place in the Societas Solis, and now even the smallest mistakes can still take everything from me. I could be put aside as easily as an unfashionable gown.

Margot will never know what it's like to have her best still not be enough.

I reach for her cold hand, eyes pleading, needing her to sense that there's more to me than I can tell her, but that I'm always, always on her side. "I don't want you to be unhappy. But you can't command me to destroy my life. It's not fair. We both know . . . We both know you wouldn't be happy with me forever."

Margot snatches her hand out of reach.

"You are a coward, Jac." She draws her peignoir more tightly around herself, every word dripping with hurt. "You never fight for what you want—not even me."

Coward. The word burrows under my skin, the itch unbearable.

My hands begin to shake. I should stop. I should apologize and reassure her all is well. It's what any courtier ought to do. But I'm angry and sad and tired. So very tired.

"Not all of us were born princesses. I'm sorry you've been told to do something you don't want to do for the first time ever."

Margot's pout dissolves into fierce white lines bracketing her mouth. "Apparently not all of us were born with spines either. Perhaps this is an ailment inherited from your father?"

Her taunting words are a blow to the chest. I go breathless. The room narrows to nothing but her furious face. The trembling moves up my arms, into my body, until every part of me trembles.

In all our years of friendship, even when I broke her heart, Margot never, ever made me feel like I was less than her.

How can she accuse me of cowardice when she's been handed everything she's ever wanted—whether she asked for it or not? How can she say this when she knows the truth of my birth, how I've spent my entire life proving the mocking whispers wrong, proving I belong, whether I wanted to be a part of this world or not?

The silence is cold, colder than the winter night when I thought nothing could come between us.

The princess finally lifts her head. "Get out of my sight." There is no trace of Margot in her face, only the formidable, cold authority of Princess Marguerite de Valois.

I curtsy to her, my mouth a grim slash. "Happy to oblige, madame."

I leave before I cave and apologize like I always do.

Perhaps a part of me is a coward after all.

CHAPTER NINE

SOMEHOW, MARGOT AND I both make it to the Navarrese ball before we would be considered inexcusably late, but not by much. I feel Oncle's reproachful gaze as I'm announced, feel the crushing weight of the court's curiosity as I slink across the pink and white marble floor to my seat.

The Navarrese colors decorate the Louvre's largest ball-room. Cloth of gold and ribbons of scarlet tumble from the musician's gallery above the four towering marble women guarding the ballroom's grandest entrance. Roasted game—made strange by exotic spices—lies barely touched. I spy one French lord feed his entire plate to a dog, his Navarrese neighbor going crimson with anger.

A cold finger zips down my spine, tensing my shoulders. Margot's rage will be like a torch held above a dry field. A single spark turning everything to ash. If she treats the Navarrese delegation horribly, it would give everyone else permission to treat them horribly as well.

"Her Royal Highness, Marguerite de Valois!" the herald cries.

Margot appears between the grand statues. She is laced into a gown of the brightest red, the red of the Navarrese coat of arms, not a trace of her Valois blue to be found. And . . . the gown is ugly. An unfashionable cut in an unflattering color.

She smiles beneath her golden tiara and black braids, daring anyone to laugh.

When King Henry rises to meet her, in a matching doublet of the same too-bright red, her smile falls away completely.

Margot refuses the Navarrese wine, barely touches her food. She does not smile at Henry's entertainers, not even as the court gets drunker, her king-brother laughing louder with a flushed face. I take a too-big gulp of wine. The alcohol burns and does nothing to ease the building pressure in my chest. Oncle pulled strings to seat me beside Margot to make certain she and King Henry had an agreeable time together. But the space betwixt us remains a stubborn patch of snow on spring's first warm day.

Frantically, I wonder if I should spill my wine on the princess, stomp on her foot, create some sort of scene that forces her to leave.

On Margot's other side, King Henry drags a ringed hand through his hair. It tumbles into his eyes, which darken with barely tempered frustration. If we were friendlier—if the sight of him did not remind me of our mortifying encounter and flood me with embarrassment—I might catch his eye and lift my glass in solidarity. *Yes, the princess is a lot. No, it's only a little bit your fault tonight.* I'm so careful to avoid getting caught looking at him that I miss it when he slams back his wine and stands. Oh God, no. I need to pull him back. Tell him whatever he's planned will not improve things because once

Margot is in a foul mood, nothing can save us from it. My hand even lifts to catch his sleeve behind Margot's back—

But he slips away.

Henry goes before King Charles, wine cup carelessly caught between two fingers, his appearance just on the side of disheveled that tips toward dashing and not disrespectful. "Come now, how about a toast?" He flashes the court a smile bashful yet bold, and even the French roar their approval. Henry lifts his cup at the preening King Charles. "I thank King Charles IX for welcoming me and my kinsmen so decadently in Paris." More cheering, more drinking. "I also hope my brother-in-law to-be shall forgive me for bringing his lovely sister a gift."

He beckons someone forward.

Feverish whispers break out among the lesser nobles seated at the back of the ballroom. I grab great fistfuls of the lace tablecloth on my lap, straining to see whatever fresh hell is coming, and then through a gap in the crowded tables—

I gasp, my wineglass and plate lurching dangerously close to my bodice.

There is an adorable pony in Catherine de' Medici's pristine ballroom.

She is shaggy and black, her belly as round as a kitchen pot. Her head barely reaches her attendant's waist. Her halter is dressed in bright red ribbons and golden bells. Unlike on Margot, the red suits her.

The Navarrese king descends and takes the pony's golden lead, turning to Margot with a genuine smile. He does not see how Catherine de' Medici's face has blanched, how her mouth pulled into a frown at the sight of the little hooves striking her marble and gold floors, how King Charles is already holding back his laughter.

"This is a Pottok pony from the mountains of Navarre. I thought she might please you, Marguerite."

Margot ducks her head, a pretty pink blush on her cheeks. If I did not know her better, the blood could be mistaken for a maidenly blush and not the flush of rage. She makes no effort to move to take the pony's lead or sink her hands in her soft fur.

"It would please me if this creature was shown to the stables, my lord, for in our court everything has its place and the place for horses is outside."

Half the court laughs, the other titters uneasily, and I can feel the change sweep through the French nobles like a fickle wind, their princess's rude words tipping the court from happily drunk on Navarrese wine to mirth at its expense. King Charles leans forward, an eager look on his face I like not at all.

Henry of Navarre freezes, cheeks going ruddy and making the red of his doublet even more garish. Even still, he hoists up his horrible mocking smile, the one from the stable. "As you wish, madame."

The pony is whisked away, her little golden bells jingling merrily. I want to grab Margot, tell her she's being utterly ridiculous and embarrassing herself, her royal family, and me. How tremendous a royal ego must be, to be unable to be put aside for even a second! How their backs must bow under the weight!

King Henry returns to his seat, each step like the menacing

stalk of a lion. His face is still red with humiliation. I lean forward with a bright expression, speaking before he or Margot can say anything and make this disaster of an evening even worse.

"Please tell me more about these ponies, Your Majesty. I've never seen anything like them!"

For the second time tonight, I realize instantly I've said the wrong thing. Margot scoffs, and King Charles turns to me delightedly like I'm a mastiff tossed into a bear-baiting pit for his personal entertainment. The hair on my arms rises.

Henry's head tips curiously, his mouth flirting with a smile. He leans back and crosses his calf over his knee. A burst of irritation goes through me. Were he to spread himself out any farther, France would have no choice but to declare war against Navarre to reclaim our ballroom. The blue of his eyes is as black as ice. "I won't. I doubt there's anything I can say that would interest you, Jacqueline d'Argenson-Aunis."

He knows my name.

The realization is a bolt of lightning.

I blink, mouth parting softly. I never told him my name, which means despite the endless days of charming his enemies, the late nights of parties, and the long days of business, he went to bed and thought of me. A hot, wild rush gallops through my veins.

Did I, the niece of a minor vicomte, hurt the feelings of a king?

Margot leans forward, blocking Henry.

"Do not speak to Jac that way. A pony is a gift for a child. You should have known better."

He ignores her and takes a sip of wine. When he sets his cup down with a metallic clang, I flinch.

"Is that what you think, Princess? My thirteen-year-old sister throws fewer tantrums. Perhaps a childish pony was the perfect gift for you," Henry says.

Margot stabs at her meat; the knife screams against the china. "Why don't you simply carry me kicking and screaming to Notre Dame, Your Majesty? We can marry at once and do away with pretending to like each other."

The Navarrese king's expression clouds over faster than a spring sky. His hands flex, knuckles battle scarred and white with tension. "You insult my honor. I would never force a woman to do something against her will. You'll marry me when you wish to, or we shall not marry at all. Excuse me." With a savage movement, he tosses down his napkin and stalks away. His advisors rush to meet him with furrowed brows and urgent, low whispers.

I close my eyes and take in a long, unsteady breath. I want to slither to the floor and disappear. If Margot were a dragon, stomping through the streets of Paris and shattering all in her path, she would do less damage to France than she has tonight in this ballroom.

"Why? You *like* ponies," I finally whisper.

Margot slams her wine cup down, sloshing crimson smears across the white tablecloth. She looks at me for the first time all night. "You know what I don't like, Jac? Secrets."

My stomach drops. For one dreadful moment I'm certain she has seen through me, that she knows I promised to make her wed King Henry.

"Was the love of a princess not enough for your liking, so

you went for a king?" Her words slur together ever so slightly, and too late I realize she has downed perhaps five glasses of wine to my one.

"Margot!" That distant night I turned her down suddenly feels like a half-healed wound split open, the hurt raw and urgent once more.

Her eyes grow overbright with unshed tears.

And then she turns away from me.

The noise of the ball rushes back. There is a riotous dance taking place, something from Navarre, but no one is paying attention. The weight of the court's curiosity presses in on me and the princess, greedy stares drawing their conclusions. I can imagine the whispers scuttling through the corridors like rats tonight, taking the rumor to every corner of the Palais du Louvre before morning. The gossip pamphlets will write of nothing else for days.

Jacqueline d'Argenson-Aunis, a lowborn nobody, is finally out of favor with the princess.

King Charles motions for the musicians to stop playing. A fit of coughing seizes him as he speaks. It goes on for so long, a valet rushes forward with a handkerchief. The Navarrese nobles close enough to see gasp at the crimson blossoming on the fabric. Apparently, news of the French king's ill-health was kept hidden from his supposed allies.

"Enough of that Navarrese nonsense! My sister craves something French." He tosses the soiled cloth at the valet. "Jacqueline. You are a fine dancer. Be his partner."

King Charles points to the youngest Navarrese lord, a boy

who looks like he was out of his gowns and into his breeches only yesterday. The boy jumps as though the French king's finger were a thrown knife.

"M-me, sire?" His voice is still as high as a girl's, breathy with panic. "But I don't know any French dances!"

"Jac will teach you." The sound of my nickname in the king's pleased voice—inappropriately familiar in an official court setting such as this one—raises the hair on my neck.

This is an order, not a suggestion.

The rage and humiliation settle into a nauseating knot inside me. Creating a scene is exactly what King Charles wants. If I react, he will know his game has gotten to me and will have me do it again to please him. If I play along, he'll get bored and torment someone else.

I curtsy, my smile tooth-rotting sweet. "Of course, my king."

The young lord—Hubert or Gilbert, I cannot tell, for his stammer is so violent—takes my hand and tries to wrap his arm around my waist. He bobs just beneath my bodice, far too close for us to dance properly. I glance back at Margot, wondering if she'll say something, if she'll encourage her brother to do something else.

But she does not look at me.

"Play, you fools! Have your ears stopped working?" King Charles roars at the musicians.

We begin to dance.

While I am a fine dancer, like all gently bred girls, the boy doesn't know what he's doing and steps all over me. I try to lead but King Charles shouts that I sully the young lord's honor by not letting him lead, and so the bloody farce continues.

When the song ends, the delighted king calls for the musicians to play another song, to see if practice can improve us. Then a third.

The boy begins crying then, his silent tears dripping on my skirts. My feet are bruised and blistered, but still I smile serenely, giving nothing away.

You are a terrible king, and I hope something terrible happens to you, I think as King Charles roars with laughter, words I could never, ever say, for even thinking them is treason. *I hope I live to see you gone from this throne.*

I look to Margot, desperate for her to put a stop to my humiliation.

But she is as still as marble, her eyes on her lap.

I close my eyes, just for a second, and imagine what life would be like away from court. I wouldn't have to smile while humiliation and pain make me sick. I wouldn't have to keep secrets from the people I cared about. I could do whatever I wished.

I could be free.

A hard tap at my shoulder ruins the dream.

My eyes open to a nightmare.

King Henry is here, vibrating with barely suppressed rage. The collar of his chemise is unlaced, his hair mussed, as though a valet had begun to undress him for the night. "Can I cut in? Surely your king does not mind if a fellow king dances with one of the finest flowers of his court."

I gape. His body blocks out the mocking, gleeful court,

his expression like a thunderhead. He's big, both taller and broader than I'd remembered.

"I—yes?" I say, hating how it comes out as a question. *What is he doing here?*

And then Henry's hand is on my waist, the pressure bruising and confident. Behind him the boy scampers away, still red-faced and crying. An older woman—a grandmother, a governess?—hugs him to her chest.

King Charles's face goes puce. Of everyone in the court, King Henry is the only person he can't order around. But his angry expression eases back into amusement when it becomes clear that Henry cannot dance either, and all of court begins to whisper and laugh about the left-footed king in ways they dared not to do when I danced with a child.

Henry looks as if he'd like to push everyone from the ramparts into the river. "You could have stopped this." His furious whisper sends a wave of gooseflesh across my neck. His boot crushes my foot and pops a blister. A pained hiss pushes through my teeth.

How is this *my* fault? The injustice races through me. A metallic taste blooms across my tongue. "I can assure you I did not *want* to do this."

Henry swings me into a hard circle. I gasp at the sudden direction change. The ballroom blurs into a dizzying red and gold smear. "You could have cried. You could have pretended to twist your ankle. Gilbert is seven." He spins me into his chest, dipping me back so we're nearly cheek to cheek, the muscled line of his body flush against mine. He scoffs, lips brushing the shell of my ear. "You could have done anything at all, and instead you chose to wait for someone to sweep in and save you."

Our eyes meet again, ice to fire. I want to bite him. Shove him. Do anything to dash the perfect golden fury from his face.

He spins me away before I can act, yanking up my hand as the song ends, bowing to King Charles. I curtsy beside him, squeezing my eyes shut behind my hair. Two frustrated tears slip through anyway.

What if there's truth to Henry's callous words?

Coward. The word runs through me again, my skin flushing hot and cold as if with fever.

What if I'm not as talented as I thought I was? What if I can't do the Societas Solis's work? What if I'm ruining my relationship with Margot for nothing? I feel like an ambushed animal, slowly driven into a hole where there's no escape. Everyone I know is here, gathered in this sweltering room, but I feel so terribly alone I want to sob.

I never should've brought up marrying Henry today. I've got to apologize to Margot, make it right even though she was in the wrong, no matter that much of this disaster was her fault as much as mine.

But when I rise from my curtsy, her seat is empty.

She's finally left me as I always knew she would.

CHAPTER TEN

'VE NEVER BEEN more thrilled to learn that King Charles is bored and forcing all of court to the countryside. Château de Chenonceau will be a welcome change—hopefully enough to make everyone forget about my humiliating night—especially since the château is haunted.

The château's reputation is at odds with its beauty. A vision of ivory and blue perched at the river's edge; the grand façade gave way to a regal gallery built on a bridge, stretching from one side of the River Cher to the other.

But the estate's beguiling charms are marred by its hair-raising stories. Locked doors that suddenly spring open. Rancid smells that manifest to one person but no one else. Then there's the legend of the Melusine, the half-serpent, half-woman beast who undulates in the river below. Rumor has it that Catherine de' Medici summoned the monster to menace her dead husband's mistress until the other woman fled in terror and left the riverside gem to the Queen Mother.

I stare down at the restless water beneath my window as I dress. Real or not, if the Melusine also has any tips on match-making, then I'm all ears.

Oncle lowers the pamphlet he's reading, surveying my

breeches with a frown. "Dressed like a boy? Oh, Jac, disguises are so melodramatically English."

"I'm going on the royal hunt to see what else I can learn about King Henry."

King Charles brings King Henry to Château de Chenonceau to test his mettle in a grand hunt. Many deer live in the forest, including the fabled white stag who has eluded King Charles's arrows for years.

Navarre is small, easily crushed by France should war come. King Henry has far more need for peace than Margot does. A king would not linger and suffer humiliation in a foreign court unless he has a good reason. I need to learn more about King Henry, to see if there's a way in with him since Margot refuses to speak to me.

Oncle looks at my shapeless hat next, shaking his head. "I despise this idea, and you look like a mushroom."

I bat my eyelashes. "Do you hate it enough to stop me?"

His eyes drop to the paper he was reading. A line of print snags my attention.

> *Jacqueline d'Argenson-Aunis, finally put in her*
> *place by princess.*

My stomach lurches. These flimsy pamphlets are everywhere in court. Tucked in purses, stashed beside chamber pots. I even watched a footman fix an unsteady ottoman in Margot's parlor by shoving a folded-up stack beneath the leg. All topics are covered by the pamphlets, from religious sermons to the latest clashes betwixt the Huguenots and Catholics, but I know that court's very favorite pamphlets are the ones filled with salacious gossip and outrageous rumors.

I think of how many nobles were stuck in their carriages lumbering across the countryside in the sweltering heat, how many of them could be reading about me. My jaw grows tight.

I knew my work wasn't going well, but if my name is in the pamphlets, then everything is going much worse than I assumed.

Oncle folds the pamphlet so I can't see my name. "I won't stop you," he says. "But do *not* draw attention to yourself once more. Do I make myself clear?"

My smile wobbles. "Crystal."

Outside the Chenonceau stables, I look enough like the other servant boys milling around that no one gives me a second glance.

The lords, however, are dressed to impress. I'm surrounded by a sea of white-clad thighs, everyone's riding breeches cleaned and brushed to snowy brilliance. The gentlemen's riding doublets are detailed with fine embroidery and gleaming silver buttons. They rein in powerful horses, hot-blooded hunters stamping impatiently. The scent of newly sharpened steel mingles with the comforting animal musk, turning the situation sinister.

A royal hunt is all about terror and splendor. My hands are cold at the thought of all the wild animals about to be roused from their homes, the noise and violence to come. The feeling grows as King Charles parades past. The French monarch is dressed in a full suit of gold-plated armor, down to the buckles of the leather straps. There are even gold-dyed feathers fletching the arrows in his quiver, his arrows the length of my entire arm.

I swallow and pull my hat lower. The gleaming of the weapons and the panting of the hounds makes me second-guess my plan. At the first splash of blood, all these men will see that I don't belong.

I flinch as King Henry brushes past me, pulling his horse alongside King Charles. "I've been looking forward to this hunt." Unlike the other men in their riding clothes, the Navarrese king wears subtle, practical clothes that would look at place more on a poacher than on a king.

Yet somehow . . . it suits him. The sharp lines clinging to his powerful shoulders, the flex of his muscled thighs shifting in their dark hose. A lion among dogs. No one would ever mistake him for a peasant though he has dressed the part.

He turns, as if sensing my stare. I duck before our eyes meet, stomach churning.

King Charles gives Henry a smirking up-and-down look. "It appears you left your hunting gear back at Navarre." He snickers at his own joke, his cronies with him.

Henry lifts a crossbow, the weapon nothing like the huge white-and-gold painted monstrosity the king's valet struggles to hold. "We hunt wild boar in Navarre. They are ferocious, violent when cornered. You wouldn't believe how many men I've seen maimed, all of them too slow to escape."

King Charles growls, squeezing his reins tightly. "And

strength matters more than speed when it comes to the stag. Let us hope you are a better French hunter than a French dancer, Henry de Bourbon!"

King Charles and his men laugh again, the sound menacing. This hunt is no hunt, but a political battle. Whichever kingdom fells the great white stag will prove themself the stronger, cleverer of the two today.

King Henry answers King Charles's mockery with a tight-lipped smile. Suddenly I'm overcome with a fierce desire to see him triumph, to see Margot's arrogant, cruel brother lose before his entire court.

The *grand veneur*, the master of the hunt, pierces the air with a whistle. The hunting hounds pour from their kennels, stepping on their too-long ears and clambering over one another to sniff the snarl of white fur in their master's gloved hands. One starts baying, a mournful sound that makes all my hair stand on end, and then another, until their cacophony of howling surrounds us. Then, all at once, the pack rushes away. The roaring men kick their horses into a gallop.

The forest swallows our party whole.

Everything is a blur of churning horseflesh and twisting trees. I cry out as my gelding stumbles, bashed to the side. Henry is immediately lost in the fray.

This was a stupid idea. What did I imagine would happen? That Henry would reveal some secret corner of himself amid all these men? Men can hardly admit to having a single feeling even in private!

Someone screams, close.

I glance up just in time to witness one of the French nobles push a Navarrese man from his horse. He falls, one foot stuck in the stirrup. He drags behind his horse, screaming in agony. The horse stops, rearing fearfully at the weight behind him.

Right in front of me.

I rein in my horse, hard. We skid to a stop.

The hunt is gone, nothing left but the glowing dust in the sun, the thunder of hooves and baying hounds growing fainter. The whir of insects and the rustling of treetops come back with sudden force.

The Navarrese noble is alive, but unconscious, his leg twisted at an unnatural angle. His horse nibbles at a fern, completely at peace.

I release a shaky breath, a fist pressed against my breastbone.

It could've been me on the ground.

I dismount and cut his stirrup. Gingerly, I settle the man's stuck foot on the dirt. He moans, the sound painful and unsettling.

He was *pushed* from the saddle. I saw it with my own eyes.

My mouth presses into a bloodless slash.

I think of King Charles's odd choice to wear armor on a hunt that does not require it, King Henry's boast that he doesn't need such protection. A sour taste rushes into my throat.

A royal hunt would be a perfect place to kill a meddlesome rival and get away with it.

The injured man's shape goes fuzzy before me.

I must find Henry.

If he dies, the Societas Solis will have much more pressing problems than Margot's reluctant heart.

After making sure the unconscious man won't be trampled by his horse, I trail the hunt at a distance, not wanting to be caught up in its deadly thunder again. The shadows slant longer. The dogs' baying quiets, and I begin to see men in twos and threes. The party has split, likely because someone has spotted the white stag. Each man wants the glory of the kill for himself.

The forest grows wilder, so dense my horse can barely pass. I think of moving on, but the scent of newly snapped wood makes me turn. A patch is punched through the thicket, the broken branches still green and damp. The sweet whiff of rotting vegetation wraps around me. The royal forest is bordered by wetlands. No one hunts here because treacherous mud can snap the leg of a valuable hunting horse, pull a man into its depths until he drowns.

And yet, someone braved the danger.

Why?

I picket my horse and follow on foot. The ground softens, and the rotting stench grows unbearable. The thicket thins into a clearing lush with cattails. I keep to the edge of the swamp, trying to avoid the stinking water.

There's a crash as something large moves through the brush ahead. I stop as the crashing gets closer, my breath catching. One white leg appears, then another, and then King Henry's horse comes into full view, his mouth full of shoreweed.

His rider is nowhere to be seen.

My pulse stutters. Was Henry pushed from his horse? Is he

lying broken in the bracken, choking on the stagnant water? I half run, half wade through the swamp, searching for any sign I'm not alone. The royal hunt's noise is replaced by a chilling stillness.

Ivory flashes through the brambles.

I drop to a crouch, drawing my knife.

The white stag.

He stands in the water, nibbling at the cattails. Three hinds follow him as do their fawns, brown flanks freckled with white. A soft breath escapes me.

At the sound, the stag lifts his head.

He is magnificent, his massive antlers dark and striking against his pale coat.

The shape of a man materializes from the shadows, using the stag's distraction as cover to step closer.

Henry of Navarre, the crossbow in his hand. He walks like a stalking cat, each step cautious and deliberate. There is a wondrous, hungry expression on his face.

I drag a hand across my face, the sight of him perfectly fine loosening something in me even as my heart keeps pounding. I bite back the part of me that wants to shout *"RUN!"* at the stag, desperate to let his mysterious magic linger a little longer.

I brace myself for an arrow to shatter the peace, taste blood in my mouth.

But Henry makes no move to lift his bow. Five minutes pass, ten, and still, the king does nothing. He stands for so long my thighs scream, then tremble. I grit my teeth, wanting to sink to the ground, knowing the noise would give me away.

A breeze wanders past, ruffling Henry's golden hair.

The stag's head bolts upright, nostrils quivering. As one, the entire herd crashes away, deeper into the wetlands. Henry throws back his head and laughs. A delighted laugh that lifts to the trees and mingles with the birdsong. He pushes his hair from his eyes and gives the way the stag ran one final, fond look before walking away.

Just as my leg muscles finally give out.

Henry is before me in an instant. When our eyes meet, his furrowed brow gives way to open-mouthed shock.

"What are you doing here?"

My body goes cold even as the warm mud sinks through my clothes. I push myself up with a squelch, ignoring both his question and hand. My knee twinges painfully. I shake my head and push the ache aside, hating how he steps even closer.

I failed at the *one* thing Oncle told me to do. By falling on my arse.

If only the swamp could have done me the favor of sucking me in to finish the job.

"Oh, just waiting for you to come along and save me again!" I snap.

Henry pulls back, his concerned look vanishing. A delighted, vile grin takes its place. "Were you following me?" He presses a hand to his broad chest. "Did you need me to saddle your horse again? I'm flattered, truly."

Heat rushes through me. I hold back the barbed retort I want to fling in his smirking face. 'Tis bad enough the king of Navarre has discovered me—in breeches!—but he doesn't need to know what I was doing. He definitely doesn't ever need to know I was *worried* about him.

"I got lost," I say.

"Doing what?" he asks suspiciously.

"Looking for rushes. I'm very into . . . basket weaving."

There it is. The worst lie of my life. Henry brings out all the worst in me. First that humiliating ball, and now this.

He cocks an eyebrow. "You . . . weave baskets? For fun?"

I sigh, like his question is the daftest thing I have ever heard. "I wouldn't call it fun, but it's something to do. The gentlemen have fun all day long and leave the ladies at home, bored to tears."

His eyes narrow. "And falling in the mud is part of the fun?"

I stand taller, crossing my arms. "It's more satisfying to gather the supplies yourself. There's—there's all different kinds of rushes. I don't have time to explain it to you."

Henry ducks his head, making a soft, disbelieving sound. He goes still, finally noting my cursed breeches.

The water has turned the fabric translucent and clingy. And even though heat surges into my cheeks, I don't try to cover myself. Let him look all he wants. It'll take more than that to shock me. I stand even wider, smirking. The movement drags his attention from my calves, up my thighs, up to my cold stare.

"Spot something you like?" I ask sweetly.

His eyes meet mine, and his smile shifts into something unreadable. "Forgive me. Do you need me to escort you home?

The hunt is dangerous. You should look for your rushes closer to the château."

I bat my eyelashes. "So kind of you, but we both know how inappropriate that would look."

His gaze drops to my breeches again even as his mouth curls into that mocking smile. "Well, we wouldn't want to be *inappropriate*, now, would we?"

I smile back at him, the expression utterly poisonous.

This arrogant king with his obnoxious smile is not someone I can work with, but the merciful king, the one who marveled at the white stag and kept the secret of a wild thing to himself? I can work with that.

And I suspect Margot can as well.

CHAPTER ELEVEN

THE POST-HUNT CELEBRATION is, predicably, a disaster.
Since he failed to kill the white stag, King Charles is in a foul mood and sulks and drinks until he calls for a re-creation of the hunt. His loyal supporters are the stags and he, of course, is the mighty hunter. The young men race through Catherine de' Medici's perfectly manicured gardens, one of them draped in white linen, while King Charles laughs and chases them, hurling sweetmeats, stones, and whatever else he can find. One of the men already has a black eye. Another drunkenly careened into the great bonfire and was taken away because King Charles said his screams spoiled his fun.

Margot and Catherine de' Medici sit beside the king's empty throne. Every time one of them moves to leave, King Charles orders them to sit down, stay, watch what he'll do next. Margot is stone faced, her mother in furious conversation with Cosimo Ruggeri. Perhaps she is begging him for a spell to stop her son. I would not blame her at all.

King Henry and his entourage watch with shocked, scandalized eyes, half of them unable to look away, half of them pretending nothing strange is afoot.

I witness the moment my note makes it to King Henry,

passed along by a Navarrese servant's hands. How his eyebrows scrunch together as he slips it into his pocket.

Sire,

Please forgive this most urgent request for your presence. I beg you to meet me when the clock strikes eleven in the heart of the hedge maze.

Vicomte Gabriel d'Argenson-Aunis.

Eleven o'clock finds me seated inside the rose-covered gazebo tucked away in Catherine de' Medici's boxwood maze, Jehan laid out on the steps before me. While I would prefer to meet King Henry alone, some level of chaperone seemed appropriate lest he get the wrong idea about me. Or that was what Oncle said when he insisted the stammering footman accompany me.

Jehan's snores fill my ears, along with the hooting of owls and the distant laughter from the fete's bonfires. I wonder if King Charles has given up his stupid, foolish game. I wonder if Margot misses me, all alone at the high table. Most of all, I wonder about Catherine de' Medici's prophecy.

The Valois line will end when the Seine runs red.

I assumed she meant the dire consequences of my failures, but what if she spoke of my success? Would it be such a bad thing for the Valois kings' reign to end if this is the best they can offer? Perhaps Margot is better off in Henry's home as his wife instead of in her king-brother's glittering, dangerous court, where surely it's only a matter of when, not if, he marries her off to an older, crueler husband as a prize for his loyalty.

Because as much as I don't want to admit it, as much as I still don't like him, King Henry is far from the worst man in this court.

A flickering light catches my attention. A person has entered the maze. As they draw closer, the glow highlights Henry's face. I let out a shaky breath and smooth the dark green silk of my skirt.

The king stops before the gazebo, frowning at Jehan's sleeping form.

"Vicomte d'Argenson-Aunis?"

"'Jacqueline' will do just fine, thank you." I rise from my bench into the circle of light.

Henry startles, then takes in my opulent dress, the pearl-and-mesh caul pulling back my hair. His mouth hooks into a smile, as slow and scalding as molten sugar. "I believe you missed some mud behind your ear since this afternoon."

I resist the urge to scratch the spot myself, hating how his look makes me feel hot and cold at the same time, hating even more the secret part of me that's pleased we've begun here. Trading words as blows and using wits as weapons.

"Sorry for the change, Your Majesty. I know you rather liked my breeches."

His eyes grow dark, his pleased expression melting away.

You should not be tormenting the king of Navarre. Not when you need something from him.

Jehan jerks awake. He glances betwixt me and the king, cheeks growing flushed. I smile reassuringly. "Jehan, would you please give us some privacy?"

Henry glares after the footman's retreating back. "*You* sent for me. Not your oncle."

"Indeed. Your Majesty, has anyone ever told you your powers of perception are unparalleled?"

He laughs, the sound mocking. "I'm beginning to think you're obsessed with me. Have you not heard I've come here to marry another?" He leans against the gazebo wall, arms crossed, one eyebrow raised.

I roll my shoulders and meet his stare. "We both know it's not like that between us."

His smirk spreads. "If that's true, then why do you keep following me?"

I match his wry smile even though I'd like to stamp on his foot. A war wages in me. On the one hand, I need to persuade King Henry that I'm his ally. On the other hand, the desire to take him down a notch is my fiercest, dearest wish in the entire world. I want to get under his skin the way he gets under mine.

"Why didn't you kill the stag?" I say.

His sly expression slips, just as I hoped. "So you *were* following me, then." I press my lips together, refusing to answer. We both knew I was lying then, so why deny it now? He sighs and fists his hand where it leans against the gazebo wall. "You know how King Charles acts when he loses something he wants. There were other ways to gain the French king's respect without earning his anger."

I stay silent. It's a good answer, but not the one I'm waiting for, the one I'm certain is still locked up inside from how his restless fingers drum along the rose trellis, how he frowns at his feet.

Henry de Bourbon is an appalling liar. At least he has that going for him.

He sighs again, longer than before. "I never saw a creature like the stag before," he admits, still not looking at me. "I felt like this place would lose something if he were gone." His head lifts, his expression piercing. "I'm not the joyless barbarian your court thinks I am."

"I don't think that of you." The words are out of my mouth before I can stop them. I remember his keen-eyed wonder on the hunt. How he rushed to his courtier's defense at the miserable ball even if it meant he was the one humiliated instead.

His eyes flash, lips twisting mistrustingly. I open my mouth to say that I mean it, I'm not making a jest, but I stop myself. It doesn't matter that he understands me. All that matters is that he listens.

"Jacqueline d'Argenson-Aunis." He leans closer—closer than he should.

The space between us has a sudden weight. I whisper back, even though we're alone. "Yes?"

He pauses—the quiet like standing at the top of a slick staircase. "I owe you an apology. I shouldn't have lost my temper with you at the ball. You couldn't have defied King Charles to his face. I demanded you do something impossible and was rude about it. Forgive me."

There's a sudden, sharp ache under my ribs, like I've missed not only a stair, but an entire flight of them. King Henry, apologizing? Admitting he was wrong? I look over his person carefully, searching for a sign that a terrible accident has addled his nerves, but aside from the tired lines around his mouth, he looks the same as ever.

"My young lord's father was killed at my side in battle, so I feel especially responsible for him. And Marguerite was—" He breaks off abruptly, then closes his eyes. "You were not deserving of my anger that evening."

Silence.

The breeze lifts, sending the distant laughter of the fete rolling over us. This far into the garden, it feels as though we're both on the very edge of France. My hand rises, wanting to push the hair from his face to get a better sense of what he's thinking. Then I clench it, worried what he'll assume.

"I—thank you. Your apology means a lot." And I'm surprised to realize that it does. It really, truly does. I can't remember the last time anyone apologized to me, the last time someone hurt me and cared enough to take responsibility.

Henry nods, still not looking at me, his fingers tapping an aimless beat along the trellis.

I swallow back the last of my pride. "Margot—I mean, Madame Marguerite—she can be challenging at times."

He tilts his head, gaze just barely meeting mine. I didn't know an expression could be sarcastic until now. "I suppose you'd know. She's certainly the worst person I've ever met."

I bite the inside of my cheek. "She's going through a difficult time!"

"Why do you feel the need to defend the most pampered girl in all of France? She doesn't need you to fight her battles."

I run my tongue along my teeth, force my jaw to soften. It's a fair question, but I don't owe him an explanation about my feelings for Margot. He wouldn't understand them anyway. Sometimes I barely understand them myself. "Your Majesty. With all due respect, I wish to see the marriage between you and Margot happen to create peace between the Huguenots and Catholics—"

"There won't be any peace until Catholics realize Huguenots don't want to seize power. They only seek freedom for their beliefs and thoughts. As long as King Charles is threatened by any thought which he did not think of himself, there shall be no peace."

I speak of marriage and he speaks of statecraft. Of course. I fight a groan. Only a man would fail to see that the two are not one and the same. "But surely we can both see how this marriage would be a step toward tolerance? A way for Catholics to realize everyone can exist together? It certainly wouldn't make matters worse than they already are. But there shall *be* no marriage unless you can persuade Margot to change her heart, so—"

He scoffs, the sound jaded and tired. "There shall be nothing until Marguerite cares for something beyond herself. Coming to this frivolous court was a mistake. Spain and France both eye Navarre like it's the last scrap of meat on the table. Every day I spend here is another day I could be making myself useful to my people. My mother said the marriage was already arranged. All I had to do was come here and marry her. Instead her brother has made me look like a fool."

My instinct is to angrily push back, defend Margot once more, but instead I consider the situation from his perspective. Navarre is stuck between Spain and France, not powerful enough to resist either. Henry thought his mother, the late queen, had solved the problem of France, but instead he must win France once again. And not in the battlefield, where I know he's spent ample time, but in a game of hearts in glittering ballrooms.

Henry laughs, his gaze unfocused. "I don't know if I can do this without her. My mother was the best leader I knew. I hadn't learned all I needed to from her before she—"

Died.

My hand is on his sleeve as his throat closes up around that last, final word.

He glances at my gloved hand for a long, long moment. Then he looks at me. His expression is a night without stars. "I'm doing all I can. And it's still not enough."

"I know," I whisper, my throat closing up too. I know exactly what it is to never be enough, to fall short each and every time. I didn't come here to understand him more—but it's impossible for me to unsee this; behind Henry's royal title is a boy, orphaned and alone.

I know what it's like to be left by a mother too soon, to both miss and resent her absence.

With great care, he takes my hand and places it back at my side, never once breaking eye contact. Allowing us both to forget it happened. "Can you help me woo my bride, Mademoiselle d'Argenson-Aunis? All of Navarre would be in your debt."

A giddy feeling rushes through me, gusting out in a breathless laugh. I didn't even have to persuade him to let me help. He came to my hand as sweetly as one of Margot's little dogs. So trusting and guileless. Surely, it can't be this easy. There must be a catch. "We hardly know each other. How do you know I mean you well?" I say.

He rocks back from me, soft expression slipping. "God's wounds, you can't make anything simple, can you?"

I shrug, a pleased warmth flooding my body even as my brain screams, *Have you taken leave of all your senses?* This was my plan, was it not, to convince Henry to let me help? But before he found me tonight, I didn't know what helping him would mean. Now I've felt his hot skin under my glove, saw how his wide eyes clung to mine like I was the only thing keeping the loneliness from pulling him under. We have more in common than I expected, and that won't do at all.

I need the distance we had before—when he was a king who thought he knew best and all I wanted to do was best him.

His eyes glint. "Would you have me beg for it?"

"Perhaps. Margot loves a good groveling. It could be good practice for you."

Henry takes one step closer. Then another that has me pulling in a soft gasp. If I breathed too deeply, my bodice would graze the buttons of his doublet. He is too close, inappropriately close, yet something sparkling and hot builds in that single sliver of space, lifting my skin in quivering bumps. It is our ill-fated meeting in the stables all over again, the one that left me strangely breathless.

He finally drops to his knees, midnight eyes boring into mine beneath his golden fringe.

"Jacqueline d'Argenson-Aunis. Will you help me? Please?"

The words drip with insolence. He gives me a dark, smoldering look, and my belly tightens. Power. That's the word. The king has all of it, yet here he is on his knees before me.

I like it. I like him like this, and judging from the gleam in his eye, he likes something about it as well. The realization makes my blood blaze.

"Does my groveling satisfy you, Mademoiselle Jacqueline?" His sly question pulls me back to myself.

I release a too-long held breath, suddenly dizzy. "Yes. And Jacqueline will do just fine. Let's end these theatrics now before your valet wonders at the grass stains on your breeches."

He stands. "My valet would express no surprise whatsoever at the state of my clothes. He has seen it before."

My cheeks roar pink at the implication. I don't give the smirking king the satisfaction of a reply. I've already won, after all. He's doing exactly what I wanted him to do. Not even Oncle could find a flaw in how I've handled this. Were I alone, I'd be preening smugly.

I've finally found a way forward with my matchmaking work.

And I'll do such a great job teaching Henry to woo his bride, the Societas Solis will have no choice but to make me a full member. Oncle shall never dream of giving me such useless, demeaning work ever again.

"When shall we begin? I think tomorrow—"

He holds up a finger. "Not so fast, my dear Jacqueline! There is something we must do first."

I squint at him, suddenly suspicious. "And what would that be?"

He smiles, almost chagrined, but not nearly enough to undo the words he says that make me want to scream.

"Why, we must get your oncle's permission first."

CHAPTER TWELVE

WHEN THE MESSAGE arrives that King Henry of Navarre wishes to call upon Vicomte Gabriel d'Argenson-Aunis, only Jehan's quick hands keep me from tossing the paper into the fire.

I'm absolutely certain that Henry has only done this to gall me. *This*, of course, being the ridiculous rules that let him do whatever he wishes and make the world think I need Oncle's permission to do anything at all. And to think I felt something for him last night!

When Jehan bows and announces King Henry's arrival, I stab my embroidery hoop so savagely I tear the canvas.

Oncle notes the movement with a slight lift of his brows as he greets Henry. "Your Majesty. To what do we owe the pleasure of your visit?"

Today Henry is dressed extravagantly, not a single golden hair out of place. There's no sign of the boy I spoke to the night before, the one I almost liked. Today he is so unbearably kingly it hurts to look at him.

"I wish to speak to you about an . . . idea I have involving your niece. Perhaps we could speak privately?"

He adds the last bit on after I've leapt to my feet, an angry

"It was MY idea!" in my throat. Oncle catches my eye over the king's shoulder and touches his temple. *Keep it together.* He's not wrong, but I resent it. Henry doesn't need to know the extent of our closeness. The less he knows about our family and what we do, the better.

I sit back down and roll my eyes. *The king is an idiot.*

Oncle hides his amusement behind a polite cough. "Of course. This way, my lord."

When Oncle's office door shuts, I'm outside it, an ear to the wood.

At once an angry presence is behind me. "Mademoiselle, please step away." It's King Henry's advisor, Admiral Coligny. The older man slunk in after his king, looking as grumpy as I felt.

I don't move. "This is my apartment, monsieur. Are you telling me where I can and can't be inside it?"

He begins to mutter something that sounds an awful lot like *"obstinate girl."* I ignore him and press my ear to the door once again.

But I can't understand a word.

Oncle speaks a language I don't know, a dialect similar to the Provençal from the lavender-drenched south. My lips twist. Even after all these years, he still surprises me with new secrets: things he never felt important enough to share.

Judging from the long silence, Henry is startled too. In French he finally says, "I did not know you spoke Gascon."

"More people ought to, since Navarre will become a closer ally to France after your marriage. Your kingdom is quite beautiful."

I roll my eyes, holding back a disgusted sigh. What does Oncle stand to gain from flattering King Henry? If his head swells any larger, he won't be able to leave our apartments.

The sound of my name pulls me closer to the door.

"Your niece has agreed to help me, but I wanted to be certain it was something you wished for as well."

"Why would I wish to help you? I've little to teach a handsome king about the heart of a princess." There's an amused edge to Oncle's voice. I can all but see Henry's flush.

"I—I suppose so, yet nevertheless—"

"With all due respect, I prefer not to discuss my niece as if she is a fragile vase that may shatter if looked at the wrong way. I imagine she's outside the door with her ear pressed against it already, so we might as well open it."

When the door swings open, I'm standing a very respectable distance from it. Most certainly not within eavesdropping distance. King Henry glances betwixt me and his glowering admiral, frowning suspiciously. I throttle the urge to make a snide comment and instead give him my most winsome smile and a curtsy.

"Now that you've asked my oncle if he can spare me from his stable like a fine prancing palfrey, can we discuss details of our arrangement? Or do we need my oncle to approve each and every single part of that as well?"

So much for throttling the snide comments. A girl can only do so many things.

Henry's frown deepens. "It is proper—"

Oncle holds up his hands. "This quibbling will not do. Jac,

if you help the king, remember your reputation shall be on the line. The court would assume the very worst about you if you're spotted with him." *And the Societas Solis has no use for ruined noblegirls* lies unspoken in the silence.

"Which seems reason enough to abandon this mad scheme!" The admiral's voice is stern, admonishing. He turns to Henry. "Sire, I beg you to reconsider. Marry the French princess and move on. You already have her brother's permission."

Henry's mouth goes stubborn. "I won't marry a woman against her will."

Admiral Coligny's sigh is large and long enough to fill all the sails of his ships. "Your damn honor will be the death of me and the ruin of this girl, then. I don't need her oncle's fury on my hands."

Oncle's expression grows stormy. "You assume much of me—"

Suddenly both my hands are in the king's. He grips them like he would the reins of his warhorse, his voice low and serious. "Jacqueline d'Argenson-Aunis, I'll protect you against all harm—including gossip—if you help me. Let these men bear witness to my promise."

Heat bursts through every part of me. Even though he's only holding my hands, even though I was flush against his muscled chest when we danced, this feels so much more horribly intimate. The publicness of his declaration makes me want to slither into the river. Let the Melusine nibble on my body until there's nothing left. This is a hundred times worse than being humiliated at King Charles's ball. I don't need Henry's protection. The fact that he thinks I do, the fact that his admiral seems satisfied with the offer, makes me wish Oncle did have some fragile, expensive vases I could shatter.

Oncle's eyes meet mine over the king's velvet-clad shoulders. The corners of his mouth turn up ever so slightly into an approving smile, a look that can only mean one thing.

Well done.

I grit my teeth and duck my head. Oncle's praise should feel like sunlight in winter. It should warm me from the outside in.

But even his praise can't make playing the part of a submissive maiden swallowable.

I accept the Navarrese king's vow, even though my entire soul screams against it.

The king and I agree to meet at midnight in a ballroom in the château's grand gallery. The room with its chessboard floor spans the entire width of the River Cher. While its twin on the floor below has long been completed, the one I'm in remains unfinished. While waiting, I kick the dead leaves into a corner, yank the linens covering the empty window apertures. Château de Chenonceau has gone somnolent with slumber, but it will be hours before I sleep, hours before I'm calm enough to even think of it.

The restlessness worsens when Henry slips inside. He has changed into the same rough-spun wools I first met him in, when I thought he was nothing more than a stable boy. The reminder of how he made me feel back then—all pent-up fury and keen curiosity—makes my eyes skitter away from him.

"I thought we could start with dancing." I'm proud of how my voice fills the space, betraying nothing of my dreadful mood.

He scoffs, no doubt thinking of our humiliation before King Charles. "Dancing? Really?"

"Margot loves dancing. It's one of her favorite pastimes."

"Of course it is. I imagine she also loves painting landscapes and pampering her small bug-eyed dogs?"

I grit my teeth so hard, I fear I may need a visit to the court tooth-drawer before this countryside stay is over. *You need him to like you,* I remind myself fiercely. *Or at least like you enough to listen.*

I ignore his pointed slander and say, "Yes. Dancing is a beloved court activity and Margot likes it very much. If you were a capable dancer, you would have her ear all night."

Henry shrugs with one broad shoulder. "If you say so. It seems an unnecessarily complicated way to have a conversation."

"Who knows best the way to a French girl's heart—me or you?" I snap.

He bows mockingly. "Forgive me for speaking! I'll follow your lead from here on out." He lifts his head, mouth curving. "Or I suppose you're to follow mine, since we'll be dancing?"

I swear to God, this is going to be the longest night of my life.

After modeling the steps, I beckon him to take my hand, and I count out a beat.

His skin is both too dry and too clammy. And his great, stomping boots mash my toes at once. Five times I start counting the lively galliard and five times he steps all over me. I tear away from him with an unladylike curse.

"Are you doing this on purpose? Have I wronged you in some unforgivable way?"

His mocking laugh echoes in the empty gallery. "Perhaps the better question is have I offended you?" He gestures to the unfinished windows, the drop into the river beyond. "You've looked like you wanted to push me out the window since the moment you saw me."

I stab a finger at him, hissing. "There's a proper word for that!"

His mouth twitches into a godforsaken smile. "Defenestration, I know. Is this also part of your lesson? Margot's preferred methods of regicide?"

The truth bursts free, livid and raw. "I'm angry because you mock me for being helpless and then go to my oncle to see if I can really do the things I promise to do!"

He grows more serious, but not nearly enough. "I did apologize for one of those things. Just yesterday, in case you've forgotten. As for your second point, I did what any other man would do. Unwed women do not mingle with unwed men. Did I offend you by vowing to keep you safe?"

"YES! I despise these courtly rules, and you make me despise them even more!" I kick at the stone wall, the violence entirely unsatisfying in soft slippers, and now there's a throbbing in my toes that beats in time to the throbbing in my temples. I mash a hand over my face and drag it down, will my blood to cool.

Behind me, Henry laughs softly. "Poor little noblegirl. Forced to play by the rules that also keep her sheltered in a life of endless leisure and wealth. Tell me, would you rather be a farmer's wife? Or perhaps a shepherdess? Does your beloved princess wish to sully her hands with honest work and escape all courtly ceremony as well?" His voice is suddenly right at my ear. I whip around, nostrils flaring, and we're cheek to cheek. I feel his warm breath on my bare neck, see how his chest rises and falls as quickly as mine even as his cold, level words slip into me like a sword. I want to slap him. I want to scream. A part of me, smaller than the rest, yet more frightening than all the others, wants to cry.

"You know nothing of being a woman. Don't pretend like you do." My words are a brittle shield, a final sally to salvage what's left of my dignity. Perhaps wishing to have a modicum of independence in my life feels small compared to ruling a kingdom. But Henry still has no right to mock me for my desires.

He throws up his arms and walks away. I expect him to leave or to explain my own experiences to me, but all he does is lean against the carved fireplace, one heel braced against the stone behind him. "I'm no woman. But I do know what it's like to live by rules that go against my own desires. Do you think I want to be stuck in a court that mocks my people, trying to persuade a woman who despises me to marry me? I only do this because I must."

The moonlight knifes across his face. Anger and sadness war in the angle of his mouth, and I can't help it, my temper softens to see it.

"Yes, but you like being king. The burden is one you're proud to carry. I don't get to choose what I bear like you can."

He tilts his head, drinking in my raw expression. I let him stare, for once not wanting to hide, my throat going tighter and tighter. It feels like we're on the edge of something new, flirting with the unknown plunge on the other side.

It feels, against all odds, like he might understand me.

I swallow and speak again. "I was angry when you spoke to my oncle because it was you taking my decision from me and giving it to him. I thought we had spoken enough for you to respect me on my own."

It's bad enough my oncle only trusts me with the most ridiculous mission from the Societas Solis, but then to have what little independence I was given taken from me was more than I could bear.

Perhaps my work would be easier if Henry thought me some empty-headed, passive girl, but he's seen too many of my jagged edges for me to keep them hidden. 'Tis a delicate balancing act. I must let him see enough of me to trust me, but not enough that he gets suspicious about my reasons for helping him. He mustn't learn about the Societas Solis.

Henry rubs his neck, frowning like he's missed something, but he doesn't know what it is. "Of course I respect you. I thought I was doing the right thing by asking for permission," he says. "Plus, your oncle is terrifying. Surely you've noticed."

I snort knowingly. "I understand you thought you were right. But perhaps next time before making assumptions you can ask me first?"

The specter of a smile touches his mouth. "Even if what you want ignores all respectability and should get you sent away to a nunnery?"

I refuse to smile back, even though part of me wants to. "Yes, most especially then. Women dislike not being listened to, Margot most of all."

He laughs unexpectedly. "Ah, there it is."

"There what is?"

"My first lesson."

My smile finally slips free. His lips curve in response, the bottom one slightly plusher than the top one. There's the strangest tug under my ribs.

His next words are so quiet, I strain to hear them over the rushing river. "For what it's worth, I've never thought you needed saving. If I truly believed that, I wouldn't be here now putting my pride in your hands. Do you know what the court would say if they learned I begged for help to win my bride's heart? You could crush me if you wanted."

"I wouldn't." The promise slips out immediately.

"Why should I believe you?" His question isn't accusatory, only curious.

I think of the scandal of my birth. How even Margot stooped to use it against me. "I know what it's like to be gossiped about, and I don't wish it on anyone. You have my word."

He studies me again with that same quizzical tilt. Then he pushes off the fireplace, his broad-shouldered shadow filling the entire room. "All right then." He extends a hand. "Shall we dance? There are hours left before dawn."

His fingers are nothing like a lord's. They are calloused, scarred with fine white lines from a lifetime of fighting for others. After a single moment, I curl my fingers around them.

"Thank you."

I peer up from my lashes. "Whatever for?"

His thumb brushes my gloved knuckles, lighter than a damselfly, there and gone just as fast. His smile is soft and guarded. Nothing like the mocking ones I've seen before. "For being honest."

The words slip into me like stones.

Henry thinks I'm truthful, but the list of secrets I'm keeping from him is enough to fill an entire book.

CHAPTER THIRTEEN

S O WHEN YOU said we were going to the races . . ." King
Henry trails off, surveying the racing green with the sad
look of someone ordered to work on a feast day.

"It was always a *dog* race, yes." Margot's smile dazzles
more than the diamonds in her tiara.

The young people of court are gathered on the grassy lawn
beneath a robin's-egg-blue sky. Fluffy little white dogs scamper
every which way, the colored ribbons around their necks the
only way to tell them apart. Margot's dogs are adorable in a
painful, heart-squeezing sort of way, even though she and I
disagree over how many dogs is an acceptable number of dogs
to have.

"So how does this work?" Henry says.

Margot gestures to the servants drawing out racing lanes.
"Everyone chooses a dog to win, and we wager on them." Her
smile turns sharp. "Do you need me to explain more? I'm not
entirely sure if racing is a pastime in Navarre or not."

Henry smiles back, not rising to her bait. "I believe I shall
figure it out." He claps his hands together and looks at the
dogs. "Now, which of these is fastest—"

"Oh, *mon amour*, don't worry about that at all! I've picked one out especially for you." Margot stoops to a wicker basket, placing something on the ground. "My dearest Cerberus!"

The ancient dog blinks grey-filmed eyes, as if just woken up. She is at least a half size smaller than the others.

Henry gamely picks up the dog. Her geriatric bladder gives out onto his polished boots.

The gathered nobles gasp, hiding shocked looks and pointed smiles behind their painted fans.

Henry beams at Margot like nothing out of the ordinary has happened. "What an excellent name you've chosen, *ma choupette*. I quite see the likeness to the Greek monster. There is no doubt this face is the last thing many men have seen in the underworld."

Cerberus's tail wags, as if she agrees with him.

When the other nobles are distracted, I give Henry the smallest nod of approval. He shoots me a wink.

I have dutifully tutored Henry in both dancing and the details of Marguerite de Valois in the half-finished ballroom every night since our agreement. He has done well for himself, gifting her with her favorite flowers each morning (pink roses) and her favorite sweet each night (a raspberry macaron). But the fact I impressed upon him above all else is to never, ever give insult to any of her dogs. No matter how much they bark. No matter how many times they pee on him. The one constant in Margot's affections is her dogs.

The dog races are the first amusement Margot has hosted since we arrived at Château de Chenonceau, which means it's Henry's first chance at a second impression.

The king and his dog lose every race, as everyone knew they would. But Henry is a good sport about it, cheering Cerberus onward even when she decides to take a nap in the middle of the track. While no one is quite brave enough to join his cheers with Margot right there, people smile and clap politely, true delight on their faces.

The princess watches it all with a smile that doesn't melt the ice in her eyes. She heaves a frustrated sigh when Cerberus has the audacity to lick Henry's chin. He kisses the dog's brow, and several ladies-in-waiting swoon at the sight.

You tiny traitor, I think. The dog toddles over to her mistress and rests her chin on her pink slipper. Henry follows, handsome as a newly minted coin in white linen, his golden hair mussed boyishly. I hide a smile behind my fist.

"Are you enjoying yourself, Your Majesty?" Margot asks sweetly, her voice dripping with insincerity.

"I didn't expect this to be fun, and yet"—Henry gestures to the perfect blue sky, the men still enthusiastically engaged with the races behind him—"you have planned a perfect afternoon, *ma cher.*"

Margot's polite expression spasms. "I'm surprised. Most men look down on small dogs."

Most men would find it humiliating to lose lurks unsaid behind the words.

Henry drops to one knee, level with the princess in her wicker chair. He braces an elbow on her armrest. She glances at his arm in her space, surprise dashing across her face. My entire world narrows to them, to Henry's mouth at her ear with its pearl-drop earring. "Perhaps I am not like most men, then."

My fist presses painfully against my teeth, holding back a shriek. How is it even possible this man is the same bumbling king I met only days ago? Confidence becomes him, tempers his careless golden splendor to something shining.

Judging from the raised eyebrows and meaningful glances of the other ladies, I'm not the only one who has noticed this change in him.

Instead of insulting King Henry, Margot has instead given him a platform to make himself likable. She should have never assigned him Cerberus. It's impossible not to be charmed by the king's enthusiasm for the tiny, old dog. Margot will never be interested in him romantically, but he has made himself interesting, which is far more likely to hold her attention.

Margot scoffs and turns away. She notes the fluster among her ladies and scowls. "I think we can all agree King Henry has lost enough for today, yes?" She snaps her fingers, and the servants begin to clear away the race lanes and usher the dogs back into their wicker baskets. The nobles draw together like a flock of sparrows eager for their next entertainment. The men even pull Henry into their own conversation with not a single trace of malice to be found. Only Margot sits alone in her chair, jaw tensed.

I take advantage of the chatter to press closer to her.

"I miss you and I'm sorry." My words tumble out quickly, too low for anyone to hear.

When today's invitation arrived at my door, my heart had

leapt at the sight of it. But there was no extra note from Margot herself, no sign that she had invited me of her own choice at all. We still haven't spoken since our fight, and each day that passes since then feels like a splinter digging deeper under my skin.

She looks at me with wary, dark eyes. "Jac."

My chest clenches at the sadness in that single word. "It was never my intention to hurt you."

Margot looks past me. Catherine de' Medici's billowing black-clad figure strides across the lawn. She looks like an escaped abbess, sent to punish all the nuns in her care for the sin of enjoying a gorgeous summer day. At the sight of her daughter, her face draws into an angry scowl.

Margot stands abruptly, turning from me. Never has the single inch she has over me felt like a foot until now. "I know. But I can't speak to you now. It's best if you go."

The dismissal knocks the air from me. Margot leaves without a second glance, her smallest finger with its sapphire ring brushing along my arm. I touch the cold path, wondering if it was an accident, desperately wishing for it to mean *something*.

Clearly, she does not yet forgive me. But is she any closer to it? Or has this mission already shattered my only friendship?

Perhaps there's not even a point in returning to Margot's good graces. If my plan works, she'll be married in August, in Navarre by fall.

The thought chills me. I press a hot fist to my breastbone, as if I could shove the awful feeling aside, melt it away, like I never thought it at all.

If I succeed, then Margot will leave France for good.

Leaving me here alone.

The air gets stuck in my lungs. *She won't be here forever.* Oncle always warned me to guard my heart around Margot, but I didn't listen. Is this what he meant? Did he know I would be one of the people pushing her into her new future? Pushing her away from me?

The courtiers follow the princess, pastel ducks swimming in the wake of a swan. Only Henry stops for me.

"That went well, yes?" he whispers, cheeks flushed and half smiling.

My smile wobbles. "You make your tutor proud."

He steps closer, brightness fading. "Is something amiss?"

Up ahead, I see the men turning, no doubt wondering where the Navarrese king has gone. I step away from him. "No, of course not. I must go. My oncle sent for me."

Henry frowns. "I did not see you receive any summons—"

But I'm already walking away—head held high, holding closed the edges of the hollow ache in me before he can see it.

There's no point letting Henry get any closer to me.

I'm already going to lose one person dear to me when this mission succeeds. I don't think I could bear to lose another.

CHAPTER FOURTEEN

"LOOK ALIVE, JAC!" Jehan's parry knocks the knife from my hand again.

This time I let the blade lie there. Then I puddle down beside it, my skirts billowing. I've never looked more like a tragic soufflé. Perhaps Margot should cast me as one in her latest court masque. Slowly deflating is all I am good for these days.

I'm up all night teaching the Navarrese king the mysteries of courtly romance. But since the work I do is secret, I'm not excused from the duties and expectations of court the next day.

"Mademoiselle?" Jehan nudges me with his toe. "We have a lot of time still." Before I started this mission, we would parry blades in our family's private chambers to spare the court the scandalous sight of a young lady wielding a blade. It used to be the highlight of my days, the single hour when I could do something for myself.

"I wish to sleep." I dream of my mattress and its plump pillows the way a starving man dreams of a feast.

Madame Dupont sidesteps us with a cluck of her tongue. "Lovers' hours. What did I tell you about them?"

My cheeks warm. Each time she says the phrase as of late,

I swear, they get a little bit hotter. "You have said very little about them, except that they are both the very best and the very worst part of any person's life. That covers every sort of experience any person can have!"

Madame Dupont unravels the large bolt of fabric in her arms. The gown unfurls with a thump, its heavy weight trimmed in an endless cascade of ruffles and flounces.

"His Majesty's throwing another ball tonight," she says with the gravity of someone delivering the grim news of an unexpectedly dead relative.

Jehan mock gasps. "*Quelle surprise!* Who would have guessed His Majesty would do such a thing?"

Since King Charles is unable to best King Henry at anything else, he seems to have decided to outdrink the Navarrese men each and every night. I shudder, already smelling the wine.

"Come now, Jac. It shall take me at least an hour to hide the purple around your eyes." Madame Dupont, not one for displays of mirth, flashes a razor-thin smile.

I groan and they both laugh, cruel things. "Can't we say the château's curse has gotten me? Locked me in my bedchamber, perhaps?"

Another voice answers. "Best not mention the curse where anyone can hear you."

Oncle stands in the doorway, just returned from a privy council meeting. "Catherine de' Medici told us her dead husband's mistress visited her in a dream and spat curses at the Valois name."

I scoff, even as my heart beats faster. "She cannot possibly think that's true."

The Valois line will end when the Seine runs red.

Except . . . I have never seen the Queen Mother look at me the way she did when she had her vision. It was like nothing of her was inside her, like something else was pulling her strings.

Oncle doesn't think her visions are real, and he certainly doesn't think they mean anything, but I can't stop thinking about it, worrying about it when I should be sleeping.

Oncle gives me a long, searching look. Like he knows there's something I'm keeping from him. "I want you to start wearing this." He offers me a wrapped canvas parcel.

Within is a sheathed knife on a finely made waist belt. I slip the blade free and test my thumb against its perfectly honed edge. This is a true weapon, far more dangerous than the hidden blades in my hairpins. I've wanted a weapon like this for a long time. Something in my chest clenches at the sight of it now. "Why? You always told me it was too conspicuous to go about armed."

"Madame Dupont has sewn hidden slits into your skirts. If you wear it over your underthings, no one will notice it's there."

I sheathe the blade with a satisfying *snick*. "What changed your mind about arming me?"

Oncle strokes his sun signet ring, a series of emotions dashing across his face, each one too quick to read. He settles into his customary frown. "It eases my mind to know you can take care of yourself. There have been . . . strange reports from outside the château."

My hands tighten on the weapon. "Such as?"

He cups my cheek, offering up a smile that doesn't touch his eyes. "Only rumors of thieves. Nothing to worry about. Come now, let's ready ourselves for another godforsaken ball, shall we?"

I take his offered hand, nodding slowly.

If he's not worried, why would he arm me now, after refusing to do so for years?

The press of the sheathed blade against my waist keeps the question close all evening.

When Henry joins me in the unfinished ballroom later that night, I'm wearing my most comfortable yet acceptable gown, am gloveless, and surrounded by a spill of books.

He leans against the doorframe with crossed arms. "Please don't make me tell King Charles you've stolen every book from the royal library."

"His Majesty wouldn't know what a book was if it hit him in the face. Come here." I pat the floor beside me. "It may shock you to learn that most ladies of the French court would happily be buried in an avalanche of books. We will discuss philosophy tonight."

"Why?" Henry settles beside me as though the books may bite him. "I thought dancing and dogs were the surest way to Marguerite's heart."

I bristle to Margot's defense like always. "She's very well-read, actually."

Henry trails his scarred fingers over the book covers. He's pushed up the sleeves of his chemise, baring tanned forearms crisscrossed with a tapestry of silver scars. "Wonderful. Then we will have a shared pastime to whittle away the soul-sucking silence when we are married." He picks up a book and frowns at the cover. "Aristotle. I imagine she despises him. He wrote the most dreadful things about women."

I sit back, surprised. "So you've heard of these philosophers then?" I know the king spent most of his teen years fighting in the wars of religion.

"My mother only allowed me to join the military if I brought my tutors with me." His mouth pulls into a wry smirk. "Did you expect less of me? I thought we were beyond assumptions, Jacqueline."

My cheeks grow warm at his teasing. I drag my hands over my face to hide the blush. *You know better than to underestimate him.* Henry has made a quick study of everything I have shown him thus far. Why does it surprise me to learn he's always been a dutiful student?

"Forgive me. I should've asked. I'm thrilled you know this already because now I can go to bed."

Henry holds up a hand. His expression is shocked, offended even. "You mean to sleep? When the night's barely started and you're not expected anywhere for hours?"

"Ugh, why does everyone insist that these lovers' hours are an acceptable time to be awake?"

Henry's eyebrows, a shade darker than his hair, rise knowingly. I roll my eyes and begin gathering up the books. "If you make a crass joke, I'll ignore it. It's late and I'm exhausted. Good night, Your Majesty."

He reaches out to stop me. "What about a ride?"

His fingers barely graze my knuckles, but I swear, I feel it like a full-body tackle. Gloves. What was I thinking, not wearing them? "On horses?"

"On horses is traditionally how it's done. Unless there's something else about the French court you haven't shared with me?"

I snort, ignoring his joke, as promised.

It has been ages since I've left the château. My world has narrowed to nights with the king and a blur of courtly duties. It is nothing like the hair-raising adventures I'd hoped to have working for the Societas Solis. I'm exhausted, yes, but I'm also bored.

I never expected my spy work to be *boring*.

Oncle's warning about risking my reputation feels a lot less important when the entire château is snoring. No noble would leave their bedchamber at this ungodly hour, much less the château grounds.

The risk of being seen seems small. . . . Small enough that it would be worth it to ride Anémone again.

"Fine," I relent. "It must be a short one though."

Henry's delighted whoop makes me smile far more than it should.

We sneak past the sleeping grooms to saddle the horses ourselves. When we reach the road ambling along the edge of the royal forest, Chenonceau sleeping behind us, I'm able to take the first full breath I've taken in ages.

Henry nudges my slipper with his boot. "Careful. If you sigh any louder, you'll wake the château."

I laugh, hiding the zip that goes through me at his touch. "I've missed riding."

"Why not join Princess Marguerite and her ladies each morning then?" he says.

"I'm not welcome on those rides." I bite my lip and pray he leaves it at that. I've been hoping Henry doesn't notice how Margot and I are not talking, not when I'm his tutor for all her likes and dislikes.

"Is this because of your father? I've heard he wasn't a lord."

I wince, biting my lip so hard it hurts. Of course he could not leave it alone. Henry is like a hungry hound. Once he gets a meaty bone in his mouth, he'll never let it go. Anémone snorts and tosses her head, sensing my discomfort.

"Who shared these rumors with you?" I demand.

"It's just . . . something I overheard after the dog races," Henry says carefully, as if the actual words he overheard were far worse than he's letting on. They probably were. All the court has taken Margot's cold shoulder as an invitation to snub me themselves. "My admiral even warned me your tutoring might be a ruse to get me to marry you instead. Can you imagine?" He laughs, the noise too loud for the empty road.

My knuckles go white on the reins. "If my company is so disreputable, then why are you out here with me?"

Henry urges his horse into a trot, turning around to face me. The moonlight slices across his face, highlighting the strong line of his jaw, the placating hand he raises. "You misunderstand me. I don't care about your birth, and I certainly don't think you're trying to trick me into anything."

"You ought to care. Everyone else does," I mutter darkly.

I knee my horse past him, pretending I don't see his shocked expression. "This actually bothers you, doesn't it?"

My grip tightens even more. Anémone tosses her head and turns in an anxious circle. Henry catches her bridle, stopping us. He fills my entire vision, every inch of him gleaming from his polished boots to his dark navy jerkin. Even out here, he can't dim his shine. No one would mistake him for a peasant. With me riding astride in a threadbare gown, I'll be the one to get us caught. I'll be the reason he loses the court's respect and ruins the royal betrothal. This was a bad idea. "We should leave," I whisper.

Henry doesn't move. I keep my eyes on Anémone's neck, determined not to face him.

"Do you know why I don't care about your birth? You're the only person who wanted to help me. You understand what's at stake when everyone else wagers on how long the foreign king and his backward court shall last. France is the backward place, if a person's worth lies in their blood and not in their deeds." His voice lowers to a growl. "I hate that you're made to feel less for things which are not your fault."

His anger is no flare, but the burn of the sun at its zenith. All at once I imagine him on the battlefield; I think of what it must be like to have this expression be one's final glimpse of this earth. A blinding blaze, then nothing.

I turn away, unable to bear it. "That's the way things are. I have risen above my circumstances."

I feel the weight of his stare like a boulder, crushing and

unmoving. He finally releases Anémone. "That's what I mean. In Navarre, there wouldn't be anything for you to rise over."

My jaw grows tight. I don't want to talk about myself anymore.

The road unspools through the rolling countryside, a length of silver ribbon, a dare.

At my touch, Anémone explodes.

There's a surprised shout, and then I hear Henry galloping in our wake.

I lift my head, letting the wind tear my hair from its plait, feeling the damp press of the summer night lash my cheeks. Vignettes of vineyards and ripe fields flash beyond the trees. I let Anémone run until she wishes to run no more and my heart overflows with all the feelings I've kept locked up for weeks. How every day Margot's silence feels like another minute without air, how Oncle is gone more days than he's here and he still doesn't tell me where he goes. How Henry, for all his ridiculousness, has managed to nestle into my empty heart like a stubborn cat even though he's just going to leave me too.

I run until I'm too tired to feel any of it.

Henry slows to a walk beside me, cheeks ruddy, panting. "If your princess actually liked riding, there would be hope for us!"

I kick at his calf halfheartedly, glad he's decided to talk of other things. At this point, I'm certain he insults Margot only to get a rise from me. "Oh, stop that! Being a dog person is honorable in its own way."

Suddenly, he goes rigid in his seat. He grabs Anémone's bridle again, sending her skittering sideways.

Outrage surges through me. "What are you—!"

He shakes his head, a finger to his lips. Then he points.

A graveyard lies ahead, its unlocked gates yawning open.

The rhythmic thud of shovels rises over the wall.

Two men dig up a grave, and another two are already open.

The knife under my gown suddenly feels like a hideous jest. Oncle told me there were rumors of thieves beyond the château walls, but he failed to mention that the thieves were *body snatchers*! The corpse in the Societas Solis apothecary flashes across my mind, Louise spattered up to her elbows in gore. Someone is stealing parts from the dead in Paris.

Could the same people be out here? Over a hundred miles from the royal capital?

"Stay here." Henry dismounts, hand going to his sword.

I catch his shoulder, stopping him. "Don't. There could be more of them." There's also a wagon drawn by a mule in the yard. Canvas covers the cargo in the bed.

Something that looks horribly like an arm falls from underneath the fabric.

I clap a hand over my mouth, fearing I might be ill.

"How can you suggest we ignore this?" Henry whispers furiously.

Because if we chase them tonight, we'll scare them away, but if we leave now we could catch them tomorrow. The lesson I learned at Oncle's knee is obvious to me.

"You can't possibly be concerned about your reputation at a time like this!" he insists.

I roll my eyes. "Good God, *of course* not!" The king can't

know what I know. What's obvious to him is that something wrong is happening and he's in a place to stop it. If I don't let him act now, he'll be suspicious of me later.

He takes off charging into the cemetery. Surprised shouting shatters the silence. I unsheathe my new dagger.

One man hurls himself over the wall and disappears. The other follows soon after. I watch them go from the shadows, not moving an inch, hating how I can't do anything useful.

Henry storms out, mud up to his knees, fury in his eyes. "Cowards! What monster disturbs the dead?" He glances to the darkened chapel. "I should wake the priest and let him know. Come inside the gates in case they return."

The river rushes behind the graveyard. Frightened, the mule has dragged its wagon almost into the water. At the sight of us, he whinnies.

"If someone comes, call for me," Henry says. His words are a command, not a question. I almost tease him for it, but the warrior before me is not someone to tease. Any gently bred girl should be swooning by now, and that's what he thinks I am. He truly means to uphold this vow to protect me, doesn't he? How . . . sweet, in a misguided, unhelpful way.

I nod, holding my dagger in the fall of my skirts where he cannot see it. "Of course, Your Majesty."

He walks away, then turns around abruptly. "And Jacqueline?"

I freeze. I've already slipped one foot from the stirrup. "Yes?"

His mouth goes soft. "Don't look in the wagon."

I wait until he disappears. Then I scramble down and investigate.

Splintered coffins lie at the bottom of the open graves. Judging from the carvings on the weathered tombstones, the dead were people of some minor repute. Ancient chevaliers, perhaps. The Loire Valley is riddled with medieval châteaux.

Even upwind of me, the whiff of grave dust oozes from the wagon. I make my way down to the river, the smell growing stronger. I brace myself and tear the canvas off the wagon bed.

Two bodies, both long dead.

I frown, eyes skittering over the peeling skin and the greyed bone. Nothing like the newly dead bodies in Paris. Robbing graves for riches, I understand. But this? What worth is a skeleton to anyone?

I search the rest of the wagon, careful to avoid unsettling the bodies further.

My fingers brush something tucked beneath the wagon's seat.

A book, barely bigger than my palm.

I touch the cover, feeling the leather's smoothness, as if it had been safely tucked on a shelf until very recently. I open it, angling to read in the moonlight reflecting off the water.

A Book of Hours. A common prayer book with illustrated pages. I've seen them a hundred times before—there are more than one in Oncle's estate—but they're costly to make, dearly valued by the people who keep them.

Why would someone bring such a valued possession on such a disgusting errand?

Men's voices break the quiet. A lantern winks amid the

darkness, Henry and the priest heading toward me. I shove the book down into my bodice before their light catches me.

Right as something wraps around my ankle.

And yanks.

Pulling me into the river.

I slip into the water, my vision spotting black. Cold rushes into my slippers, turns my skirts and stockings into leaden weights.

A hard pressure catches my elbows, stopping my slide. Henry. I clutch at his arms, gasping raggedly.

"Did you fall?" he demands, still holding me upright.

I swallow, throat raw. I don't remember screaming. "No, something grabbed me."

I *know* I did not imagine what I felt. I know in my bones that if I were alone, I would have been dragged out into that dark, drowning current.

The priest lifts his lantern toward the river.

There's nothing in the water. It flows gently, moonlight feathering across the ripples. With a sudden burst of embarrassment, I realize the river can't be more than waist-deep as far as the eye can see. I was never going to drown. Nothing could have snuck up without me noticing.

But impossibly, something did.

Henry kneels and holds out his hands. "May I look?" At my nod, he braces my foot on his knee and lifts my soaked hem.

My stocking is slashed above the ankle, the shallow wound bleeding sluggishly.

The priest frowns, still in his humble nightdress. "Is your wife all right, sir?"

Henry drops my foot like it's a big hairy spider.

I suck in a breath, cheeks burning at the misunderstanding. Even though I want to, there's no point in correcting the priest. Not without raising his suspicions. I straighten my soggy skirts with as much dignity as I can muster. "I'm as well as I can be, thank you."

The priest and Henry share more words. I ignore them, mind racing, struggling to put the strange pieces all together in a way that makes them fit.

Bodies defiled in Paris. Skeletons unearthed at Chenonceau. What, if anything, do they have in common?

When we ride away, I feel the hidden Book of Hours beneath my bodice like a second heart.

CHAPTER FIFTEEN

TONIGHT, THE GRAND gallery of Château de Chenonceau arches like a ribbon of light over the river. But inside, it's as grim as a funeral.

Black muslin hangs from the chandeliers, and the long black-and-white checkered floors twist onward and onward as far as the eye can see. By the time Oncle and I arrive, the entire court is there in their funeral blacks.

He takes in the scene and sighs. "Another danse macabre."

I think of the mural painted on the wall of the Cimetière des Saints-Innocents, the one of dead skeletons dancing with the living above the graves, how strange it feels with the pulse of Parisian life just beyond the cemetery's walls. A stark reminder that death comes for all. A shudder inches through me. "Why is this happening?"

"Catherine de' Medici seeks to honor her husband, the late dead king." Oncle nods toward the Queen Mother, resplendent in a dress that shimmers with thousands of black pearls. She floats through the crowd, smiling beatifically as if at a wedding, an expression so out of character that courtiers blanch and cross themselves in her wake.

It's the worst party I've ever been to, which is truly saying something.

The Navarrese court sticks close together, frowning and muttering like a flock of distrustful ravens. Not that I can blame them. If someone had lured me to their country estate and welcomed me like this, I'd already be packing my trunks.

King Henry's golden head appears. He's devastating in his simple black velvet and silks, the fabric clinging to all the right places. My God, who let him come here looking like that? My heart climbs into my throat, and our eyes meet from across the room. One corner of his mouth lifts. I flash him a tight-lipped smile and turn away. Oncle takes my elbow, his voice a firm whisper. "Remember what we talked about."

When I came into our apartments last night—soggy and blood-soaked and scaring Madame Dupont half to death—Oncle had set me down in his study beneath a blanket.

"Where have you been?" His eyes sparked dangerously.

I told him everything, from our ill-advised midnight ride to the graveyard and the exhumed bodies. He listened, his silence like a noose tightening about my neck the longer it went on.

"This was the only thing the grave robbers left behind." I slid the Book of Hours across the table. In the flickering candlelight, the prayer book looked so innocent. Perhaps one of the men—almost certainly paid to do their grisly work by someone else—brought it with him as a talisman against the dead spirits they disturbed.

But when Oncle's hands touched the leather binding, he flinched as if burned.

"Do you think these grave robbers are related to the ones in Paris?" I asked.

He shook his head and tapped his thumb against the table,

his sun signet ring thudding with each movement. "King Henry doesn't know you found this?"

I shook my head, squirming. "No, I hid it from him."

"Well, at least you did something right, then." He stood abruptly, his expression lethal. "What were you thinking? Why would you leave the château grounds with the king? What could possibly have inspired you to endanger your life, your reputation, and the Societas Solis's work all at once?"

"Henry insisted." The lie rolls off my tongue a near whisper.

Oncle shook his head, turning away from me. As if my actions were so unfathomably witless, he couldn't bear the very sight of me.

"Then keep your king on a shorter lead next time. You've done good work so far, Niece. I would hate to see you fail now."

The memory of his disapproval stings my pride as much as my heart. I yank my arm from Oncle in the crowded gallery ballroom. "I remember."

His mouth twists, as if he's on the verge of saying something else, but all he does is nod and disappear into the crowd.

Lively music capers down the walls, weaving through the hush of conversation and awkward laughter. No one knows how to conduct themselves at this strange event, whether we are here to mourn the dead king or celebrate him, and no one is brave enough to ask Catherine de' Medici what she wants. Her creepy sorcerer, Cosimo Ruggeri, has even set out a portrait of the dead king beside King Charles's throne. The man stands in the frame's right side, the left of it covered in black crepe. If I peeled the fabric aside, I'd doubtless find one of King Henry II's mistresses painted beside him. The thought fills me with a strange ache. Catherine de' Medici is so devoted to her husband in death, but he never was devoted to her in life. It's sad, how much she lives in the past when she has so much power to shape the future.

I plant myself inside one of the oriel windows. The gallery is so narrow, there is no escaping the danse macabre, but at least here there's some quiet. The moonlight silvers the coursing water beyond the open window. I pillow my elbows on the sill and gaze at the dark rush. My hidden knife digs into me as I lean forward.

There's something Oncle's not telling me.

This, in and of itself, is not surprising. Oncle has kept secrets my entire life, *"for your own safety,"* he'd always assure me with a smile. Except whatever he's keeping from me now no longer feels like it's for my safety. It feels like he's hiding something on purpose, afraid I'll find it if he gives too much away.

"Don't get too close to the water, *ragazza*!" a sly voice laughs.

I spin around. Cosimo Ruggeri leans against the wall. A pleased, leering grin splits his face at my surprise.

I force my hand away from the knife hidden in my skirts. "Why do you address me so informally, monsieur? I didn't think you were welcomed at events like these." Which is true. Or it was true in Paris, where his unpopularity often shuttered him away in the Valois apartments. But more and more on this trip, I have seen him trailing the Queen Mother like a hideous shadow, waiting at King Charles's side with a glass of tonic whenever the king spots a handkerchief scarlet with his cough. He must be concocting a miracle cure for King Charles's consumption if Catherine is willing to extend him invitations to court events.

Cosimo draws closer, his voice dropping to a whisper. "The Melusine tasted your blood once and thirsts for more of it."

The cut on my ankle stings. A chill gusts through the open window, raising the hair on my exposed skin. How does he know I was at the river last night? Was Cosimo one of the men digging in the graveyard?

I lean away from him, revolted by the very thought. "The Melusine isn't real."

He grins again, and I swear, there's something pointed about his teeth. "Just because you don't believe in her doesn't mean she's not real."

A bright voice rises above the din. "Jacqueline! It has been *ages*."

I've never been happier to see Lady Hélène and Charlotte. Cosimo slinks away as the ladies-in-waiting approach, flashing me one final greasy smile.

Lady Charlotte stares after him, giggling. "Was he courting you?"

I frown, certain I've misheard. "Of course not."

She giggles and bats her eyelashes. "Pity. We thought you finally set your sights on a husband befitting your birth."

Heat bursts through me, relief blackening to shame in an instant. Of course they're not here to save me from an awkward conversation. They get nothing from being kind to me. The ladies lean closer, expressions vivid and lustful. I smile with as much sweetness as I can muster. "Actually, we were talking about you, Lady Charlotte. We agree you'd look quite fetching with cat ears. Cosimo has a spell that could help you grow them. Wouldn't that be marvelous?"

Lady Charlotte gasps, hands patting her jeweled hair combs. "*Cat ears?*"

My smile grows cloying. "Yes, to better match your catty personality!"

Their mouths drop into identical shocked expressions.

There's suddenly a towering presence at my back. A throat clears behind me, as if holding back a laugh. "Mademoiselle, I've been looking for you." King Henry smiles. The expression is polite, bordering on friendly, but his eyes narrow at Lady Charlotte and Hélène. He leans closer, blocking them from my sight. "May I have a word with you? Privately?"

Hélène and Charlotte scamper off with hasty curtsies, leaving the king and me alone. Beyond Henry, I see their heads swoop low together, then Hélène glancing back at me with a pouting, suspicious look. My stomach clenches.

"You shouldn't speak to me here," I hiss. "It's too public."

He frowns, as if he truly doesn't understand what I'm saying. "They were being cruel to you."

"Yes, but that doesn't matter. The court loves to be cruel, and I can handle myself."

His courtier's smile slips. He leans closer, until he's all I can see, until it's only me and him and the night beyond the window. "All right. You called my bluff. I was bored and wanted your company."

He burns like a fire even with the cold of the night at my back. I press my eyes shut, not wanting him to see how the question ripples through me. "Why?"

His scent fills my head, more overwhelming than his presence. "Because you're the most interesting person in this room. I want to know everything about you."

You can't, I think helplessly. A shiver skates down my skin, impossible to hide.

But by God, sometimes I wish he could.

His thumb grazes the bare skin above my gloves. His breath catches when he feels my goose bumps.

A herald's trumpet shatters the moment. Henry finally pulls away, his full mouth soft, eyes hungry. I drag myself away from him, farther into the window's safe corner.

"A toast to King Henry II of France, may his legacy live on forever!" Catherine de' Medici cries, her wineglass aloft. She glows with happiness, a lovelorn girl at last reunited with her prince. *"Ut decus suum vivat aeternum!"*

King Charles echoes the Latin with far less enthusiasm, his expression sour with duty. No doubt his mother had him practicing the single line all day.

The court all joins in the third time, chanting until the toast made to the dead king shakes the château's foundation.

Until the candles all flicker out.

I blink in the sudden darkness. There's a moment of hushed confusion before a bloodcurdling scream shatters the quiet.

A body crashes into me, pinning me against the wall. I scramble frantically for my knife until another hand closes over mine. "Don't. Move." Henry's voice is silkier than a shadow.

The acid reek of terror bolts through the shifting bodies. Each one of my shaky breaths is louder than a thunderclap. After what could be seconds or minutes—the darkness distorts my sense of time—the light returns bit by bit, candles smoldering blue, then orange, the rosy light illuminating the shocked and horrified faces of the lords and ladies.

And Catherine de' Medici's tearstained cheeks. She spins to the crowd, laughing. "He is pleased with us! The king accepts our well-wishes!"

Lukewarm applause breaks out among the crowd, none of it loud enough to quite drown out the fearful murmurs. A quick glance at Margot's blanched face reveals that not even she knows what happened. Her eyes ricochet frantically around the room until they find mine. They latch on and widen.

Too late, I realize Henry is still standing there, *guarding* me like some sort of overly zealous sheepdog in full view of the entire court. I push out from behind him, face burning.

He tries to grab my wrist. "Jac—"

I sidestep him, shaking my head. I've got to find Oncle. This didn't feel like a prank or a courtly gimmick done for sensation. Something about this felt bone-chillingly *wrong*. I need to know if he felt it too.

Oncle cuts through the crowd, chasing after where Cosimo Ruggeri has just slipped away. I catch up to him just as he disappears into the servants' hall.

"Oncle, something's wrong."

"Obviously." He spins to me, jaw hard. "What do you *want*, Jac?"

I swallow, determined not to quail under his stare. "I think Cosimo is behind the grave robberies. He knew I was outside the grounds last night. I saw him—"

Oncle grabs my upper arms with bruising strength. His eyes are dark with rage. "And tonight the entire court saw you and King Henry, together." His fingers dig in deeper. "Stop worrying about things that aren't your concern. Do *not* let the king and the court get the wrong idea of you, Jac."

I stifle a cry as the pressure finally lets up, then stagger backward. Even though my nerves are a mess, I hide behind a coolly lifted chin. "I'm not *encouraging* Henry to do anything. He's a bloody king. He does whatever he wants."

Oncle looks down on me, his threat softer than snow. "Then do not make him want you."

Ice stops my heart.

Oncle closes his eyes and lets out a long, low breath before pursuing Cosimo again.

I watch him disappear around the barely lit corner, copper flooding my mouth.

I wasn't certain before, but now I am.

Oncle is keeping something from me. Something he absolutely does not want me to learn more about.

Except he's figured out that I'm hiding something from him, too.

CHAPTER SIXTEEN

WEBBED HANDS WITH gruesome claws swipe through the darkness. I twist away, my body wrenching. The fist slams beside my head. A gasping sob tears from me.

I'm going to lose this fight.

The water reaches my chin now, its currents hungrily pulling my feet. A grinning rictus with needle-sharp teeth flashes just beneath the surface. Skin sloughs from the creature's bones, tattered sinew brushing my skin. I scream, mouth filling with water.

The Melusine swipes again.

My eyes snap open.

The bedchamber is milky with blue light. The linens twist and tug at my legs, and for one wild moment I'm still drowning, still writhing away from those piercing claws.

There's a pounding at the door, low and urgent. My mouth goes dry.

No one should be here.

Only Oncle, Jehan, and Madame Dupont have access to our chambers. Everyone in our household is well aware I'm not to be awakened before midmorning, which means—

Someone else is outside my door.

I swing one leg out of bed then the other. I pick up my knife and inch toward the door on bare feet, wishing I was dressed in something other than a white nightdress with a drooping pink bow at the throat.

Another knock sounds. This one louder than the last.

I shove the door open, spinning outside with a vicious snarl. My forearm presses the person against the wall, my dagger at their throat.

Madame Dupont's mouth opens in a silent scream.

The knife clatters on the floor. I slap a hand over my face. "Please forgive me! Are you all right? I thought you were someone else!"

"That much seems obvious." Madame Dupont massages her collarbone, frowning at my dagger like it's a nasty carcass dragged in by a cat. "I'm fine. But I must say, if this is how you and his lordship continue to answer unexpected calls, I shall look for work in another household."

I duck my head. My bare toes twist against the tiled floor. Strange, late nights with even stranger kings have made me lose my wits.

Of course it's only Madame Dupont. There's no one stalking me. The Melusine isn't real, and even if she were, she'd never crawl through my window because she has a *fish tail*, for Christ's sake—

Madame Dupont braces my shoulders. Her no-nonsense expression is the same as always, but there's a softness around her eyes. "Jacqueline. It's fine. Just consider a less violent greeting next time someone knocks at your door, hmm? I woke you to bring you this."

She presses a folded letter into my hand. The sight of my name in a familiar, looping hand sends my pulse into a gallop.

Meet me at the stables now. Dépêche-toi!

M

After days of silence, Margot has finally sent for me.

"How—who—who gave this to you?" Messages from the princess do not arrive via our household staff, but by royal courier. Royal messages also, as a rule, do not arrive before the sun has fully risen. Something has happened. But what?

"One of her lady's maids. I believe the princess bribed her to bring it to me personally. Come now, let's get ready. Unless you don't wish to go?"

Her suggestion that I have a choice—that it would be perfectly acceptable for me to return to sleep, and Madame Dupont would blink wide innocent eyes if Margot demanded to know where I was—tempts me like a newly forged blade.

The princess has not been kind to me and everyone in our household knows it.

But I can't ignore her now. Not after she saw Henry and me together last night. Not when she sends for me so urgently after days of silence.

Soon I'm running down the sleepy hallways, past the maids carrying freshly laundered smallclothes and the footmen replacing the endless vases of flowers, and then I'm outside, racing across the dew-damp grass glinting gold in the first shimmer of sunlight.

There's a silhouette in the distance that makes my heart lift.

"Jac!" We fall into each other's arms. Margot squeezes me like it's been years since we last spoke. "Thank goodness! I was worried you wouldn't get my note in time. There's a merchant in town who just might fund my school, and Mother isn't awake to stop me from going. Quick, into the carriage!"

Margot seizes my hands as soon as the footman closes the door. "You must forgive me. I wanted to take every evil word I said to you back the very next day, but Mother forbade me from seeing you."

My hands go cold in hers. Oncle meets with the Queen Mother or the king almost every day, and he did not see fit to tell me this? Or—my stomach gives an uneasy lurch—perhaps Catherine de' Medici did not tell Oncle my presence was unwelcome. Which would mean she no longer trusts him.

His cover as a Societas Solis member might be in danger.

"Did she have another vision of me ruining the royal family?" I try to keep the question light, verging on playful with a smile and a laugh, but it's hard when Cosimo Ruggeri knows things about me that he shouldn't. When Catherine de' Medici's dire prophecy keeps me twisting restlessly each night since I saw the desecrated graves.

Margot laughs. "No, it's because of the rumors that you fancy King Henry. She thinks my unmarried ladies-in-waiting are making eyes at him for themselves."

Heat explodes across my face and down my neck.

"Of course I don't fancy him!" I finally choke out. "He's a king and I'm . . . well, I'm me."

Margot loops her arms over the back of her bench and props her feet on the edge of my mine. "I saw how he looked at you last night. He seems . . . fond."

The heat spreads down my chest and belly. Henry *is* fond of me, but that doesn't mean he wants me. Not the way Oncle suspects. Denying that the Navarrese king is handsome would be like denying that a sunny summer day is gorgeous. No one would believe me. Of course I'm attracted to him. "He has sought my company once or twice. He is pleasing to behold, so I let him linger."

Margot arches her eyebrows conspiratorially, as if she doesn't quite believe me. "But he seemed to *know* you, Jac."

I lift my chin, needing her to drop this. Nothing would kindle Margot's anger faster than me admitting I've been helping Henry court her. "Was I supposed to snub him? He's a king, Margot. You might be able to ignore him, but I can't."

Her mouth twists. "I suppose so."

Her begrudging tone chafes my nerves. "Tell me why you sent for me today. We both know you don't listen to your mother."

Margot glances out the window, her jaw working from side to side as ripe summer fields scroll past the glass. Already stone cottages line the road, gardens overflowing with flowers and children who point and gasp to see the royal carriage pass. Soon we shall be in town, under the guards' and the footmen's listening ears, unable to speak freely with each other.

I hold my breath, hoping against all hope she answers.

Carriages, bedchambers, parlors. Darkened rooms late at night. These are the places where women are allowed to be ourselves, to release the truths in our hearts and minds without fearing the consequences. It near embarrasses me, how desperately I want Margot to be honest with me even though I can't be honest with her.

The princess tilts her head back. "I was avoiding you." Each word is reluctant, sheepish. "When you told me you wouldn't help me escape my engagement, it felt like you were abandoning me. I was reminded of the time you turned me down. I was angry and hurt all over again."

I laugh disbelievingly. "*You* felt abandoned? You ordered me to leave and didn't talk to me for weeks. I thought you might send me away for good. I felt abandoned by you."

Margot has the good grace to look guilty. "I know. And I'm sorry."

I nod slowly, struggling to hold in a flare of anger. "You can't always get your way. I'm your servant, but you asked for too much. Do you really think your mother or brother would let me stay in court if they knew I helped you defy their orders?"

Margot's lovely face blanches. She twists the edge of her cloak, brow furrowed. "I—I had not considered how it would look to my family."

I nod again, straining to keep my expression neutral. I think of King Henry's apology to me, how easily he gave it as soon as he had the chance. Why is owning up to her mistakes so difficult for Margot?

Even still, my hand drifts across my lap, palm up, beckoning for her to take it. "We're friends, but we're not equals. You could destroy me if you felt like it."

"I would never!" she cries, outraged.

"But you almost did." All the hurt I held in a tight little ball is suddenly right beneath my ribs. I think of the pamphlets and their ugly rumors. The snide looks and comments from the other noblegirls. I have such little standing in court already and Margot's silence was almost enough to take that away too.

She takes my hand and places it over her heart. "I won't hurt you again, I swear it."

The heat of her words, the gleaming at her lash line she stubbornly refuses to let fall, loosens the hard knot in me. "I will hold you to that."

She dashes away the moisture in her eyes and hugs me. I squeeze her back, her floral scent washing over me, making me feel fully like myself for the first time in weeks. Margot is difficult and stubborn, but I can't imagine a world where I don't care for her. Marguerite de Valois is the brightest flame in France, and I will always be the senseless moth plunging straight into her fire.

Margot pulls away, keeping my hand in hers. "I've given thought to what you said about the marriage of convenience."

I swear, my heart stops beating. "You have?"

"Henry has surprised me of late."

A rush of embarrassment goes through me. Even his name

turns me over like a beetle, all my soft bits exposed for the world to poke at. "Are the surprises pleasant or unpleasant?"

"Pleasant." Margot's brow furrows. "He's nothing like the blustering warlord I met in Paris. He agrees that women ought to be educated like men. He has even heard of Sappho, Jac!"

Relief breaks over me like much-needed rain. I laugh, my lingering distrust and anger washing away. "Are you going to invite him to one of your salons?"

Margot tosses her head, black curls flouncing. "An invitation to one of those must be *earned*, not merely given."

I laugh again, hiding how I'd rather groan with frustration. All those sleepless nights coaching the king on how to court Margot, and she still remains unmoved? A rock would be less obstinate than the princess's will.

Her painted lips pull into a coy smirk. "Which is why, of course, Henry shall lead my first salon back in Paris himself. If he impresses me . . . well, perhaps he'd be worthy of my hand after all." The carriage lurches to a halt. "I swear, Jac, he's completely different! Even you might like him now!"

The door swings open and blinds us with sunlight before I can respond. Which is for the best. Otherwise Margot would see my stricken expression.

I've returned to Margot's good graces. But for how long? Today she showed me the most honest, rawest parts of herself, but I can't do the same with her. She started this fight, but I was avoiding her as much as she was avoiding me.

What happens when Margot figures out that I'm manipulating her? Between Henry's honor and my own inability to resist her, it's only a matter of time before she discovers I've lied to her for my own gain. And when she does, I'd deserve her wrath.

I hold up the princess's magnificently embroidered hem as she greets the townspeople, sourness gnawing at my stomach and clawing up my throat.

I'm hoarding secrets, and the longer they linger, the more they fester into something dark and spoiled.

Even if she were not getting married, how can this summer possibly end with Margot and I staying close?

CHAPTER SEVENTEEN

ARGOT'S FAVORITE JEWEL is a diamond." Henry's smile glitters. "Now tell me yours."

I make a show of sighing dramatically. "Must I? This is taking *forever*."

His grin grows wider, the brightest thing in the dark ballroom. "You must, I insist."

Tonight is our last tutoring session. Tomorrow the court returns to the Louvre, and Henry and I shall return to our own lives. *This is good,* I remind myself. It means that I have come that much further in my mission, a task which once seemed impossible weeks ago. There's finally a chance the royal wedding will actually happen.

"Jac," Henry wheedles. "The sooner you answer, the sooner we can leave."

After years of keeping secrets, my instinct is to hold everything back. It takes me a moment to remember. "A ruby. Now, what about Margot's favorite place?"

It's late—so late, we should be gone—but neither of us says a word about the dawn drawing closer. Neither of us makes a move to leave.

Henry steeples his fingers. "Marguerite's favorite place?

Clearly it's wherever she's the center of attention."

I snort because he's not wrong. "I think you meant to say Paris."

He looks at me expectantly, arching a brow. I roll my eyes and oblige him. "I suppose my favorite place is . . . my oncle's country estate."

He frowns. "Didn't your mother die there?"

I gesture to the slumbering château, all the court's dreams of revenge and power. Oncle's estate is lonely, but not lonelier than here, where being surrounded by hundreds of people only reminds me how few of them truly care for me, how few people I can trust. "I don't like my oncle's estate, but it's the one place where I don't have to hide."

Henry contemplates me with too-blue eyes, a muscle pulling in his jaw. "Perhaps you deserve better, then."

I shrug and glance out the window, not taking up the argument.

Sparring with Henry gives me a delicious rush, but this time his words brush along a seam in my heart. This question skirts too close to the secret parts of myself. Caves and corners of feeling better left unexplored. A woman should also have some mystery about her. Perhaps even from herself.

After all, what's the point of wanting things I can never have?

When all this is over, I'll have earned my place in the Societas Solis. I'll be using my skills and rank to make the world better. I'll have achieved my lifelong dream, which is more than most people ever get.

Henry doesn't press me. He shifts forward, scarred fingers tracing patterns in the dust. The moonlight drapes across his broad shoulders like a silver cloak. This moment already feels like a memory. A heavy feeling curls up in my chest.

I shake it away, frustrated. Why can't I stay in the present? Why must I aways rush to the end of something nice before it's over?

I expected Henry of Navarre to be many things. Cocksure and stubborn. Challenging to work with.

Never in a hundred years did I expect to *like* him.

Too late, I notice Henry has stilled. He's caught me watching him. I look away quickly, down at the chessboard floor.

"Can we talk about the danse macabre?" he says.

My heart drops.

I've tried to forget, but that night lingers like a stubborn fever. His closeness, his warmth. How he stood between me and the darkness without a second thought.

How he saw me shiver.

"What about it?" I ask sharply.

He cants his head, studying me carefully. "What's going on with Catherine de' Medici and her dead husband?"

I exhale softly, stomach twisting. I have a feeling this isn't the question he wanted to ask.

"She never got over his death. Even though my oncle says Henry II was over her before she bore him his first heir."

He glances at the half-finished carvings along the windows, the twinning *H* and *C* of Catherine and Henry II's initials. How the letters form a phantom *D*, long thought to be a sly reference to Henry II's favorite mistress, Diane, who once called this river palace home. "Is all the Valois family cursed with sadness and cruelty, then?"

I've always thought of my family as a cursed one, one patched together by grief and secrets. The powerful Valois seemed to have everything they ever wanted or needed. But Henry's right, heartache trails the royal family like a ghost. Margot has lost a parent too, but sometimes it feels like she's lost much more than that. I think of us curled up head-to-head in her royal bed. I always thought she was indulging me, knowing how lonely I got when Oncle left. But how many nights did she call for me because she had no one else?

"I promise Margot is the best of them. She's considering a marriage of convenience. Fund her school and she'll accept your hand. I'm certain of it," I say softly.

Henry shifts, accidentally brushing my shoulder. He wears the same simple clothes I first saw him in at the stables. I can't believe I ever mistook him for a servant. The imperious tilt of his golden head, the way he takes up all the space around him, all of it screams of kingliness. He smiles, the expression not quite reaching his eyes. "But do you think Margot could ever love me?"

My throat closes, blocking back all the things I could say. All the reassuring lies I should offer him.

His smile turns soft and sad. "That's what I thought."

The quiet grows vaster and vaster, until we might as well be on opposite sides of the river. I want to break it, to go back to when our words were light and teasing. *This was always about the royal marriage and nothing else,* I remind myself. *You don't need to make him feel better.*

But somewhere along the way, his feelings started to matter to me. And they need to matter less if I'm to make it in the Societas Solis.

"We should go. It's late," I whisper.

Henry scrubs out the shapes he drew in the dust before I can take a closer look. "All right."

Somewhere in the distance there's a thud of a door slamming.

Then laughter, drawing closer. Quickly.

Too quickly.

He stiffens. "Bloody hell."

My pulse doubles. I scramble upright, but it's too late.

The servants' door bursts open behind us.

"A tryst!" a delighted male voice yells. Another man lurches behind him, giggling madly, wineskin in hand.

I seize Henry's arm and yank him after me, sprinting for the half-finished grand doors at the room's other end. I shove them open and we spill into the hall, colliding with a statue of a venerable ancestor. Henry rights it before it can fall and wake up everyone sleeping in the bedchambers.

All of Oncle's warnings flash through me, pushing my feet faster.

If I'm caught with the king, it'll cost more than my reputation. Oncle and Margot will be furious and hurt. She'll never trust me again. He'll send me away. I'll never have another chance to prove myself.

We sprint down the white stone staircase. The two men tumble after us, their faces a mystery in the scant moonlight. They crash into a flower arrangement in the stairs and send the roses and silver crashing, loud enough to wake the dead.

An angry sob tears from me.

"Here." Henry catches up with me at the bottom and motions to a smaller door. The servants' stairs to the cellars.

I ease the door open. There's a thin wail from the hinges, barely audible.

But it's loud enough.

The men give chase again, laughing drunkenly, like this is all some sort of marvelous game.

We plunge into the cellars. A servant gasps as we explode into the vaulted kitchen, a loaf of floured dough in her hands. We sprint past her, past the skinned game hanging on hooks, past the great fire, and out another door I've never seen.

We're outside on a dock. The river flows at our feet, and the château soars above. A moored boat bobs in the water, filled with produce. There's nowhere left to go. We're trapped at the very bottommost level of the château.

Henry grabs the boat oars. "There's still this."

I shake my head. If we run, all we'll do is prove we're guilty of something. We couldn't sneak back before breakfast. By then, it'll be clear the king of Navarre is missing, and Oncle will know I'm with him.

I can already see the jeering pamphlet headline.

Jacqueline d'Argenson-Aunis, a backstabbing king-climber.

Catherine de' Medici would send me away before noon.

Henry spins around, wild and urgent. "There's a way out of this, but it's dishonorable."

My answer is a ragged pant. "I don't care. Do it." There's a fumbling on the door, like someone can't quite figure out how to open it.

Henry crosses the dock in shuddering steps. I back away until I hit the wall, my hidden knife digging painfully into my back. He leans over me, the color high in his cheeks. His fingers scrape down the stone, a hairbreadth from my bare arms. "Can I touch you?"

His gaze darkens, dropping to my lips, my heaving chest. There's nothing polite or hesitant in those depths. He's not doing this to help me. He's doing this because he *wants* me.

And I can't pretend that I don't want him anymore.

His stare upends the box where I've shoved every unwanted feeling I've had for weeks. Each touch, every time our eyes collided across a crowded room, all of it was adding up to something I should've saw coming.

"Jac?" He inches closer. He won't make a move unless I give him my word. The fact that he's asking, when he so desperately wants to take, makes me want him even more.

Each near touch of his is a lick of fire and I want to burn.

I gasp out a *yes*.

We crash into each other.

His mouth is even softer than I imagined. And sweet—sweeter than honey and sugar and the sip of the pale gold wine I once stole from Margot's cup, each bottle reserved only for royalty. I sigh against his lips, and then his tongue is in my mouth, his knee nudging my legs apart to crush me closer to him.

It's not close enough.

I rise onto my toes, and he picks me up, holding me against the wall. When my nails scrape down his spine, he shudders and groans, our kiss growing deeper. I can't get enough of him. I don't think I could ever get enough of him. I'm so used to going hungry, I didn't know I was starving.

When the drunken men burst through the door, leering and laughing, they find the king of Navarre in a compromising position.

"What is the meaning of this?" Henry thunders, turning his head as I duck mine so my face remains hidden. "Can you not leave a man to his pleasures?"

Screaming with glee, the men leave.

But we don't stop kissing. We kiss until my lips are bruised, until pink gilds the sky visible from under the château's belly. We kiss until there's no possible way we can pretend we're doing it for anyone other than ourselves.

When Henry finally sets me down, my entire world spins with too much champagne. He makes a weak, vulnerable noise and leans his forehead against my brow. He trembles against me, as if caught in the throes of a fever, a leaf in a gale.

I reach up and push the hair from his eyes, as I've longed to do for days. He tilts his head, resting his cheek in my hand. "Forgive me. This was the only thing I could think of."

I swallow several times before I find my roughened voice. "I understand. We did what we had to."

He sighs. The warm rush sends gooseflesh rippling all

down my back. "Right." His hands skim down my sides one last time before falling away. "I do have one question though."

The warm, shimmering feeling pops like a bubble. I glance up at him, gut churning.

I kissed the king of Navarre.

I just kissed the king of Navarre, and there's absolutely, positively no way I can pretend I didn't want to. There's not a *chance* he missed how much I wanted him.

"Yes, Your Majesty?" I ask, heart teetering on the château's highest peak.

He laughs, like he can't quite believe what he's about to ask. "Can you tell me why there's a knife under your gown?"

CHAPTER EIGHTEEN

THE PARIS WE return to is far different from the one we left.

Shouting and laughter has been replaced with whispers and silence. The city's hustle and bustle remain the same, but now with downcast eyes and suspicious looks. Even the buildings are quiet, shutters drawn against the streets. The sense of wrongness grows when we reach the arrondissement farthest from the grand boulevards and the bourgeoisie neighborhoods.

"What happened?" I finally whisper.

Oncle frowns. With a single, gloved finger, he raises a spray of dried purple flowers hanging from the door, their stems smeared scarlet. A talisman against evil. The back of my neck prickles.

"I don't know. Stay close." He hurries toward Louise's apothecary, faster than before.

Louise's letter was waiting for us when we arrived back to the Palais du Louvre. At first glance, the letter only listed prescriptions ready for us. But when Oncle held it over the fire, I watched with wide eyes as the hidden message appeared in dark letters like a summons.

Urgent trouble in the city. Come at once. Bring
Jacqueline too.

A small boy opens the apothecary's back door before we reach the threshold.

"Thomas! I've told you a thousand times not to answer that one," Louise says, yanking him back. From the way her hand lingers on his shoulder, I realize Thomas must be her son, someone she's been careful to keep from me until now. Louise's irritated expression deepens when she sees my stare.

"Took you long enough."

"We came as soon as we could." Oncle unfastens his cloak.

"Well, it's not fast enough. There've been more murders, and this time they're children."

A wave of revulsion washes over me. "Children?"

"Aye, and the entire city knows about it," Louise says grimly.

My hand goes to my throat. This is why Paris feels different, so dark and suspicious. "Do you think it's related to the trouble from before?"

"Come decide for yourselves."

Louise ushers us inside. She takes us through the private back room—blessedly body-free—and into the apothecary's shop. Drying plants hang from the ceiling, and I see a table scattered with herbs, a well-used mortar and pestle. With murmured apologies for the sudden closure, Louise ushers her customers outside. She locks the front door and draws the threadbare drapes closed. She sends Thomas upstairs.

Then she brings out the charcoal sketches.

Dead bodies, most of them unbearably small. Something wretches deep inside me at the sight.

"Last week there were six murders. The victims were Catholic and Huguenot alike, but you wouldn't know it from the way the Catholic majority talks about it." Louise taps a tangle of black on their chests. "All found with their hearts missing. Whoever killed them cut them out and took them."

The hair rises along my arms. The wrongness of it makes me feel ill, unmoored from my body. "Who would do such a thing?"

Louise lifts her head, her mouth a grim slash. "I don't know. But I suspect it's related to the corpses with their missing parts. I'm wondering if someone's getting desperate enough to kill for what they want."

My hand fists, pressing into the soft skin of my neck. "Which would be what?"

Silence falls. Louise traces her renderings with downcast eyes while Oncle glares at the shuttered windows.

"I don't know," Louise finally says. "That's why I sent for you. I think the Societas Solis needs to patrol the streets of Paris at night."

Oncle scoffs. "We don't have enough men to guard an entire city."

"Then why don't you come up with a better idea?" Louise flutters her lashes, her voice all false sincerity. "This could affect the royal family, too, you know. People still think Henry of Navarre is behind it."

My heart drops at his name. Hopelessly noble Henry? Behind something as grim and disgusting as *this*? "Henry would never hurt children!"

Oncle lifts one sly brow. "I didn't realize you and the king of Navarre were on a first-name basis, Niece," he says.

I square my jaw, willing away the blood that wants to rise to my cheeks.

"More and more people believe that the Huguenots let something monstrous loose to terrorize Paris and force Princess Marguerite into saying yes . . ." Louise trails off, letting our minds fill in the blanks.

If Margot refuses the king of Navarre, then she must have a good reason to do so. And as much as her family is happy to see Margot married off for their own gain, the people of Paris do not want to lose their beloved princess to a foreign king. Especially if she despises him.

They would be willing to fight for her.

This is my fault. They should be engaged already.

I lean against the worktable, my insides hollowing out. My fingers trace my still-tender lips, the memory of Henry's kisses boiling beneath my skin.

Except Margot is open to marrying him now. And Henry knows it. Navarre could never stand against France's might. He needs this marriage even more than she does. He knows what he has to do. What he *must* do.

Louise turns to me with sharp eyes. "And how is the royal betrothal coming along, Jac?"

Every spot where Henry has touched me burns. I focus on

her as I respond, Oncle's frame a blurred figure behind her. "It goes well. The king and the princess are nearly engaged. Give it a week at most."

Louise nods. "That will help, but I'm afraid it won't be enough. Too many people already distrust the Huguenots, and these murders have given them another reason to harden their hearts. This is how wars begin. The Societas Solis must discover who killed these people and why."

The words send a shudder down my spine. *War.* Could several murders really lead to such greater violence? The darkness of the room seems to draw closer, the cold truth settling into me like a stone. Of course it could. A single spark is all it takes to start a fire.

Oncle investigates the drawings again, pensive. "Some people kill and maim for the pleasure of it."

"What does that mean?" Louise crosses her arms.

"It means you might be making too much of these murders. It might not concern us," Oncle says.

"It could be a mad killer," Louise agrees. "But people believe it's supernatural. Do not scoff, Gabriel! You might not think magic is real, but people's beliefs have their own power. The space betwixt madness and magic is but a sliver to most."

Magic. It lingers heavily, like an ugly curse word whose meaning I don't fully understand. I think of the danse macabre, how strongly terror—honest, true terror—gripped the court when the ballroom went dark. I think of the men who ran when Henry entered the cemetery, the unearthed skeletons. The book I found beside them.

"Is that what happened in the graveyard? An attempted spell?" I say.

Louise goes curiously still. Her eyes whip to Oncle. "What happened in the Loire Valley?"

Oncle's frown, impossibly, grows even deeper. "Nothing that concerns the Societas Solis. Only grave robbers outside the castle walls."

I shake my head. "It wasn't only grave robbers. Catherine de' Medici's sorcerer *knew* I was there."

Oncle scoffs again. "Cosimo Ruggeri is a dangerous fool who enjoys frightening people."

"But why would Catherine de' Medici's sorcerer rob a grave?" Louise's eyes gleam catlike in the candles. "How do you know that what happened out there doesn't have anything to do with what's happening here?"

My heart thumps faster. I'm eager to continue our conversation, this feeling of finally being included in something real for the very first time. "Could Catherine's vision have anything to do with it?"

"Tell me more, Jac," the apothecary owner demands, her fist gripped tight around her sun pendant.

"She had one before we left. '*The Valois line will end when the Seine runs red.*'"

The candles shudder in a sudden draft. I hug my arms against the unexpected cold, uneasy at how the room has gone silent, how Oncle looks at me like I've committed a faux pas too gauche to be mentioned.

This time, I know I don't imagine Louise's sudden stillness, how her wide eyes pass over me to Oncle, a feeling hardening in them that I can't read. "That sounds like a vision of war. You didn't tell me about this, Gabriel."

"It felt beneath our notice. The Queen Mother has visions near once a week."

Louise raps the charcoal drawings, her words a hiss. "Do you not see these tiny bodies here? Have you not heard what I've said? It *all* matters now!"

I stuff my hand into my pockets, thumbing my sheathed knife for something to do, chastened by the strange sense that I've disappointed Oncle.

After a final lingering glance at me, Oncle takes out a cloth-wrapped package. "Jac found this in the graveyard."

It's the Book of Hours, the prayer book with its illustrated pages. Louise frowns, peering closer. She touches the cover and draws away with a soft gasp. "Now, *this* is a strange thing to leave in a graveyard."

"Perhaps one of the grave robbers had cold feet about his work," Oncle jokes grimly. "If you want the Societas Solis to patrol the streets of Paris, so be it. I'll send messages now to bring more of our people to the city."

My thumb stops caressing the knife. "Let me do it. The king and princess are almost engaged. I'll need more work to do soon."

Henry may have bought my half lie about why I carried a knife at Château de Chenonceau ("My oncle told me to!"), but it would be another thing entirely if he learned I can actually *use* it.

He can't get any closer to you.

This has been true for weeks, but it matters so much more now that my foolish heart has stumbled. I thought this match-making work beneath me, but if there was one thing I could say in favor of it, at least it was safe. I wasn't likely to end up hurt.

But the awful lurch in my stomach when Henry glances my way? How my heartbeat hitches every time his name ambushes me in a conversation? How the memory of his hot body pressed against mine keeps me up each night, replaying on a horrible, tantalizing loop? These unruly feelings leave me raw and stinging.

I need a new mission. I needed one days ago, the moment I realized I couldn't resist the golden king. Then, perhaps, I wouldn't have been stupid enough to let feelings for another royal fester in me.

Doing more work for the Societas Solis will earn me my place in the world. It'll let me have a life like Louise's, a life where no one can tell me what I can and can't do. I will not let hopeless, mewling *feelings* distract me from the future I want.

Louise claps her hands together. "Oh, that would be useful! Do you think you could come—"

"Absolutely not." Oncle's words strike faster than an adder. He looms over both of us, his face a cold, icy mask. "My niece will *not* be roaming the streets of Paris."

Louise sighs and rolls her eyes. "Why not? She's here and willing, and we need people. You want to make a name for yourself in the Societas Solis, don't you, girl?"

"*I said no!*" Every muscle of Oncle's body quivers, his spine a rigid line. His outburst is so unexpected, so loud, my heartbeat races like I've discovered an intruder in our home. I try to remember the last time Oncle raised his voice and can't. He glances at me—a feeling like shame in his eyes—then drags a hand down his face. A dark beard shadows his jaw, like he ran out of time to be shaved this morning. "Forgive me. Until the king and princess are wed, nothing is certain. The most useful thing Jac can do is make sure this wedding happens."

Louise looks away. Like she's embarrassed for me.

Familiar frustration wends through me, turning my calm to anger, restraint to recklessness. Why does Oncle bring me here, into conversations about things he'll never let me do? He claims he trusts me enough to let me into the darkness of his secret world, but he doesn't trust me enough to give me a candle to make sense of anything there.

By the time we leave the apothecary, twilight drags a violet cowl above the rooftops and church spires and solemn universities that make up the wild, beating soul of Paris.

Oncle takes my arm when we're out of the apothecary's sight.

"What?" I snap.

His expression is thunderous. "Don't even think of investigating these murders on your own."

I laugh darkly. "Is marriage no longer a fast enough method to be rid of me, then?"

"I'm not trying to get rid of you. I'm trying to keep you *safe*." Fine lines frame his eyes like river deltas, exhaustion

178 | ERIN COTTER

flooding his gaze like I've never seen before. "Promise me you'll listen, Jac."

My mouth twists. "If Margot asked King Charles for a favor, he wouldn't let you send me away."

Oncle's expression grows hard; he's no doubt remembering how I convinced Margot to help me frighten away my one-time suitor, Gérard. "Do not test my mettle, Niece. Disobeying the king is nothing. I'll disobey God himself to protect you. I promised your mother."

He means it, every word.

I see it in the line of his clenched jaw, how his fingers press divots into my skin. He means to seem angry, but he's not.

He's terrified.

Like a dog who snarls and barks to keep his enemies from drawing closer, Oncle's anger is supposed to keep me from drawing close enough to see what he's hiding from me.

A widowed queen's bloody vision. Dead children with missing hearts. A prayer book abandoned in a country cemetery.

What does it all mean? Why is Oncle so frightened?

He walks so fast, I can barely keep up. I hear anger in every strike of his bootheels.

When the ivory sides of the Palais du Louvre begin to peep through the Paris rooftops, I decide to let loose the final arrow in my quiver. I exhale slowly, gathering my cloak more securely about my shoulders.

"I promise I'll listen."

He lifts an eyebrow, not believing me at all. "Do you, now?"

I duck my head obediently. "Yes, I swear it."

He scoffs and turns away. "Time shall show me the truth of this."

He walks ahead of me, so he does not see the fingers I have crossed behind my back.

Oncle may not share more with me, but I have a feeling Louise will.

CHAPTER NINETEEN

M ARGOT'S SALON INVITATION arrives by eagle.

The bird screams down the hallway, bronze dust motes eddying in the wake of its flight, and drops the gilded envelope at my feet. The royal falconer beckons the bird back with a whistle. The nobles nearby clap as though they've witnessed a marvelous trick.

The envelope is not addressed to Jac, but to Artemis, goddess of the hunt and wild animals.

Suddenly the eagle makes sense. It's a nod to Hermes, the Greek god of messengers and, of course, his winged sandals. I bite the inside of my cheek.

So this is to be a masque as well.

Margot's salons are renowned for their intellectual rigor as much as her masques are known for their splendor. I have spent many evenings watching the candles melt to puddles as Margot plans them. It's a dazzling fiction, members of court bringing the story to life.

My teeth sink into my bottom lip. I have no doubt Henry is getting one of these invitations this very moment. Knowing Margot, she ordered it sent during one of his endless meetings with her brother, so all the men of court would know and see that she willingly invited the king of Navarre somewhere.

Which means Henry and I will be together for the first time since we kissed.

And it won't happen again.

A buzz in my veins grows louder and louder as the night draws closer, the rumors surrounding it growing more and more fantastical. The princess has had ice sculptures of winged horses dragged in from the Alps. She has summoned the pope's personal musicians from Rome. The notorious professor of philosophy Petrus Ramus himself will lead the symposium dressed as Apollo, the god of education.

When the rumor goes around that Margot has decreed all invited should wear as little as they please to honor both the ripening summer and the goddesses of fertility, I finally crack and ask her what's true and what isn't. The mere memory of Henry's chest crushed against mine still leaves me breathless: the sight of it might be enough to undo me entirely.

Except Margot only laughs merrily and pats my head like I'm one of her dogs. "All shall be revealed, my dearest Jac. I especially hope that you like it!"

I swallow, remembering how vital orgies are in the symposiums.

When the night arrives, I'm strung tighter than a new crossbow as I follow the flickering candles to the Tuileries Garden.

Soaring faux marble, crafted from God knows what, rises from the ground. Bright bursts of laughter and the heady perfume of roses waft from the Olympus hidden beyond high hedges. Two guards flank an elegant arch, their pikes strung with gold ribbons.

"Is the answer . . . God?" Lady Hélène says cautiously.

The guards slam their pikes on the ground. Their faces are hidden by Sphinx-shaped helmets. "That is not the answer, mademoiselle."

Hélène laughs, snapping out a fan to hide her reddening face behind it. "Why, you can't keep me here all night! I don't know the answer and the princess invited me personally."

"I'm afraid the princess said that no one can enter unless they can answer their riddle."

I snort and clap a hand over my mouth lest Lady Hélène notices me laughing. Of course Margot has made this a test, locking out everyone too dull to hold their own at the salon.

Maybe Henry won't get his riddle right, I think wistfully. Then he won't torment me all night with his sweet, wicked mouth and midnight eyes. Then the chances of me embarrassing myself would go from very high to very low.

The other guard takes my invitation. "It is greater than God and more evil than the devil. The poor have it, the rich need it, and if you eat it, you'll die. What is it?"

I tilt my head, considering. "Why, it is nothing."

The guards step aside to let me pass. Lady Hélène's envious groan follows me in.

Margot has indeed brought Olympus to Paris. The Tuileries Garden is lit with so many lanterns it appears as though all the stars have tumbled from the sky. Rugs and blankets, everything a pristine white, softly drape over chaises and chairs. Hidden musicians play a lilting, ethereal melody, and the air is already syrupy with honey cakes and the tang of wine. No fewer than a hundred servants must have sweated all night and all day to bring Margot's vision to life.

The princess herself is like a beacon at the garden's heart. She reclines on a chaise flanked with golden swans and an obscene number of roses. Her bare feet peep out from the hem of a petal-pink gown so diaphanous, it leaves little to the imagination. She catches my eye and winks. It hits me like a punch. I don't know whether to be more struck by her beauty or by her boldness. Margot has cast herself as Aphrodite, the goddess of beauty.

I suddenly feel childish in my own Artemis costume, a plain, pale green length of linen wrapped over my body and secured with so many knots, Madame Dupont has already told me to wake her when I return to our chambers so she can help me untie them.

The Valois court, promiscuous enough on its own, needs only the flimsy excuse of a masque and everyone pretending to be someone else for a night to toss away all modesty. Too late, I recall Artemis is also a virgin goddess, and the thought of the sly looks and comments this will bring me all night already makes me flush.

My attraction to men and women both is a puzzle I cannot solve. I envy Oncle and Margot for how easily they know themselves. Neither of them understands why I can't explain what makes my heart gallop for one person and not another.

Margot only blinked at me, bewildered. "But why do you feel anything for men when the world is full of women?"

"Preferring men would make your life simpler," Oncle told me in his blunt, pragmatic manner when I stammered I was both like and unlike him. "Have you tried *not* kissing girls?"

I've tried to convince myself that it's a good thing. That I can have whoever I wish and isn't that delightful?

But it never feels good in moments like these, when the freedom to embrace whomever I want without consequence hangs before me like a gloriously ripe plum, and the longing in my breast grows near painful. At moments like these, it feels like reaching for anyone at all is impossible.

"Mademoiselle, may I tempt you?" A servant offers me a tray of a sparkling wine. Nodding furiously, I seize two glasses and down both at once.

From a rose-filled corner, I take in the rest of the guests. There is King Charles, a brooding Zeus who, judging from the red on his lips, has already managed to guzzle at least half a barrel of wine. Most of Margot's other ladies-in-waiting are nymphs or muses. Even the little black Navarrese pony is there, a pair of wire and paper wings on her back. A tiny, perfect Pegasus. When the servant holding her velvet lead passes, I brush my fingers through her lustrous mane.

I sense Henry's arrival the way animals sense an incoming storm.

He wears nothing but a leather skirt and a length of red silk pulled across his chest, fastened with an iron brooch. His golden hair is swept back irreverently, hastily. I imagine his French valet begging this foreign king to let him do more, to make more of his entrance into the one and only event his

intended bride has invited him to, and Henry dismissing him
with a smile, shrugging into his silks mere minutes before
gracing us with his presence. He is a sliver of sunlight, golden
and lean and so bright, he blinds.

He greets Margot with an elegant kiss on her hand. She
draws forward, whispering something to him. His loud, bold
laugh scrapes against me like the blunt edge of a blade.

The wine I drank too quickly hits me all at once.

I have seen the male form before. Each year, Catherine de'
Medici brings great, straw-stuffed boxes of marble master-
pieces from Florence. When Margot was not there to tease me,
I ran my fingers up the carvings, marveling at the smoothness,
how the stone itself seemed alive with its curves and twists.

Henry reminds me of those statues. He is a masterpiece
made flesh, and I know the stone's spell shall never bewitch me
again. Every new inch of him laid bare feels like a glimpse of
hallowed ground, a place I prayed to but never fully believed in.

My throat swells shut. Am I being punished for wanting
too much? Must the only two people I've ever fallen for be here
tonight looking like this? I wish that the night would end now,
leaving me with nothing but this image pressed and hidden in
a book like a flower.

I worried Margot would turn this event into something
hungry and prowling, but this is so much worse. I feel undone,
inside out, my innermost thoughts and feelings obvious to all.

Henry turns toward me, and I flee deeper into the garden before our eyes meet. But soon, a familiar figure makes
itself known. It takes far more than a pointed snub to deter

the king of Navarre. He is as persistent as he is unbearably good-looking.

"Why do you look like you're trying to disappear?" he asks.

I swallow. If the hedges could send out their tendrils and pull me into their quiet green depths, that would be lovely. "Artemis is the goddess of the woods as much as the hunt, so standing at the garden's edge is exactly where I belong."

His grin unspools slowly, honey tipped from a jar. "Of course you would be Artemis." He steps closer, so close I can smell the soap still clinging to his skin. I add him bathing to my fantasy of how he got ready for tonight. And my cheeks go so red, I drop my eyes to my sandaled feet.

"Would you care to guess who I am?" he says.

"Adonis?" The fair youth Adonis was a mortal so beautiful, Aphrodite left her husband for him. The idea that Margot told Henry to play the part of the goddess's forbidden lover and not her blacksmith husband, Hephaestus, the god of forge and fire, makes my chest squeeze.

A coy smile lifts his lips. "No, I'm Ares. But I'm *very* flattered you think me the epitome of male beauty. It's a treasured compliment coming from you."

My stomach swoops even lower, churning with acid and regret. How soon is too soon to leave? Perhaps I could spend the symposium under a blanket. Or perhaps locked inside a wardrobe.

The tiniest line appears betwixt Henry's eyebrows. "Is all well with you?"

I want to laugh off his question, but I can't. I don't know

how I feel. All I know is that coming here was a mistake, a foolish, stupid mistake, and it's too late for me to leave without drawing attention to myself.

"It's nothing. My costume itches." And it's true. For once, my hair is unbound, and the unfamiliar sensation of hair brushing my bare skin makes me squirm. I claw the mass over one shoulder. Except that feels worse so I shake it over both shoulders instead. I feel virginal and prim compared to the abundance of silk and skin that swirls around us. Only Henry is clad as simply as me, but the similarity brings me no comfort, only a formless anxiety that builds and builds the longer we stand apart in our own corner.

Someone is going to know something happened between us.

"I like you like this," he says, his voice a low murmur. He moves closer, shielding me from the crowd's view. He takes the end of a wave and curls it about his finger. The gentle pressure tugs on my scalp, makes my entire body throb even though he barely touches me at all. It makes me want to slant against him, ask him to touch me other places—

I tear away from the thought with a gasp.

Mon dieu, it's been five minutes. I'm never drinking wine around beautiful people again. It makes me witless, makes me forget everything I should care about.

Henry lets my hair slip from his fingers. "Jac—"

"Don't." The word is too loud for our quiet corner.

He freezes, hand outstretched. A too-deep breath would put his touch on my waist. Slowly, he steps away, confusion and hurt in his eyes. Guilt smacks my knuckles at the sight of it.

"Sorry," he says. "I didn't mean to offend you."

Something knots up in me, small and hard and just as annoying as a rock in a boot. I give Henry a scornful look, the sort of look one might give a troublesome pupil. "You're here to impress Margot. You're the king of Navarre, and I'm the princess's lady-in-waiting. I've done all I can to help you win her hand. The rest is up to you." I lift my chin, forcing out the words that feel like peeling away my own flesh. "We shouldn't talk to each other anymore."

If he can't be strong enough to do the right thing, then I must be strong enough for both of us.

He recoils, a barely there shift that I feel like a tremor in the earth. "Did our kiss mean nothing to you?"

I clench my fists and turn away from his wounded expression before it devastates me. Before I'm forced to painstakingly explain my embarrassing and inappropriate feelings for him. Why is he so determined to talk about *feelings* all the time? Why must he flush them out like a hound on the hunt? "Because it can't mean anything. We both know that."

A muscle flutters at the base of his neck, the movement rippling all down his gloriously naked chest. His fingers just barely graze the knot on my hip. "When you realize you're wrong, you'll know where to find me."

I clamp my eyes shut, my voice a hiss. "You are the most frustrating person I've ever met!"

A trumpet sounds. The symposium, the salon section of Margot's fete, is finally beginning, and if Henry and I appear together it will cause questions. I flee before he can follow me.

• • •

The symposium is not led by the famous professor but by one of Margot's old Greek tutors, a man so wizened and ancient, I half wonder if she dug him up from his grave to serve as her *maistre* for the night. I hardly pay attention to his commentary. Something about Aristotle, as it always is. All I can see is Margot at Henry's side, the way she looks at him with a coy smile, his answering smirk.

When Henry gets to his feet to speak, his skin rippling golden in the torchlight, I fear I might explode.

"How is it that the Greeks worship goddesses, and yet the philosopher Aristotle remained steadfast in his belief that women were inferior to men?"

Margot smirks and crosses her legs. "How indeed, Your Majesty?"

Catcalls and jeers ring out among the pantheon of gods.

The king smiles, a glittering, dangerous expression that makes me grit my teeth. "Aristotle spent too much time at his studies and not enough time in the company of the women who raised him. I was raised by a queen, and I've come to France for a queen of my own." He turns to Margot, hands outstretched and bare.

"I have little to offer you that you don't already have, Marguerite de Valois. But if you'll have me, I promise to create a place where girls can seek an education equal to their brothers'. If you marry me, there shall be a school for you in Navarre."

Scandalized gasps burst among the crowd. Even King Charles reels back, fumbling his wine cup and staining his front a vivid purple. No one knows if Henry is making a jest or not, if this is a promise or a part of his performance. Margot's dearest wish has been dismissed for so long, no one ever took it seriously.

But I see the seriousness in his expression, and how Margot's eyes grow shinier each passing second. She hides her incredulity behind a delighted laugh, a courtier's smile. "Why should I believe you, warrior king?" Her smile curls into a smirk. "You could just be trying to conquer me."

Henry bows. "Because I've been in enough battles to know when I've lost." His eyes catch mine behind Margot. My insides twist up too tight to breathe around, the entire world narrowing to his stare. I couldn't break eye contact with him if the Louvre was on fire.

He smiles, the expression razor thin, his voice as soft as silk: "I can assure you this is a battle I'm happy to lose."

CHAPTER TWENTY

MARGOT'S SALON RAGES late. I spend the night at her side, afraid to leave, afraid of Henry finding me, afraid of what I might do if he does.

He makes it so very hard to do the right thing, I don't know whether kissing him or killing him would make me less frustrated. "Did you hear what Henry said?" Margot snakes her arm through mine.

I hate the way my traitorous heart lifts at his name. Like I haven't been thinking of him the entire night. Like I haven't let him tie me up in angry knots for hours already. "We all heard what he promised you. Though I imagine some people will struggle to remember it after the fete you threw." I know I won't be the only person to wake up tomorrow with a pounding head and a sour mouth. King Charles has already fallen asleep on his throne, his laurel crown askew.

Margot laughs and elbows my side. "Yes, but do you think Henry will remember it?"

The look she gives me, her mouth still smirking, her eyes huge with hope, makes my chest ache fiercely. I pull her closer and lay my head on her shoulder. "I think he meant every word, Margot. He doesn't say things he doesn't mean."

She nestles closer, her cheek against my temple. "The school wouldn't be in Paris like I wanted." She twists a ripple of her skirt over and over again, fingertips going red. "But it could be something. A start."

I squeeze my eyes shut. "It could be something."

It could be everything.

It hangs unspoken between us, how the scale has tipped in Henry's favor, how marriage might be worth the risk to Margot so she can have the one thing she's wanted more than anything else. A dream impossible until this night. Something her mother or brother could never take from her.

Margot wears her jokes and cynicism as finely as she does her jewels, one more barrier betwixt her feelings and the world. Seeing this single crack in her armor strengthens me. Shows me what I need to do next.

Murmuring something about needing more sweets, I kiss Margot's cheek and disappear into the garden. Henry's waiting beside a marble statue tucked in a secluded bower. He jerks up at my approach, gaze intense beneath his tangled fringe. My pulse leaps at the sight of Ares undone, his beauty more stinging now than at the night's start.

"Hmm." I take in the familiar Artemis statue, one of Catherine de' Medici's favorites. I can't believe Margot convinced her mother to let it out of the Louvre. "Seems a bit on the nose for you to wait here, doesn't it?"

He leans against the priceless marble, leather skirt parting and baring his muscled leg midthigh. "I knew you'd come eventually."

My teeth grind, hating how want flares in me. He takes up nearly all the space in the shady bower already. I don't think there's a single space in France big enough for him and his ego. "Don't get any ideas. I didn't come to talk about us."

His teeth gleam wolfishly. "Excellent. I was hoping I could get you to listen."

Anger ripples through me like a beast undulating beneath the sea's surface, mere inches from bursting forth. Must everything be a joke to him? "If you were lying to Margot tonight, I shall never, ever forgive you. Opening a school is all she's ever wanted. If you're playing games—"

Henry holds up a hand. The smugness has slipped from his face. "You think I was lying to her?"

I roll a stone beneath my foot, sulking up at him. I let the silence speak for me.

He shakes his head, his taunting smile slipping away. "I can't believe I've won over Margot but not you." His words are low and furious. "After all this time, you still treat me as you did the very first day we met. As though I'm an insolent boy who needs to be put in his place."

My temples throb. "That's because you haven't learned your place yet. You say and do whatever you want, regardless of the consequences. Margot deserves something real."

Henry laughs. "That's rich coming from you, Jac."

My anger bursts forth, roaring. "Have I not helped you get exactly what you wanted?"

I want him to roar back. To meet me in a fight where I know I can hold my own.

His voice goes rough. "I want you to trust me. Are you capable of that? Can you trust a single person other than yourself to do the right thing?"

His words cut straight through me. To the soft truth running along my bones, which I've done my best to protect. Not trusting people is what keeps me safe. It's only animal instinct to leave before I get hurt. Before I'm hurt by people like *him*, who have everything and don't realize it.

"You don't understand," I say. "You're a—"

"A king, yes. I'm quite aware. But by God, Jac, I've tried to show you again and again the kind of man I am beneath the crown, and still you find me lacking." He paces, tracing Artemis's bent arm, the antlers of the white stag at her side. "I'm giving the princess what she wants because I know *you* want her to be happy." His unwavering stare locks onto mine. "I know you love her."

"Of course I love her. She's my lady—"

"No, Jac, you *love* her." He stops right before me, expression more serious than I've ever seen it. "And you're afraid of being alone."

The final threads holding me together snap. It's nothing but me and him and that dark, knowing gaze stripping me bare. I take a shuddering breath, grasping for the control that's already slipped from my fingers.

I always knew Margot was going to leave me, but her leaving with the only other person who's cracked my heart wide open? It's so hideously unfair, I want to scream.

Henry will never know this. Especially not the part where

once I thought Margot returned my feelings. He sniffed out my secret, but I won't betray Margot's. It's not mine to share. For the first time, I wish the king was as stupid as I once thought he was. I can't bear the thought of one more piece of myself in his hands, one more part of me I can't take back.

Henry still watches me, waiting. I pick up all the soft, tender things he's torn out of my chest. Hide them behind a lifted chin and a mocking smile. "Well done, Your Majesty. You figured me out. What are you going to do about it?"

He shrugs, the movement a careless flex. "Nothing."

"Why not?" My words are barbed, hot. "You could get me to agree to anything. It's unnatural for women to be with other women."

His look is scathing, offended. "You think I'd use this against you?"

Shame licks up my spine. I should apologize, but instead I stand even taller. I'm being vicious, but I don't know how else to get him to leave me alone. This—me—it's none of his concern. "Why bring it up at all if you aren't?"

He holds my stare for so long, I wonder if he'll respond at all. "Because I'm like you, Jac."

I laugh, the sound short and shrill. "What, that you too possess unexplored abandonment issues?"

His lip curls. "No. I'm like you because I also desire men and women both."

My heart thrashes against my ribs so loud, I'm certain he can hear it. "Stop jesting."

He scoffs, turning away. "Why would I jest about something

like this?" Why indeed? When there's nothing to gain and everything to lose? Not even Margot or Oncle understand this part of me.

I nod slowly. The world feels off-balance. Like I held a map sideways and someone has righted it for me, revealing a place I've never seen before. Never knew existed. This feels like it changes everything even though it changes nothing. "I'm sorry. I just—I didn't expect this. Do—do other people know?"

Henry fists a hand in his hair, all of it peaking in damp spikes. I have a sudden certainty that he's never shared this part of himself with anyone before. My hand itches to take his, tell him that it's all right, he's safe with me. What a privilege it was to discover this part of myself and have Oncle accept it. He has never made me feel alone about this.

"Only my former lover. We were soldiers together. I hoped it could be more, but he said his love for his king was more than his love for me." His lashes lower, fluttering against his cheekbones. "When I was a mere prince, I could fight at men's sides as their equal. Now that I'm king, when they look at me all they see is Navarre itself. How can I ever live up to their expectations? How can I ever ask someone to love the man more than the king?"

My throat swells shut, the image of a lonely boy with aching, mortal shoulders carrying the soul of an entire kingdom. I know how carefully Oncle shields this part of himself from court, how unfair and cruel the world can be to men who prefer men. How much worse this must be for kings.

I skim my smallest finger down his wrist, reminding him

that he's not alone. He turns to me ever so slightly, his little finger catching mine and holding tight. We're barely touching, but I've never felt closer to him. We have so very much in common. Is this why I've been so drawn to him? This boy whose soul feels carved from the same stone as my own?

"You can love whoever you want, Henry. It's the joy of being what we are," I whisper. "Don't let one boy let you doubt."

He flashes me a wry smile, as if he doesn't quite believe me.

"I came here for a queen, and I found you instead. Clever, infuriating, beautiful you, Jacqueline d'Argenson-Aunis. Please don't send me from your side without giving me a chance. I'll be your spaniel, your knight. Whatever I can be for you, let me be it."

All my blood has rushed into my smallest finger, the skin there more sensitive then everywhere else. His chest heaves, and his face is all aglow with a frightening fervor. I shiver and pull away.

"I don't need you to be anything."

"Yes, but do you want me to be anything?"

His question skirts the very edge of where I've allowed my heart to wander. Beyond it lies a grey unknown, a place of shadows and danger and God knows what else.

I shake my head, my words a whisper. "You can't."

He draws closer, so close, I could lean my head on his chest. "As you have noted many times, I'm a king. I can be whatever I wish."

He holds out his hand. I trace a single fingertip down the lines, across his unsteady fingers. They wrap around mine again, and I make no move to stop them. So slowly, so carefully, the last distance between us disappears. My head under his chin, my cheek to his chest. His heart thrashes like a fledging leaving its nest for the very first time.

"What do you want, Jac?" he says.

I close my eyes. My fingers dig into his skin. He's been so honest with me. What do I lose from being honest with him, just this once, when I know this aching moment must vanish by dawn? "I want so much it crushes me."

He holds me closer, lips in my hair. "Tell me more."

It all swirls before me. "I want independence. I want to do work that matters and have no one look at me sideways for it and say a woman's place is in her husband's home. I want my oncle to be proud of me for who I am and not what I can do. I want a house of my own and a garden and enough space for Anémone to run. I want to believe that things will get better instead of worse. I want to never feel lonely again." I burrow deeper against him, my last wish barely a breath. "I want to be enough to make someone stay."

The quiet is louder than thunder. I immediately want to take the words back. Shove them into the secret chambers of myself. But I couldn't even if I tried. The ropes holding them back have all frayed and snapped.

Henry holds me so I don't shatter. "You ask for the entire world to change then. Let me help you bend it to your will."

I laugh wetly. Tenderness overwhelms me for this golden boy who refuses to accept the word "no," the foolish king who makes impossible promises but means every word of them.

I press a kiss above his heart, finally letting myself have a taste of what I want. Tomorrow I'll return to being an acolyte for the Societas Solis. Tomorrow he'll return to being a royal. "Not even a king can do that."

His hand, heartbreakingly tender despite his fierce expression, combs through my hair. "Watch me."

I let myself sink against him again, taking as much as I can until the spell finally breaks. "Why did you swear to protect me when you're already promised to so much more?" The question has long burned in my mind, but his confession today makes me feel like I can finally ask about it. Something raw and vulnerable holds us together. A spring vine, creeping inch by inch across a rough stone face, settling thin roots into inhospitable cracks.

"I couldn't bear the thought of anything harming you because of me. You were willing to risk yourself to help me. It was the absolute least I could do."

My insides twist guiltily. Would he still think I was so noble if he knew about the Societas Solis? That I wasn't just helping him from the selflessness of my own heart? I shake my head, laughing. "I did very little. Save your oath for when it's worth it. Don't feel like you still owe that to me."

Something ripples across his face, there and gone too fast for me to read. "I wish I could convince you that you're worth it."

My breath gets caught. I square my jaw and look away, needing this terrible, bright, buoyant feeling in my chest to lessen.

I step away, holding out my hand. "Shall we have one last dance? There's still time before dawn." Still time before we must go back to the world where this never happened. The world where nothing more can happen.

Because after tonight, Henry will propose to Margot, and they will marry.

For the good of France and Navarre.

For the good of all the people who need the endless civil wars to stop.

They will marry, and it will be the best thing for everyone except for me.

Henry's fierce expression fades, as if finally realizing I can't take any more of this. I've burned so hot for so long there's nothing left but ash. He takes my hand, presses a kiss to my palm. "Whatever you wish, love. I'm yours to command."

CHAPTER TWENTY-ONE

N O ONE STOPS me when I disappear into the streets of Paris.

Why would they? In Madame Dupont's stolen cloak, I'm another feminine silhouette, face hidden in the shadow of my hood. To the royal guards, I could be a servant heading to the market. A lady's maid visiting a sister in the city. No one would ever suspect that I'm the unchaperoned, unmarried niece of the royal spymaster who believes that I'm with Margot while Margot believes I'm with my oncle.

My lips curve as I slip past the iron gates.

I've never been in the city alone.

Many times I've come here with Oncle, but today, the boulevards leading into the city's heart beckon like a treasure map.

I pass through a bustling market on my way to Louise's apothecary. Canvas stalls and open wagons selling everything imaginable. A display of tiny carved animals draws me closer. I stroke a little dog, his likeness reminding me of Margot's beloved creatures.

A shadow cuts over me. "You gonna pay, or keep fondling them for free?"

Too late, I realize I don't have any coin. Money didn't cross my mind once as I donned my disguise. I drop my gaze and move on with murmured apologies.

Then I notice the drawing on the ground.

A crude likeness of King Henry, commanding some sort of vile doglike beast to chase a terrified rendering of Margot.

"It is disgraceful, *non*?" The carpenter toes the pamphlet distastefully. "If our princess marries that vile man, all of France shall be under his yoke. He'll destroy what it means to be French! He already sends his evil creatures to butcher our boys!"

The air is punched from my lungs. It's one thing to hear people disapprove of the royal marriage; it's another to hear their disapproval with my own ears. A sour, hot feeling surges up my throat. "I don't know—"

The carpenter is in my space, towering above me. "Do you sympathize with the Navarrese king, then?"

I smile up at him, the expression all sunshine. I force my outrage down into a hard knot. "No, monsieur. The crudeness of the drawing offends me. It's not fit for ladies' eyes."

And then I'm weaving through the crowds before he can say anything else, my heart hammering. When I glance over my shoulder, he's still standing there, his stare an arrow aimed at my back.

I scramble down the next alley, and then the next. I don't slow my step until I reach the apothecary.

"Mademoiselle!" Louise's eyes go wide when I step inside, disheveled and panting. "What are you doing here?"

"I want to investigate the murders," I say.

I'm tired of pretending not to want the things that I want.

There's no future for me and Henry. I can't make Margot stay. But I can do this: make myself so useful to the Societas Solis, Oncle won't have any choice but to make me a full member. If I can earn his respect, if I can claw out a place for myself here, it'll be enough to fill the hungry hollow in my chest. It must be.

Louise nods slowly. She touches the sun pendant on her bodice. "Did your oncle send you?"

Dust motes hang in the afternoon sun like specks of gold. I open my mouth, ready to lie, then think better of it.

"No. He doesn't know I'm here."

Louise drops her pendant, eyes oyster-pale and sharp. "Lying to your oncle is a bold move, mademoiselle. Do you know how many people have lied to him and lived?"

My smile wavers. The silence grows, big enough for me to be frightened of it. I shift, suddenly aware again of the distance betwixt me and Louise, the vast gulf separating our worlds even though I'm so close to her right now.

This isn't going to work.

The thought is like a stone through glass. To Louise, I'll always be Gabriel's niece, a noblegirl good for matchmaking and nothing else. I step closer, desperate to make her see I'm more than that. "Look, I—"

The shop doors open and a trio of women enter, their conversation filling up the small space like a noisy flock of rooks.

"Do you mind waiting, mademoiselle?" Louise hooks a thumb over her shoulder to her back room. "I know you're very busy and I don't want to waste your time, but I can't close early today—"

"Call me Jac, please." I hold up a hand. "I'm happy to wait."

Louise flashes me a close-lipped smile that could mean anything.

Thomas, her son, is already in the back room. As is an entire basket of wriggling kittens.

"That's quite a lot of cats you've got there," I say.

Thomas looks up from his mortar and pestle. With his stern brow and serious expression, he bears more likeness to a crabby priest than a child of ten. "Their mother was struck by a carriage."

I wince at the matter-of-fact tone. "Oh. I'm sorry you had to see such a thing—"

Thomas points to the basket's side. "She's there. I splinted her leg."

I spot the striped creature on a pile of linen scraps. Her back leg is a neatly tied lump of wood and linen. At my look, her ears flatten back, and she clambers into the nest alongside her babies.

"You splinted the leg?" I say, certain I've misheard.

"That's what I said, isn't it?" the boy snaps.

I blink, taken aback.

Thomas ducks his head and mutters, "Maman doesn't like it when nobles come by. She says you only want to use this place so you don't dirty your hands or your fancy silks. That's why none of you will protect Paris."

My heart thumps unevenly. So the Societas Solis still doesn't have enough people to search for the murderer. There might be a chance for me.

"Can I tell you a secret?" Thomas nods solemnly and leans closer. "I don't think I want to be like the other nobles. If I start acting like one of them, will you tell me?"

"I will." Thomas clenches a fist and presses it to his heart. "And you'll promise not to agree with Maman when she complains there are too many animals inside."

I mirror Thomas and press a fist to my heart. "You have my word. Besides—" I put my mouth close to his ear. "I completely agree with you. There's *always* room for more animals inside."

He giggles, stern façade finally cracking.

"What are you two laughing about?" Louise stands in the doorway. This time I recognize the strain in the expression, the wariness at seeing me carousing with her only child. Guilt pinches me. I'm here to do business, not to play with children. I stand and smooth my skirts. "Sorry, I was just—"

Thomas interrupts. "She told me I can have as many animals inside as I want!"

Louise smiles. "Could you mind the storefront, darling?" She lays a hand on Thomas's shoulder. He squeezes it and nods.

"Yes, but don't touch my things. I'm making something for the cat."

Louise kisses his curly head as he passes. "Of course not, my love."

Then it's just me and Louise and the anxious silence again. I clear my throat. "Your son has a gallant heart." Paris hardly cares for its people. The animals live even more sordid lives.

Louise sits across from me. "He can't stand to see a living

thing in pain. This world needs more people like my Thomas in it." Her posture straightens, her soft expression vanishing. "Which is why you'll be patrolling the streets of Paris for the murderer tonight and every night until we find answers. My son won't be a victim."

Her fierce words leave me breathless. "Truly? Do you mean it?"

"You're here and willing, aren't you? Your oncle may think a royal engagement will be enough to ease the city's fears that these murders are part of some awful Protestant plot, but I know a royal wedding doesn't mean shit to anyone who's worried about their son coming home."

I bite my lip, thinking of the ugly drawings I saw on my way over. I know Louise is right. And yet.

Do you know how many people have lied to your oncle and lived?

Getting what I want so quickly has knocked the wind from my sails, leaving room for the doubts to tiptoe back in.

"You'll have to lie to Gabriel with me." I hate even saying the words. But I know Oncle would deliver upon his threat to send me away. If I am gone, then my chance for a future of my own is also gone. "I know that's a lot to ask."

Louise laughs, the sound razor sharp. "Well, of course we'll be lying to him. That goes without saying."

I bite my lip, not entirely sure she grasps the danger. "It would be daring. He's not always reasonable—"

"I have overseen your oncle's work for years. I know exactly what he's like." Her smile turns glittering. "Or did you assume because Gabriel was a man and a noble that he out-ranked me?"

Scarlet explodes across my cheeks. That's precisely what I assumed.

I duck my head. My memories of Oncle dashing from the Louvre for days at a time rewrite themselves. It was never his choice to leave me; it was always a summons. From Louise. Who is in charge.

Which means women don't just work for the Societas Solis. They *run it*.

This is what Oncle has been hiding from me. The fact that not only was my dearest desire entirely possible for him to grant, but that another woman was already living the life I wanted. The betrayal is a bone-deep ache, something broken and barely healed. I ring a hand around my throat and bite my lip.

Why would he lie to me about this?

Louise claps my shoulder. "Be easy on yourself. You're not the first to make this mistake. The entire world underestimates us, Jac. It's one reason the order is open to women. We can go places men can't."

I lift my head. Her stare already bores into mine. "The Societas Solis does not care for titles and wealth. Such things are useful, of course, but merely tools in the end."

Despite the betrayal still stinging me, something twists hopefully in my chest. "What else is useful for your work?" This is already more than Oncle has ever been willing to share with me about the Societas Solis. It feels as though Louise has finally unlocked a door whose handle I've rattled for years.

"You, for one." Louise nods toward the blade hidden on my hip. "I never knew Gabriel had trained his niece. He's kept you a secret for far too long."

The praise is a delicious confection, all the sweeter for its rarity. I close my eyes, mortified to feel them filling with tears.

"He regrets it. He promised my dead mother he'd keep me safe."

Louise smiles sadly. "A chivalrous promise, of course, but no one in Paris is safe if war breaks out once again."

All I can do is nod. There's a lump too big in my throat to speak around. Louise has done so much more than listen to me; she sees me in a way that Oncle never has. A secret worth sharing.

My entire life I've been reaching for something that's felt just beyond reach, my muscles screaming to cross those last few impossible inches.

Here, at last, the future I want is within grabbing distance.

My heart squeezes painfully. How I wish it was Oncle offering it to me instead!

"Here." Louise slips her sun pendant over her head. It glimmers on her palm, as bright as an earring abandoned on the ballroom floor. "You'll get your own once you take formal vows to serve, but this will do for now."

My breath catches at the sight of it. How many times did I trace Oncle's signet ring as a child? How many times did I draw the sun in the dust of the locked-up rooms of our estate, as if drawing it would summon him home to me? I reach for the sun pendant, but Louise pulls it back, one eyebrow raised. "Are you certain this is what you want, Jac? Once you start working for the Societas Solis, you can't go back. It can be a lonely life."

I laugh, the sound dry and humorless.

As if my life could get any lonelier than the life Oncle wants me to have. Me, married to a man who doesn't care about me, tucked away in the middle of nowhere. Oncle forever off on his adventures, Margot and Henry married and gone to Navarre.

Me, safe, but dead inside.

I came to Louise today because I don't trust Oncle to make good on his promise to let me do more for the Societas Solis. He's made it clear, over and over again, that I'm only useful as his royal matchmaker. What happens after Henry proposes to Margot?

What happens once I've outlived my usefulness to him?

I'm not going to find out.

"Of course. This is all I've ever wanted." I've fought too hard to wrench this door open to leave now when I'm on the threshold.

Louise's smile shows all her teeth. Her sun pendant is strangely heavy in my palm. "Then welcome to the Societas Solis, Jacqueline d'Argenson-Aunis."

CHAPTER TWENTY-TWO

W HEN THE GILDED invitation arrives at our door, it feels like a jest.

Oncle tosses the parchment on the dining table after he reads it. "An engagement ball. The princess has at last consented to be wed."

All I can do is nod tightly, my heartbeat thick in my throat.

A public betrothal is pointless because the wedding date has long been set. I know the invitations have already been sent out with the royal couriers. They race along the roads, blue cloaks flying, to summon the marquesses and vicomtes and ducs from their châteaux to Paris to witness the wedding of a century. Already I have seen the swans being fattened and the royal gardeners painstakingly coaxing the roses into a lusher bloom.

There is only a month until the wedding, after all, and nothing but the very best of everything shall do.

Oncle turns to me, an odd look on his face. It takes me a moment to recognize his close-mouthed smile. Then he pulls me into an awkward embrace, all the more awkward for the fact that we're not a family prone to displaying affection.

"Congratulations, Niece. You've done excellent work. Better than I could have imagined."

I hug him back, knowing it's to be expected, hating how his approval now goads when it once set my spirits soaring. Louise's sun pendant lies hidden in my pocket, as heavy as a stolen diamond.

"Does this mean I can do more work for the Societas Solis now?" I ask.

Oncle goes still. Then he pats my back, stepping away. "Not now, but I'm certain something needs to be done after the wedding." His smile doesn't reach his eyes.

He's lying.

I squeeze Louise's sun pendant even more tightly, the tines cutting into my skin.

He's lying, but so am I.

For three nights, I have walked the crooked arrondissements of Paris. Three nights I've gone to Louise's apothecary to tell her what I have seen, and she has greeted me as an equal each and every time.

I don't need Oncle to get what I want anymore. But he doesn't need to know that yet. He'll find out soon enough, when Louise decides it's time for me to pledge myself to the Societas Solis and earn a sun of my own. By then, it'll be too late for him to stop me.

Tonight I'll have to play the part of the vicomte's dutiful niece once more for the betrothal ball, even though the thought fills my veins with iron.

I enter the ballroom in my finest emerald silk gown with its pearl-studded sleeves and wonder if I'll be sick when Henry arrives. Seeing Margot is bad enough.

She's a dream in white, her delicate skirts scudding like summer clouds across the floor. Her bodice sparkles with an ocean's worth of pearls. Her sable hair is braided and set with a silver crown. She's so beautiful, it aches to look at her.

I watch her, fist pressed just beneath my collarbones, as if it'll be enough to hold back the surging nausea. Soon, she will see me and draw closer. Soon, Henry will enter and I'll be one more spectator in the crowd, watching and waiting for him to drop to one golden knee and ask the question everyone's been dying to have him ask for weeks.

Acid fills my mouth, the vision stinging like a slap.

Oncle looks back, frowning when I no longer follow him. "Is everything well?"

I shake my head.

I don't want to be here anymore.

I don't want to see Henry ask for Margot's hand or to hear her pledge her future to him.

I plead a sudden headache and leave as quickly as I came, fleeing the sticky camphor-scented air for the outdoors. The night air is a cool relief for my too-hot skin and too-hot spirit. I press my back against the Louvre's stone foundation and will my breath to slow.

Then I go to the stables.

I take out the honeyed damson I pocketed and feed it to Anémone. Not even her velvet nose can calm me as much as I need. I'm a jumpy wreck, straining to hear any noise from the ballroom. I don't want to witness the proposal, but I want to know when it happens.

"No more balls," I grumble into her neck. "I've been to enough balls to last me a lifetime."

"Then we have that in common."

I turn around slowly, so slowly, dizzy with dread, hoping I'm wrong.

But no.

Henry of Navarre stands behind me, painfully handsome in his splendid garments. Every inch of him is polished and shined to a gleam. He looks nothing like the boy who has stolen my wits and heart. He looks like a king.

Margot's king.

My heart crawls into my throat, so heavy I could choke on it. The tinkle of dice and laughter comes from the hayloft. The stable boys must have the night off. Any one of them could recognize Henry, and then the entire palace would know the king has left his own engagement ball to be with another girl. The scandal it would cause would be like nothing else.

"You shouldn't be here."

Henry slinks into an empty stall, his smile dangerously soft.

"I wanted to see you first."

The sentence rolls down my skin like warm oil. I close my eyes, clenching my fists like he'll somehow vanish if I wish for it hard enough.

"You've seen me now, so go." I glance meaningfully from his feet to the long path back to the Palais du Louvre, a blinding torch against the night. "You can't be here."

He angles his body closer. Someone has combed back his hair and corralled it with a silver crown. The order does not suit him at all. My fingers rise ever so slightly, itching to muss it.

"Do it." His gaze is dark and imploring.

Something quivers in my stomach.

He stretches a hand to me across the aisle. "Please, Jac."

With an incensed growl, I storm across the narrow aisle. He dips his head lower, and the heavy crown tumbles into the crook of my elbow. I reach on my toes and drag my fingers through his golden hair, relishing the pull against my palm.

The sound he makes is worth more to me than the diamonds in his crown. I let it wash over me, shuddering. This is enough. More than enough. Him being here, him wanting to find *me*, when all the most distinguished nobles of France and Navarre wait on *him*, does a strange thing to my chest I like not at all. The sooner he leaves, the sooner the feeling will go away.

I tug his hair gently, admonishingly. "It's time for you to leave."

His gaze slivers like a purring cat's. "You can't tell me what to do."

I give his hair one last tug and set the crown back on his head, stepping out of his reach. "I can. You told me you were mine to command, remember? Perhaps you should listen before you get us in trouble."

He straightens reluctantly. "I want to show you something."

"Can it not wait until later?"

He beams, the expression breaking through all his flirtatious swagger like the sun through clouds. "No, I think you'd like to see it tonight."

I roll my eyes, but his clear excitement disarms me. He stands on the balls of his feet like he'd rather have left a minute ago already. Whatever he wants to show me can't be too bad if he's acting like a boy that's been promised a gâteau.

I cross my arms and sigh. "Fine. But after this you have to *leave*, Henry. We can't be seen out here."

He winks and presses a finger to his lips, gestures for me to follow down the stable aisle. We duck out the side door to the adjoining barn. There, Henry opens an empty pen and motions for me to go inside.

Inside is the tiny pony Henry gifted Margot, but she's not alone. Beside her is a foal, a scrap of shadow who cannot be more than a few hours old. I gasp and kneel beside the baby. His tiny, fuzzy head just fits in the crook of my neck. He's perfect.

I marvel at the foal's teensy hooves and long-lashed eyes, the softness of his baby hair like dandelion heads. I close my eyes and breathe deeply, the sweet smell of hay and horse a welcome departure from the loud, sweltering ballroom with its cloying perfumes and seething bodies.

When I open my eyes again, Henry is grinning. "Are you glad you stayed?"

I stroke the foal's little head. "I think my heart just burst into bits."

Henry laughs lightly, like it's nothing to him, but it's everything to me.

He knew tonight would be hard for me and made sure I would have one happy memory of it. He is so *good*, so teeth-achingly sweet, it hurts.

A hollow place suddenly opens wide in my chest, the dreadful loneliness already clawing at me. Margot gone, and Henry with her. What am I supposed to do?

You have the Societas Solis, I remind myself savagely. *You finally have what you've always wanted.*

Henry kneels in the straw, heedless of his fine clothes. I wipe away the stinging in my eyes before he notices.

He holds out his hand. "There is something else I wish to show you."

A ring glimmers on his palm.

It's exquisite, a dainty ruby surrounded with a spray of diamonds on a slender silver band. I reach out and trace the circle thoughtfully, a hot rush in my throat. I wonder if I'm the first person to sully it with my commoner's touch. "Margot will like this. She hates blue. It reminds her of her family."

I withdraw, but Henry's fingers catch my hand, holding me close. His eyes meet mine, steady and more serious than I've ever seen them. "This isn't for her."

Only when his hand starts to tremble do I understand what's happening.

I gasp, eyes locked on the ring.

My ring.

His eyes are so huge with hope, I stop breathing.

"When I'm asleep you're all I dream of, and when I'm awake you're all I can see. Marry me, Jac. I want my dreams to be real."

The words reverberate through my bones, down to my toes. All of me rattling to pieces like the inside of a church bell striking noon. A high note rises above them all, defying all sense and reason. *The king asks me to* marry *him.*

My whisper is barely a breath. "Henry. What are you doing? You need to marry Margot."

For France. For Navarre. For a thousand reasons that we both already know.

That's what tonight is for. That's why the most important people in two kingdoms are gathered in the gilded ballroom, all of them doubtless murmuring and wondering where the guest of honor has gone by now.

His voice is full of fiery conviction. "That's what I thought too. But above all else, I need to be a good king." His eyes find mine, dark and searing. "You would make me a better king, Jacqueline d'Argenson-Aunis."

A long, shuddering breath floats from my lungs. It feels like I'm out of my body, peering down on two people kneeling knee to knee in a barn. Both covered in straw, one wearing a crown. One shaking so hard she might come apart.

Me, make him a better king?

A peasant's daughter?

A secret spy, becoming his queen?

My voice is as unsteady as the foal's little legs. "You're mistaken. Margot was raised to be a queen and I wasn't. She—"

"Margot was raised knowing that people would lay cloths of gold at her feet wherever she walked. The princess of France doesn't enter a room and wonder if she's important enough to matter. But I do. You do. We know what it's like to wonder if we'll be enough to carry the people we care for." His lips brush the shell of my ear. "Please, Jac, make me yours. Enter that ballroom on my arm, and we'll show them what we can be together."

My pulse rages in the hollow of my throat. For a breath-stopping moment, I see it all. The roughness of his scarred hand in mine as we enter the ballroom together. His face soft with sleep beside me in the darkness. Our breath mingling in the crisp morning air, each of us lost in our own book. Each vision feels like a treasure box, brimming with possibility, countless quiet moments adding up to everything, an entire universe of belonging. What would it be like to have another hand to hold up the lantern and chase away the darkness that haunts us both?

But Henry's not only asking me to marry him. He's also asking me to be his queen. I think of Margot's measured smiles when she reads vitriol about herself, how she must lift her head and pretend to be above the wounded feelings raging through her breast. I think of Catherine de' Medici and how her dead husband is still the most important part of her life.

How Henry would become the most important part of mine. How my dream of independence would be crushed beneath my crown.

Henry knows what it is to be king, yes, but he knows nothing of what it means to be a queen. How it might be different.

What would happen if I entered the Louvre on Henry's arm?

I imagine the herald beginning to announce the Navarrese king, sputtering to a halt when he sees the king isn't alone. The musicians falling quiet with a discordant squeal. In the absolute silence, jeweled heads would turn to stare at us, one by one, Margot's last of all.

Margot, in her matching silver crown.

Margot, whose reputation would never recover.

And there's Oncle. His resigned sigh, as if he always expected me to fail anyway. Catherine de' Medici's white, furious face. She would blame Oncle for this, for bringing his wanton, lowbred niece into her dazzling court to seduce her daughter's royal bridegroom, for making Margot a laughing-stock in France and beyond, the Valois name becoming a punch line along with her. Oncle would be dismissed from his spymaster's post, perhaps even stripped of his title and estates. The Societas Solis would turn its back on him.

After all, what use is a publicly disgraced, penniless lord to an order of spies where secrecy is valued more than life?

What use is his niece?

Acid ravages my stomach. I don't deserve Henry's lovely words. I'm a liar, a silver-tongued snake willing to shove aside my best friend's happiness for my own. I can't take Margot's future from her, not when she's finally excited for it. Lying to her about my work with the Societas Solis has been devastating.

Lying to Henry is somehow even worse.

I feel the ring betwixt us, how it grinds into my palm. I pull away from him, and it falls to the straw.

He reaches helplessly. "Jac—"

I slip away. "I can't." Tears rush down my cheeks, too quick to catch. "I'm sorry, Henry. My oncle has many enemies. I can't risk what they might do to him."

A lie and a truth woven together, dust on my tongue. But it's the best I can offer. I thought we both knew how this had to end, but I was wrong. So terribly wrong.

Slowly he picks up the ring. His face has gone pale.

"But—but I thought—" He stops, and I know he saw it too. Our life together. That whole, wild universe just out of reach, a night sky across a strange land. He looks up from his tangled fringe, his stare dark with betrayal and hurt.

"I love you," he says. "Does that mean nothing?"

The words tear into me. Is that what this feeling is? The one that burns me up whenever I think of him? Love should be soft and tender, but this love has teeth. It latches on to me, jaws locked, refusing to let go no matter how hard I try to pull away. The wound will leave a ruinous scar, if it heals at all. An agonized sound slips from behind my teeth.

I love him, but I can't have him.

I can't have him, but I want him.

I want to say it back—to tell him I love him too, to give him something to take with him—but I can't. Why must he make it so hard—so brutally, unfairly hard—for me to do the right thing? My lungs are punctured, filling with water. My words are a damp cry. "We both know there's more to marriage than love!"

He stares, the lovely panes of his face filled with nothing but devastating loneliness. "No, Jac. There isn't for me. Love and marriage are the same."

I close my eyes, unable to look at him any longer.

I hear him leave, imagine the long trek back to the glittering palace, each step putting more and more distance betwixt us.

It's not enough.

Minutes or even hours later—time leaping and pausing in strange bursts—a roar echoes from the Palais du Louvre. I press my face into the foal's fur and let the sound gut me.

CHAPTER TWENTY-THREE

THE QUIET IN Margot's parlor is as thick as custard.

"So there's truly been no word from King Henry, then?" Lady Charlotte finally bursts out, unable to keep it in any longer.

My embroidery needle stabs through the canvas straight into my thumb. I curse and throw the entire hoop down. A spot of crimson blossoms across the fabric.

Six pairs of shocked eyes turn toward me.

"Oh—*oh my*. Where on earth did you learn to curse like that, Lady Jacqueline?" Lady Charlotte's face is as wide and tremulous as an unset soufflé. If she spent a single second in a Parisian market she might faint.

I flee across the room, dipping a handkerchief into a swan-shaped ewer and wrapping it tightly about the wound. All the chaste and good maidens of the Bible mock me from the ceiling fresco with their gentle smiles. I scowl. I wager none of them has ever ruined a royal engagement before.

King Henry never made it to his own betrothal ball. The roar I heard—the one I was so certain meant he and Margot were engaged—was from King Charles proclaiming he was bored and it was time for brandy for all.

Henry's advisors claim the king is ill. Each day they stand and stammer before King Charles and Catherine de' Medici and tell them His Majesty is recovering but can't yet leave his apartments, and each day Catherine de' Medici's mouth grows thinner and thinner.

No one believes it. But only I know the truth.

Henry had every intention of attending the betrothal ball.

Just not with Margot.

Soft footsteps behind me, and then a cloud of rose-scented perfume that makes my stomach drop. Margot. I force a smile, betraying nothing of how I'd rather be alone, how her presence makes me feel ill with guilt. "If I die from this wound, make sure my oncle doesn't dress me in something hideous for the funeral."

She laughs. "So *not* the puce velvet, then."

We share a secret smile, both of us remembering the frumpy dress Oncle made me buy last season. For a moment, everything is as it was before, when it was us against the entire world. The time before I betrayed her.

Her smile dissolves at the sight of Lady Charlotte and Hélène whispering furiously.

"Jac . . . can I talk to you about the betrothal ball?"

My expression grows strained. "Of course."

Her voice goes quiet. "I think it's my fault."

I twist the handkerchief even tighter. "Why would you think that? He's the one who left you waiting."

Every time I hear about it, the agony and guilt nearly pull me in two. Imagining how Margot's perfect smile wilted a little more each quarter hour that Henry didn't appear, how the court's whispers grew louder and their smiles sharper as the night dragged on. They came for a betrothal and left with a scandal, something infinitely more delicious. Catherine de' Medici has even forbidden pamphlets about the embarrassing night from being printed, a decree which, of course, only makes sure even more of them are printed.

All of Paris and half of Europe must know Henry of Navarre jilted Princess Marguerite, and it's all my fault.

Margot draws closer still, her lips brushing the shell of my ear. "I told Henry the only lovers I take to bed are women."

I twist the handkerchief again—too much—and hiss at the bright plume of pain. "Margot! Why would you do such a thing?"

A stab of hurt flickers across her face, there and gone so fast, I could've imagined it. "I thought if I must marry him, then he must know this about me. Would you rather I lie and cuckold him instead?"

"No, of course not!" My injured finger is cinched so tight in the fabric, the skin purples. My guilt burrows even deeper, a hideous, flesh-eating worm. Margot blames herself, but this is all my fault, and I can't even be supportive right now when she needs me. "Did it seem like what you said displeased him?"

Margot's brow furrows, the rest of her sharp lines softening. "That's what I can't figure out. He thanked me for telling him and meant it." Her lips tremble, her dark eyes glassy with tears. "He accepted me as I am and still left me alone in that ballroom. What if I ruined my chance to have a school? I trusted him with everything, and he tore it to bits." Her face crumples. I take her in my arms before anyone can see, one hand stroking her hair. My shame curls into a steely knot.

No one is allowed to break my princess's heart.

King or not, Henry is going to answer for this.

Paris is eerie tonight.

I walk deeper into the city. Each pool of shadow, every soft movement makes my skin skitter. Perhaps it's the rain-slicked cobblestones, how earlier today the clouds cracked and sent everyone cursing and muttering inside. Even now, the storm lingers like a foul mood, the clouds still sullen and black over the slick streets.

Or perhaps it's because Henry ignored my demand to speak with him all day.

I delivered the letter myself to the sour-faced guard outside his apartments. I hardly expected Henry to come greet me himself, but hours later, his silence had slipped under my skin. Whatever might lurk between us unseen and unsaid is going to claw its way out eventually. Why wait? He can be cross with me, but he can't be cruel to Margot.

It was almost a relief when the evening grew late enough that I could go to Louise's apothecary and forget about the king. At least for a little bit.

"Only one murder took place in this arrondissement." Louise's finger had traveled an X over the map earlier tonight. "But it's the only place where there was a witness."

I splayed my black-gloved hands on the table, Louise's sun pendant wound around my fingers, staring at the place where the streets tangled. "What did they see?"

"The girl saw a shadow over her brother's bed. When she screamed, it bolted out the window."

"So it unlocked the window from outside, then."

Louise frowned, the candlelight carving dark lines along her mouth. "Not quite. The glass was just missing. Like someone had cut it out neatly with a knife. I went and saw it myself."

I walk faster past the Cimetière des Saints-Innocents, with its paupers' graves and its tall *charniers* full of bones, still dwelling on Louise's words. People do not move like shadows, nor can they make an entire glass window disappear without leaving something behind.

Louise clearly missed something. But what?

Something moves along the cemetery wall.

My pulse riots, all the rumors of the monster knifing through me.

I inch backward, pressing myself into a building's shadow.

But the shape draws closer. Grows larger.

This is how people die. The fear bolts across my heart.

My blood thunders where my palms press against the wall. One small movement feels like enough to give me away, to have it leap toward me—

The shape suddenly sharpens.

A cat, prowling along the cemetery wall. It stops to lick its paw, utterly oblivious.

The tension shudders out of me. I take a deep breath.

Louise wouldn't have given me this task if she thought I would fail. Replace these dark houses with trees and it's no different from stalking a wolf who's developed a taste for lamb.

I touch the daggers on my hips and wade deeper into the city.

My reflection in the puddles is unfamiliar when the light of the full moon cleaves through the roiling clouds. A fine young man, but not so fine you would think him noble, strolling back from a pleasurable night in some house filled with sighs.

A grey fog rolls through the crooked streets when the church bells chime two. Men move through the mist, laborers whose work pauses for nothing and no one. I round a corner and nearly collide with someone.

"Watch it, boy!" the man snarls.

I step backward, dagger still drawn. "Apologies, monsieur!"

He spits, giving my blade a contemptuous look.

I sheathe the weapon unsteadily. *Get it together.*

Each step I take feels like too much. Too big, too loud as the city grows quieter, the night racing toward the bottom of its glass in a seedy tavern where nothing good happens.

As the fog grows thicker, I become certain of it.

Someone is following me.

And has been for a while.

A cold breeze whines through the streets, freezing up my courage. A copper tang fills my mouth.

It could be a pickpocket. A hungry soul who has watched me pass and thinks me an easy target. I duck down an alley, hurrying ever so slightly to get to the better-lit street beyond it.

Except the torches are guttered and damp, victims of the storm. The barren braces mock me like empty places in a jewelry box.

Swallowing, I keep walking, an animal instinct howling in

my chest to turn back, to run to Louise's apothecary. I make it only a block before I feel it.

The itch of an arrow betwixt my shoulders.

I whip around, dagger drawn.

No one is there.

My eyes strain, searching the black, broken cobblestones and twisted shutters.

There. Movement at the alley's edge. Right where I came onto the street.

My pulse goes jagged.

"Who's there?" I whisper.

No answer. Except—I squint harder—is that a glow? Eyes glinting green?

My nostrils quiver. The only steady part of me is my knife arm. "If you don't show yourself, I'll hurt you!"

A scoff answers me. From *behind*.

A man stands there, broad shouldered and menacing.

"I could ask the same of you, monsieur."

I take one staggering step back. Then another. My grip goes soft on my blade.

It's *Henry*.

His hair hangs in humid spikes, his glare burning beneath. He's here, after refusing to leave his apartments for days. A thousand questions gallop through me, one more urgent than all the rest together.

"Why are you following me?"

His silhouette goes still.

"Well?" I press, more savagely.

"What business do you have with the d'Argenson-Aunis family?" he demands.

He doesn't recognize me. The low pitch of my voice must've fooled him as much as my men's clothing. I square my shoulders and stand taller, praying the illusion holds. He can't recognize me out here. I'd have to spill my secrets, explain to him why I'm dressed like a boy, carrying a dagger like it was born in my hand. Any single one of those things would be enough to cause a scandal on its own—all together? I don't want to know what they add up to.

"Go home, king of Navarre. The city already blames you for its troubles. Don't give them another reason to distrust you," I say coldly.

His surprise is a barely there tremor. Perhaps he thought no one would recognize him out here, alone in his hunting leathers. But I would recognize him anywhere, under any circumstances.

He steps forward, fingers flexing on his sword hilt. "Not until you tell me what you were doing in the palace."

The sight of that confident movement sends fear wrapping around my ribs. His weapon is heavier and longer than my dagger. If we fought, I'd be at a severe disadvantage.

My jaw is clenched so tight it aches. I wish I could tell him the truth. Poke his chest and tell him to go home and forget he saw anything. He would listen to me, even though he wouldn't like it.

But this is not the Henry I know. This is King Henry of Navarre, the stranger I met so many weeks ago. There's an aggression in his shoulders and a supercilious glint in his gaze

I've never seen before. Too late, I remember his prowess in battle, how he led his own army.

No, this is worse. Not Henry of Navarre, but Henry the warrior.

"I think it best you leave," I say.

There's a cold metal rasp. His sword shivers free.

"You leave me no choice, then."

He attacks.

The blade catches on the X of my crossed daggers. Sparks illuminate Henry's furious face, beautiful even in rage. I barely got my guard up in time.

He spins away. I sidestep another blow, mind racing.

I won't hurt him. But I also can't let him win.

I parry another blow, gasping. If I don't end this quickly, he'll wear me down with strength alone.

Black spots across my vision as the king flourishes his blade and comes at me again.

I duck, just a hair faster.

There's an opening at his side as he sails past. Enough for a dagger.

The hesitation costs me.

Henry's sword knocks my right dagger flying. The force sends me stumbling backward. He gives me a shove. My back thuds against the cobblestones, pain cracking at the back of my skull. A strange numbness races along my limbs.

Henry looms over me, chest heaving, his expression terrible. I can't move, some soft-bodied bit of me still trusting him even as wrath fills his face. Even as my mind shrieks at me to get up and do something. Except the very action of turning my head makes my stomach churn. A warm wetness spreads under my head.

Is this truly how my spy work shall end? Henry defeating me in an empty Paris street, asking me questions I can't answer? The Societas Solis has no use for an unmasked spy. I wasn't good enough to survive a single fight.

"Why won't you answer me?" It's started to rain again, and Henry glowers beneath the spiked fringe of his hair. In a breath, he'll be close enough to recognize me. He'll know.

I twist away, panting hard. "I—"

A shadow crashes into Henry, dashing him from my sight.

I freeze, shocked, and then his battle bellow drags me back to my senses.

A dark figure sits on Henry's chest, stabbing at his face again and again. Sparks fly from his vambraced forearms. He barely manages to counter each blow.

I scramble upright—the entire world spins—and fly at the intruder blade first. My dagger squeals against his armor.

The attacker jerks toward me so fast I startle. He wears a vizard—the full-faced mask favored by courtly ladies so the sun does not darken their complexions. A luminous stare burns from the eye holes.

The distraction is all Henry needs. With a roar, he leaps to his feet.

But not fast enough.

More sparks light up the street as the masked attacker parries Henry's blows again and again, forcing him from attacking to defending in seconds. Sweat gleams on Henry's brow, his teeth gritted furiously. He can't hold his own for much longer.

My heart races. I need to help, but they're both too fast, the attacker too strong. If he blocks Henry's blows, he could block mine just as easily. The king is outmatched in every way.

His sword clangs to the street. He leaps to the side, just barely escaping a mortal blow.

"The ground!" I scream.

Henry drops.

The attacker straddles him, blade held high.

I inhale. My vision narrows to the knife in my hand.

I exhale and send it flying.

It sinks into the attacker's neck with a wet, warm splat.

With an unholy scream—so high and strange, my hair goes on end—the dark figure collapses.

For a single second there's nothing but shocked silence. Then there's a barking of dogs, the throwing open of windows. My second dagger clatters to the ground. The killer's blood licks my boots, thicker and more sluggish than I'd imagined. The edges of the world begin to spin.

"Are you injured?"

Henry's hands are in my armpits, keeping me from falling. He gives me a shake when I say nothing, voice commanding. "Answer me." Already his hand unlaces my jerkin, presses upon my ribs, seeking hidden fatal wounds.

"I've never killed someone before." The dazed confession walks right out of me.

His hand stills on my breast. A shock goes through me at the unexpected contact.

His mouth goes soft in surprise. "*You* saved me?"

I clamp my eyes shut. A hundred things hang on that *you*.

But I don't have it in me to lie to him anymore.

I reach for him. My hand presses a bloody handprint to his cheek. The crimson streaks swirl, not making sense.

He inhales sharply. "*Jac.*"

People flood from their doors now. Henry's shoulders tense. They can't find a noblegirl dressed as a boy alone with the king of Navarre with a dead body between them. We should move. I *need* to move.

But when I try to get up, the nausea overwhelms me. Sick splatters to the street, half of it on Henry.

His voice becomes urgent, louder than the onlookers drawing closer. "Your head is bleeding."

Stupid, useless tears prick my eyes. This isn't how I wanted him to see me again. I need to disappear. I need to apologize.

Instead I curl into his chest, whimpering with pain.

Even though I shouldn't. Even though I don't deserve to, not with how I've treated him.

His heart thumps, steady and certain. The most peaceful sound in the world.

I don't deserve him.

And he certainly deserves better than me.

My eyelids grow as heavy as stones. The last thing I feel is Henry lifting me before everything goes dark.

CHAPTER TWENTY-FOUR

THE FIRST THING I notice is the scent of flowers.

The deep burgundy anemones slowly pull into focus. I touch the petals, still damp with dew, wondering where they came from. Madame Dupont isn't one for touches of whimsy. No one in our household is.

The second thing I notice is that I'm not alone.

I bolt upright only to double over with nausea. A silver chalice appears before I can befoul myself. A hand grabs my hair before it joins the mess.

I wipe my chapped lips and lift my head.

Henry sits at the edge of the bed, clothes wrinkled as if he has been wearing them a long time. There's an older woman behind him, dozing on a tuffet. A physician's bag rests at her feet.

The attacker. Henry. The night spinning as wetness pooled beneath my head. There's a dizzying swoop in my stomach, the feeling of falling and waiting to be dashed on the rocks below.

Henry takes my shoulders, stilling me. "Moving makes it worse." He places the bowl of sick beside my chamber pot. "The physician said the headache will pass in a day or two."

I stare at the pots, a rush of embarrassment spearing me. "Where am I?"

"In the Navarrese apartments of the Louvre."

My stomach drops even lower. The blue light filtering in behind the draperies means it's near dawn, close to the morning.

I can't be found in the king's apartments. Not when he's refused to show his face since the failed betrothal ball. Everyone would assume there's something between us.

And they'd be right.

Henry should have left me bleeding on the streets.

I swing my bare feet to the herringbone floor. The movement echoes in my head, making the room sway. "This—this is horribly improper! I need to leave now."

Henry takes my shoulder again. "I've already written to your uncle. I told him you fell and hit your head coming to speak to me on Margot's behalf. It's already been a day. Everyone knows you're here."

Everyone knows you're here.

The words settle like a fever, too awful and clammy to think about.

It's already too late to avoid a scandal.

I laugh, the sound hopeless and harsh. "My oncle won't believe it."

A shadow passes over Henry's face, the moon over the sun, a look there and gone too fast for me to parse. He leans closer, dragging the bed linens over my legs. His size forces me to back up or risk touching him. "And will your oncle believe that you were out in the Parisian streets in the dead of night? Clothed and armed as a man?"

My back hits the pillow. Something in me ices over, growing colder even as my mind races.

If Oncle hears I was out in the streets, he'll know exactly what I was doing, who I was working with. He knows I wanted to investigate the murders. He'll know I didn't listen to him and did the one thing he forbade me to do.

And he'll send me away for disobeying him. Just like he promised.

Another surge of sick overcomes me. Henry holds up the chalice, once again tangles his fingers in my hair.

I groan and pull my knees to my chest. I hear the telltale clink of watered wine being set beside me. I don't have the strength to drink it.

Henry's voice is deadly quiet. "Your nighttime stroll is safe with me. But know that all of my advisors are outside this door right now, wondering why you're here, waiting for me to give them a good answer. So answer me, Jac. What were you doing in Paris?"

I touch the throbbing spot on my head, reminding myself that it's not a nightmare. And I'm certainly not dead, which might be preferable to enduring the chat I'm about to have.

I can't lie my way out of this. There's no reason for a gently bred lady to be armed and dressed as a man in the city at night.

But the secrets I carry don't belong to me. They also involve Oncle, Louise, all of the Societas Solis and their clandestine work. I can betray myself, but I can't betray them. I lift my chin, meeting the king's stern expression.

"My oncle is the royal family's spymaster, and he trained me as his apprentice. I help him with his work. It's"—I let the word stick for effect—"it *was* a secret."

The best lies always have a scrap of truth stitched into them. Everyone knows my oncle is the Valois spymaster—how much of a stretch would it be to imagine his ward would help him?

Henry's mouth is a suspicious slash. "So your oncle sent you armed and alone to the streets."

"Surely you've heard the rumors that you set something loose to terrorize Paris. Oncle ordered me to find the real killer to clear your name. He told me to do whatever it takes to make sure the royal marriage has the city's full support. The thing we want more than anything is peace between the Catholics and Huguenots."

Henry pulls away from me. "You didn't help me woo Margot because you wanted to. You helped because he told you to do it. You've been *spying* on me the entire time," he says, voice rough with betrayal. "My advisors were right. You were lying to me."

How can he accuse me of being entirely in the wrong when all I've done is help him and all he does is refuse to listen? Anger and shame and misery tangle so hopelessly, I can't begin to unsnarl them. "I was following orders, yes, but I also wanted to help you. I *told* you I wanted the marriage to work from the very beginning. Or did you forget I tutored you with my oncle's permission?" My voice cracks and my composure along with it. The messy feelings pour from me, a dam finally overspilling its banks. "I didn't ask you to propose, Henry! *You* made assumptions about my heart. *You* let yourself get distracted by love. You may have forgotten what you came to France to do, but I never once forgot why we were together."

He flinches. "And was seducing me part of your orders as well?" he demands, voice dripping with contempt.

The accusation sinks into me like a knife. I cringe away from it, hating how deeply it hurts.

He hates me.

And why shouldn't he, after all I've done to him?

I played with the passion of a king, and now we're both burned, a hundred places oozing with hurt.

I thought if I kept all my feelings locked away, I would be the only one wounded. Instead I've hurt everyone I love. Margot's reputation, Henry's heart, and after tonight, Oncle's trust. Why did I ever think this would work?

Everything I touch falls apart. I wanted too much, and now I'll be left with nothing.

Hot tears prick my eyes, too heavy to hide. I glance at the open window, the vast sky. I need more space to fall apart. I need to leave this stifling dark room.

I heave myself up. The room tilts at a sickening angle.

Henry catches me before I can fall. He squeezes my upper arms, scowling. "You're not supposed to be out of bed."

I jerk myself away and stagger to the window. Tear aside the drapes. Step one bare foot on the blue roof beyond.

With a growl, Henry scoops me up and steps outside. He

presses me against the dormer window, his face a mask of fury. There's still a bit of my blood on his cheek.

I pound both fists on his chest. "Let me go!"

He holds me tighter. "I'm not letting you go, Jac. You're too sick to stand. I swore an oath to protect you, and I'll protect you from yourself if I must. Hate me for it all you want." His dark stare drags like a current. A scrap of memory returns, a dream largely forgotten but not yet gone. Me in Henry's arms, the city hurtling past as he ran back to the Louvre. His voice, splintering, screaming for help.

A sharp, terrifying feeling wells in me. Something I can never take back once I say it out loud.

My nails dig into him as I grab fistfuls of his shirt. "I could *never* hate you!"

And then I kiss him.

My mouth is hungry, bruising. He crushes me to his chest, a hand traveling up my back, anchoring me to him more solidly than any pillar of this ancient palace. My skin burns where he touches, and there's an answering burn deep in the center of me. I press closer, giving him all of me until I'm weightless and untethered. The kiss softens like a retreating wave, a tender, secret thing left unearthed in the tide's wake.

His nose traces the curve of my cheek until we're brow to brow. "Jac." He draws a shuddering breath. "I'm sorry. I thought I had lost you and it was my fault. I pushed you. I'm the reason you're hurt."

The back of my head twinges. The crack of my skull on the cobblestones, Henry looming over me, frightening in his fury.

"Perhaps I deserved it. I did break your heart."

"A head for a heart isn't a fair trade. And you did save my life." His fingertips drag cool and light across the back of my bruised hand, turning it over. He presses a kiss where the hot pulse jumps. "I owe my entire life to you from this moment forward."

The tears burn again and this time I make no effort to hide them. "It was my duty to protect you."

"This is why you turned me down." He brushes the wetness from my cheek. "Your spy work. Your independence. It's the thing you want most of all. The one thing I couldn't give you because I didn't know."

I murmur a "yes" and sink into his chest. It's as honest as I can be. He doesn't need to know about the Societas Solis for this to be true.

He kisses me again, endlessly, each kiss the velvet brush of a feather. One to my stinging temple, one to the crease of each eye, his lips kissing away my salty tears. He kisses the curve of my shoulder where it throbs from the fall. We ease down to the rooftop tangled together. As if we break the rules to some secret game if he stops kissing me.

I thought our love a passion, a battle, a clashing of desire. Never did I expect it could be so achingly gentle. I wish we could stay like this forever, hidden from all the world's demands.

I settle deeper into his lap, my head tucked beneath his chin and nightgown rippling in the breeze. His fingers comb through my hair, each touch a shivering marvel; I lean back into him, my eyes drifting closed.

"I thought if I caught your oncle's enemies, then you'd reconsider my hand. I've been watching your apartments. That's why I followed you." His whisper tickles the delicate curve of my ear. "But you never needed my protection, did you?"

I smile, even as gooseflesh ripples across my skin. "I did tell you not to swear your silly vow."

He laughs lowly. "But you liked having me around, didn't you?"

His hands slide up my arms, teasing the pebbled skin to new heights. My insides go molten. I keep my eyes closed, letting the want spread like golden oil, giving over to it in a way I never have. "Yes. I wanted you since Chenonceau."

He nips my ear, sending a shock through me. "I wanted you the moment you demanded I saddle your horse."

A startled laugh slips from me. "You did?"

His hands slide to the ends of my hair, lifting the weight from the nape of my neck. I quiver as the air whispers across the too-hot skin. He smirks, heavy lidded and pleased, letting my hair fall. "I like being told what to do, Jac. Surely you've noticed."

I bite my lip, belly cinching tight. I *have* noticed and I love it. I move to take his mouth, but he cups my cheek, stopping me. "You must know that I love you. Knowing what you are doesn't change anything for me."

I close my eyes. An entire chorus swells in me, the glorious feeling drowning out all else. "I love you too." The words feel like throwing open a door to a room no one's ever been in. I step inside it, marveling at everything I've never seen, everything that's been here the entire time. For ages I was afraid anything I gave him I would never get back. I hoarded parts of myself like my secrets from the people I care about.

I didn't realize this meant I was closing off parts of myself from *me*.

Something unbearably tender passes across his face. He traces the line of my jaw reverently, even as his eyes darken with desire.

"My offer still stands. You would do me the honor of a lifetime if you would marry me, Jacqueline d'Argenson-Aunis."

A melancholy note slips beneath my joy, bringing me down. "I couldn't, Henry. You don't want me to be your queen."

His mouth pulls wryly, as if he doesn't believe me. He presses a kiss to my knuckles. "Then come to Navarre and be my queen of spies instead."

I laugh, the sound coming to a choking stop when he doesn't join in. Surely this is a dream, a cruel jest from my addled brain. I dig my nails into my thigh to be certain I'm awake.

"Your council wouldn't accept a woman among their midst," I hear myself tell him.

He squeezes my hand, the pressure another reminder that this is real. "I am their king. My council *will* accept it because anyone who doesn't will find himself in need of a new position." The cool command in his voice makes me bite my lip.

Queen of spies. A delicious tremor runs through me. It's more than I ever hoped for. More freedom than the Societas Solis could give me. Henry offers me a place and a purpose. A home for my heart. I'm afraid to imagine it too vividly, like the vision might dissolve to nothing if I press upon it.

I want to accept Henry's offer, but my wants are not the only things that matter.

I pull in a soft breath and go still, struck with a sudden terror of suffocating this brave, soft thing with my honesty. "And what of Margot?"

"She'll get her school. I don't break my promises."

My heartbeat crescendos painfully. "What of your kingdom? What about France? You came here for a bride, not a spymaster."

It's simple to make promises beneath the moonlight, where we can pretend there's nothing in the world but us and this beautiful feeling bigger than the whole sky.

But Henry is a king, and I'm no Valois princess. Millions of people matter more than our tender, tremulous love. I would break his heart again and again to stop France from bleeding.

He frames my face with both hands. Draws me in again. "I'm certain there's a way for all of us to get what we want. Let's speak to Margot. She must be a part of this."

I shiver, suddenly cold despite Henry's warmth. He has seen all my ugly mistakes and loves me anyway. But Margot doesn't know how I've betrayed her. How I've worked against her happiness from the very beginning. What if she hates me for it? What if in gaining Henry, I've lost the only other person who cares for me, jagged edges and all?

The dull pounding in the back of my skull redoubles. "I don't—"

He kisses me softly. "Do you trust me?"

My hand runs up the planes of his chest, feeling the muscle, the ribs beneath it, the rock-solid certainty of him. If confidence alone were enough to keep a fire burning, his rooms would never go cold.

"I'll try," I murmur against his cheek, surprising myself.

After all, what harm is there in trying? If Henry thinks there can be peace with no royal marriage, why not explore the possibility? If peace prevails, I don't see what issue the Societas Solis would have with my work. The Parisian murderer is dead, slain by my own hand.

My work with the Societas Solis is nearly over.

And there's a dazzling, new future waiting for me just on the horizon. One I never saw coming because I needed someone else to notice it first.

I draw an unsteady breath. Maybe there truly is a way for us three to get everything we want.

"'You'll try?'" Henry teases, nuzzling my neck. "For someone who's made a great fuss over kings always getting their way, I'm wounded you doubt me now."

I laugh and kiss him. "If anyone can make this dream come true, it's you."

The look he gives me is more brilliant than the rising sun.

CHAPTER TWENTY-FIVE

HEN MY ARRIVAL is announced to Margot's parlor, the entire room goes silent; the sea of shocked eyes should make me laugh, but instead they make my throat grow tight. Lady Charlotte's embroidery thumps to the floor. Cerberus, the most ancient of Margot's dogs, barks and skitters across the floor at the noise.

The princess scoops up her dog, not bothering to hide her surprise. "Jac! It's true then?"

I touch my head, still tender with its gash. "It's all true."

The ladies-in-waiting flock around me, tittering and gasping.

"Oh, the poultice has made your hair *so greasy* though!" Lady Charlotte cries, as if that's the very worst thing she can think of. "It smells a little strange too."

I hold a fist solemnly over my heart. "My suffering has been immense. Thank you for noticing."

Lady Hélène nods gravely. "You've suffered so bravely."

Margot's painted mouth pulls. She studies me curiously, searchingly. Only she has not stood to investigate my injury herself. "Is it true you recovered in the Navarrese king's apartments?"

The question makes my pulse stutter. "Yes. I went there

to speak to him. It was wrong of him to abandon you at your engagement ball. He needed to hear it."

Margot's mouth settles deeper into its frown. I run a finger along the silver cord of my gown, every stitch rough against my clammy skin. Each second that passes feels like a dropping stone. "How . . . inspired of you to worry about me," she finally says.

I bite the inside of my cheek. I wish with my entire heart that Margot had been alone, that there wasn't a rapt audience witnessing this fraught union. "I live to serve you, madame."

The princess's lovely face splits into a grin, all dimples and flashing white teeth. "Of course you do. How very *generous*. Tell us, is it true that when you were ill, Henry attended you himself?"

Lady Charlotte and Hélène gasp, gloved hands over their mouths. No one dares to speak in the wake of Margot's question, one that all but accuses me of being with the king. The stony seconds pile up, enough of them to build a fence. I rush over and take Margot's hand before she walls herself off from me completely. "Can I speak to you? Privately?"

I drag her toward her massive canopied bed, as far away from the other ladies as I can. She tears her hand from mine, eyes blazing. "What's really going on between you and Henry?"

My head injury prickles. My fingers twitch, wanting to scratch it, to feel the sweet pain of the scab splitting open. The shorter question at this point might be what *isn't* going on between me and Henry. "We need to speak to you."

"*We?*" Her head jerks back. "You two are a '*we*' now?" Her voice pitches up incredulously.

A metallic taste blooms in my mouth. I glance back at the other ladies, hoping they can't hear us. I wish there had been a better way to get Margot's attention, but Henry and I agreed the best way to minimize questions was to reach out to her as soon as possible. Oncle took me from the Navarrese apartments—his eyes burning with question—straight to our own suite and now I'm here. The sooner we explain all to Margot, the sooner we can take control of this scandal before it spirals out of our control.

"Jac." Margot steps closer. Her rosewater scent overwhelms me, sending my sensitive stomach turning. "What are you keeping from me?"

Her words are angry, but this close I see how her hands tremble. I want to take them in mine, press soothing circles into her skin, and reassure her that all shall be well, that Henry believes there's a way for all of us to get exactly what we want.

She just needs to trust me one last time. Even though she's right to doubt me. Even though I don't deserve it.

Before I can say anything, the door bursts open. Catherine de' Medici storms into the room, a gale through a badly latched window. She has a fistful of paper crushed in her hand. When her eyes land on Margot, they go wide.

"*You!*" She stabs an accusatory finger at her daughter. "*You dare make a mockery of our family name?*"

Margot flinches, a hand going to her throat. One of her dogs whines and slinks behind the sofa. "What are you talking about?"

The Queen Mother steps closer, black skirts billowing.

The other ladies-in-waiting shrink back as the dowager queen passes, her eyes as hard as flint. Margot squares her shoulders, refusing to be cowed even though I see how her hands tremble. Catherine's eyes flicker to me at Margot's side. "I was willing to overlook your foolish fumbles with girls, but this is unforgivable."

I cease to breathe. *She knows.* Margot's mother knows about her trysts with girls. After how careful Margot was, how carefully I tried to protect her.

Margot's nostrils flare, her face going pink. "If you were willing to overlook them, then why are you here now?"

There's a *crack.* Margot doubles over, her hand clutching her reddening cheek.

"Don't play me for a fool!" Catherine de' Medici shouts. "I know you've spent time with men. Does your lust know no bounds? This is why King Henry has refused to propose!"

There's a series of gasps around the room, a collective recognition of horror.

The princess of France was alone with a man.

To accuse an unwed woman of such a thing is very serious indeed. It calls her reputation into question, the reputation of her entire family. In the court, a woman's reputation matters more than her life. More than an illness, more than an illegitimate pregnancy that can be hidden in a country estate—nothing is more deadly to a girl than scandal.

"I've done no such thing!" Margot says, hand still to her face.

"Here." Catherine drops her ream of paper. The leaves slide every which way across the floor. The gossip pamphlets. Margot bends to get a closer look, but Catherine snatches her arm in an iron grip.

"You'll confess what you've done or so help me God. This marriage alliance won't fail because of your foolish, sluttish ways!"

Catherine de' Medici drags Margot from her own parlor. With a furious screech, the princess grabs the gilded doorframe on the way out, and at a cool nod from her mother, the guards pry her hands from the sill. Her pale, panicked face disappears around the corner.

My entire heart leaps after her. "Margot!"

The other ladies-in-waiting follow me like panicked horses. Margot screams and drags behind the guards, refusing to go pliantly, her lilac skirts going grey with dust. More guards come to help until she's all but carried.

Nobles and servants stop and stare at the princess's humiliation. A scream burns in my throat, demanding that they look away, for God's sake! Catherine de' Medici strides ahead of the chaos, head held high and face smooth. As though nothing at all is amiss. As though this is exactly what she wanted.

Catherine drags us to the royal family's chapel. The guards throw Margot into the confessional booth.

"Confess your sins!" Catherine shouts.

"I've done nothing wrong!" Margot fists her hands.

Catherine slaps the confessional. *"Confess!"*

"There is nothing to confess!" Margot roars back.

Catherine falls upon the confessional, screaming and kicking the holy structure. Lady Hélène screams when her foot goes

250 I ERIN COTTER

through the priest's door. Catherine de' Medici acts demon possessed, an unholy fervor behind each blow and shout. I take a step back and then another. Some of the other ladies-in-waiting cross themselves, tears streaming down their faces.

Finally, the priest appears in his flapping cassock, hands lifted, begging for peace. The sorcerer Cosimo Ruggeri slinks after him. Both men approach the raging queen carefully and whisper placating words. Soon nothing but Margot's sobs fill the stone sanctuary. Catherine de' Medici stares at the curled-up ball of her daughter with utter contempt.

"Won't confess now? Then you'll stay with me until you do."

The guards haul up Margot by her armpits. She's limp and pale, her face a mess of snot and shock. I snarl at the sight, my wound throbbing in time with my racing pulse. I want to tear Margot from her mother even though it won't fix anything. Margot reaches toward me, wide eyes begging me to help as I always have.

Then she's gone, carried away into the Queen Mother's private rooms.

A shuddering breath leaves me. *What in God's name just happened?*

Lady Charlotte reads a crumpled pamphlet beside me. Her bottom lip trembles as her eyes rove across the text.

"Give me that," I snap, snatching it from her.

The pamphlet speaks of the court's time in Château de Chenonceau, the scandalous news hitting the printing press days later.

Seen every night in the unfinished ballroom—

—fled the room and found embracing—
—alone in the gardens—

I stop reading.

The pamphlet flutters from my hand. There's a ringing in my ears like I'm standing right outside the church bells at mass.

Margot was never alone with a man at Château de Chenonceau.

But *I* was.

My insides clench like I'm about to be sick. Guilt runs straight through me, splits me open. Margot is being punished for things *I've* done.

I knew tutoring Henry was a risk, but it was a risk that felt worth taking. A risk Oncle even approved of. I never once worried anyone would mistake me for the princess. She shines like a diamond, and I'm a tarnished denier.

I clap a hand over my mouth, a low, aching moan escaping me. What consequences face Margot? What will King Charles do to punish her for this? Public humiliation before the court could be only the beginning. She could be sent away for this. She could be married to a man twice her age who lives at the very edge of France just to make her disappear. France's beloved princess has been brought to her knees by a scandal of my making.

"Even Jac is overcome and she's the least proper of us all!" Lady Charlotte falls upon me, weeping. I pat her back while also trying to shove her away, the shock and shame twisting up my insides until it all comes up and I'm heaving on the chapel floor.

CHAPTER TWENTY-SIX

WHEN I STORM into our apartments, Oncle is already waiting for me. He holds up a hand. "I heard what happened."

The images flash through my head. Margot screaming, her mother falling upon the confessional. The shocked, scared faces of the ladies-in-waiting. I release a slow breath and brace my back against the wall. "So you know it's my fault. It was me spotted with King Henry, not Margot."

Oncle's mouth twists. "I had suspected as much."

I swallow, sinking lower. I'd do anything to erase the disapproving look on his face. "I'm sorry. If I'd been more careful—"

"It wouldn't have made a difference."

"But someone thinks I'm Margot—"

"And now all of court finally has an explanation for why Henry hasn't proposed." Oncle goes to the sideboard and pours two glasses of claret. He hands me one of them. "Drink. You look dreadful."

The bitter liquid cuts through the fog in my head. Whether it's the alcohol or the confidence of Oncle's answer, I feel like I can think again. These rumors about Margot aren't true. We can set this right still.

"When will you tell Catherine de' Medici it was me and not Margot?"

Oncle's glass freezes at the edge of his lips.

"You . . . you plan to make this right by sharing the truth, do you not?" I say, heart crawling into my throat.

A muscle twinges in Oncle's jaw. "Catherine de' Medici doesn't know of your work with Henry, and it will stay that way."

I blink, not understanding. "But—Margot is being punished for something she didn't do!"

"Which is unfortunate. I wish things had happened differently."

A hot feeling begins in my gut and spreads. "This is wrong. I won't stand for it."

Oncle goes perfectly still. "You *will* stand for it, Niece! I told you the Societas Solis would ask you to do awful things."

I flinch away, his shout landing like a blow.

He leans across the table. His expression is terrible, more terrible than I've ever seen it. "If Catherine de' Medici knew you were with the king, you would never see Paris again. The damage it would do to your reputation would forbid you from court. Your disregard for discretion would prove you have no place in the Societas Solis, and you would have nothing!"

I gape at Oncle in the ringing silence. A cold, smothering quiet. I already have so little; how would it be possible to have less? To be even smaller and less significant than I already am?

"Not even you?" I mean the question to be imperious,

demanding, but instead it sounds small and weak. A child begging for a parent.

Oncle looks away, mouth pulled sideways. "I can't unmake the fabric of court or the rules of my order, Jac. You know that."

I only ask you to choose me first! The old wound splits open, more painful than ever. I grit my jaw to hold back the hurt. I'm already too emotional—I don't need to give him another reason to dismiss me.

"So that's it, then? You won't lift a finger to help Margot?" I say.

Oncle slaps a pile of papers. More of the odious, hideous pamphlets and their life-ruining lies. My fingers flex, yearning to toss them in the fire, as though burning the words alone would be enough to make them disappear from people's minds.

"You fail to understand how serious this is." He gives me a cool, sidelong glance. But there is nothing calm about him. The expression is a thin sheet of ice over a rushing river. "It doesn't matter if the rumors are true or not. The princess's honor has been called into question. There were whispers she had done something wrong when Henry didn't propose, and these pamphlets have finally explained why. They're believable, which is more important than being true. Even if you did confess it was you with King Henry, no one would listen because it's more delicious to believe the princess has done something scandalous. King Henry's advisors already demand that he call off the marriage negotiations. King Charles tries to appease them with talk of finding another bride. All our careful work could be gone in an instant. I will do whatever I must to see this marriage go through."

My teeth grit at the unfairness of it all. The pamphlet's horrible words swim before me, pages and pages of slander. Physical proof that I've ruined my friend to save myself.

Alone near the garden fountain . . .

The pamphlet's words snag me, pulling me back from the edge.

Henry and I were many places, but we were never near the fountain. I snatch up the paper and read it more closely. For every time Henry and I were spotted together, there is also an outright lie. My pulse starts to race.

Someone has framed the princess. But why?

My mind whirs through the possibilities. Who stands to gain something by ruining Margot's reputation? Who gains what by endangering the marriage alliance?

"Someone has printed lies. We can figure out who did it—"

"Jac—" Oncle begins warningly.

My fists clench, crumpling the paper. "Why do you keep fighting me? Someone is trying to sabotage the royal wedding! Does that not matter to you?"

Oncle tugs the pamphlet from my shaking hands. "Hundreds of Catholics oppose the wedding. It doesn't matter if we find the liar or not. The best way to clear Margot's name—the only way for her to escape this shadow—is for the king to propose. If King Henry doesn't care about Margot's indiscretions, then everyone else will stop caring about them as well." His eyes bore into me. "Use your influence. Get him to propose, Jac. Convince him to give the princess his ruby ring. You're so very close to finishing this mission. Do not fail now."

My lungs are a size too small. All of this is happening too fast, too soon. Henry and I never got a chance to talk to Margot. If she's forced to marry him because of rumors I've caused, she'll never forgive me. I can figure out who's behind this, but I need more time, more information.

"There's got to be another way out of this," I say quietly. Desperately.

Oncle slams his hand down. "There isn't, Jac! I must leave tonight on business for the Societas Solis. If I return and the king and princess are not engaged, then you will have failed your mission, and I will send you away from Paris. Do you understand me?"

I steel my jaw, blinking back the fierce stinging in my eyes, hating as always that *this* is how anger manifests in me. Is there any weapon more feared or scorned by men than a woman's tears? One of them falls, too quick for me to catch.

I bow my head dutifully so Oncle can't see the storm raging in me. Let him see my weakness and not my strength. "Yes, but I hate it."

A relieved sigh loosens his shoulders. He reaches across the table and takes my hand unexpectedly. I stare at his fingers, the callouses that have been there as long as I can remember. Which of these scars came from battles he'll never tell me about?

"I know this isn't easy, but I'm proud of the work you've done so far. I don't say that enough," he says.

His eyes are so earnest it nearly kills me. My gaze drops to his desk, and I squeeze his hands. The sour aching feeling pushes up into my throat. "Thank you, Oncle."

I use the moment to memorize the printmaker's shop name on the gossip pamphlets before he dismisses me.

The next morning, the cobblestones are cool beneath my slippers. Judging from the sun slanting against the Sorbonne college, it won't stay cool for much longer.

I send up a prayer to whoever might listen that I'll be gone by then. Oncle is already gone, and each morning, Jehan and Madame Dupont attend to their chores. I only have an hour before someone notices I've disappeared, and I need to make the most of it.

The Quartier Latin is a quite different beast from the rest of Paris. Students swarm through the twisting streets in their university robes, their loud Latin debates scattering the pigeons. More than once, Margot has begged me to give the other ladies-in-waiting and servants the slip so she can dash disguised to the college and sit in on their classes. Being here without her feels wrong, another betrayal added to all the other ways I've betrayed her this summer.

You can bring her here once you clear her name, I remind myself fiercely. After all, that is why I'm here.

All of the city's printmaker shops are located near the university. In response, the bouquinistes blossomed alongside the Seine's left bank. Already the booksellers are unraveling their green awnings, setting out the day's gossip pamphlets still wet with ink alongside the books. I once overheard King Charles grumble that the bouquinistes multiply like fleas on a dog's arse, and I can't say he's wrong. Each year more of the booksellers appear and bring strange, new ideas from all over Europe to Paris. More than once, the Valois family considered shutting down the bouquinistes to slow the trickle of Protestant beliefs into their city, and every time Oncle told them that forbidding something only makes it all the more appealing.

I tear my eyes away from the still-damp headlines and walk to the shop across the street. Inside I see the wooden printing presses with their great screws, the letters in careful rows around them, great sheets of paper littering the tables and floor like autumn leaves. The men working the presses glance up and freeze when I enter.

"Can I help you, mademoiselle?" a boy asks, his face bright with thinly veiled curiosity.

I smile, knowing what he must see. I wore my most understated dress and cloak, but they still see I'm a noblewoman. A noblewoman out alone, unchaperoned, in the printmaker's shop that prints the vilest things about noblewomen and their misdeeds. I slide a silver denier across the counter, preemptively paying for his silence.

"I was hoping to speak to someone about Princess Marguerite."

The boy's face shutters. "We haven't broken any law or done any wrong—"

I flutter my eyelashes. "Oh, you misunderstand! I'm not here to defend her honor. I'm here because I know a few things

I believe this shop would *very* much like to print." I'm tempting them with something far more valuable than a single silver coin—the promise of delicious, scandal-making, pamphlet-selling gossip.

Except the boy doesn't take the bait. He bites his lip, glancing over his shoulder. "I'm—I'm afraid you're in the wrong place. We're not interested in printing about the princess at this time."

I keep my smile pretty and floating even though my molars grind.

A printshop, not wanting gossip? It is as unnatural as a dog that doesn't want a bone, as King Charles refusing a glass of wine. There are hundreds of printshops in the city, and all of them are in constant competition with one another.

Someone must have paid this shop off not to work with anyone else.

But who? And why?

Could it be the same person who told them to print the rumors about Margot?

"I am so sorry, mademoiselle, but I'm afraid we are closed right now." The boy quickly turns a sign over from OPEN to CLOSED on the counter. He smiles at me, the expression not reaching his eyes.

"Good day!"

I reel back, the door slamming in my face.

Someone is paying this shop handsomely indeed if they're willing to offend a noblewoman. And the only person with deep enough pockets to do it must be noble themselves.

I heave my eyes toward the sky and groan.

It's good to know, but it's not enough. It won't clear Margot's name. I need to find out who has paid off the shop or this trip has been in vain. Already the bells are chiming the half hour. Time is slipping through my fingers like sand, and I don't know when I'll next be able to escape the Palais du Louvre.

I turn my back to the shop and face the riverbank. A bouquiniste catches my eye and gestures for me to come over.

"Oy, mademoiselle! You want news from the palace?" He fans his arms over his wares with a wink. "I have everything you would desire over here."

The last thing I want to see is more lies about Margot, but I slip him some coins and browse the papers anyway. I'm not the first noblewoman to creep across the Seine for sordid gossip, too ashamed to be caught reading the pamphlets in the palace itself. If this bookseller thinks I'm like all the other women, then he'll have one less reason to remember my face.

Someone bashes into me, knocking the pamphlet from my hands. The bouquiniste snatches it from the air with a scowl. "Hey, watch it, you!"

The man doffs his hat, already walking on. "Pardon, monsieur, mademoiselle."

The familiar voice freezes me.

My pulse roaring in my ears, I take the pamphlet back from the bookseller and hold it up. Glance over the top of it.

I watch the man approach the closed printshop. He knocks on the door, glancing over his shoulder at the bridge leading back to the right bank, back to the Louvre.

I step to the other side of the bookseller's awning, out of sight, heart hammering.

I don't need the boy from the printshop pointing me out to Oncle's footman, Jehan.

CHAPTER TWENTY-SEVEN

O NCLE IS BEHIND it.

Oncle is paying the printshop to print the scandalous, hate-filled words against Margot.

I cross the bridge, weeping. It feels like my chest has been torn open, the shock and treachery and sheer lowness of it all leaving me raw and bleeding.

Oncle has taken shears to Margot's reputation and cut so savagely, the tatters may never be whole again. It's an act of treason. It's a betrayal of me. Why would he do it?

What does he gain from casting doubt on the royal wedding—the thing he's wanted for weeks? What does he possibly get from sabotaging my work and that of the Societas Solis? It was his idea that I helped with the royal marriage in the first place.

Why would he turn on us now?

I sift through all our conversations searching for the thing that would make any of this make sense.

Convince Henry to give the princess his ruby ring.

It's what he urged me to do after he refused to help Margot. Which means it's the thing he wants me to do next. Oncle says Henry's proposal is the only thing that can save Margot's reputation. By threatening Margot, he hopes to get Henry to finally propose. Oncle has seen how honorable Henry is. How he's the kind of man to marry a girl to get her out of trouble.

I shiver, remembering the ring in Henry's hand, how it winked like a drop of blood when he held it out to me.

Why would Oncle know what it looked like?

Perhaps Henry showed it to King Charles's privy council to be sure it would please Margot. But then why would he turn around and give it to me? Henry would never give me Margot's scraps. He knows it would insult both her and me. For all the time he has courted us, me privately and her publicly, he has never once made either of us feel in competition with the other.

Henry had no reason to show the ruby ring to anyone other than me. Which means—

I stop and slow. I brace myself against the palace wall, feeling the ghastly truth slip through my ribs like a dagger.

I'm the reason Oncle did this.

Somehow, Oncle knows Henry proposed to me and not Margot.

My stomach lurches. All my worst fears have come true. Oncle has ruined Margot's name to take Henry from me. To force the royal marriage to happen as quickly as possible. How else would he know about the ruby ring?

And if I stand in the way of the royal engagement again, I'll be sent away like a lamed horse who has outlived her usefulness.

I dash away the last tears on my face. Something iron and hot coalesces inside me.

Oncle thinks I'm a silly, lovestruck girl, foolish enough to endanger France and Navarre with a feeble crush. He doesn't think I take my work seriously; he doesn't know that forsaking peace is the last thing I would ever do.

He doesn't know because he didn't ask.

He *never* asks me anything.

And even if he did, he still wouldn't trust me to do the right thing.

I want to scream. I want to rend the stones from the palace's foundation, and I hate that I can do nothing except bottle my rage up inside me.

Oncle never gives me any choice. He gives me just enough slack on my lead for the illusion of freedom and yanks me back when I test the limits of where he'll let me roam. Even Louise, someone who barely knows me, trusts me more than the man who raised me.

Bitterness floods my mouth. To Oncle, everyone around him, nieces and princesses alike, are pieces to be moved on a vast game board. No one except for him knows the rules. No one else can succeed without knowing his rules.

I will clear Margot's name of my mistake. I will make sure France and Navarre are at peace before I dream of a future with Henry.

But to do this, I need to remain on Oncle's game board awhile longer. I must pretend to play his game while I play my own.

"Mademoiselle, is all well?"

I jerk up at the voice. A Valois guard eyes my tears like they are poisonous spiders set loose to murder his king. Two more guards lurk behind him, clutching their pikes awkwardly.

I duck my head and dash the wetness from my eyes. "'Tis nothing, monsieur. Would you escort me to the stables?"

A figure already paces restlessly at the stable's edge, two horses' reins in hand. It's bustling midday all around me, but it feels like twilight in my heart, the day already edging into something darker and cold.

Henry jerks up at my approach. Fatigue has stamped purple half-moons beneath his eyes.

"I saddled Anémone for you. I hope you forgive the liberty."

My throat grows tight. "You're forgiven."

I catch my horse's face in my arms, pressing her velvet nose to my heart. For the first time ever, it doesn't make me feel better. My feelings swoop low like vultures, guilt and shame and horror all plucking at my chest.

"It's our fault Margot's locked up."

"I know." Despite his exhaustion, Henry's voice is low and urgent, a warrior on the verge of victory. "But not everything the pamphlets printed was true. We must find out—"

I press a finger to my lips and nod toward our horses, the gardens beyond. The stable is milling with servants. I've no doubt they're as desperate for gossip as the rest of the Louvre. "Let's talk out there."

Henry barely waits for us to pass the garden's edge. "We could go to the printshop. We'll bribe them to tell us—"

"I already went there." There's a spasm in my chest. "I know who did it."

"Who?" he demands, eyes flashing.

I look straight ahead, unable to bear his reaction. "My oncle."

His gasp pulls like a serrated edge, his shock and betrayal hurting me as much as my own. "But why?"

My hands tighten on the reins, turning my fingers purple. "It's because he knows about us. He knows the only way to clear Margot's name is for you to propose to her. And he knows I'll insist that you do it to save her."

Henry laughs disbelievingly. "But I don't want to marry Margot. She doesn't want to marry me either."

My eyes bore into his. I need him to stay with me. "I know. But maybe you two must marry for now. We can get it annulled later on."

Henry's mouth pulls into a frown. "A marriage annulment? From the Catholic church? Isn't this how England ended up with its own religion?"

I bite the inside of my cheek and taste blood. I understand Henry's skepticism. The English king's efforts to divorce his wife led to years of bloody religious war. Just like the one France is in now. "It's a gamble, but—"

"You know what I think, Jac?" Henry's tone is pleasant, but his expression has gone cold. "I think you're getting exactly what you want. The royal marriage your oncle asked for, the lover and work you wanted. You're asking Margot and me to risk a lot, but I don't see what you're willing to risk." His voice goes lower, softer. "Why are you so afraid?"

My heart closes up like a fist. I want to hit things. I want to make someone else hurt as much as I'm hurting, but I know I can't.

Not yet.

Because Henry's right. I'm afraid of what the Societas Solis is hiding. Of what it might mean for us.

I kept something from Oncle, but there's also something he's keeping from me.

The murders, the dead boys, the strange Book of Hours. I can't help but feel it's connected to the royal marriage. Why else would Oncle betray me and command, on pain of exile, to make sure Henry and Margot are engaged when he returns from his errand? Why else would Louise be so willing to accept the help of a mere acolyte to hunt a murderer? Why is Oncle now being ordered away from the capital city by the Societas Solis when France feels like it's teetering on a cliff?

There's something I'm missing. Something everyone is keeping from me.

I'm going to sniff out Oncle's secret just as he found mine.

But Henry can't learn about the Societas Solis. It would put him in danger, make him a threat to their secret plans. He needs to stay in the dark for his own good, even though lying to him feels like tearing off my own fingernails.

I swing to face him, grabbing his hand even though anyone can see us out here.

"I haven't asked you for anything yet, Henry. But I'm asking you for this. Please."

His mouth pulls, a maelstrom of feelings flitting across his face. His fingers move over mine. He lingers on the third finger of my left hand, caressing the empty space slowly. I feel it all the way through my body.

"I will do anything you ask of me, Jac. Even this."

I lift his hand and kiss it. Relief runs across me like cool water. "I swear, I'll make this right for all of us."

"There is just one thing I ask of you in return." He smiles unexpectedly.

I don't like the look of that smile. "Anything."

He leans closer, his whisper tickling the soft skin of my ear.

"You've got to be the one to ask Margot for me."

I laugh, even though the thought of talking to Margot makes me want to hurl myself into the Seine. "Of course I will. She wouldn't want it any other way."

CHAPTER TWENTY-EIGHT

WELL, THIS IS a first, even for me." Margot stares at the ring Henry has just slipped on her finger with an unreadable expression. "Are you *both* proposing? Because I think if we asked the bishop to cry the banns for us it might actually kill him, which wouldn't be the worst because he says *horrible* things about women—"

I push the words out from my clenched throat. "I'm not. But Henry is. Or he will, later, after I explain things."

"After you explain *what* things?" she demands brusquely.

Her curtness makes everything cinch up even tighter in me. A single wrong word, and it feels like my skin might split from shame alone.

When Henry told Catherine de' Medici he wanted a word with her daughter, *alone*, she was all too happy to oblige him. As long as someone was there to chaperone, of course. Someone Henry insisted must be me.

Henry steps closer, sensing my nerves. "It'll be all right. Tell her what you told me."

Then there's his hand on my elbow. Two fingers, barely a touch at all. But I feel it all the way down my body, through my feet, into the ground. It feels like a promise. *If you fall, I'll catch you.*

I don't deserve him. If this works out, I'll spend my entire life trying to be half as good and honest as he is.

But Margot *does* deserve the truth. Or as much of the truth as I can give her.

"Jac, you're shaking. Out with it now." Margot's patience thins.

The words tumble out in a hot rush. "It's my fault you were humiliated."

Henry takes my hand and steps just behind me. "No, it's *our* fault."

Margot's eyes dart to our braided fingers. She gasps, brows flying high.

"I knew it!" She stabs a single triumphant finger into the air. "I always suspected and did a fine job keeping it quiet, if I do say so myself."

"Ah yes, the famous Valois restraint. They will weave tapestries about your patience, Margot," Henry says dryly, thumb brushing the back of my hand.

The princess squeals and clasps her hands together like someone has given her an entire basket of puppies. "You two are adorable and disgusting! Look how he growls behind you like a loyal wolf! Look at your blush!"

My body burns from the inside out. I glance longingly at the window in her parlor, wondering if perhaps it's not too late for me to escape this. What Henry and I have feels too tender and too new to withstand Margot's sharp wit.

Her reaction makes me feel ambushed, too helpless and surprised to react. I expected Margot's brow scrunched in rage, a snarl. I expected anything except her delight, a knowing curve to her lips.

"Of course I knew. You've never fallen in love before. It was painfully obvious something new was going on. Give me some credit, please. I can be self-absorbed, but that doesn't mean I'm shortsighted."

Henry's eye roll could move mountains. "Your humility, too, Margot, must go in the tapestry. I shall commission it as a wedding present to you."

Her smile turns pointed. "How thoughtful, dear Husband. I shall have the students practice their letters on it in my school."

I slide between them. I need to speak the truth before I lose my courage. "I'm one of my oncle's spies, Margot. He told me to make sure you married the king and swore me to secrecy. I was helping Henry court you."

She snorts and looks pointedly to where Henry and I touch. "Ah yes, and look how well that's gone! You two, together, and me forced to marry Henry to avoid my mother locking me away forever. Everyone wins!"

Her biting laughter fills all my wounds with salt. "Be serious."

Her mirth goes cold, suddenly the rush of a river beneath the black ice. "I'm serious, Jac. None of this would've happened if you'd been honest from the start, but you weren't, so here we all are."

I wince, her words stinging like a slap.

She leans closer until we're brow to brow. Her diamond earrings brush my cheek. "Tell me: If you hadn't fallen for Henry, if your oncle hadn't figured out you were endangering his plan and slandered me, would you have ever been honest with me? Or would you have been your oncle's good little apprentice and seen me married and sent to Navarre and said nothing?"

I want to tell her no. That I didn't have a plan, and I never thought that far ahead. But that would be a lie.

I expected to keep this from Margot. Just like I kept the assassin's attempt on her life from her. Just as I've kept Oncle's work and the Societas Solis secret. Lying is as easy as breathing for me. Runs in the family, you could say.

A realization shudders through me that hurts more than anything else.

I never trusted her at all. Not the way she trusted me. I'm no better than Oncle when it comes to trusting the people close to me.

Margot's mouth pulls sadly. Her free hand goes to a spot on her wrist, a vivid bruise barely covered by her sleeves. A mark from her mother's wrath. "That's what I thought."

The sight fills me with soul-crushing guilt. I think of all the times we've been alone, all the chances I had to be honest with her and chose not to. My voice is a wretched, tremulous whisper. "I'm so sorry. I didn't want to hide from you." *But I did anyway* hangs there unsaid, heavy as a rotten fruit.

She shakes her head. "I don't accept your apology, Jac."

My chest cracks wide open. All my fears and doubts rush into the space.

You lost her—

She has every right—

You *deserve this.*

"Margot—"

She holds up a hand, stopping me. "You misunderstand. What you did was wrong, but I can't be angry about it. You act like you were born already owing the world a debt, and I didn't make it easier for you. I owe you an apology myself. I'm sorry I didn't make you feel like you could be honest with me. I'm sorry you ever had to call my love into question."

My throat closes around a mortifying sound that might be a sob. This is love, isn't it? The pearled tears gleaming in Margot's lashes, the warmth of Henry's hand on the small of my back. The word shines with iridescence.

Perhaps a part of my heart was born broken. It let anything in, even when I tried to shut everything out. I grew up feeling like I must earn my seat at every table, a corner of my oncle's heart. I poured myself into the shape of whatever anyone wanted me to be.

I take in a long, shuddering breath and turn to Margot. Her understanding disarms me, scatters all my carefully rehearsed words. My surprise must show, because she takes my hand and presses soothing circles into my wrist. "I listened when you spoke. There are pressures in your life I can't understand. I'm trying to do better."

"So you're not angry?" I whisper, hardly daring to believe it.

She takes in a big breath and releases it all in a huff. "No. I'm absolutely furious with myself. I thought the worst of you when I heard you were in Henry's apartments. I imagined you thought me silly and foolish and not worth your time." Her eyes fill with tears. "I thought you were moving on to better things."

I rear back, shocked. If Margot were the brightest star in the sky, she would be the sun itself. "Better things? Never!"

She raises one brow, mouth curving. "I've been angry for all the wrong reasons."

Henry bows his head and nods solemnly. It might be the first and only time he's ever agreed with Margot. The princess smacks his arm. "I'm not talking to *you*, Henry of Navarre! You deserve all my anger and more, I daresay."

He laughs mirthlessly, dragging a hand through his hair. "And what have I done to offend you this time?"

And then—as familiar as my own reflection—there's Margot's mischievous smirk. "Why, you've made my closest friend in the entire world fall in love with you. Now I must share her with you, and that is quite unforgivable."

His mouth lifts, his smile a glimmer of gold.

The servants' door to Margot's chamber eases open.

Henry and I are on our feet at once, hands to blades.

Jehan stands in the doorway, mouth a grim slash. "Mademoiselle, I bear urgent news from Louise."

The sentence is a slide of sleet. The world narrows to the letter in his hand, its dripping wax seal.

Jehan doesn't know I'm working with Louise, which means

two things: First, whatever she sends to me is so important, she doesn't care if Oncle finds out.

And second, as soon as Oncle returns from his Societas Solis errand, he'll know I've gone behind his back to help Louise.

He'll send me away for disobeying him, just like he's always threatened.

"What happened?" I ask, dread and anxiety sharpening my voice.

He bows, a muscle pulsing in his jaw. As if he's already guessed the extent of my double-crossing. "Another man was found dead in the city."

When no one moves, Margot goes to take the letter herself. I leap up, snatching it before she touches it.

"Jac!" she says crossly, but her frown fades when she sees how I quiver.

"It's mine," I say. Except the defense has no teeth at all. I know there's no possible way for me to avoid sharing whatever the note says with Margot and Henry.

Jehan bows and leaves. I stare at his retreating shape, my nails digging divots into the paper. Did he give this to me in front of them on purpose? Did Oncle leave him a note to make certain to destroy every happiness that might happen to me in his absence? Perhaps Jehan's gone to saddle a horse now and ride to meet Oncle, to tell him how I've been a naughty girl, how I've unraveled his schemes. He's Oncle's man through and through and I can't blame him for it, but I'm angry about it.

Henry places both hands on my shoulders. "It's all right, love. We can read it together."

I squeeze my eyes shut, wishing I could make him and Margot both disappear. Doing this together is the last thing I want. But if they can trust me, I've got to trust them. After all, it's not like I have a choice anymore. I give the paper to Margot with numb fingers.

Her lovely brow furrows at the words. "A priest was found with his heart torn out."

A terrible dread grabs my ankle and pulls me under. "Then the killer still stalks the streets of Paris," I say.

The killer *I* killed.

"But . . . that's not possible. I saw the body," Henry says.

It's hard to forget the wet squelch of my knife sinking into his neck. How warm the blood was against my boots. I dealt Henry's attacker a mortal blow, and there have been no attacks since.

"Maybe there was more than one person. A larger operation than I thought," I say. "Just because we fought one person, it doesn't mean they were working alone."

"There's a murderer?" Margot is aghast. "Cutting out *hearts*?"

Her face is a full moon, wide with shock and fear. She doesn't know what I'm capable of or what I've done, and now she's being dragged into this. For Margot, I hide my fear behind a lift of my chin. "Yes. Someone is killing boys in Paris and taking their hearts. It's part of my spy work. The last mission I need to finish."

The one I thought I'd already finished.

The iron tang of blood is in my nose again. My head throbs where it struck the cobblestones. There's something we're missing. Something huge and obvious just out of sight.

I must find the answers before Oncle returns. Before he even thinks of sending me away from Margot and Henry.

But Henry and Margot also can't know about the Societas Solis. Louise outranks Oncle, and I'm afraid of what might happen to him if I reveal the order to the royals. I'm angry and upset with Oncle, but I'm not here to tear out his life by the roots.

"Don't even think about it," Margot says sharply.

I startle back to the moment. "Think of what?"

"Doing this alone."

My mouth pulls wryly. She knows me too well. "It's dangerous. If something happened to one of you it would cause even more problems. This work is for someone who has nothing to lose."

Henry pulls me to his chest. "And you're everything to me."

"To us," Margot corrects. Her hand slides down mine to circle my wrist.

Bracketed between them, the deeply inconvenient truth becomes clear.

I might stand a chance against whatever haunts Paris, but I don't stand a chance against Henry and Margot.

"You can't cut us out, Jac." Margot grins triumphantly. "It's too late."

A shudder goes through me. "I know," I whisper. "That's what I'm afraid of."

CHAPTER TWENTY-NINE

MARGOT, IN A plain gown with her dark hair hidden by a fair wig, almost looks like a commoner, but not quite. While we have toned down her brilliance, nothing can diminish the grace in her movements and the subtle command in her voice. It is obvious she's used to getting answers to her questions.

"You heard nothing? Truly?" she demands of the shopkeeper beside the church, an edge to her words. "Not even the barking of your dogs?"

The old woman clutches her basket closer. "That's what I said, isn't it? My story isn't likely to change in these past few minutes!"

I take Margot's arm and guide her away, whispering, "Subtlety's the word here. People don't like it when you don't believe their truth."

"I *was* subtle!" She stamps a fine-slippered foot. "She said she heard nothing and then brought the dogs up the second time and not the third!"

I twist the end of my braid anxiously. I spent years learning from Oncle how to best get people to talk when they don't want to. How could I expect Margot to take to the work after an hour?

You didn't have a choice, I think despairingly. *She's the one who insisted on coming with you.* I half wish she were still under her mother's house arrest, but as soon as she emerged from the parlor on Henry's arm, his ring on her finger, Catherine de' Medici said she could do whatever she wanted.

"I need to get inside to ask questions." The church looms beside us, a somber, gothic building with people milling around out front. Many of them talk in hushed whispers; many more of them don angry, mistrustful expressions. I'm glad Henry's royal duties forbade him from accompanying us so he could not hear their words. This latest murder—of a Catholic priest, nonetheless—has done nothing to endear the Protestant king to the Parisians.

"This is what that priest gets for preaching religious tolerance—"

"—a dog would be more welcome at my table than a Huguenot!"

"The likes of them don't belong here—"

All at once, Margot bursts into tears.

Great shuddering sobs tear through her body. She sinks to her knees on the church's steps, hands clasped before her breast. In her blue cloak and grey gown, she looks almost as saintly as the ugly Bible maidens frescoed in her grand royal apartments.

I gape in surprise, but several men step closer, doffing their caps, hands outstretched. Drawn toward a beautiful woman's tears like moths to a lantern.

"Sister, what ails you?"

"Oh, I *must* pray on this dreadful day! Please, don't lock up the church doors for those of us grieving the murder of Father—" She falters ever so slightly.

"Father François," I whisper.

"Our dear wonderful Father François!" She ends in a fresh wave of wailing.

The men mutter and decide perhaps it's best to let the church serve its purpose during this troubled time. Margot flashes a wink when no one is looking and I can't lie, I'm impressed. Subtlety may not be her strength, but bending others to her will certainly is.

With more heaving sobs, Margot draws a crowd on her way to the confessional. No one notices when I split away and wander around the vast stone sanctuary, searching for anyone who looks like they might have information.

A boy kneeling before a pietà statue in a quiet chapel catches my eye

I cross myself and kneel beside him. "I'm sorry for your loss." And I mean it. The little I've learned about the late priest is that he was one of the people who fervently believed in religious tolerance. He was exactly the sort of person Paris needs, and I can't help but wonder if he was targeted for it.

The boy lifts his tearstained face. He can't be more than twelve. "Father François was the only reason I joined this place. He was a foundling like me. He actually *cared* about the downtrodden."

A foundling. I tuck this away for later. It's not uncommon for orphaned children to be called into the church's service, but it's rare for a foundling to rise as high as François did without outside help.

"He sounds like a great man, all the greater for his humble beginnings. Tell me, what orphanage did he hail from? I shall make an offering there in his and your honor."

Perhaps there is a connection. A record we can go through.

The boy snivels and wipes his nose. "L'Hôpital des Enfants-Rouges."

I thank the boy and dip my head, lest he see my disappointment. He has just named the largest orphanage in Paris. Between years of civil war and the diseases that cut through the filthy crowded city like a scythe, thousands of children have called the Enfants-Rouges home. Another dead body, another dead end.

"Did you learn what you needed to learn?" Margot's curious eyes are raven bright when we leave. Like she's been having fun, of all things.

I shake my head. "All I learned was that Father François hailed from l'Hôpital des Enfants-Rouges."

Her face brightens. "I've been there!"

"You have?" I say, surprised.

"Yes. Mother sends me there twice a year. I'm named after my great-aunt who founded it, so she says I have to go. She insists I have a gift with children that my brothers lack." She rolls her eyes. We both know Margot's brothers would never be allowed to set foot in an orphanage because none of them has ever made a child smile.

"Can you get me in?"

Margot laughs, looping her arm through mine as we cross the bridge from the Île de la Cité. The Louvre hovers ahead like an ominous moon rising above the roofs and smoking chimneys. "Of course I can get us in."

My heart leaps. "How soon?"

"Today. No one is going to stop the princess of France from visiting orphans." She grins, the expression all teeth. "Honestly, Jac, how did you ever do all this work without me?"

I shake my head, dazzled and a little frightened at how easily the world throws open its doors for Margot. "You are terrifying."

"I know," she says smugly. She stops when we reach the right bank and catches my hand. "Just—follow my lead when we get inside the orphanage, all right? They might make assumptions about you, and it's best to let it happen."

I lean away from her, brow furrowing. "What kind of assumptions?"

Her dark eyes dance. "Ones you won't like."

CHAPTER THIRTY

O
H, MADAME! WHAT an honor, what an absolute gift it is to welcome you." The abbess of l'Hôpital des Enfants-Rouges shakes Margot's hand so vigorously for so long, I wonder if she'll need to call for a cold compress when we return to the Louvre.

Margot smiles demurely and lowers her eyelashes. "The honor is all mine, Abbess. As soon as King Henry proposed, I knew I needed to make a gift to God for my good news."

The abbess's eyes fill with tears as footmen carry in the trunks of gifts Margot brought. "Bless you, child! Truly, your great-aunt's generosity lives on in you!"

I stand behind the princess's splendid cloak, heroically resisting the urge to roll my eyes. The orphanage is located in le Marais, its great stone shoulders brushing against the Knights Templar's massive fortress. The austerity of the fortress seems to have rubbed off on the orphanage, with its grey façade and iron fences. The solemn lines of children in their red cloaks are jarring against so much drabness.

Margot's voice gets thick. "May God rest my dear great-aunt's soul. I feel lucky to share her love of children." She sighs prettily and makes the sign of the cross.

I turn a laugh into a cough. I've watched Margot grimace in the royal nursery enough to know her love for children is as sincere as her belief that not every meal requires a dessert course.

The abbess turns to me. "And who is this?"

I make myself as small and pathetic as possible. It's not hard in the shabby, unfashionable beige dress I'm wearing.

"This is one of my ladies-in-waiting," Margot begins carefully. "I brought her along with me today because . . . well, because I thought you might be the only person who can help her."

The abbess clucks her tongue and leans closer, voice dropping. "Do you fear she may be in a delicate condition?"

I don't understand for a moment.

And then heat explodes across my cheeks when I do.

I gasp, horrified. Suddenly the abbess is taking my hands, pulling me against her bosom. "Oh! Oh no, dear girl, please do not feel humiliated. This is a safe place."

I grimace. This is Margot's plan? Letting the abbess assume I'm pregnant and looking to see where I could discreetly give up my child?

"Tell me, is the child's father fond of you or not?" the abbess asks gently.

I chance a glance at Margot, unsure what to say. She draws a finger across her throat behind the abbess.

"No, he very much is not, and I—I fear for our safety."

The abbess draws me into a crushing embrace. "Of course you do, dear girl! And the princess has brought you to just the right place. Perhaps I can show you where your child would live?"

I glance at the austere courtyard beyond the windows of her office. Even the summer garden looks grey and shriveled.

"I think," Margot says, placing a hand on my shoulder and gently easing me from the matron's clutches, "her condition is too delicate, perhaps, to see the children given that they are so very . . ." She trails off, trying and failing to come up with a word other than "sad." She gives up and smiles. "I think you understand what I'm saying."

I wail and bury my face in a handkerchief, a woman overcome with despair. Out of all of Margot's absurd schemes, this one might top the list. Laughter shakes my sides, barely held in. Margot shushes me gently and pulls me closer. "There's no need to cry. I'll look at where your child would stay for you."

"Of course, of course!" the abbess cries. "Come this way, madame. The children would be honored to see you. They have heard so many stories of your greatness and—"

The abbess's voice cuts off as the office door shuts behind them. They soon appear in the grim courtyard beyond.

I stop pretending to cry and go for the records stacked on the shelves.

The records are massive tomes with badly pasted bindings. Each one is thick with handwritten notes, recording a child's admission date to l'Hôpital des Enfants-Rouges and their release date from the orphanage, including where they went afterward.

I comb through the shelves until I find the books for the years when the priest could've been born.

When I crack the first one open, my heart falls.

There are *hundreds* of entries.

I search the page for names with the symbol of a Christian heart beside it—the indication that a child has gone into the church's service—but there are so many names and so many symbols, I keep losing my place. Five minutes pass, then ten. Then I hear Margot's tinkling laugh, drawing closer. She and the abbess are striding back across the courtyard, and I'm nowhere close to finding what I'm looking for.

I eye the too-full shelves.

Surely no one would notice a few missing ledgers, would they?

I tug frantically on the front of my stays—ribbons tear—and the books drop beneath my bodice.

Right as the door opens.

Margot brushes invisible dust off her satin skirts, smiling benevolently at me. "Well, I think this place will suit any child of yours quite nicely. Shall we leave?"

One of her eyebrows rises, asking a silent question. *Are you done?*

I clasp both hands under the books in my bodice and nod. It won't do for them to fall out from under my skirts.

Margot's eyes fly open. She turns a snort of laughter into a cough.

"God keep your soul, Daughter!" The abbess steps forward, hand outstretched toward the slight bulge at the front of my gown. "May I say a prayer for your child?"

My glare for Margot is sharp enough to draw blood.

• • •

"Your *face*, Jac. It was incredible. I should get it painted so I never forget." Margot is still gloating of her great success back in the Palais du Louvre gardens.

"Always happy to amuse you," I say grumpily. "You could've warned me l'Hôpital des Enfants-Rouges is where ladies of court go to give up their illegitimate children."

"Perhaps, but I didn't think you'd play along if you knew."

Perhaps not, but I'm not giving Margot the satisfaction of knowing she's right.

The records are scattered on the blanket around us. Even with two people going through them, the progress is slow. There must be at least a hundred children named François taken into l'Hôpital des Enfants-Rouges each year. Margot insists we'll know what we're looking for when we find it, but I'm not so certain.

The sun is perched on the westernmost wall of the Louvre. It's been nearly an entire day with nothing to show for it. Long enough for Jehan to find Oncle. He could be coming back here right now, his cloak streaming over the flanks of his galloping horse. Rushing back to stop me.

"I'm good at this work, aren't I?" Margot nudges my shoulder. "Admit it."

"There's no denying that." Her privilege made our search go faster in a way I never thought possible, but it still doesn't feel fast enough. "We did better together than I could've done alone."

She pokes me again.

"Margot, I'm trying to read," I grumble.

Her half-lidded eyes snag mine. Pull me in.

"Do you ever wish we had done more together?"

A rush of embarrassment goes through me, the urge to leap past this with a jest or a dismissive comment near overwhelming. With a look like that, she must be talking about our romantic past, and the memory of all those nights tangled together turns my insides to ribbons. "Is now really the time to talk about this?"

Her stare is like a peat bog, and I'm drowning in it. "I'd like to, if you want to."

She's giving me a choice. I bite my lip, teetering on the edge. "Margot . . . I saw you with another girl the very next day after you'd been with me. And you told me that's how you are, and I thought I could handle it. But I suppose—I suppose I realized I needed to go before you found someone else, because I couldn't bear it. My heart isn't big enough to love more than one person like that. It's not like yours."

Margot closes her eyes. Her lashes are sooty smudges on her cheekbones. Even like this, rumpled and tired, she's the most beautiful girl I've ever seen. "My royal blood feels like chains tying me to a legacy I never asked for. The thought of willingly tying myself to one other person forever . . . I couldn't." She tucks a length of hair behind my ear, lingering on the soft spot where my jaw meets my throat. "But you deserved to hear that from me instead of guessing it for yourself. I'm sorry I hurt you, Jac. And I'm even sorrier I made you feel like you couldn't tell me why you had to end things."

"Yes, but I should've told you about Henry. Then maybe you wouldn't have been hurt too." The words hurry from me, raw and honest. Like if I don't say them now, I'll never say them.

"Can I ask why you hid your feelings for Henry from me?" Margot says. At my alarmed look, she raises a hand. "I'm not asking out of judgment! I'd just like to understand."

"Aside from the peace treaty?" I roll a blade of grass between my fingers, not looking at her. "I suppose . . . I suppose I didn't think it mattered how I felt. You *hated* him, and when I have feelings for men and not women, you seem to . . . dislike it. I worried you'd hate me for caring for him."

Margot squeezes her eyes shut. "I could never, ever hate you, Jac. You know that, don't you?"

"Fine, then. I worried you'd give me such a difficult time it wouldn't be worth sharing my feelings."

She ducks her head, chin wobbling. "I lost your trust when I broke your heart."

I laugh awkwardly, unable to deny it, hating how she's pinned me so neatly. "Well. I don't think you meant to—"

She seizes my hands suddenly. "Do not make this small! I've hated not being close to you this summer. Knowing that it's my fault hurts all the more." Her lashes gleam wetly. "Promise we'll be honest with each other even when it's hard."

I stroke the back of her hands, the bump of her engagement ring, and crush her to me. "Of course we will."

She squeezes me back, her familiar rose scent falling over me in soft waves. I'm only realizing now how much I've gotten wrong. I thought Oncle was my whole family because I owed him so very much, but there was Margot, too. Who chose to keep me by her side, as close as any sister.

Margot pulls away with a wet sniff. "My God, you're thinking sisterly thoughts about me, aren't you?" she groans, and pushes me away. "No, don't insult me by denying it! We'll be stuck together until we're dead. There's still plenty of time for me to win you away from Henry."

A shadow covers us, followed by a deep voice. "To win what away from me?"

Henry. The setting sun knifes into my eyes, making him blurry with gold, his expression hidden in shadow.

Margot bats her eyes at him. "Nothing, dear Husband. Here, Jac and I found out where Father François is from."

She flips a book around and points to a name on it.

My mouth falls open. "How long ago did you find that?"

She laughs smugly. "I knew you'd leave as soon as I showed you, and I wanted you to stay. See those two Cs written there? That means the dead priest had two noble parents."

I slowly sit up from the blanket, feeling all the blood rush back to my body.

It could be nothing. Nobles secretly hide their illegitimate children away in the orphanage all the time.

But I have a feeling it's not.

Henry sits cross-legged on the edge of our blanket. He's dressed for dinner, in snow-white hose and a dark blue doublet. A sapphire earring hangs from his right ear.

"I could ask my men to investigate the other dead boys.

Discreetly, of course, to see if there are other connections to the orphanage or the priest," he says.

"Can you ask them to do it now?" I ask.

He shakes his head, chagrined. "No. I was sent to summon my fiancée. Margot's mother is hosting a dinner in her honor, only for family."

It stings more than it should, that "*only for family.*" "Of course. You two have to go."

They leave, promising to send for me once they've escaped Catherine de' Medici's clutches. I stay out until true darkness falls before going inside the Louvre.

Bored and dreading running into Jehan and his questions, I enter through the celebrated entrance and its grand corridor. I only walk down here for official court events, five steps behind Margot, my eyes on her gown's hem to make sure it doesn't tangle. This time I look over the austere portraits in the great hallways.

Despite the fact that King Charles sits on the throne, I feel his father, King Henry II—Catherine de' Medici's dead husband—glaring down his long nose at me from all sides. Since he no longer sits on the throne, it would be more appropriate to replace his portraits with portraits of King Charles, but rumor has it when Catherine's council suggested such a thing, she fell upon them with curses and blows and no one dared bring it up again. Not even her son, the king.

My feet slow and stop beneath the oldest of the portraits, one of the long-dead king as a young man. The dauphin of France is garbed in intricate red and black armor, his head bare. His shorn hair and soft face are startlingly young. He cannot be older than seventeen here.

I have seen his proud brow on Margot's brothers. I have seen his dark eyes in her face.

But there is something else I have seen before here as well. I draw closer to the portrait, my hands tracing the ridges and whorls of the paint.

I have seen his nose somewhere else too.

I think back on Louise's sketches of the dead boys.

And a bone-chilling premonition sweeps through me.

King Henry II had many mistresses. Even now, speaking their names near Catherine de' Medici is courting death itself. But still, everyone knows. It's the worst-kept secret of the Valois family.

I tear away from the portrait, my heartbeat thick in my throat. I feel the long-dead king's eyes on my back as I walk swiftly down the marble hall, going faster and faster until I'm flying through the Louvre.

Could it be that the dead boys are King Henry II's royal bastards?

CHAPTER THIRTY-ONE

I RACE TO LOUISE'S apothecary, heartbeat staggering. The world is a patchwork along the way, angry faces, sullen muttering. Word of the latest bloody murder has spread. Paris feels like a hunting hound snarling in her kennel, frothing for the taste of blood in her mouth.

Louise glances up calmly when I burst through the door. As if she's been waiting for me.

"You shouldn't be here," she says.

I throw back the hood of my cloak, feeling the night air burn against my cheeks.

"They're all royal bastards. Each child killed was an illegitimate child of King Henry II."

The words linger, catching and gathering weight like moisture in the air before a storm.

Louise's face blanches, then grows even paler.

An iron hand descends on my shoulder.

"What an interesting theory about the murders." Oncle stares down at me, his expression thunderous. "Especially from someone I specifically forbade from looking into it."

Oncle leads me outside. The silence is so thick and cloying, I could cut it with a knife. He says nothing, save a soft command to mount his horse. I hold my breath, waiting for the storm to break.

His horse's saddlebags are dusty and soaked with sweat, and I swear, there's more silver at his temples now than when he left. Oncle has ridden fast and hard from wherever he was and went straight to Louise's. Why?

Did Jehan find him and tattle about my naughtiness? Did Oncle come here to wait knowing I'd be unable to resist disobeying him while he was gone? Has he been laying another trap for me just as he did with Margot and the pamphlets?

His anger stalks beside us, nearly casting its own shadow. I flush, torn between chagrin and resentment. I hate how being with him like this makes me feel like a child.

"I would rather walk, Oncle," I say stiffly.

He finally looks at me, a barely there tilt of his head. As if he cannot stand to see me. "No. You have a head injury. You shouldn't be out here at all."

"The Louvre is not far, and you leading me there will attract far more attention—"

"Jac." Oncle turns to look at me fully, his expression more grave and menacing than before. "You will *stay* on the horse. You have attracted far more attention than I had imagined possible."

I sit up straighter, mustering all the dignity I can grasp. "Just send me away, then! To our home, a convent, into the arms of a henhearted husband. Don't make this worse by drawing it out!"

"You're angry." He says it so calmly, so matter-of-factly, I want to snarl.

"You are too! Don't pretend to hide it from me like you do everything else. I know it was you who printed the rumors about Margot. I know you found out about my feelings for Henry. You let me think the scandal was all my fault, but it was *yours*. You did it to *use* me. So don't lie to me now!" My shout splinters, breaking against the houses pressing in on both sides. A woman glances up from her vanity, startled, but her eyes slide right past me.

Oncle turns down a street I've never seen before. Behind him torches sputter to life, one by one, until the entire street flickers with orange.

"I did lie to you," he finally admits. "And I am angry. But not with you. On the contrary, you've been very useful."

I sit back, hating how the word "useful" still plucks hopefully at my heart, how it feels like a compliment even though I know it's not. How long does it take to unlearn a lifetime of wanting the wrong things? "What do you mean by useful?"

"Do you know why I had to leave?" he says, ignoring my question.

"Of course I don't. You never tell me why. You just go and forbid me from questions," I growl, hands tightening on the pommel.

He glances at me, something akin to guilt dashing across his face. "I was looking for the missing pieces of this." He pulls out the Book of Hours I found in the Loire Valley graveyard so many weeks ago.

I don't know what he means. The book is entirely whole, nothing missing. He could've bought it from the bouquinistes

296 | ERIN COTTER

just today. I wrestle back another frustrated growl. "Speak plainly! Don't dangle half-truths in front of me and expect me to grasp them."

"I didn't find what I was looking for," Oncle says like I haven't spoken. "But *you* did."

I feel his laugh on the nape of my neck like insect legs. I want to slap the feeling away, but I'm afraid to move. I don't want him to see how unsettled I am. He won't make me feel small anymore. "I'm never going to guess what you're thinking. Unless you plan to explain things to me, we might as well return to the palace."

There's nothing but the strike of the horse's hooves on the cobble. And then he speaks. "Some believe the hearts of kings contain powerful magic."

With a startle, I realize we're at the city's edge, the ancient Gallo-Roman wall crumbling ahead. The Louvre is far behind us. My heart crawls into my throat, suddenly too big to swallow.

"Oncle, you're scaring me." My words are a whisper.

He stops and places a hand on my knee. His expression is almost friendly.

"I will show you. Hold this." He folds my hand around the cold sun pendant in my pocket. He's known exactly where I hid it the entire time. "Now touch the book."

The cover ripples and shifts. The beautiful green leather vanishes beneath my fingertips.

Now the cover is a torn scrap, splattered with dark stains.

Most of the pages are missing, and the ones that remain are jagged and warped. They no longer contain prayers, but lists of bones and phases of the moon, grinning skulls and broken femurs. I draw away with a gasp, and the book is suddenly as it was, the green leather cover innocent and pristine. Fear explodes into a gallop in my veins, racing through every inch of me.

"It is a grimoire. A book of dark magic," Oncle explains.

My breath picks up faster and faster as I stare at the green leather. A cover that plainly belongs to a Book of Hours.

"It is ensorcelled. Only one who has devoted themselves to the dark arts can see it."

The sun pendant suddenly scalds my palm. A scream crawls up my throat. I want to leap off. Run into the darkness. But there's nowhere to go, and the city guard who tipped his head to Oncle as we slipped beneath the city wall's saw-toothed gate would only deliver me straight back into his arms, a ward wild with hysteria. If only those who have pledged themselves to dark magic see the book, then the Societas Solis—

Oncle gently unfolds my clenched fist and caresses his own sun ring—the one he's worn for as long as I can remember. "Our order does not practice dark magic. We seek to stop it."

I close my eyes and will my ragged breath to slow. "I don't understand." Oncle has spoken of reason and logic all my life. He has always looked down on Catherine de' Medici's preoccupation with the occult.

Oncle sighs as though he expected more of me. "Magic is real, Jac." He twists off his ring. "The rumors about Catherine de' Medici practicing dark magic are not mere rumors. They're all true. It's why the order pushed for me to become the royal spymaster. I was watching her and her sorcerer the entire time."

I think of the wild things, haunting things, Catherine de' Medici has done. The strange potions she makes Margot drink. How she asks Cosimo Ruggeri to consult the planets' movements before making a decision. Margot even once said she scried in the entrails of lambs.

And her visions.

Oh God no, her visions.

The Valois line will end when the Seine runs red.

My voice cracks. "Are all the rumors true?"

His smile turns queer. "Most of them."

He presses the center of the sun and the ring pulses with light.

I gasp, flinching away. The horse beneath me merely flicks her ears as if she has seen it a thousand times.

Perhaps she has.

Oncle smiles, his face yellow in the glow of the ring. "Jac. I cannot protect you any longer, and perhaps I protected you for too long. Come now, it's finally time."

I lift my head. We have stopped before a temple so old, it's more a rugged pile of stones than a temple. My hands grow white knuckled on the saddle pommel. "Time for what?"

"It's time for you to speak your vows to the Societas Solis."

I think of Henry and Margot, doubtless in a panic back at the Louvre, wondering where I've gone. How I've pulled them into this dark mess without knowing a thing about what we were getting into.

If the hearts of kings truly contain magic as Oncle claims—a shudder jerks down my spine—if magic is real, then the attempt on Henry's life takes on a new nauseating meaning.

He could be in danger.

We could *all* be in danger.

The guilt splits me open like a pomegranate, every seed a burst of bitterness in my mouth.

I glance over my shoulder, but the Louvre is long gone.

"What if—what if I need more time to decide?"

Oncle's smile sharpens even as his eyes grow sad. "I'm afraid it's too late to change your mind, dear Niece. You already know too much about us."

CHAPTER THIRTY-TWO

THE TEMPLE IS in ruins.

It rises from the darkness like a slain body, slowly swallowed by the earth. Broken colonnades jut from the ground, velveted with moss and lichen. A shattered stone floor crunches beneath my feet. Even though the roof is long gone, stepping into the embrace of crumbling walls makes me feel closed in.

"This was once a Roman temple."

Oncle ties up the horse and then offers me a hand. I swallow back my fear and take it. "A new member's vow must be witnessed to ensure the binding takes hold."

"What binding?" My heart races so fast, I worry he can hear it. Then he'll know about the scream filling up my ribs, the way my entire soul shouts at me to leave. I need to get back to the Louvre, to Henry and Margot.

I have an awful feeling it's too late for me, but it's not too late for them.

Oncle halts before a statue. A naked woman, half her head gone, left hand missing. Dark stains splatter the marble.

But that's not why I gasp.

There are two people already there, their faces hidden. A

man in velvet and satin and a woman in the fine skirts of a wealthy merchant's wife. They must be other members of the Societas Solis. The witnesses.

How many of them have I seen before unknowingly?

How many of them recognize me?

"Your vow shall not be made with words alone, but also with blood." Oncle takes out a knife, flashing me a doting smile. "This won't hurt much."

I jerk away, too late.

The pain is a dazzling white slice.

I stumble, clutching my left hand where an angry red line is opening along the meat of my thumb. My blood spatters on the broken white stone. My breath comes out in short, hard gasps. The pain is nothing, but the shock of Oncle grabbing me, hurting me *on purpose*, makes my head spin.

"Where is Louise?" the woman asks. "We cannot do this without the divine light."

As one, everyone bows their heads. *"The divine light, the ichor of the gods."*

The words susurrate, heavy with meaning. They echo in the trees, into the night beyond. A dark prayer that makes me shiver.

Oncle lifts his head first. "Louise keeps the bottle for our order, but this will do just as well." He twists the sun on his signet ring, and a blazing liquid spills forth. It glows like molten iron in a blacksmith's forge but moves with the lightness of water. It shimmers in Oncle's cupped palm. I gasp, stepping back.

He steps closer. "There are other worlds that brush against ours. Worlds of darkness and worlds of light. The Societas Solis searched long and hard to find the fountain of the divine light."

"The ichor of the gods, the divine light," whispers the circle once more.

"A fountain?" I imagine the fabled well deep in the forêt de Brocéliande where Sir Ywain met and married his faerie wife. The elixir of life whose very mention sends Margot reading for hours, spellbound by visions of the philosopher's stone, wondering aloud if such an object could truly be made.

Oncle speaks of fountains and gods, but for my entire life he only spoke of secrets and shadows. How could he hide this for so long? How could I have missed the signs? Oncle knew things he shouldn't. He knew about Henry's ruby ring. He knew about the places Henry and I have gone. He was always one step ahead of me, and I never stopped to wonder why.

And now I've pulled Margot and Henry into it.

I should've stayed away from them. The thought beats in time with my dripping blood. The future we dreamed of together feels so childish now under the blue-black sky. An impossible dream, something only a princess and a king would ever dare think was possible. I know how stories like mine end. I always have, but I let myself forget for one reckless summer.

Oncle bows again. "The divine light lets us see the dark magic that seeps through this world like a sickness. When touched, it reveals and protects us from the darkness. You saw how it revealed the Book of Hours to you."

"The divine light, the ichor of the gods."

This time the whisper does not vanish. A cold wind rises, tugging at my skirts, my hair. The blood runs down my fingers, as hot as oil. I clench my fist, and the trickle becomes a stream.

This is what Oncle chose over me. All the lonely evenings I cried myself to sleep as a child, all the questions he's evaded with lies and half-truths. He tried to hide it from me, but I opened every drawer and searched every cupboard until I found the answer for myself. I was a dog. A dog swallowing a stolen bone, too senseless to realize it's big enough to choke on.

He warned me about the Societas Solis at every turn, and I never listened.

Oncle's fingers light on my elbow. His whisper is soft with admonishment. "You wanted this, Niece."

My throat swells shut. How could I ever forget?

I close my eyes, unable to bear it. "When did you swear yourself to them?"

He hesitates. His words are a soft confession. "Before you came into my life."

I should be terrified. I should be angry. But instead, grief swallows me whole—blunt edged and bruising.

I made a promise to your mother. My entire life, Oncle was torn in two, split between his promise to my mother and his vow to the Societas Solis.

I thought joining his work would close the hole my mother's death had carved in both of us. But I had it wrong. The Societas Solis was the darkness at the heart of our family, always hungry, always pulling Oncle away when I tried to pull him closer.

And now it's finally pulled me in too.

Just like I wanted.

I clap both hands over my mouth. A sob escapes anyway.

Oncle's fingertips press divots into my arm where no one can see. An apology. A promise.

"Gabriel, the night grows long," the man snaps.

Oncle steps back, hiding behind the cool mask I loathe more than anything in this world. "Give me your pendant."

The tiny sun winks. I suddenly see it for what it is: a collar whose clasp binds so tight, it would choke me before I freed myself of it. Regret surges up my throat, all burning bile.

I don't want this anymore. I have spent my entire life pledged in the service of kings and queens and princesses, and I know this isn't what independence looks like. But it's too late for me to change my mind.

Oncle holds out his cupped palm. The golden liquid pooled there trembles.

"When your blood mixes with the divine light, you'll be bound to us. Your vow will forbid you from speaking of our magic."

"The ichor of the gods, the divine light."

I hold back a shudder.

"What happens if I try to speak of it?" My panic shoots into a higher register. If the magic is a muzzle, how am I supposed to warn Margot and Henry to stay away from me?

Oncle laughs, as if I've said something amusing. "Pain, then death. This magic is ancient and binding. To go against it is to go against the very fabric of your soul."

I lift my chin. "And what if someone writes about it?"

"Then we kill them. Traitors have no place in our ranks," the impatient man says. He has taken another step forward.

"Does your cut still bleed, or do you need another slice, girl?"

Oncle's head snaps toward him. "Don't threaten my niece."

There's a gleam of teeth from the hood's shadow. "Once she takes her vow, she won't be your niece anymore. She'll be our newest initiate." His thumb strokes his sword pommel. "And I think she's asking too many questions."

The other member whispers and nods. My stomach drops. Oncle takes the smallest step in front of me.

All the blood rushes from my face.

I'm furious with my oncle—a fury heavy with grief and regret—but I'm even angrier at this order that let a still-mourning boy of seventeen bind his life to something that would never let him become the person he wanted to be. Hate rages through me for the shadow that the Societas Solis has cast over both of us.

Oncle's right. He's protected me for far too long.

I gather up all my boldness and step between him and the rest of the order. "I'm ready. What do I say?"

The furrows on Oncle's brow ease, just barely. He lowers his palms. "Speak your own words, and the divine light will judge your commitment. Spells can be twisted by their speakers."

I bite the inside of my cheek, tasting bloody flesh. If I speak, I won't mean a word of what I say. If I open my mouth, my body will shake like brittle winter reeds. I'll be burned from inside out, my bones will become coal and then ash, and neither Henry nor Margot will ever know what became of me. They'll suspect Oncle and come after him, and he'll never be able to tell them.

There's no escaping this.

Frustrated tears race down my cheeks.

Everyone I care about is about to be undone by a single sentence.

And there's nothing I can do about it.

Oncle tips his palm. A bead of the divine light cuts across my bloody palm and pools in the wet gash. The power sets my teeth on edge, fills my ears with the clash of phantom swords. Heat scalds my veins. My mouth has gone dry. The edge of the wound starts to knit closed.

"Speak quickly, Jac, before it burns you!" Oncle shouts.

Except I can't. My tongue already feels charred. The fire pours into my lungs. I sink to my knees and start to cough. Each one shakes me like a leaf.

It won't be my words that end the people I love. Silence can kill just as well.

"Wait!"

The woman in the fine skirts has raised her gloved hand. Her masked face is pointed away from us, into the dark opening we came through.

Running footsteps.

The ringing of steel as the men unsheathe their swords.

I curl in on myself, drowning in fire, forgotten at everyone's feet for an instant.

No one notices me scraping my burning, weeping cut on my already bloodied skirt.

No one looks when I come back to life with a shuddering, gasping wheeze.

Just as someone bursts into our circle.

CHAPTER THIRTY-THREE

KNOW WHO HUNTS the hearts," Louise pants.

I stay hunched over, my heart slamming against my breastbone. The burning has vanished from my body, just as the unearthly substance has sunk into the dark fabric of my dress.

I've escaped the magic's thrall for now.

But for how long?

Behind Louise another shape emerges, slower and stranger. Jehan, holding the scruff of a terrified-looking boy.

"When Jac said the hearts were from the king's bloodline, I was reminded of dark magic I read about long ago. I believe it's the spell missing from our Book of Hours. A spell that takes the life from one and gives it to another."

The gathered Societas Solis members go perfectly, eerily still. The silence is broken only by the distant scream of some small thing meeting its death. I shudder and hug my arms around myself, heedless of the blood and sticky ichor.

"Taking life to beget more life is the darkest magic there is," the impatient man finally says. His voice is softer now, feathered with apprehension. "Stopping magic like this is the entire reason the order exists."

The silence falls again, heavier than before.

"What does he have to do with it?" Oncle nods toward the boy. He shrinks against the broken marble statue, his terrified eyes latched on me. As if I'm the one person who might help him.

"This is one of the gravedigger's boys," Louise says. "Tell them what you told me."

The boy swallows, throat bobbing. "He left a list of names with the gravedigger. Said to tell him when the bodies got to the graveyard. Then he came and he—" The boy breaks off with a shudder.

I clench my fists so tight, my half-healed cut reopens. I suddenly don't want him to finish his sentence.

Oncle kneels to the boy's level, cloak dragging in the dirt. "He did what?"

The boy swallows. "He cut into the bodies and took *things* from them. Like the scraps from a butcher you'd feed a dog."

My stomach drops so fast, I fear I might be sick. The impatient man isn't so lucky. He barely turns before vomiting. A repulsed shudder goes through the group.

Only Oncle remains calm. "Can you describe this man?"

The boy shakes his head. "I don't know his name. He spoke with an accent and only to the undertaker. He paid us well to shut up, but he unsettled us all. My boss lost the list of names to get him to stop coming around, but then I heard about the murders in the city and I knew. . . . I knew it was him." His voice gets smaller and smaller. "We didn't stop him from doing anything. He just went out and did it worse."

Oncle's mouth pulls disdainfully. "Sounds like the Queen Mother's man."

Cosimo Ruggeri, Catherine de' Medici's sorcerer.

"Perhaps, but even if Cosimo's behind it, we don't know enough to do anything," Louise says. "Who did he hire to act as his assassin? How did the assassin know whom to target?" She whips toward me. "Jac—tell us what you remember when you killed the Paris murderer."

Four pairs of eyes latch on to me.

I stand slowly, a fox flushed out before the hounds. There's a high keening in my head. Whatever I say next will make or break me.

"I felt someone following me for blocks. They attacked when I was on an unlit street."

Louise presses closer. "Did anything happen before they attacked?"

I meet her stare, my expression level, even as my pulse starts racing once again.

I never told anyone Henry was there.

And it was Henry following me the entire time.

Henry saw me leave and followed after. It was only after he confronted me, only after he attacked me, that the murderer showed himself. The killer never once went for me. I was an afterthought, collateral damage. His single-minded viciousness was only for the king.

Henry was the target the entire time.

My vision blurs—a senseless smear of color.

The two kings in Paris could not be more different.

King Charles of France, weak and consumptive.

King Henry of Navarre, powerful and hale.

Would Catherine de' Medici willingly drain the life of one king for her sickly son's?

"Jac?" Louise asks, drawing me back to myself. "What is it?"

I snap out of my thoughts with a wild-eyed look, breathing hard. "I'm sorry. I have a hard time remembering that night." I touch the back of my head, its still healing cut. "The attacker said nothing. He fought like no one I had ever seen. I defeated him with luck, not skill. It's a wonder I'm alive at all." I don't have to try to put the fear in my voice—it's already there.

If I'm right—and given what I've learned tonight, I feel more and more certain I'm right—then Catherine de' Medici needs to kill Henry to complete her spell.

Even though she wants him married to her daughter.

Even though it would destroy peace between France and Navarre.

King Charles's life—the Valois family legacy—matters more to her than anything else.

It doesn't make sense, but we're beyond sense. Dark magic is real, and it's coming for the man I love. My pulse thunders in every one of my fingertips.

"Can I go now?"

Everyone turns to the gravedigger's boy. At our look, he stands straighter, skinny chest puffed out. "I've answered all your questions."

Oncle sighs and rubs his nose. "Was there not a more subtle way to do this, Louise?"

Louise drags an unsteady hand down her face, her expression utterly shattered. "I chose speed over subtlety, as you would've done yourself."

Oncle turns to the boy with a sad, regretful expression. "I'm afraid you know too much."

The boy's face falls, confused. "But I don't know anything."

Oncle's hand moves to his belt. My pulse goes jagged.

"Let him join us, then!"

Heads whip toward me. My chest heaves. There's not enough air to fill my lungs. "Give him the same choice you're giving me. If he says the vow, he can't speak of the order."

Oncle's face is so terribly sad, his voice unbearably gentle. "We have no use for him, Jac. I hate it when things must go like this. Hold her."

I lunge for the boy, but not fast enough. Hands seize me, yanking me back. Louise tucks my thrashing body under her arm, wrenching my head away.

The boy screams.

I scream too, twisting my face back. There's a spray of warmth across my body—and then silence.

When Louise releases me I fall to my knees.

I'm drenched in blood. It drips into my eyes, stinging and body-hot. Revulsion spasms through me, flooding out everything else, letting numb terror fill every inch of me. Oncle and the other man already drag the body into the darkness. I stare after them, mouth open in a silent scream. My hands rise, unsteady, to hold in the high keening noise leaking out of me.

The Societas Solis means it. They will kill anyone who might reveal their secrets, even children.

Even me.

Especially me. If they find out I'm lying about Henry.

Oncle returns, rubbing his bloodied hands on his black cloak. "Let's leave. There's work to be done."

I turn away, unable to look at him.

"Wait." The impatient man looks at me. "She never said her vow."

"She'd be dead if she hadn't said it," Oncle says.

The man's smile glimmers in the shadow of his hood. "It's best to be certain, no?"

Oncle's ring already spins in his hand. I swallow, turning to face him, the largely healed cut on my hand already burning.

There's nowhere to hide. Nowhere else to run.

Oncle catches my frightened look and smiles reassuringly. There is still blood on his face. My knees start to shake.

Would he tremble holding the blade to my throat?

Louise pushes past him. "Let me. This is faster." She fumbles with something at her side. An entire flask of the divine light swings from the belt around her waist.

"Hurry, we've been here for too long." She pours the liquid into my bloody right hand.

I clutch the pendant tightly. "I swear myself to the Societas Solis."

The pendant flashes once and goes dark.

One by one, each member bows their head to me, murmuring a welcome.

I bow my head back to them, keeping wild eyes hidden beneath my lashes, holding back the terror raging through me. I wipe the leftover blood and ichor on my skirt and shove both hands in my pockets.

No one needs to remember that Oncle cut my left hand and not my right.

CHAPTER THIRTY-FOUR

MAGIC IS REAL, my mother is a witch, and your oncle is in a secret order tasked with stopping her." Margot's eyes burn with accusation. "And you *kept* this from me!"

I cringe. I want to dash the nightmarish sun pendant from her gilded dressing table. I want to toss it into the Seine and pretend I had never even seen it.

I kept the Societas Solis secret from Henry and Margot for too long, and now we're all in danger.

Henry, from Catherine de' Medici's magical machinations. Me, for double-crossing the order, and Margot for merely trusting the wrong people. Trusting *me*.

"We had a right to know. This was never just about you, Jac!" Margot makes a sweeping gesture to her opulent parlor, to Henry standing with his head bent, as if he can't bear to look at me. "We agreed to be honest with each other, and you still lied to us!"

"I'm telling you now, aren't I?" My voice is so small, stooped beneath the weight of guilt. Even Cerberus, Margot's ancient dog, glares at me from her lap.

I wish I'd never come to Paris. I wish I'd never met Margot

or Henry. I wish I'd taken my oncle's advice and married Gérard de Montbéliard and exiled myself to his country estate.

If I had, none of this would be happening.

If I had, perhaps we'd all be safe.

I reached for things I shouldn't have, and now everything is crashing down.

The breeze soars in from the window, sending the rose-colored draperies fluttering. Across the river on the Île de la Cité, I spot the spire of Notre-Dame Cathedral piercing the bright blue sky. The wedding is next week, and I know laborers still toil away to make the ancient cathedral fit for royalty.

I saw the preparations from Anémone's back, when Oncle insisted we ride into the city. How yards and yards of golden cloth and scarlet and blue ribbons were unspooled from the carts. How the air rang with hammers to build the raised dais where Henry and Margot would speak their vows, tall enough for the crowds, hundreds of feet deep, to see them.

We were far from the only onlookers in the cathedral square. Some of them even wore unfamiliar clothes from distant lands, doubtless wedding guests here early to marvel at the might of France, where blood and beauty live hand in hand.

"I think the wedding may be part of Catherine de' Medici's spell," Oncle mused. "Remember how the candles went dark at Chenonceau? There's power in having so many people gathered in one place."

My fear felt like swallowing glass. "Then shouldn't we warn Margot or King Henry?"

Oncle shook his head. "There is nothing we can do. We must wait and see what happens."

"But why?" Some of my sharpness slipped out, just a little. "If something happens to them, then the peace treaty—"

"The peace between Catholics and Huguenots doesn't matter anymore," Oncle said coldly. "Peace is nice to have, but the Societas Solis exists to stop dark magic at all costs, even peace, if needed. We don't know what the spell does or what it needs. To tamper with its pieces now might do more harm than good."

"But—"

"You got what you wanted. Isn't that enough?" he snapped unexpectedly. "Secrets stay among family. You know this."

The Societas Solis is not part of our family! I wanted to scream.

Instead I ducked my head, slipping into the role of the obedient girl he's always loved best. "Of course."

His disappointed look lingered. It sliced through the noise and bustle of the square, the rhythmic pounding of hammers and the scream of the gulls. "I forbid you to speak of it to them, Jac."

I felt the hot rush of power where my sun pendant pressed my skin, the magic of his words, the effect of a vow I made with blood that wasn't mine. A risk, a wager.

And it worked, because here I am now, speaking of the Societas Solis with no ill effects.

For now.

But it's only a matter of time before Oncle figures out I've double-crossed the order.

And when he knows, I'll only have hours left to make things right.

Perhaps even minutes.

I know what they'd do to me. But to Margot and Henry? I glance at them now. Margot, her chin pillowed on the windowsill, skirts frothing to the floor. Henry, as cold and exquisite as a marble statue. My heart squeezes painfully.

I'll do anything to protect them.

I force the words out, each one like the tearing of a fingernail.

"You two have to leave before the wedding."

Margot laughs. "And how do you suggest we do that?"

"We'll make it look like an elopement," I say.

Henry turns, his handsome mouth all stern lines. "I can't run. What would my people think? This alliance matters too much to Navarre."

Good God! Would it kill Henry to set aside his honor just once? "I'm sure there's a country priest willing to conduct the ceremony. We can send word back to Paris you two are married."

Margot tosses her black curls, scowling. "I think not. I won't marry Henry anymore. I've said that from the beginning. Especially now that there's *dark magic* involved."

Henry takes in her measure and scoffs. "Poor Princess. How difficult it must be to stand there and be beautiful."

Margot stabs a vicious finger into Henry's chest. Her diamond engagement ring glitters. "Don't act like you're better than me! How would it look if you died at your own wedding? Do you truly think your *death* wouldn't threaten the peace more than whether or not we marry?"

A plate shatters. A startled maid's eyes meet mine from the doorway. Broken china and crushed macarons surround her feet like rotten flowers.

Margot tears around, cheeks stained pink. "I asked to be alone! Does no one in this place listen to me?"

The maid scuttles out, whimpering. I leap to my feet and step betwixt them, hands raised. "Stop fighting! The two of you are supposed to be in love!"

Angry tears spill down Margot's cheeks. She thumbs them away with a rough, impatient gesture. Her hands tremble, like little birds on the verge of flight. How many times have those perfectly manicured hands saved my life? Not from bodily harm, but from a more gruesome fate: the social death of a woman who dares to defy the court's rules.

Margot looks to Notre-Dame Cathedral's distant spire as if it were a gibbet to hang a criminal. "We're supposed to all be in this together. I'm not a pawn for you and Henry to move around wherever you need me to go. Excuse me." She picks up her skirts and storms away. The gilded double doors slam shut behind her and send all her dogs barking.

A sigh shudders out of me. I drag cold hands over my hot face, torn between anger and self-loathing. "Why can't she see that I ask this of her for her own protection?"

Henry says nothing.

I take him in through my fingers. He's all square jawed and staring determinedly at the mocking frescoes. He won't look at me even though I'm right at his side.

"Is everything all right?" I ask, biting my lip.

He laughs darkly. "Why wouldn't it be? We're doing everything exactly to your plan."

The unexpected sarcasm stings. I pull away from him, smarting. "What do you mean?"

He takes my arm and guides me into Margot's office. He braces himself against the wall with one hand. He drags the other hand through his hair, leaving it in rumpled chaos. "Do you know how I felt when I couldn't find you last night?" He towers over me, his anger filling the too-small room like a pacing lion. I feel the velvet brush of its pelt, belly clenching. *You were always going to disappoint him.*

I lift my quivering chin. Force myself to hold his black stare.

"I should've told you about the Societas Solis sooner. I'm sorry I didn't. I'm trying to make things right now."

He steps closer, too close. I bump into Margot's overflowing desk. Her letters cascade to the floor, quills raining after them. "I wanted to mount a search for you. I told my advisors I was going to ask my men to find you, perhaps even court danger to find you, but you can't trust me to even know your thoughts."

Shame fills my mouth, thick and sour. "And what did they say?"

Henry draws a shuddering breath. "My advisors said you were not worth the effort. That you were the lowborn niece of a minor vicomte and I was too addled by my feelings to remember what was best for Navarre."

The words strike my jugular. A killing blow. There's no

use arguing with them. Henry's men are right. I've known I'm no good for him the entire time, but I let Henry convince me otherwise for a few breathless weeks.

I never should've let our romance get this far.

Even though there's barely space, I sink into a trembling curtsy for a king. Not a foreign king, but the one of my homeland, my heart. My eyes burn with regret. "I know. I'll do anything to make this up."

He snarls, both hands slamming down on the desk behind me, boxing me into his chest. "You misunderstand! I'm angry you disappeared to face the danger alone." He leans forward, lips dragging a hot path along my cheekbone. His voice drops lower. "I was terrified something had happened to you. Do you know how it feels to instead learn you chose to leave me behind? Even after we agreed to trust each other?"

The room grows suffocating. I squeeze my eyes shut, breathing in the scent of his skin, the animal heat of his body.

He doesn't understand. No, worse. He's stubbornly choosing not to understand. There is no place in my sordid world for golden kings.

I clench my teeth. "Someone has already tried to kill you once."

"Then let them try a second time!" His voice shakes dust from the ceiling.

"You can't tell me what I can and can't do." I lean away from him—onto the desk, the only space left. "The choice was mine to make!"

Henry laughs against my neck. I shiver, feeling it everywhere. "Don't insult me by pretending I have ever tried to command you, Jac. I haven't asked for anything except to be at your side. For you to trust me, as I trust you. But you won't let me in, even when I stand at the stone doors of your heart begging. You ease open an inch, and each time I pray you've finally let me in for good. But then the doors slam shut. You keep me outside no matter what I do." He looks at me, his expression heartbreaking. "I don't know how much longer I can last out in the cold."

I place a hand on his chest and feel the thunder of his pulse, how strongly he believes what he's saying.

In his lovestruck gaze, I am made gold.

He can't see how the gilt flakes, revealing the rusting steel beneath. He deserves better than me. But he refuses to admit it even when I've proven myself a villain time and time again.

"It's not that I can't trust you, Henry. I can't trust myself."

My heart has turned against me my entire life. It's untrustworthy, traitorous. I believed in the Societas Solis and they turned out to be liars. I trusted Oncle with my life and he brought me to hell. Even Louise told me exactly what I wanted to hear to get me to do her dirty work.

Once more, I feel the hot spray of blood on my face, see Oncle wiping it from his hands. That innocent boy is dead because I told the truth to the wrong people.

What if I get it wrong again?

What if I bring down someone I love next?

What if I already have?

I'm crying now, huge, ugly sobs that I'm certain the entire palace can hear.

Henry's arms curl around me, holding me together.

"Do you know what happened when my advisors said you weren't good for Navarre?" His fingers slide up my back, into my hair. "I told them to write up an abdication notice."

I rear backward. "You can't do that! You've spent your life preparing to be king."

Henry doesn't let me go. "No, Jac. I spent my entire life waiting for *you*." His midnight eyes meet mine, more steadfast and serious than I've ever seen them. "I told you before. You're my everything. If you're not enough for Navarre, then I'm not either."

I want to tell him he's making a mistake.

I want to tell him this is folly, madness, but I stay silent. He's asked me to trust him again and again. The least I can do is listen.

"If you won't have me as a king, I'll come to you as a man. What do you say, Jac?" His mouth curves shyly. "Will you let me stay at your side?"

I think of Henry's first love—the man afraid to be with his future king—and my throat closes up. I know what it means that Henry's willing to do this now for me. He means every single word. I know the abdication papers are written, waiting for his signature. If I asked him to leave his throne, he'd do it. If I told him this was the only way I would be with him, he'd do it. He'd undo years of diplomacy with France. He'd send Europe into a political tailspin.

He'd do it all for me.

Because despite every mistake I've made, all the times I

trusted wrongly, the countless times I doubted myself, he's never once doubted me.

Because he loves me, jagged edges and all, even when I hated myself.

I kiss him in answer, burying both hands into his hair.

Saying yes feels a million times better than all the times I've said no, all the times I thought I was doing the right thing but instead fenced in my own wild heart. I can't stop crying. Henry tries to wipe away the tears, but he's crying too, and our kiss becomes softer, more tender, so sweet, I melt to nothing.

Sometimes trusting someone is harder than loving them. I hope I have years to get better at it.

After I don't know how long, the door opens. "All right, I think I have a plan if you'll listen to me for once in your goddamn lives—"

Margot cuts off abruptly. She recovers with a coy laugh. "Crying on my desk is all well and good, but may I recommend another desk activity that's *far* more satisfying?"

"What is that?" I ask. Royal blue fabric cascades from her arms, an absolute riot of it, enough to trim the sails of the entire French navy.

"Oh, this?" Margot shakes out the shape. "This is my wedding dress. I was thinking it might just fit you."

I laugh wetly. "And why would I want to wear it?"

"It was your uncle's pamphlets that inspired me, really. I was thinking about how people say we look alike, and how your horrible little sun trinket lets you see magic. If Henry so stubbornly insists on being married before half of Europe even though my *mother* wants to *kill him*, then it might be best if you were at his side? Under my name, of course."

My eyes go wide. "You want me to fake-marry your fiancé?"

Her painted mouth hooks into a mischievous smile. "It's for the good of France and Navarre, Jac! You don't have to say it judgmentally."

If the spell that Catherine de' Medici weaves is as fragile as Oncle says it is, then perhaps I could see it and stop it before something happens. If I'm at Henry's side, I'll see it first. I'll be close enough to act.

I fall out of Henry's arms, racing over to kiss her cheek. "Margot, you brilliant rogue!"

A woman is a pawn, and in the game of court she only has one move: marriage.

Why not use the one move available to us?

"I know," the princess says humbly. "This is why I'll make an excellent headmistress."

Henry's mouth softens with surprise. "You would do this for me? Let Jac borrow your name?"

"And wear my gown—let's not forget that. It's a *very* nice gown." Margot flashes him the wink that unlaced a thousand bodices.

When Henry's gaze cuts to me it's like plunging into a hot bath in midwinter. "You would marry me after all, then?" His voice is low, soft with hope. His thumb traces the silkiest circles against the scar where Oncle's knife sank into my skin.

God, it does things to me, his softness! I take in a deep

breath and loosen it in something almost like a laugh, but not quite. "I don't think it counts if I'm pretending to be someone else."

But it could, if we wanted it to. If I choose to let it mean something.

Henry kisses the blue veins in my wrist, his whisper just for me. "Tell me if you want it to count when it's over."

His words make me fizz like a glass of champagne. I braid my fingers with his and then take Margot's hand as well so no one feels left out. I catch both their gazes and hope they see the fire in mine and know better than to dampen it. "I'll do this for us."

Margot gets her school. Henry gets his peace.

And I can make things right.

Henry's arm comes around my shoulders, drawing me closer to that broad chest with its proud, thumping heart that I would do anything to keep beating.

"I love you, Jac," he murmurs into my hair. "Have I told you lately?"

Margot rolls her eyes and says something that sounds an awful lot like *"disgustingly adorable,"* and I pull them both closer. For the first time in my life, my heart has finally gotten something right.

I'm so glad I finally trusted it.

CHAPTER THIRTY-FIVE

PRINCESS MARGUERITE DE Valois blazes with diamonds the day of her wedding.

All of us, her ladies-in-waiting and a half dozen lady's maids, have labored since dawn to bathe and array the princess like a rare hothouse flower in a royal blue gown trimmed in snowy ermine fur. The gown has a train the length of three men. Under our hands, Margot is transformed from a girl to an emblem of France itself.

Looking at all of Margot's silks and furs and heavy gems makes sweat trickle under my stays. We'll have a quarter hour, if that, to swap clothes.

And if we're caught?

Then Henry will be left defenseless against Catherine de' Medici's dark magic, Margot will be forced to marry him against her will, and Oncle will know I've double-crossed him and the Societas Solis both.

All we've worked for would come to nothing.

I squeeze my shaking fingers on the back of a brocade chair, bracing myself. Margot's eyes catch mine in her great gilded mirror. Her eyebrows lift in a question.

I nod.

"Crown me with the veil and let us call it done," she commands in a tone that allows no argument.

The head of the lady's maids frown. "Your mother made no mention of a veil, madame."

Margot stamps her slipper, eyes flashing dangerously. "And this is my wedding, is it not?"

The maids stammer apologies and quickly pin the heavy diamond-crusted mesh into her hair. Margot sweeps the veil over her face and turns to the mirror.

There's nothing to see except her profile.

I release a relieved breath, my death grip easing on the chair. At least this part of our plan works.

Margot's voice is pleased. "Excellent. And now, my ladies-in-waiting shall join me. Come, there is a veil for everyone inside my bridal trunk."

Lady Charlotte's nose wrinkles as she holds up the fabric. "Oh, but must we? My maid has spent hours on my makeup!" Her dismay is echoed in the distraught expressions on the other ladies-in-waiting. I pin my veil on quickly to hide my smile.

Margot takes Charlotte's hands. "Why, yes, you must! I sewed some of my wedding diamonds onto each veil myself, as a gift to honor you all for helping me today."

Lady Charlotte's mood improves dramatically at this news. With many thank-yous and fawning compliments, Margot's bridesmaids hide their faces. Once every girl has fastened her veil, Margot bows her head to us. "Thank you. Now I must ask you to leave so I can meditate in prayer." A pious woman, it turns out, is a handy disguise indeed.

The lead maid's face flushes bright red. "But you're not to be alone! Your mother said—"

"Jacqueline shall attend me then. Now leave." She makes a shooing motion, and the women all hurry out.

Leaving us alone.

We share a single breathless look before crashing into each other.

Stays are yanked, hair is pulled, and more than one diamond scrapes painfully against my skin as we rush to swap our clothes. Margot mutters a steady stream of curses the entire time. Why must women's clothes be so bloody complicated?

After what feels like seconds, there's a knock at the door.

"Madame! Your mother would like to see you."

Margot fumbles her engagement ring and sends it skittering across the floor. I wince, each strike of the diamond on the tiles louder than cannon fire. "The princess is busy in prayer!" I cry.

"We need to leave," Catherine de' Medici answers crossly. The door begins to open—

I race across the room and throw myself against it, holding it shut. The Queen Mother gasps, scandalized.

"Madame, I'm so sorry, but the princess wishes to be left alone!" I settle the sun pendant beneath Margot's wedding gown as she pins the veil to my hair with frantic fingers.

Catherine's laugh is cold, a current of menace just beneath its surface. "And even princesses don't always get what they want. Open the door. *Now.*"

Margot finishes with one final stab.

I only barely manage to throw myself to my knees before

the effigy of the Virgin when the door bursts open. Beside the door, I hear Margot suck in a soft breath and sink into a flawless curtsy.

The back of my neck prickles beneath the too-hot veil and crown of pins and braids.

Catherine de' Medici clicks her tongue disapprovingly.

"Why do you hide your face and linger in prayer, Daughter? You're a bride today. Not a nun."

I stand and curtsy to the Queen Mother. Up close, she smells faintly of sulfur and something herbaceous that makes my nose itch. She is dressed in her customary black, adorned with only a single cross on a golden chain. I imagine it's supposed to seem festive, but it only gives her the air of attending a funeral.

I swallow and force my gaze to meet hers through the veil. "Because I'm frightened, Mother. This wedding is so big." My voice is soft and vulnerable, nothing like Margot's.

Catherine's mouth hooks into a sharp expression.

Margot shares her mother's eyes, a rich, dark bistre whose color has been immortalized in more than one courtly poem. My eyes are far lighter—the brown of early autumn leaves. All at once, my knees begin to shake. Margot and I are nothing alike. Perhaps in passing, but not up close like this when only the rush of blood in my ears and my unsteady voice stand between success and failure.

The silence bends and stretches, wrapping around my neck. My hands begin to tremble.

Catherine pulls me into an embrace.

"Don't be afraid. You look more lovely than I could've

imagined. Your father would be proud of you, God rest his soul, were he here to see you crowned a queen."

I sink into the embrace, a long, shuddering breath leaving me. Margot, standing behind her mother with eyes downcast, lets out her own relieved sigh.

We have duped her mother.

Now it's time to trick all of Paris.

Catherine de' Medici stands back. "If you are frightened, perhaps Cosimo Ruggeri can bring you something for it?" My teeth clench to see the sorcerer standing in the doorway. I imagine him slinking through the Paris graveyards, coins at his belt and blood under his nails, waiting for the body of the next boy to be delivered to him. I take a tiny step back before stopping myself.

Margot doesn't like Cosimo, but she has no reason to fear him.

"No, I'll be fine." My voice is a shade too sharp to be casual.

Catherine de' Medici frowns. "It cannot hurt—"

I stand up even straighter. "I wish to have my wits about me today."

"Very well." Catherine's mouth twists. "But I must insist you take these with you."

A pair of sapphire drop earrings lie in her palm.

My heart slams into my rib cage. I don't know if the earrings are spelled, but I don't want to wear anything Catherine de' Medici gives me. I know too little of how the divine light works, how her dark magic machinates, to trust anything from her. "Must I? They're far too fine—"

She crushes the earrings into my palm, voice flat, eyes dark. "You are a princess of France marrying a king. You will do as I say today."

Or else. The threat hangs over my neck.

I murmur a "thank you" and fasten the earrings myself before Catherine de' Medici lifts my veil and does it for me.

The roads are so packed heading to Notre-Dame Cathedral, it takes the royal carriage an hour to make a journey that should take five minutes. People push in from all sides, tossing summer flowers before the carriage's gilt-painted wheels. The bright scent of crushed roses trails me all the way to the cathedral. Paris has turned out to see their princess wed to the foreign king, wondering if this means the end to war is finally in sight. Horns blast a triumphant fanfare when I step outside, the noise almost as overwhelming as the crowd's attention. The cathedral's stern gothic face is festooned with cloth of gold. A dais rises above the tallest steps where a familiar figure already stands with clasped hands and bowed head.

Henry.

The world slivers to nothing but him. He is a vision in yellow silk, a slice of golden twilight, too bright for this overcast morning. Even though so much is at stake, even though he's not here for me, and this wedding isn't for us, my ribs suddenly feel too small for my heart.

When I appear, every line of him lifts toward me. One hand rises, a barely there wave.

I nod my head, just once.

His hand falls, but his smile grows more brilliant in return, and even though no one can see my face, I grin back.

This might just work.

But when King Charles escorts me down the long aisle, my hope wilts.

A sautoir hangs from Henry's neck, the chain thick with pearls and diamonds.

A shimmering haze clings to it like a miasma.

The sun pendant against my chest suddenly flares so hot, I gasp.

It's spelled.

"Where did you get that?" I whisper when I reach Henry, my words lost to King Charles beneath the crowd's roar. Getting closer to the sautoir sets my teeth on edge, makes the hidden pendant burn hotter.

Henry's eyes cut to King Charles.

My heart sinks. It would have been too suspicious for Henry to refuse a gift from his supposed brother-in-law, and it's far too late for him to refuse it now, here before thousands of people, the French king behind me, Catherine de' Medici in the first row beneath us.

"Silence, girl," the bishop barks, glaring. His expression grows even graver when he takes in Henry.

If I were ranking all the people who oppose this marriage, the clergy would be at the top of my list.

If this were a Catholic wedding, it would take place inside the cathedral with a proper mass. The compromise—being married on the cathedral's steps—seems sacrilegious to

Admiral Coligny, who frowns behind Henry like he'd rather be anywhere else. Beyond him the more conservative Catholic courtiers mutter among themselves, outraged to be attending a wedding outside the doors of their holy place.

When Henry takes my hands, it's not two people joining, but Navarre and France, Huguenot and Catholic.

The ceremony rushes past me. Never have I seen so many people in one place. I half wonder if the streets shall groan and split beneath their weight, the Seine swallowing us all. Only Henry's gaze grounds me in the moment, a slim spar in the sea of stares, but even his hands are slick with sweat.

I trust you, his expression says. I feel his trust in how he strokes my fingers reassuringly where no one can see, in how he stands here doing exactly what I've asked of him, trusting me to find a way out of this.

My sun pendant burns so close to the sautoir. The magic crawls over the chain like ants, a nauseating movement that sets my stomach spinning. Is it my imagination, or does the haze grow stronger the longer we stand here?

An ominous feeling creeps through my veins, as soft as a choking vine.

If the divine light only lets me see things when the pendant touches my skin, does Catherine de' Medici's magic work the same way? Can she see me up here blazing gold, waiting to undo her spell?

The sautoir must go. I need to get it off Henry. But how? With so many people watching? It can't look like a deliberate action. It must be an accident.

"I take you, Marguerite, to be my wife." Henry's ringing, confident words jerk me back to the ceremony.

The solemn priest turns to me. "Repeat after me. I, Marguerite, take you, Henry, to be my husband."

Movement catches my eye from the side.

Catherine de' Medici presses closer, her white face rapt.

Her golden cross has started to shimmer with the same haze as Henry's sautoir.

I gasp, squeezing Henry's hands so tightly, he winces.

"My love," he whispers. "What is it?"

I shake my head, throat tight, unable to speak with so many eyes and ears on us. The magic grows stronger, pulling from Henry like a leech, just as Louise feared it would.

A puzzled murmur rises from the crowd, a buzzing hornet's nest.

All the Navarrese nobles lean forward, their stares scorching. Too late, I realize what I've done, how my distracted silence looks like I've just rejected their king in front of the entire city. Henry's mouth drops.

The priest clears his throat. "I say, repeat after me—"

"She accepts!" King Charles snaps before I can speak.

The old man frowns. "She must accept of her own accord."

With an annoyed sigh, King Charles's rude hand grabs my neck and forces me to nod. The sun pendant burns hotter than a coal.

Henry's hand goes to his throat.

My pulse goes jagged.

There's no more time.

"I accept!" Throwing back my veil, I pull Henry to me right as the bells toll.

I kiss the king of Navarre before every soul in Paris.

It's a rude kiss, hungry and desperate, full of everything I have. My teeth sink into his lip, a plea, a promise. *Don't leave me.*

Wrapped around the king's neck, my hands seize the sautoir and *pull.*

My pendant stops burning. Henry gasps like a man saved from the sea.

The snapped chain of the sautoir dangles from my fist, hidden behind Henry's shoulder. When I drop it, he sweeps it into a crack in the platform beneath our feet.

Henry turns us toward the roaring crowd. But his eyes stay on me, a proud expression unfurling in the corner of his mouth.

I lean into him, smiling a small, secret smile, just for him.

No one will find the sautoir until it's too late. I imagine as soon as the court leaves, it'll disappear in the pocket of some lucky lad who searches the dais.

Henry and I don't need to feign our joy as we walk hand in hand toward the waiting carriage. The white horses are dressed in harnesses of Valois blue and Navarrese crimson. We barely fall upon the velvet seat before the carriage lurches off to catch up to King Charles.

"You saved me." Henry pulls me onto his lap, refusing to let me claim my side of the seat.

I run a gloved finger down his nose. "For now." It was more luck than anything else that saved us. I don't want to linger in France long enough to see if we're lucky a second time. "Did you tell your court to pack their things?"

"I did." Henry nuzzles my neck. The crowd pressing in on all sides roars even louder. How quickly would their cheers turn to screams if the Navarrese king died mere days after his wedding? The long-awaited peace feels even more vulnerable after the wedding, fragile and small.

Easily crushed.

Henry, Margot, and I need to escape to Navarre, where Catherine de' Medici can't follow us. Now that Margot is Henry's wife, Catherine can't forbid her from following him anymore. We need to leave before she figures out how her spell went wrong. Before the Societas Solis realizes I faked my vow with them.

Catherine de' Medici waits for us in the Louvre courtyard. I sweep the veil over my face again before stepping out of the carriage. "My king, I wish to pray for our union. May I retire to my chamber?"

The Queen Mother frowns. "I'm certain God is pleased enough with your devotions today," she says, an edge to her voice.

Henry laughs and presses my knuckles to his lips. "My queen shall pray as much as she desires! Was the freedom to pray however one wishes not the point of this marriage today?"

The people closest to us, Huguenots one and all, cheer at Henry's words. The Queen Mother has no choice but to acquiesce.

Henry seizes my hand and races to Margot's chamber. I chase after him, laughing, and watch how the servants smile and clap to see their princess galivanting like a girl in love. It means something to them, to see France and Navarre together and happy. I understand now why Henry insisted on going through with the wedding. It's a political win for both kingdoms.

Inside Margot's chambers, servants have already begun to pack up her trousseau. The sight relieves me, sends my shoulders easing down from my ears. No one will stop us from leaving. This is the last time I'll have to look at the cursed cherubs and virginal Bible maidens on the princess's ceiling ever again.

Henry lifts my veil and kisses me against the ornate bedframe. I give myself over to it, fire racing down my limbs. He presses a kiss against my neck before glancing at the wide-eyed servants frozen beyond. One of them fans herself.

"Leave us."

They scatter.

Henry steps back, keeping one of my hands in his. "Let's get you out of these things."

The unintended meaning behind his words makes me shiver.

He flushes, the double entendre only reaching him now. "Apologies. I meant—"

"I know what you meant." I drag a fingertip down his throat, pausing at its hollow. Where the very top button of his doublet lays. "I would very much like to explore that other meaning with you."

Seeing how my boldness makes him blush makes my insides clench.

I haven't considered the wedding night and the duties expected of husbands and wives. Thinking of them now fills me with a desperate curiosity.

Henry reaches over my shoulders to undo the top buttons of the wedding gown. His gaze darkens.

"You would want to do such things with me?" His fingers circle the first knob of my spine.

I shiver as he undoes another button, his fingers dropping to the next vertebra. "I would like to do many things with you, Henry of Navarre."

He swallows, his exploring touch growing tender. "I know our wedding wasn't true, but . . . I need you to know I meant every single word today. Whether or not we marry, whether or not you ask me to abdicate my throne, you'll always be my queen."

My entire body melts. "I know." I nestle against his chest, reveling that he's here. That he's *mine*. Of course he must say this. He would not be my Henry if he were not making promises. "I love you for it."

He makes a soft noise. "I thought you despised my oaths?"

I press a kiss to that wondering mouth, smiling. "They're growing on me."

Well before Henry has freed me from all the wedding finery, there are knocks at the door. Two long and two short, just as we discussed. Margot comes in when we beckon her, still disguised as me. She takes in the chaos, her half-packed trousseau, Henry's missing doublet, and the froth of diamond-studded silk on the floor. The wedding dress will be hopelessly wrinkled when we put it back on her. She tuts at the mess, shaking her head.

"History shall record my wedding day as an absolute scandal, and it's all your fault, Jac!"

I roll my eyes, seeing how her sly grin grows. "Oh, hush. This is no worse than the trouble you'd get up to on your own."

When Henry of Navarre and his new queen step out to a chorus of catcalls and cheers, no one pays attention to the lady-in-waiting with the knowing look trailing after them.

No one sees when a palace maid seizes my arm, stopping me from following the newlyweds.

No one notices when my face pales with dread.

"Hello, Jac." Louise smiles down at me, the expression almost friendly. "Seems you've had a busy day."

CHAPTER THIRTY-SIX

N O ONE NOTICES me being led by knifepoint through the palace—not the nobles in their finery dripping with gems and ribbons, nor the servants with their glistening vases of cut flowers.

Everyone's eyes slide from me and Louise like water down a glass. We even go through the crowded banquet hall and still no one stops us. No one questions why a maid would be bullying a lady-in-waiting out into the courtyard.

Noble carriages are still arriving with guests, each one pastel painted and as perfect as a cake.

When Louise pushes me toward the sole grey carriage amid the riot of color, I dig in my heels.

She tuts. "Come now, Jac. Don't be obstinate. Being obedient is one of your very best qualities."

"Where is my oncle?" In all my nightmares about how this would unravel, it was always Oncle who held my arm, always him asking the questions. It's his absence—more than anything else—that makes my knees lock with dread. "Did you hurt him?"

Louise uses magic to hide us from everyone. That much is obvious. And I'm utterly unarmed except for the pendant, and

I don't know how to use it. But perhaps if I get her talking, get her distracted, I could make a run for it. Break her grip on me and shatter her spell along with it.

There are a hundred steps to the bustling stairs where footmen are welcoming visitors into the royal palace. The torches flanking the open doors burn like beacons. Only seconds of running. A hundred steps. Then, safety.

When Louise's illusion falls, she'll be taken by the Valois guards. Questioned by Catherine de' Medici, who will recognize Louise right away for the sorceress she is. The role I failed to notice her playing all these weeks.

Louise laughs. The knife flashes in her hand. "Your oncle is gravely injured. You've broken his heart, Jac."

I leap—but not fast enough.

Plain explodes at my temple. All I see are the Louvre's blue rooftops as I slump into Louise's arms, and then all goes dark.

I wake up in a windowless room. The floor is swept clean, and the faint scent of cooked onions wafts from under the door.

I'm imprisoned.

Or at least I think I am. I rise from the mattress, wincing at how my head swirls with pain, and give the door a good, firm yank.

Nothing happens.

My body goes cold. I bite my lip, trying to fend off my growing panic. My sun pendant is missing. Oncle would not let the Societas Solis kill me without questioning me first. Would he?

The Societas Solis will ask you to place your loyalty to the cause above country, kings, and even kin.

The dreadful words rush back to me with needle-sharp clarity.

Whether I live or die is not even Oncle's call to make.

It's the order's. The magical order I've lied to and double-crossed. The order whose secrecy I violated as soon as I told Henry and Margot about it. If there are any rules left to break, I can't imagine what they are.

I draw in a shuddering breath. Panic catches me in its jaws. Bites down with crushing might.

No one will look for me for hours. Even if Margot and Henry notice I'm gone, they can't leave their wedding banquet to look for me themselves. All they could do is send a servant to check the d'Argenson-Aunis apartments. Would Madame Dupont or Jehan tell them they haven't seen me since before dawn? Or are they in on this? Would they tell the servant I'm fine, that there's no reason to worry about me?

My chest heaves. I brace myself against the wall, black spotting my vision.

Does Oncle know where I am?

A stab goes through my temple. Shame and pain tangled into one wrenching ache. I curl up on the thin mattress, facing the wall, tracing the whorls in the wood in a hopeless effort to anchor my spinning head. I remember how Henry cared for me the last time I was sick like this. How he held my hair and never once made me feel ashamed.

When he discovers me missing, Henry will know something has gone wrong. That he should leave France. But I know he won't go without me because of his stupid oath, his useless honor. He's going to get himself killed because I was careless enough to get caught.

I clamp my eyes tight, the guilt making me even more nauseous.

I've damned him and Margot both, just as much as I've damned myself.

My cell door opens. A trencher clatters and the onion smell grows stronger. My stomach rolls. I'm too weak to even stand.

"I'm not hungry."

The person stays unmoving just beyond the door.

I don't lift my head. I don't want to see who's here. I don't want to see their smug expression, hear taunting words about the hubris of a stupid noblegirl who thought she could defy the Societas Solis and win.

I curl up even smaller and let the darkness take me again.

I'm sitting the next time the door opens.

Louise flashes a tight-lipped smile. "Good. I was to force-feed you, if it came to it."

Force-feeding is good. This means the Societas Solis doesn't want to kill me yet.

I touch the bump on my skull. "You concussed me again. You're lucky I wasn't sicker."

Her mouth twists. "Put your hands where I can see them." She uncorks the flask at her waist and dabs golden ichor on the wound. The pain eases at once. "The divine light has healing powers in small doses."

"What about large doses?" Perhaps the magic can help me escape if I can learn how to use it. *Give me enough time to tell Henry and Margot to leave.*

Louise corks the flask. "The secrets of the divine light are not for the likes of you. Precious few in the Societas Solis study it."

She leans against the wall, taking in my torn bridesmaid gown, the flinty gleam in my eyes. I drop my gaze to the floor to seem less defiant, but the tendons in my hands still tremble angrily.

"I see how Gabriel was so misled by you. You truly do have the makings of a great spy, but not the heart or spirit of one, I'm afraid."

I roll my eyes. "Thanks for the compliment."

"I mean it. Twice now you've discovered what we needed to know with hardly any training."

Twice I've helped the Societas Solis learn something? One is that the murdered boys all share dead King Henry II's royal blood. *What could be the second?* I trace the scar Oncle's knife tore into my flesh, the knotted line where the ichor of the gods stitched it back together not five minutes later.

"What do you mean?" I demand, my insides going cold.

Louise smiles. Like she's glad I asked. "We suspected the king of Navarre mattered. But when you protected him today, when I saw how the princess tore the sautoir from his neck, I knew it was *you* up there instead. And we knew we were right." She cups my bruised jaw, her hand cool. "You showed us exactly what we must do to stop Catherine de' Medici's spell."

I gape, not understanding.

Then the truth runs through me, gutting and devastating.

The Societas Solis exists to stop dark magic at all costs.
Even peace, if needed.

"You plan to assassinate Henry." It's not a question.

Louise's mouth twists ruefully. "It's the only way to be certain Catherine doesn't get him first."

"Please don't." My heart slams against my breastbone. "He's going to leave Paris. Once he's gone, Catherine de' Medici can't get him."

"The Queen Mother's sorcerer is very shrewd. Cosimo probably already planned for a possible escape."

"What about the peace between France and Navarre?" I ask, wheedling, desperate to keep her talking, to see if she spills anything useful. "Why spend so much time and effort to make sure the wedding happened only to kill the bridegroom?"

Louise's sigh is deep and regretful. "The Societas Solis's work is not as simple as mere peace. Sometimes sacrifices must be made to do what's best. Even when it's hard."

My fists clench, teeth gritting. She has the gall to suggest I don't understand sacrifice?

As if I haven't sacrificed my own happiness trying to become the person I thought Oncle would love. As if I have not seen Oncle again and again choosing duty over love, secrecy over honesty.

The Societas Solis's dark magic cursed my family years ago.
But I'm ending the curse now.

I won't let them get Henry.

"When do you plan to kill him?" I say.

Louise laughs prettily and pushes off the wall. "Oh, come

now, Jac. I'm not cruel. I know you care for the king, and it's best you don't know."

When she leaves, I close my eyes and breathe, trying to rein in my galloping heart, my racing thoughts.

Buildings have a language of their own. The creaks and moans tell a story. I hear quiet footsteps, no more than a handful of people at most. There's also the tolling of church bells marking the hours and bursts of distant laughter. Revelers, celebrating the wedding. I'm not far from the Palais du Louvre if I can hear the merrymakers.

I'm still close to Henry.

When the light under the door becomes candlelight, I pound on the door, groaning.

The shadow of boots appears on the other side.

"What is it?" a male voice asks.

"Monsieur, my monthly courses are upon me. Please bring me fresh linens for I have dire need of them!"

He makes a strangled sound. I sigh impatiently. Often, I've wondered if men fear the battlefield less than the mention of a woman's monthly courses. I pound on the door again for good measure. "Please, do hurry!"

I hear stammering, and the boots scamper away.

I'm ready when they return.

When the man steps inside, I step from the wall beside the door, water ewer clutched in both hands, ready to cudgel him into sleep—

The maid turns to me with a gasp.

I swerve at the last second.

Never leave a witness behind. I can hear Oncle's voice in my head admonishing me.

I ignore it.

"My lady!" The white linens tremble in the girl's arms.

I fumble for the sapphire earrings hanging from my ears. I forgot to swap them with Margot, and now a king's ransom is in my hands. "Say you didn't see me, and these and my endless gratitude are yours."

With shocked, wide eyes, she stares at the jewels in her palm. "They say you're his niece." Her throat pulses. "You could've killed me."

My smile is cold. "Fortunately, killing innocent people doesn't run in the family."

Her eyes fly open. She nods once and mimes buttoning her mouth.

I enter the hallway. The building feels empty now, as quiet as a graveyard. I walk quickly, wishing I had thought to ask the girl for her clothes. But there's a shrieking sense in me warning me to move *now* or it'll be too late.

Two people come around the corner talking in low, urgent voices.

I press myself, shadow smooth, into a recessed doorway.

"—just left to kill him—" a man with a horribly familiar voice says as he passes.

The woman beside him clucks her tongue. "Such a shame. He had such promise—"

I turn my head, holding my breath as they pass, the woman's skirts brushing the hem of mine.

Henry.

Someone has gone to kill him.

That's why the building is quiet.

That's why the maid didn't try harder to stop me.

She thinks it's already too late.

Maybe she's right.

I take off flying down the hall, no longer caring who sees me.

I explode from the building into the street.

The Louvre hovers over the grand noble mansions lining the street. I rack my brain for where to go. Weren't Henry's men staying in this area? Is that why the Societas Solis is head-quartered here and not at the apothecary? I take off toward the half-remembered address.

I don't make it far.

A flash of gold in the dying sunlight. Henry. My heart nearly bursts with relief at the sight of him. He hurries away from me, his advisor the Admiral Coligny at his side, both of them bickering.

I hoist my skirts and run. "Henry!"

He turns, stunned. The admiral's face pulls into an ugly grimace.

A brilliant spark behind the men catches my eye. The muzzle of an arquebus, peering from a doorway.

Pointed at Henry.

A scream tears from me.

Henry and the admiral turn around, too slow.

I don't think.

I throw myself in front of Henry as the arquebus sparks from the darkness.

I squeeze my eyes shut. Wait for the bullet.

A spatter of hot wetness.

An agonized shout.

The admiral writhes, clutching the tattered remains of his hand.

Henry shouts, down on his knees.

I glance at the assassin's window, at the pale oval face in the shadows.

Oncle.

He holds the smoking arquebus at an awkward angle, as though he jerked it up at the last second.

Jerked it up to save me.

Our eyes lock for an endless moment, and my entire world turns.

Oncle went to kill Henry though he knows I love him.

Oncle saved me though he was oath-bound not to.

People pour into the street from the magnificent houses. Admiral Coligny barks orders from his spreading pool of blood. Navarrese guards surge into the building where Oncle stands.

Oncle broke his oath to the Societas Solis and shattered his cover with the Valois family for me.

I feel dizzy. There's no coming back from this. The Valois family will know Oncle doesn't work for them, and the Societas Solis will know he can't be trusted.

Oncle will die, and it'll be my fault too, just like everything else.

I take a stumbling step to the window, hand lifted helplessly.

Oncle shakes his head oh so slightly, a wan smile on his

face. He kisses his fingers once, turning them toward me, right as the Navarrese soldiers fall upon him.

Then he's gone.

An angry, gasping sob slips from me. I fall to my knees, heedless of the blood seeping into my skirts.

"Jac."

Henry towers over me, gore spattered and red. I wipe the tears from my cheeks only to leave behind a scarlet smear. The onlookers flinch at the movement.

"The Societas Solis means to kill you before Catherine can. Nowhere here is safe. You *must* leave Paris!"

Admiral Coligny spits. "Don't you listen to this lying creature! She has bewitched you, Your Majesty! The Valois sent her to ruin you!"

Shocked gasps break out among the crowd, all of them Huguenots, anger and suspicion thickening the air in an instant. Henry stares at me, his expression unreadable. His guards circle him.

I see myself as they must: blood spattered and sobbing for a man who tried to kill their king.

Time slows and stops. The Navarrese entourage knows my oncle is the Valois spymaster.

And now my oncle just tried to kill Henry.

The awful truth fills every inch of me

They think the Valois family brought Henry of Navarre here to assassinate him.

Henry gestures to his guards. They step closer, pikes raised. "Take her to my apartments and send for my new queen."

CHAPTER THIRTY-SEVEN

THE FRENCH ROYAL *family tried to kill the king of Navarre at his own wedding.*

I can feel the dark rumors forming beyond this door, scampering down the hall and out racing along the streets. By dawn, all of Paris will know. By tomorrow, the city could balance on the edge of a knife. The slightest jostle would make it fall.

When Henry and Margot enter his guarded office, I start talking.

Henry snorts contemptuously and storms forward, his arms slipping around me. "Never mind that for now. Are *you* well?"

I blink, surprised by his sudden possessiveness, his severe expression.

"You were just—gone, Jac!" Margot says, her hands fisted tight. "I looked for you, but you had vanished. We didn't know—" Her voice catches.

I blink, taken aback by their concern. *It's because they love you.* The thought still feels surreal, something for other people but not for me. *You matter more to them than what you can do for them.*

"I—yes. I'm fine." As fine as anyone can be when their oncle may have started a war.

"Jac." Henry turns my face softly. "Tell us what happened."

So I do. When I'm done, Henry's brow is furrowed deeply. "Why would Catherine de' Medici try to kill me now? I've been in France for months. Why go through all the expense of the wedding to have it be a funeral?"

"Perhaps you had to be married for it to work?" Margot says. "Jac thwarted the spell at the wedding—"

"But the Societas Solis tried to kill me as soon as they knew Catherine de' Medici was after me," Henry says. "If Catherine's only chance to kill me was at the wedding, then why would the Societas Solis still be worried enough to kill me?"

I shrug. "I don't know! The Societas Solis are the only ones with answers, and they know I've betrayed them. They won't share what they know with me now." I hate not having answers. I hate hearing Henry discuss his death so calmly, as if him dying would not kill something in myself.

The air turns restlessly. The tinny sound of glass shattering somewhere else sends Henry jerking toward the window, vigilant as a watchdog.

"My oncle might know," I say. After all, there's more than one traitor to the Societas Solis in the Louvre's walls.

Margot scoffs, crossing her arms. "He had you kidnapped!"

But that's not all he did.

I'll never forget our eyes locking across the street, the smoking arquebus barrel, the tang of blood on the hot cobblestones.

He spared my life when he shouldn't have.

Which, yes, is a rather low bough, but it's one I'll reach for anyway. I don't have much else to grab.

"I don't think we have a better plan." But by God, I wish we did! I can't hold back the daunting, childish fear surging at the thought of Oncle's disappointment. I'm nervous, even after all this, afraid of his flashing eyes and his fickle approval.

He told me I was never enough.

But he saved my life.

Was there something in me worth saving after all?

Or did he just do it out of obligation to my dead mother?

Henry steps behind me and pulls my back against his chest. His warmth chases the chill away, pulls me back from my dark thoughts. "You won't go alone. We'll go together."

I was wrong about Henry's oath. I don't need someone to handle my big battles, but I need help to fend off the small ones like these. The tiny cuts that bleed until I'm exhausted.

I nod once, my throat swelling closed. "Together."

He tucks my hair behind my ear, presses his lips against my cheek. "Always."

I've never seen the dungeons of the Palais du Louvre. They're tucked in the bones of the old medieval keep the old French kings tore down for the glittering palace of today: a reminder of when there was more blood than beauty in the royal halls. Each descending step grows colder and colder, until it feels more like autumn than summer, and I draw my simple cloak more tightly around myself.

A guard dressed in Catherine de' Medici's somber black

stands at the end of a corridor filled with flickering torches. He holds out a hand.

"You cannot come any closer."

Henry hesitates, but then his shoulders rise. "I'm the king of Navarre. My brother-in-law, the king of France, gave me free rein of his home. You must stand aside."

The guard's throat bobs nervously. "Please don't ask me to disobey my lady's orders."

"Go back. Let me handle this," Henry murmurs to me. He turns to the guard with a jolly laugh, the sound near offensive in the quiet. "My good soldier, if a man tried to take your life, would you not wish to question? Isn't that my right as the wronged party?"

The guard's hands tighten on his pike. "Monsieur, please, I can't go against my orders!"

I retreat step by step, mind whirring. It's strange that Henry would be barred from the dungeons. Stranger still that his access would be barred by one of Catherine de' Medici's own guards and not one of the Valois family's guards. This means Catherine herself, not King Charles, has forbidden anyone from seeing Oncle.

He knows something she doesn't want people to know.

Henry and the guard argue in earnest now, Henry laughing and needling, the guard sweating and begging. I backtrack until I find the pot I saw abandoned on the stairs.

I return to Henry and the guard, eyes downcast. Margot made me change before we left, and the plainness of my dress almost passes as a maid's uniform.

"Pardon me, messieurs, the Queen Mother has asked for a chamber pot for the prisoner."

Surprise ripples through Henry at my implication that Catherine de' Medici is with Oncle. But of course she must be, for why else would she post one of her own guards down here, trembling and alone, to turn away all who would come, including a king?

The guard blinks, his grip loosening ever so slightly.

"You may go ahead. But you, monsieur, please, you must leave!"

Henry huffs and crosses his arms as I slip past. "I shall return within the hour, and mark my word, if you still deny me passage, the king of France will hear of this. . . ."

Their conversation fades as I hurry around a bend in the corridor. With each step the shadows grow larger, sprout teeth and talons. A jumbled pile of ivory sticks gone yellow flashes in my periphery. I rush faster, hairs rising all along my arms.

The dungeons are not a place anyone returns from.

There's a murmuring up ahead, and when I turn another corner, a horribly familiar voice becomes clear.

". . . ask again, shall I? Who do you truly work for? You've lied to the Valois family for too long. Tell me or your leg shall be forfeit."

Catherine de' Medici, her black skirts melting into the darkness, a single candle in hand.

Oncle groans. "Why would you flirt with war by killing the king of Navarre? Don't deny it. I know you want to kill the boy. I know about your dark magic—"

A wet crunch sounds. I clap a hand over my mouth. Oncle gasps in short, hard bursts. Catherine talks over his agony, voice cool and pleasant. "I need to kill the Navarrese king because I have seen the future. Henry de Bourbon will take my son's crown if he's not stopped now. There's only one king in France worthy of sitting on our throne."

The Valois line will end when the Seine runs red.

I think of King Charles's cruelty, how his only interest is his own pleasures. After all this time, Catherine de' Medici still believes in her son?

Or does she fear losing her own power if he's ousted from his throne?

"Using dark magic won't save your son or the Valois legacy," Oncle says firmly. "If King Charles succumbs to his illness, it is the natural way of—"

"Enough! If you won't tell me who you work for, I'll find your niece and perhaps she can help you talk. I know you've hidden her. Mark my words, I *will* find her, and you'll wish she were dead before I'm done with her."

I flatten against the farthest corner of the empty cell moments before Catherine de' Medici passes, her candle highlighting the angry lines of her face in a fierce orange light.

Her footsteps still echo when I get to Oncle. He sits braced against the wall, leg bent at an unnatural angle out before him.

There's a vial in his hand. Something that looks horribly like—

I bolt forward. "No, wait!"

Oncle freezes, poison a hairbreadth from his lips. "You're not supposed to be here."

"Then perhaps you should have hired better kidnappers." I fall to my knees, at his eye level. "I can fix things if you help. Please trust me."

Slowly, Oncle tucks the bottle back into his doublet. He laughs. "You, fixing things! You stopped me from fixing this when you saved Henry from my bullet. Now Catherine will kill him and use his death to usher in some unspeakable evil. If you think she plans to let him leave Paris alive, then you're even more foolish than I thought."

His disapproval stings like a slap. I dig my nails into my skin, biting back the urge to apologize. I'm finished apologizing for things that aren't my fault. "There must be a way forward that doesn't involve Henry dying."

Oncle scoffs. "If there were, don't you think the Societas Solis would've tried that first?"

I grit my teeth, his words stirring my anger. "I stopped someone from killing Henry thrice already—"

"Only twice. I should have succeeded the third time." The words hang low and heavy between us. The burst of the bullet, the spray of blood. It should be my blood darkly staining his front, mine and Henry's both. The most dangerous man in France was undone at the last instant with a shot that he shouldn't have missed.

I grip the bars tightly. "Why did you hesitate?" I need to know. More than I've ever needed to know anything in my life. "You said that kin doesn't matter to the Societas Solis. Taking your vow means leaving family behind."

Oncle sighs, the sound like a death rattle. "I lied, Jac." He tilts his head back, eyes closed. "You are the most important thing in the world to me. The moment you were in my arms, I knew one day you'd be my undoing. I've regretted the vow I made to the Societas Solis every day of your life. I lied to you again and again to protect you." With a shuddering groan, he leans forward, cold fingers slipping over mine. "I've always loved you."

Everything in me suddenly feels too small. My heart, my lungs, all of it. The wall could crack and fall into the river and I would still be rooted to the spot, too spellbound to move, too stuck to save myself.

"Why did you never tell me?" I whisper.

He holds up his signet ring. "You know how the magic binds. I couldn't tell you anything. I could only warn you away from making the same mistakes I did." His head snaps up, stare furious. "But you could never listen! I should've sent you away as soon as you were old enough. It was selfish of me to keep you close. You never belonged with me."

The words would have once devastated me. Served as confirmation of my pathetic, mewling fear. I was right after all. Oncle didn't want me around. I have been a burden to him.

But now they anger me. I finally understand the dark threads that bind his hands, bought his silence, but I refuse to be blamed for them.

My fingers curl more tightly around the bars, rough metal biting. "No, why did you never tell me you loved me? Why did you always put the Societas Solis first? My entire life, all I ever wanted was a kind word or a scrap of your attention. But you were so cold and distant. Sometimes I wondered if you cared at all."

Oncle bows his head. He draws each breath so slowly, I wonder if he's hiding another injury, a weeping mortal wound.

But then I realize he's crying.

When he finally speaks again, his voice is a rough rasp. "Then I have failed as your oncle and protector both. God protect me from your mother's shade on the other side."

A damp wind moans down the hall. The torches flicker and spit. We must be riverside, the mighty Seine lapping the stone nearby. I sit with the silence, let it twist and curl.

Oncle has always loved me in his rough, brusque way.

He has always loved me, but he could never tell me. Not in a way that I could feel.

It's the saddest, loneliest thing I can think of.

Love doesn't have limits, but there are limits to what others can accept of love. My oncle has been miserly with love, doling it out a few coins at a time from a beaten old purse. I went hungry, wanting more of it. I wanted him to be more for me than he was capable of being.

I can't forgive him for it. But I understand him better now. Perhaps one day that understanding can lead to something else. Something more.

"You haven't failed me yet. There's still one thing you can do to help me."

He lifts his tearstained face. "I will do anything you ask."

"Tell me the spell Catherine de' Medici seeks to cast with Henry's blood."

It's a gamble, a guess, but when Oncle's eyes fly open, I know I'm right. It doesn't matter that I tore the cursed sautoir from Henry's neck. Whatever spell the Queen Mother has woven is almost finished, waiting for one final splash of blood.

The Societas Solis thought it was already too late for Henry. Killing him was a last resort.

Oncle moans, dragging a hand through his tangled hair. "Ah, Niece, ask me anything but that! It's too dangerous."

"Please. Trust me enough to let me try. You taught me how to be my own protector."

His mouth presses into a white line. I make no move to school my features into something soft and dutiful, no effort to hide my desperate want. If he won't answer me, then everything I want is already gone.

Oncle leans forward, whispering, even though there's not a soul around us. *"Ex sanguinis cordique regii monarcha vivat."*

May the monarch live from the blood and the heart of the king.

I shudder at the words, how they wrap across my shoulders like a clammy arm.

"And this spell takes Henry's life and gives it to King Charles?"

"In theory, yes. But spells are fickle. A wrong word or interpretation from the sorcerer can make the entire spell turn on them."

"Can I stop the spell if the words have already been spoken?"

Oncle shrugs, shaking his head. "If it can be stopped at all—and I don't think it can—I would try destroying the physical element of the spell. Catherine de' Medici practices her dark magic in a workshop under the palace. The entrance is hidden in her private apartments. Whatever you do, don't let the king of Navarre set foot in that place. Otherwise his death can be used to finish the spell. And be careful, Jac! Defying death is a monsterous, unnatural magic. The Societas Solis fears the dark promises Catherine de' Medici may have made with creatures beyond the veil to do this. There could be worse things in her lair than Cosimo Ruggeri."

I kiss his hand. "Thank you, a thousand times thank you, Oncle. If you—if you escape, come find me in Navarre. There'll be space for you there."

Oncle laughs, the sound a hollow scrape. "We both know there's no escaping for me. I always knew protecting you would be my end." His gaze holds mine, serious and soft all at once. "I have many regrets, but that isn't one of them."

I want to tell him he's lying, that it's not too late, but my throat closes tight around the words. I'm not as good at lying as I used to be. "Like I said, Henry and I will keep space for you."

He sucks in a quiet breath. "You truly love him, then?"

"I do." I give him a long, measured look, trying not to smile. "I didn't appreciate you trying to kill him."

Oncle smiles and tugs his sun signet ring from his thumb. Pushes it through the bars. "The divine light in this might help you. Only unleash it when all hope is gone. The magic has a mind of its own and might do more harm than good."

I move to take it from him, but he pulls it back, eyes dark and serious. "I cannot emphasize enough how dire the stakes are. We might be dueling with magic, but to France and Navarre it looks like I tried to kill King Henry during his wedding fete.

Starting another war would be easier than drawing a breath."

His words are heavy. They sink down into the deepest part of me. I bow my head, a chevalier to his king. "I will do everything in my power to prevent war."

A razor-thin smile dances across his face. He presses the ring into my palm. "France may yet stand a chance, then. God keep you safe. I pray we see each other again in this life before the next."

I grab his hand one last time. I don't try to stop the tears from rolling down my cheeks. "I'll make you proud, I swear."

Oncle brushes my cheek with bloody knuckles, his smile the softest thing I've ever seen. "You already have a hundred times over, Daughter."

CHAPTER THIRTY-EIGHT

Y MOTHER'S HIDDEN workshop?" Margot repeats my question, eyebrows rising. "If I had known about *my mother's magical workshop*, don't you think I would've mentioned it by now?"

"Can you get me into your mother's apartments to look for it?" I ask, voice tight.

I don't know how much time we have left.

Every quarter-hour chime of the bells feels like a count-down to some dark, dire fate. Henry has been stuck in end-less meetings with his remaining advisors since we returned. I wish he were here even though Oncle's instructions were clear. *Don't let the king of Navarre set foot in that place.* Whatever comes next, Margot and I must face it alone.

Oncle's sun signet ring weighs heavy on a slender chain beneath my bodice. How much time does he have left?

Is there still a chance to save him?

When I came up from the dungeons, Henry held me for as long as he could. He went to his people with my tears on his velvets, the salt staining them white.

Margot's expression softens. "We'll go this evening. My mother has gone to pay respects to my father at Saint-Denis."

I frown. Saint-Denis is a cathedral beyond the city walls, the royal crypt of the French kings. It isn't strange for Catherine de' Medici to go there, but it is strange that she would go now, when the tension betwixt two kingdoms is so taut, it seems a single finger flick could ignite war.

"You're certain she'll be gone tonight?" I say.

Her mouth twists wryly. "Trust me. My father is still her favorite of us all. She'd rather spend time with the dead than the living."

I wait for Margot at the appointed hour in the corridor outside her mother's apartments with downcast eyes, dressed as a maid. While the Queen Mother may be gone, her doors are still guarded and locked. Margot will need to make a show to get us inside to look around.

Late as usual, Margot tears around the corner in a swirl of sapphires and lace.

"You!" she snaps, pointing at me. "Come with me. I have need of you."

The chamberlain outside the Queen Mother's door straightens to wakefulness at Margot's furious approach. His eyes widen, and he hurriedly stoops into a low bow.

"Why, madame, how may I be of service—"

Margot interrupts him with regal fury, just as we had discussed. "You can serve me by letting me inside to find the necklace promised to me as part of my dowry! When I dressed this evening, the jewel was not among my things."

She clasps her bare throat, which does indeed look naked considering all the other gemstones dripping from her bodice, arms, fingers, and ears. I hide a laugh behind a cough. There isn't a sapphire in all of France that won't be pressed into Margot's service tonight.

The chamberlain blinks owlishly. "Are you certain? The Queen Mother doesn't wish for others to enter her rooms without her permission, and I fear—"

Margot stamps her foot. The candelabras catch the light of her gems in the movement, scattering dazzling scintillations everywhere. "Do you accuse me of not knowing where my things are? I may be queen of Navarre but I'm still a princess of France, and I demand my bride gift!"

The chamberlain cringes, wincing at how Margot's voice carries down the hall. She has put him in a cruel position. Deny the princess's request, and others shall nod and agree that he defied the royal Valois will. Allow the princess inside, and they shall agree that he broke the Queen Mother's decree in her absence. I watch the debate play out in his pained eyes, watch him decide.

It's best to listen to the queen before you than the queen who is elsewhere.

He bows and unlocks the door with the key tied at his waist. "Of course, madame. Please forgive this inexcusable delay."

"I'll think about it." Margot tosses her haughty head and sweeps inside. She demands I follow with a snap of her fingers, not even looking.

The door shuts behind us.

Catherine de' Medici's private apartments are grander than

Margot's, by far the grandest place I have been in the Louvre. The Valois blue covers the walls, the plush rugs, and even the upholstery of the exquisitely carved chairs in her vast parlor. Sparing no glance for the astounding beauty, Margot begins moving the heavy furniture away from the walls. I hurry to help her.

"You'd never guess she's Italian given all this," I say, peeling back a tapestry woven with French fleur-de-lis.

"She loved my father even though he was an unfaithful husband and a middling king." Margot stops looking behind a large mirror and glances up. The ceiling is painted charcoal and white with a pattern of skulls, spades, and feathers flanking the intertwined initials of Catherine and her dead husband. Where most queens would paint their ceilings with visions of heaven, the Queen Mother has painted hers with reminders of death. How many meetings with her advisors has she held here, beneath the shadow of a dead man?

Sudden movement startles me. I flinch, spotting my wide-eyed face in the mirror—a dark, heavy thing, out of place amid the blue and silver splendor. I lay my hand on the glass to hide my tired reflection.

The mirror unexpectedly swings upside down, revealing a stone stairway beyond.

I swallow and take a step back, fighting the animal instinct to run. The yawning darkness is thicker than it has any right to be. I can't shake the unnerving image of that mirrored door slamming shut behind me and locking me down there forever. I'm not afraid of closed-in spaces, but this passage feels so hair-raisingly *wrong*.

To step beyond that threshold is to step into a world that only existed in myth and fable. I know whatever I see beyond this point will change me forever.

Oncle was right. Magic doesn't only live in superstition. It's real and right here, in the bedchamber of the most powerful person in all of France.

"God Almighty," I whisper, crossing myself.

Margot turns, her lovely face a mess of confusion. "What's wrong?"

I glance from the stairs to Margot. "You see nothing there?"

She shakes her head, face growing pale. "It's just the wall, Jac. I already looked behind it."

My hand goes to my throat. Slowly, I pull up Oncle's ring from its slender chain.

The ring glows with an eerie, eldritch light.

Margot draws in a sharp breath. "Is that—"

"The divine light, ichor of gods, the thing currently ruining all our lives?" I place the ring in my palm and hold it out to Margot. "It reveals illusions. Take my hand and see."

Tentatively, Margot laces her fingers through mine.

And gasps.

She shakes, pulling away, blinking eyes huge with fear. "I saw the stairs."

We consider the long, dark tunnel, thinking the same things. How we used to run rampant through the Palais du Louvre and its grounds, so certain we had found all its secrets.

We were so certain of everything back then.

"You don't have to come with me," I say, even though going down alone is the last thing I want to do.

Margot swallows and clasps my hand again. This time, her touch is steady.

"When I was a child, I always imagined the pathway to hell was a staircase. Our priest was filled with fire and brimstone and encouraged my fear. I was so frightened hell was a place you could go to by accident, not knowing where you descended until it was too late," Margot says.

"He sounds like an inspiring priest."

She snorts. "Mother had him dismissed because she was tired of our nightmares." Her head tilts, her lips twisted in that mischievous smirk that heralded so many of our foolish, dangerous schemes. "What say you? Shall we go down together?"

I squeeze her hand with as much strength as I can muster, my throat tightening. "There's no one else I would want to go to hell with."

Margot laughs and places her gilded slipper on the first step. "Let's see what the devil looks like."

The stairs twist downward for a long, long time. I try to count our steps but quickly lose track. Are we even still on the Louvre grounds? Or are we somewhere far beyond, deep in the heart of Paris? There's no light save the ring's haunting glow between our sweaty palms. Our journey is silent, each of us lost in our own thoughts. I graze the dagger sheathed at my waist and hope it's enough for both of us. I wish I'd thought to arm myself more thoroughly. I wish I had thought to ask Oncle more questions. And—something in me grows small and scared at the very thought—I wish I had said goodbye to Henry.

I don't notice the door until it's right in front of us.

"Jac." Margot tugs me back to her.

It's just a door, made of plain wooden slats and banded with iron.

A key already lies in the keyhole.

I've seen hundreds of doors like this before. Doors to stables and doors to storerooms. Doors to stacked cellars and doors to secret rooms in apothecaries that are not what they seem.

Even still, at the sight of this door, a scream rises in my throat. Every nerve shrieks to flee, to turn around and forget any of this was here at all.

I reach a trembling hand toward the key and turn it.

The door swings open noiselessly on well-oiled hinges.

The room beyond is all cavernous darkness. The shadows snatch away our ring's dim light.

"Hold on." Margot releases my hand and steps inside.

"Come back here!" I cry, terrified of what might happen if she's not at my side.

She waves something before me. "I found it!"

Thrice there's the sound of flint striking stone, and then a candle fizzles to light before Margot's pleased face. "Mother always insists on keeping a candle close. She says the servants are too slow when she calls for them. Come now, let's go."

The area is shaped like a catacomb, all small, stony rooms

with sloped ceilings, each one leading to the next. For all I know we might very well be in some church's catacombs, the priest wholly unsuspecting that the hallowed ground of his holy place hosts dark magic.

Some of the rooms are empty, but many of them are not. One is filled entirely with astrolabes, another with orreries. With each chamber we pass through, Margot uses her candle to light the half-melted ones already there.

The extra light isn't reassuring. One area I had assumed empty is full of shelves holding canopic jars filled with organs. We both nearly scream when the candle reveals a wall of grinning skulls.

"What is this place?" Margot demands, almost angrily, as she drags me into the next room. This one is lined with books, all books save the desk with its inkwell and quills. "What's my mother doing down here? What does her life lack? Was being queen not enough for her?"

I want to take her wrist, to remind her that I know what it's like to uncover a parent's dark lies, but there's no time. "My oncle said to destroy whatever we find."

Margot nods, her nostrils quivering. "Let's get to it, then."

We smash the strange instruments against the walls and tear pages from the books. The only room we leave undisturbed is the one filled with canopic jars, each of us too afraid to disturb the remains of the dead. I wince at the noise, but Margot doesn't care. She even hovers over the torn books with her candle until I remind her that starting a fire belowground would suffocate us.

"Fine!" she snaps, abandoning the books with a huff. In the faint light, I see one page has the body of a man with the skin flayed open, his insides all rendered in vivid detail. I cringe away. "Let's keep going."

The next room is the largest one yet, four men tall and four men wide. It contains nothing but a draped bundle on a slab of marble in the very center. A long, jagged breath tears from my lungs.

It looks like a body.

Margot freezes, her bravado all gone. "Do you think . . . ?"

I swallow hard. "Yes."

She nods slowly, what color she has left leaving her cheeks. "Then I suppose we should see who it is."

The walk to the body feels longer than the whole walk down here, hours to cross a single room.

Margot sets her candle on the lip of the slab. Her hand in mine begins to tremble.

A breathless whisper. "Together?"

I nod, my words all caught in my throat.

We peel back the shroud from the face.

A man of middle age, his parched pale skin gone grey and tight over his skull, the eyes long sunken into the space behind. His too-long teeth are bared in an eternal grin, the lips having shrunk back from the bone. He's been dead for quite some time, skin papered over jutting bone. It looks like a single touch would make his flesh crumble to dust.

A shuddering breath escapes me, chasing away my light-headedness. Long dead is better than newly dead. We must be in some church's catacombs after all. Maybe the man's family has asked the priest to rebury him. Perhaps that's all there is to it.

Margot cries softly.

I turn to her, and my relief dies as I see how she trembles, how tears cling to her eyelashes and her mouth drops open in a silent scream. Even still, she leans closer to the corpse's face, a shaking finger nearly tracing one sunken cheek.

"Father?"

Her whisper is a thunderclap.

I jerk backward, like I've seen something I shouldn't. As if I'm staring rudely.

King Henry II has been dead for years. He is buried at Saint-Denis, well outside the wall of Paris, in a gallant crypt with a carved marble sarcophagus of his powerful body with his sword in hand. He wouldn't be here uncovered and alone in the dark of some nameless catacomb. Where is his crown? Where is his kingly cloak, his casket? Margot must be mistaken.

If King Henry II's body went missing, we would've known. Catherine de' Medici would scream and rend her hair. She would send all the soldiers of France away to find him. She would—

An eerie moan gusts through the tunnels, blowing out the candles behind us one by one until only Margot's remains.

The floor shudders beneath our feet.

And then, the dead eyes roll beneath their shrunken lids, popping up and opening.

The greyed-out orbs latch on to our faces. Something twitches beneath the shroud.

A force throws me to the ground.

Margot screams.

Our final candle sputters out.

CHAPTER THIRTY-NINE

SCRAMBLE FOR MY dagger, too slow. Something wrenches my wrist behind my back. I cry out. Soon my other hand joins the first, a rope slipped around them.

Margot's screams begin anew. There's a scramble of movement—the candle falls, hot wax splatters my skin—and then she lands roughly beside me, also bound.

Oncle's ring is missing. I search for it frantically, twisting my neck, wriggling in my bonds until—there it is! A faint glowing ember against the wall.

From the darkness comes a slow, languorous clap.

"Very, very good, *ragazza*. You were far more destructive than I expected."

A murmur, and then every candle whooshes to life.

I gasp at the sudden brightness, blinking against the pain of the light after so much shadow.

Cosimo Ruggeri, Catherine de' Medici's sorcerer, stands before us, which is no surprise at all.

But what is a surprise is the black-clad and masked figure beside him. The assassin who tried to kill Henry that night in the Paris streets.

The one I dealt a mortal blow.

Very much alive.

The masked face tilts, birdlike. He takes a step toward me.

Cosimo pats the assassin like he's performed a marvelous trick. "Ah, yes, you dealt my poor pet a dreadful wound. That was very rude of you."

"But I *killed* him," I say numbly. There's a handkerchief tied around the neck wound I dealt him. As if it was nothing more than a scrape.

"Yes, you did." He runs a finger down the assassin's shoulder. "But this is no mortal man."

The sorcerer doesn't look well. He appears to have aged years since I saw him right before the royal wedding. His hair has grown sparse, and his beard has gone completely grey. Lines carve deep valleys across his face. Even his robe hangs looser, his figure gaunt and skeletal beneath it.

Cosimo takes in my look and smiles, revealing the bright red gums of a dire disease. "I'll forgive you, Jacqueline d'Argenson-Aunis, because you brought me exactly what I needed."

His hand creeps up the assassin's arm to the vizard mask. Then he yanks it off.

Margot screams bloody murder.

The assassin is unmistakably dead, greyed-out eyes staring at nothing. Its skin is loose, sloughed off in parts, jagged and missing in others. It reminds me of slimy things that lurk under damp rocks.

"Chevaliers make the best revenants. Even in death, the body seems to remember its battle skill," Cosimo says conversationally, a tutor with his pupils. He prods the corpse, and it lurches forward, sending Margot into another scream. "I made this one to kill the king of Navarre."

I was right about that night on the Parisian streets. The assassin *was* only targeting Henry. Its unnatural strength and speed, its single-minded viciousness: it all makes sense now.

Catherine de' Medici and Cosimo created and compelled a revenant to kill the king of Navarre.

"It was you digging up the bodies outside Chenonceau," I realize.

"And it was you who stole my little book," Cosimo says sullenly. "That was also very naughty of you. My mistress was most vexed with me."

"What do you want from us?" I demand boldly, lifting my chin. I'm glad he tied my hands so he can't see how they tremble.

He grins wider, the expression more haunting than everything else I've seen down here. "Why, the blood of a king, of course."

There is only one king in France worthy of sitting on the throne.

That's what Catherine de' Medici said to Oncle. We assumed she thought of her son Charles.

But we were wrong.

She spoke of her dead husband.

The king she has mourned for nearly fifteen years as if he had died just yesterday. Certainty, cold and heavy, settles into my bones like stone. This was never about King Charles's life.

"Yes, indeed. You have brought me the last thing I need to bring His Highness back to the throne. Royal blood."

I think of the poor dead boys, Henry II's royal bastards who did nothing and suffered so much for the sin of their father's wandering eye. Anger roars in me, as hot and explosive as gunpowder. I wrench my body upright, planting myself before Margot and the grisly sight of her long-slain parent.

Cosimo rocks backward.

I lift my chin even higher. "I see no kings here."

He smiles again, the expression more sinister than before. "The blood of a king is all well and good, but the blood of a queen will do just as nicely."

The undead assassin falls on us again. Margot screams as its dead, clammy fingers tie her ankles together.

I leap—Oncle's ring is right there, just behind the sorcerer—but the assassin kicks me to the ground again, unnaturally fast. It seizes my bound hands and drags me away. I scream, vision spotting white with pain as my joints strain, almost popping from their sockets. It throws me against a vertical support beam and lashes my hands to the wood. The ceiling sags ominously above me, the beam already fissured with cracks.

"The blood of a king is best just to be safe, but the Latin *regii* can refer to either a king or queen."

Cosimo snaps his fingers. The assassin hauls a howling Margot to the room's center, just beneath her dead father's feet. She turns and spits at Cosimo, angry, hate-filled tears streaking down her cheeks. "You'll regret killing me. My mother tasked you with this evil work, but I'm still her daughter."

Cosimo tuts disapprovingly. He glances at the spittle which has landed far from his boots and drops a finely embroidered handkerchief on it. "When did I speak of killing you, *piccola regina*?"

The assassin lumbers back with a jar filled with a gross writhing darkness.

Leeches.

Bile surges in my throat as Cosimo plucks out the thick bloodsucking creatures and places them all over Margot's bare arms. She thrashes, but to no avail. There are too many of them. Their sucking, greedy mouths eagerly latch on to her skin no matter how many she squashes.

I clench my jaw so hard, pain spikes through my skull. There was no making this right. I brought Catherine de' Medici exactly what she needed. I blink away the angry tears gathering in my eyelashes, the tiny spark in the opposite corner like a secret wink.

Oncle's ring is still here.

The Queen Mother knows Oncle has betrayed her, but he never told her he worked for the Societas Solis.

Does she know about the divine light, the ichor of the gods?

Could it stop this?

Oncle warned me not to use the ring unless the stakes were dire. I can't imagine anything more dire than this.

Cosimo lays kindling on a spiked brazier. When the flames catch, he begins chanting. The fire dances and grows taller. He feeds something grey and small into the flames. Then he mutters in Latin and does it again. By the third time, I realize with a burst of horror it's the dry, dead hearts.

Then he moves to Margot.

She screams and kicks, catching Cosimo's knee. He stumbles, the joint making a wet snapping sound, but it doesn't stop him. He tears the fat leeches from Margot until they're both covered with a fine crimson mist.

"*Ex sanguinis cordique regii monarcha vivat!*"

With that final, terrible invocation, he tosses the blood-filled leeches into the fire.

An awful cry tears from Margot's throat.

The writhing bodies burst in the flames, showering the embers with her blood.

The world stills. Stops.

Nothing happens.

Cosimo's nostrils flare with each ragged breath. He turns his gaunt stare to Margot. Then he's over her in two angry steps, grabbing her chin with bony fingers. "What sort of witchery is this, *piccola regina*?"

Margot's breaths come in raw bursts. White rings her terrified eyes. They meet mine for a single second.

I go stone-still with understanding.

Margot was betrothed to Henry, but she didn't marry him. *I* did.

I stood before all of Paris, under her name, in her clothes, while a priest proclaimed my vows for the king of Navarre. Legally, this is no marriage.

But what laws govern magic?

Love and marriage are the same, Henry said to me once.

Perhaps that's also true for magic.

Cosimo whips toward me. He takes in my long, dark hair, my dark eyes, how similar they are to Margot's.

He straightens and claps again. I cringe at each slap of dry flesh.

"Well, well! My mistress will be very upset when she learns about this. What a greedy girl you are, taking things that aren't yours."

The leeches are slimy and wet. I don't feel their bite, but I see how they suckle, how their bodies grow fat and bloated with my blood. I gag and heave at their disgusting touch, but only bile comes up. Cosimo tears them off ruthlessly, each wound stinging so fiercely, I scream.

He repeats the final words of the incantation one last time and tosses the leeches into the fire.

This time, with each bursting, blood-filled body, the flames burn slower, shift darker, black-red—the darkness of blood in the farthest reaches of the body. Shadows appear in the fire. A clawed hand. A sharp-toothed mouth.

I feel the boom of the midnight bells in my bones, all of Paris's clocks with their two hands pointing straight up at the full moon.

Cosimo's fevered eyes bore into King Henry II's body.

The body twitches. Once, twice. Then jerks.

Then it explodes into movement.

CHAPTER FORTY

OSIMO HITS THE wall with a wet crunch. He crumples. The undead king rushes me next, roaring, eyes two ghastly grey lights. He swings a vambraced arm. I flatten to the floor.

His blow breaks the beam above my head. I squeeze my eyes shut against the hail of splinters and stones. Then there's a crash behind me.

The room is a haze of dust. The king's momentum carried him into the wall and shattered the stone. Another crack appears as I watch. A trickle of gravel begins to pour from overhead.

The room is going to collapse.

Panic floods me. I scramble upright and slip my bound hands over the snapped support beam.

The king charges from the dusty shadows, roaring once more.

I drop to the floor with a whimper. I'm free, but my hands are still bound and he's so fast. How am I supposed to get past him? How do I get Margot?

The king stops. His head whips back and forth, gruesome eyes never blinking. More of the stone wall collapses with a crash. The undead king charges the slide, bellowing.

His movement eddies away a cloud of dust, revealing Margot still bound on the floor, her body curled around the marble plinth. A cut bleeds sluggishly beneath one of her eyes. Her face wears the intense expression I only see when she debates philosophy. She mouths, *"It only senses movement."*

I crane my head toward the lumbering creature, now standing unnaturally still, face inches from the crumbling wall. The stones had stopped sliding.

My heart pounding so hard I fear it'll give me away, I wriggle toward a sharp bit of broken stone. Biting my lip, I start to saw the rope binding my wrists.

The rope begins to fray.

Another groaning rockslide, another roar as the king assails the wall, doubtless hastening its collapse.

I saw faster, sweat trickling down my brow. One by one the threads snap, but not fast enough.

The last thread snaps just as the undead king notices me.

I roll to the side. A gauntleted fist slams into the ground right beside me. I gape at the cracks radiating out from the blow.

The undead king fists his hands and roars right in my face. I cry and wrench away. This close, the sound has an uncanny keening high note in it, a sound not of this world. Something I more feel than hear.

I twist again. Another blow lands where I was. Then I'm on my knees, dagger in my hand.

The king reaches out to grab me but I'm already running.

"Margot, free yourself!" I kick a jagged bit of rubble toward her. She catches it with her bound hands. The king storms after me, teeth gnashing. Each of his footsteps sends the entire room shuddering. The broken wall finally collapses.

A vinegar stench floods the air. The wall fell into the room of the canopic jars, all of them shattering and spilling their preserved organs.

I run up the pile of rubble, the king charging after me. He gets stuck in the wreckage as I hoped. I backtrack to Margot and slice through the bonds on her ankles.

"Jac!" she screams, terrified eyes on something behind me.

A tug on my skirts and then I'm swinging weightlessly, the floor below me.

I spin in midair until I'm face-to-face with the undead king.

There is no light of recognition in his stare, no feeling in the rotting face. No one would mistake this being for a living creature, despite its man shape. The only thing about it that echoes the old king is the tarnished armor with its royal Valois emblems. Everything underneath has gone threadbare and rotten.

Catherine de' Medici's dream of France's one true king is a nightmare made of dust and bone.

The king puts his revolting face to mine and shouts. His breath smells of grave dirt, the rush of air as stale as a coffin and as cold as autumn. I grit my teeth against the foulness, shoving down the part of me that wants to scream back, and thrust my dagger with all my strength.

It pierces his right temple, easy as a spoon into an eggshell, a boot through the thinnest ice. There's hardly any resistance.

The dead face doesn't react. Hideous fear chokes me.

He can't be killed, just like the assassin.

And he's still holding me.

I thrash, laces and seams digging into my flesh. Something rips, and I drop lower with a sob. The king's other hand inches forward. Moves to crush my skull, have it burst like a full, ripe grape.

This is how it ends. Worse than Oncle feared, worse than anything I could imagine.

I gave Catherine de' Medici exactly what she needed.

How fitting that I'll be her first victim.

His fingers wrap around the back of my skull—

"Father!"

His head snaps to Margot. She stands in the corner, picking up shattered bricks and throwing them again and again against the wall.

"Over here, you great giant oaf!"

He charges at her. I drop six feet to the ground, hip first. A pained hiss slips through my teeth.

The king gathers speed with each lumbering step until he runs at Margot like an enraged bull.

But the Valois princess isn't the finest dancer in France without merit. She pirouettes at exactly the right moment.

The undead king misses her and slams into the wall even harder than before.

Goes through it.

A thundering crash, and then I'm squinting against the sudden light, the peach sky beyond. We are indeed in the city of Paris, and dawn is rising, transforming the dust billowing out from the broken wall into a gilded cloud. The undead king lifts his head in the sunlight, nostrils quivering.

Then the screams begin.

With a roar, the undead monarch gallops away, disappearing.

Catherine de' Medici's monstrous king is wild in the streets of Paris.

My hands press over my mouth. I'm too horrified to scream, too horrified to move even as the Parisians' confused cries reach me.

My God, what have we done?

What have *I* done, with the strange royal magic in my veins?

Margot helps me up. Her splendid gown is torn and grey with dirt, only the smudged facets of her sapphires still bright.

"Jac, we must leave. We've got to warn the palace."

We both flinch at a distant bloodcurdling scream, the roar that follows, and—my gut sinks—the clamor of battle. No mortal man stands a chance against the undead king. I shake my head and grab Margot's trembling arms. "We've got to warn *everyone*."

Our eyes lock for an endless moment. Then she nods and steadies, gripping my arms with renewed strength. "All right."

A faint wet cough distracts us. The sorcerer.

We scramble back into the ruins through the settling dust to find Cosimo. He sits where he fell, a damp starburst of blood behind him. I kneel to his level, my dagger hand braced on my knee so he can see the sharpness of my blade.

"You made it. Tell us how to stop it."

He coughs, blood trickling from his mouth. "Another

monarch must destroy the undead king's true heart."

I glance toward the canopic jars in the other room, destroyed in the rampage. Cosimo sees the movement and laughs darkly. "You won't find the heart there. It's in the Saint-Denis Cathedral. But you'll never succeed." His eyes grow glassy, raptured. "Our king shall be an emblem for his people. When others see him fighting in the Valois colors, they'll pick up arms and help him remove the imposter king from his beloved city!"

Henry. My stomach plunges to my feet.

Paris is a powder keg, growing fuller and fuller all summer. The undead king is the spark it needs to finally explode. He will kill indiscriminately, but that isn't how it will look to the angry, frightened Catholic majority who would see his Valois colors and think the royal family slaughter themselves. They will see the king fighting and join him.

"Saint-Denis is where my mother said she went tonight." Margot's voice is small and scared. "Do you think—did she—"

My throat tightens. "I don't know what your mother has to do with this."

But I imagine we'll soon find out.

And it won't be good.

Cosimo laughs, the sound wet. "My mistress won't be stopped by the likes of you!"

I sheathe my blade and stand. "I wouldn't be so sure if I were you." I keep my hand on the hilt, looking toward the Louvre gleaming copper in the dawn. My smile is sharp; Cosimo flinches as it lands point-first. "Haven't you heard? There's another queen in Paris."

CHAPTER FORTY-ONE

R ACING THROUGH THE hidden passageway back to the Louvre, I don't feel especially regal.

Pain splinters through my hip; Oncle's ring, recovered from the rubble, feels small and silly bouncing against my chest. Even my dust-covered dagger feels like a plaything, a toy in a child's hand not to be taken seriously. Why should Henry or anyone else believe us? A princess who claims her dead father came back to life and the niece of a traitor?

No, a queen without a crown, a bolder part of me whispers.

I giggle helplessly, wincing as it jostles some secret hurt.

This is the most ridiculous thing of them all, the thing that makes us wholly unbelievable and foolish. Perhaps Cosimo was right. Perhaps I'm nothing more than a girl who wished so desperately to be something more that she brought destruction and bloodshed everywhere she went.

We burst into Catherine de' Medici's bedchamber. I half expected a ring of guards, their blades pointed to our throats, but it's empty. We're alone. The single petticoat laid over the back of a chair is near offensive with its normality. Why isn't anyone looking for us? How is it possible that this room can be exactly the same, when we have seen the once-dead king of

France rampaging through Paris with his bloody fists?

A hysterical laugh bursts from me.

Margot turns with a sharp look, her brows rising. "You're sobbing."

And so I am. The ripping sounds I hear aren't leeches pulled from flesh, but from my own chest.

Carefully, like I'm an orphaned foal in need of comfort, Margot wraps me in her arms. She forces my head beneath her chin even though she is a scant inch taller than me.

"Hush now. We'll make it right."

I jerk away, scraping my eyes with a blood-speckled sleeve. "There is no making this right. My blood was the final part of the spell!"

Oncle told me not to start a war and I started one anyway.

Margot tilts her head, nostrils flaring. "Your mistakes caused all this?" She gestures toward the window, where her undead father carves a path of destruction through the city she loves. "I'm the one who told you to marry Henry in my place." She steps closer, her eyes blazing. "If you believe that you're responsible for this, you're wrong."

I swallow, shaking my head. "It doesn't matter. We can't fix this."

She tosses her head and laughs. "Of course you can."

Her laughter shocks me from my tears. What is there to laugh about, to be confident about, at a time like this? She comes closer, drawing me back into her arms again. Even though the laughter lingers in her smile, her eyes are more serious than I've ever seen them. "I don't know how you'll fix it.

But I know you can because you've solved every problem I've ever had, whether I've asked you to or not. It's why I loved you, first as a friend and then more. I believed in you first, Jac."

I shake my head again, but there's no vigor in it. Margot's unwavering gaze holds me like the hand of God. I couldn't look away even if the undead king came crashing through the wall.

I didn't know she noticed what I did in secret. I hadn't known she felt like this about me.

She brushes mortar from my hair, her hand staying at my temple. "I have made countless mistakes like anyone else, but I don't make mistakes about who is worthy of my love. If you don't believe in anything else at all, then believe in this."

And then she kisses me.

Her mouth is commanding, fierce, and I swear, she still tastes of almonds from that winter night so many years ago. The flavor brings me right back to the wordless wonder, the very first time I felt like things could be different. The inkling that perhaps my entire life could be different. I kiss her back like I've wanted to for months, years, letting her convictions fill me with fire.

We part with a gasp. She holds my face close, voice low and urgent. "My greatest mistake was not making sure I stayed in your heart when I was there first. But Henry is a worthy king, and you are a worthier queen," she growls, fingernails nipping my skin. "He better appreciate my sacrifice!"

I laugh breathlessly and lean my forehead against hers, filled with a feeling so vast and aching, I fear my ribs might crack.

"I'm certain you'll find a way to remind him of it every day."

She kisses the corner of my mouth one last time, whispering, "Let's show both Navarre and France how brightly you shine outside of my shadow."

Margot insists that I change before we leave. As she helps me into one of her mother's dour black gowns, a church bell begins tolling incessantly in the distance. Then another joins. And a third.

Alarm bells. Ringing all across Paris.

By the time we head to the Navarrese apartments, it seems the entire Palais du Louvre shakes in the chorus. People scurry through the halls, all fearful gazes and hushed whispers. A few stop and stare at Margot's ruined dress with its sapphires barely hanging on, at my dark bloodstained presence beside her.

Henry's doors are guarded by four men in scarlet livery, all heavily armored. Gauntleted hands go to their swords' hilts at once.

Margot raises her hands pacifyingly. "Please. We mean no harm."

No one moves. For one wild second I think they mean to cut us down, but then they grab us and force us inside.

The room is in pandemonium, men milling everywhere, half whispering, half shouting. Only Henry remains seated, a still point in the chaos. He wears dark silk corded with black velvet and trimmed in gold braid, as if going to a funeral. He only looks up when we are forced to our knees at bladepoint before him.

His eyes widen.

A stern advisor shakes Margot roughly. "Madame! Tell us

if your family has declared war upon us, or we shall slay your companion."

Margot's face flushes red. "Is this how Navarre treats unarmed people who come to you with no ill intent?"

I move to place a hand on Margot's, willing her to remain calm. But before I do more than twitch, there's a blade at my throat. The stern advisor grabs my hair, wrenching my head back. One jerk is all it takes to end my life. My dagger is gone, taken by the guards at the door.

Henry bolts upright, a half-drunk goblet clattering to the floor. "Stand down! I didn't order you to draw your blade, monsieur!"

The blade digs in deeper. "The Valois and their allies *slaughter our people in the streets*, my king! And you would have me stand on ceremony?"

All the men stare at Henry. But he stares at me, taking in my mortar-dusted hair, the bloody scrapes on my knuckles, and the fire in my eyes. I see him follow the column of my neck, the golden chain on which hangs Oncle's ring beneath my bodice.

He knows that I have something to tell him. Something on which the fate of everything hinges.

I swallow even though the movement opens a hot line in my throat. "I know how to stop the slaughter."

"She lies!" The advisor pulls my hair. A pained hiss whistles from my clenched teeth.

Henry's stare goes wild, every line of his body stiffening. "Enough! Release her!"

The advisor scoffs, not moving. "Her lies are obvious to

all except you, Henry! Surely you don't mean to listen to your whore over your own men?"

Whore. The word slaps me. I suck in a breath and drop my eyes.

I ought to expect it, given all the time I've spent with Henry. The Navarrese entourage isn't daft. They came here for wedding bells and got alarm bells instead, and they know me and my oncle have something to do with it.

But still, the word makes something quail in me, stokes the old, secret fear that a lowborn girl can never amount to anything.

Margot leaps to her feet, her fury palpable. "How dare you slander the queen of Navarre!"

Shocked, angry gasps explode around the room. A kicked hornet's nest moments before the entire swarm buzzes out. The pressure on my neck eases. I gasp at the sudden relief, a hand fluttering to the skin above my lace collar. My fingers come away sticky scarlet.

Henry slowly kneels before me, a look of puzzled wonder on his face. "Queen?"

I bare my forearms and their bloody pockmarks. My voice is loud enough for all to hear. "The spell needed my blood."

Only Henry knows what I truly mean. He mouths the spell to himself, lips parting softly as he thumbs away the worst of the filth from my tender skin.

"What did you think when the magic recognized you as mine?" he says.

A hundred answers wheel through me. That I had resisted

my own happiness for so long, I couldn't recognize it when it was within reach. That I spent so much effort becoming someone else, I lost sight of who I was. That I trusted both too much and not enough. How he was the first person to see how I could be so much more than I let myself be.

There are so many things I want to say to him, but time races away, its tail nearly out of reach. I must trust there will be time later on to say all the things he deserves to hear.

I smile, the expression crooked and raw and so, so big, it hurts my face. "Why, I thought I should find my husband and command him to help me right this wrong."

He takes my hands in his, feather soft and shaking. "Swear you mean it. Swear you're truly my queen." Quiet, so quiet only I hear it, he says, "Swear this is truly what you want and not what you think I want."

I twist our hands, lacing my fingers through his. "I swear it with all my soul."

Joy, incandescent and wild, blazes across his face for a glorious moment. Then his kingly expression is back, the earnestness I once ridiculed, the honesty I now love.

I feel how tenderly he helps me to my feet, how he turns to his court so all can see my hand in his, the respect he pays me.

"The princess of France is right. Jacqueline d'Argenson-Aunis is queen of Navarre. I'll hear no further words against her."

There is not a single sound in the entire apartment. Then a boy, the youngest of them all, the young lord I once danced with so many months ago, ducks his head and bends his knee.

"Your Majesty, I welcome you!"

The stern advisor sucks in a long, scandalized breath.

Then one by one, the men fall like waves, knees sinking into the fine, rich carpet. *Your Majesty* nestles into each nook and every corner, loud enough to drown out the alarm bells outside. Margot catches my eye and sinks into a flawless curtsy. A marveling breath moves through me.

Henry turns, his mouth curved proudly. "My queen and I must leave to save our kingdom."

CHAPTER FORTY-TWO

T HE SEINE RUNS red as Catherine de' Medici foretold
so many months ago.

Later, Paris would learn of the massacre. How
the river current dragged bodies as far as Saint-Cloud and
Auteuil. How the cobblestones glistened with bloodlike rain.
How there were bodies stripped naked in piles, bodies tossed
in wells, poisoning the water for months afterward. We would
hear how the sight of the undead king in his Valois blue became
a rallying cry for the murderers who shouted, "Long live the
king!" when they rampaged through the bloody streets.

God willed them to do it, the killers would claim afterward.

But there was nothing godly about it. Fear, plain and
simple, motivated the attackers. They believed that making
room for new ideas and people meant their own lives would
be smaller.

It would come to be called the St. Bartholomew's Day massacre, and the horrible day will be a bloody stain on history
forever.

Right now, as Henry and I exit the ruined catacombs into
the Paris streets, we step out with bated breath and drawn

blades. The church bells still ring in warning. Sluggishly now, far fewer of them than before. The city is eerily silent, but if I strain my ears, there's the distant clash of arms, terrified screaming.

Margot begged us not to go through her mother's dark chambers again, but we had no choice. The gates of the Palais du Louvre are already locked and chained, the terrifying truth spreading from mouth to mouth like fire.

Slaughter in the streets. The Catholics have fallen upon the Huguenots and seek to murder them all.

Henry blows out a misty breath and rubs his hands together. "Where's the cathedral where the king's heart lies?"

I point to the north. "Saint-Denis is six miles or so beyond the city walls."

He says nothing, but I know we're both thinking it. Six miles through the war-torn streets might as well be the entire length of France. Making it there without being spotted feels like a fool's dream. Making it there without being apprehended or worse feels impossible.

Henry adjusts the baldric crossing his chest. I take in the sword on his hip and the bow on his back. Nothing about him shouts that he's the Huguenot king that Paris would love to kill, but with his golden hair and furious eyes, his lack of crown won't fool anyone if they get too close. I caress the dagger hilts at my hips nervously, feeling exposed. Nothing feels like enough. Our leather armor is too thin for the raiders and our weapons too weak for the undead king. I don't know if we can do this. But I'll never forgive myself if we don't try.

"We could wear the white armbands of the killers and hide among them."

Henry's mouth hooks disapprovingly. "I shall do no such thing!"

I cross my arms, stung. "Your honor may get us slain, then!"

He laughs carelessly, spreading his arms wide. "Honor is all I have left. My people followed me here to see me wed only to find their deaths. I don't want a single account of this slaughter to say that the king of Navarre dressed in the clothes of his enemies and slunk through the streets like a coward."

"Fine. Then I say we stick to the roofs if we can."

He shakes his head, running a hand along the fletched arrows in their quiver. "Too steep. We would be easy targets for archers."

Something falls nearby. I flinch at the clatter, spinning around. A dog sprints past. Henry stares at my trembling dagger. I sheathe it savagely.

"Would the Societas Solis apothecary have anything that could help us?" he asks. "Something to turn things in our favor?"

I move to touch Oncle's ring and find armor instead. Margot quickly altered men's clothes to fit me before we left, but the armor is still a shade too large, leaving my neck exposed. I think of the undead king's crushing fingers on the back of my head and shudder. "Maybe. Let's look."

I don't know how the divine light works, but perhaps someone at the safe house does. Even though I'm a traitor to the order, even though Henry is safe from them now that Catherine de' Medici's spell has sprung, the thought of seeing any of them again fills me with dread.

Does the order even consider the massacre its problem? Do they know of its dark origins, how the undead king tears through the streets with sightless eyes? Or have they chalked up Paris as a regrettable loss, already fled their safe house like rats from a sinking ship?

We head north. Everything has an eerie, abandoned feel. Many buildings boast crushed walls and broken windows, the undead king's path of destruction. His victims are harder to witness, the bodies broken not with blades, but brute strength. Henry curses softly as we pass a body pulled to pieces like a soft roll. He draws closer to me, nocking an arrow to his bow.

The bodies slain by mortal hands are no easier to bear. Slashed throats and bleeding chests. From the locked houses above, I feel the dozens of eyes pressing into us, following each mincing step, flinching at each swivel of Henry's head.

A market lies flattened in an open square ahead. Already flies buzz over the bodies, the scent of blood mingling with the burning of abandoned cooking pots over smoldering fires.

I stop us at the alley's mouth. There's jeering laughter, not more than two blocks away.

Henry nods and lifts a finger to his lips.

We creep over the spilled brassicas and trampled flowers, the shattered pots of honey and puddles of wine. I try not to look too long at the bodies, but I can't help it. Open, terrified eyes, desperate reaching arms. Some lie hunched over things hidden on the ground, as if the people died defending something dear to them.

A high, thin wail comes from one bundle.

Henry and I both stop, his face going scarlet.

A baby, alive beneath their slain parent.

He storms over to the body before I can stop him.

"NO!" An explosion of movement from a splintered market stall. My dagger almost flies before I realize it's only a girl, nine or so, her face bloodied and eyes wild. "Leave my sister!" A jagged stick trembles in her hand.

Henry stops moving. "Who did this?" he demands in a rough, low voice.

The girl's weapon clatters to the cobblestones. She sniffs and drags a bloody hand across her face. "There's a cross on their hats and a white sleeve on their arms. They guard every exit out of the arrondissement. They took my brother. I should've stopped them, but—" Her words end in a sob.

Henry lays a steady hand on her arm. "The path is clear behind us. Take your sister and hide. The king of Navarre has come to end this."

The girl lifts her head, shocked from her tears. "You—you came yourself to save us?"

He fists a hand. Presses it over his heart. "Until this stops beating. You have my word."

I close my eyes and grit my teeth, unable to bear the sight of her gratitude, unable to witness how the breeze teases Henry's hair into a boyish mess, as if he were just a lad. My new husband. A golden soul among men.

A shining target for all his enemies.

The girl's fleeing back fills me with sour fear. "Why would you tell her who you are?!" I say. "Are you trying to get us murdered? Shall we ask the cathedral to announce you next so everyone knows?"

"The Huguenots need to know I won't hide behind the Louvre's walls!"

I grab him roughly. Red rims his eyes. He doesn't try to stop the rage-hot tears running down his face. My anger scatters like a palmful of dust. I thumb the wet tracks away, holding his gaze like he's a rogue stallion on the verge of spooking.

"I know. But if you're caught, I don't know if I can push on alone. If you can't keep your identity hidden for yourself, can you keep it hidden for me? Just for now?"

He steps away, eyes darkening recklessly. "I see you invoke my vow of protection whenever it suits you. That's not fair, Jac."

I don't deny it. I know exactly what I'm asking. I ask him to ignore his people's pleas to help me instead.

It's the cold calculus I learned at Oncle's knee, a ruthlessness I can don like a cloak. I don't like it, but I'll wear it if I have to. The best way to save more lives is to end the bloodshed at the source: we must stop the undead king.

The hard edge of his jaw eases. His head droops, brow resting against mine. I feel the sigh shudder through him, feel how thousands of lives settle across his shoulders, how heavy it weighs. I pull him into my arms, trying to take on some of the weight myself.

"You ask for too much," he finally whispers.

I press my lips to his cheek. "I won't ask you to set aside your honor ever again, I promise."

He sighs against my neck, as soft as silk. But nods all the same.

We continue walking north.

At the crossroads ahead where one arrondissement ends and another begins, we spot them.

The killers in their Catholic feast day whites, jeering and laughing around a pile of strongboxes. One man cracks them open with a blacksmith's hammer while the rest comb through the contents. The oily torchlight catches on their shining weapons. Five men. Two of us.

And the quickest street to the Societas Solis apothecary lies just beyond them.

"Walk proudly. As if we belong." My blood already races.

Henry nods. My pulse roars louder as we draw closer, walking straight down the street's middle. The tallest man spots us first. He tucks the fat coin purse from which he was counting behind his back.

"'Tis a good day for killing heretics, is it not, my brothers?" he says.

"Aye, it certainly is!" I shout back.

Henry goes still and silent. I step on his foot, reminding him of the promise he made only minutes ago.

The men smile and nod as we pass. I exhale as they vanish behind us, already bending over their piles of stolen coin and treasures.

We've nearly made it to the next arrondissement when a new voice speaks.

"Oy! What's the password?"

I turn, even as dread pulls every part of me toward the opposite direction. Another two men have arrived, damp with fresh bloodstains. One watches us with a drawn sword. The second kicks the treasure pile to the cobblestones, swearing at the others for letting greed overtake their vigilance.

I scoff, lowering my voice. "Password? You would waste our time with such nonsense while heretics still live?"

The marauding men cheer drunkenly. I realize part of their treasure is a barrel of Armagnac. The brandy's alcoholic burn almost covers up the reek of blood, but not quite.

The man closest steps forward, brow furrowed. He opens his mouth—

An arrow buries itself in it.

Henry tucks his bow away, already turning. "Run!"

An arrow whizzes over our heads. Another strikes the street at our heels. The men scream and curse behind us.

We keep running well after they fall far behind us, until my side splits with pain and I'm forced to slow, stop.

Henry pants, chest heaving, taking in the houses all around us. "Are we close?"

I nod, pointing. "The apothecary is around that corner."

He nocks another arrow and rounds the corner first, bow drawn. His brows lift in surprise at whatever he sees, face blanching.

"It's on fire, Jac."

CHAPTER FORTY-THREE

BRIGHT RED TONGUES lap at the windows, creeping ever taller.

Deadlier than a plague, more destructive than war, nothing levels the city faster than fire.

Henry seizes my shoulder. "Don't!"

"I must!"

His eyes widen as he hears it too. A child screaming from inside. Louise's son, Thomas.

The street-side door is wedged shut with a barrel. A shiver of rage goes through me. Who barricades a child inside a burning house? Who decided to do this at all?

Has someone else discovered where the Societas Solis lurks in Paris?

The metal bands of the barrel are already too hot to touch. Cursing and sweating, I race into the courtyard. The smoke gathers thick and grey. I yank Oncle's ring out and press it to the sun signet burned on the rear door. A spark of light, and then it unlocks with a gush of hot air. I race inside, eyes burning. More hot smoke billows outward, so dense I can hardly see, but then through the darkness swim tearstained cheeks, the terrified whites of his eyes. Thomas.

"Come on!" I cry, gesturing for him to go.

He shakes his head. "The cats!"

I join him in the tiny back room and hoist his terrified kittens into his bag. None of them like it—I'm clawed endlessly—but I know Thomas won't leave until he has them all. I understand saving the creatures you love even if it puts you in danger.

Popping noises sound from the shop's front room, glass vials bursting. The flames burn strange colors.

"That's all of them!" Thomas cries.

I sling the bag over my shoulder and haul him outside.

The small courtyard is now so filled with heat and smoke I wonder if we're too late, if the fire has already spread outside.

"Jac!" Henry's panicked face appears in a window overlooking the courtyard. "Hurry! It's going to—"

With a shuddering groan of stone pried from earth, the apothecary collapses.

Thomas screams and presses into my side. I shield him from the scorching wave of heat, bracing for the burning beams to crush us, smother us in their flames, then burn and blister our skin.

But when the fiery avalanche subsides, I crack an eye open.

The building collapsed into the street, not into the courtyard where we stand.

We're safe. For now.

I wipe the sweat from my brow and steady my nerves. We'll go through the alley to the street. It's not ideal and someone has surely heard the commotion by now, but I've got my blades and Thomas has his long legs. We can face whatever is out there.

We must.

We turn the corner and stop.

The alley to the street is gone. Blocked by burning rubble at least eight feet high.

Worse, the fire has grown, the yawning dark red center like a gateway to hell. Tentatively, the flames lap the wall of the adjoining building. Then they sink their teeth in hungrily.

My stomach drops.

We're trapped in the courtyard with nowhere to go.

"What now?" Thomas stares up at me with round, tremulous eyes. The look of a child whose last hope lies with my answer. The kittens meow and wriggle against my back, their movements growing frantic.

Three stories of timber and stone surround us, no way out save through the windows, all of them ten feet up. Ember-filled ash blows against our backs, a cascade of orange.

Copper fills my mouth. I rushed in without thinking and damned us both. Maybe damned us all if the burning flames get me and leave Henry to undo the spell alone.

"Henry!" I shout frantically.

But the king is gone. Fire trims the window where I last spotted him. Another few minutes and we'll be trapped on two sides. *What will get us first?* I wonder. The smoke or the heat?

Another explosion. I jerk my head up.

The lowest window has burst open. Henry stands there, unrolling a rope of tied linens. I sob as the end hits the ground.

"Go, now!" I shove Thomas.

But he just looks at me, hugging the mother cat with her splinted leg. "How do I climb with her?"

The kittens wriggle against my back, the bag too full for another animal. He must leave the cat behind. That's the only way forward.

But I can't force myself to say it.

"Give her to me. You go first."

He scrambles up the rope, his skinny arms trembling, until Henry pulls him inside.

I tie the canvas bag to my belt, tuck the mother cat under my left arm, and begin to climb with my right. The entire world narrows to that open window. The sill is painted pink. It looks like a screaming mouth.

But it gets closer. Even though each jerk upward makes my abdominal muscles shriek. The kittens wriggle, upsetting my balance, and I slip.

"Jac!" Henry leans all the way out the window, hair bronzed by the light, the fire reflecting in his determined eyes. "My hand!"

Linen frays on the rough stone sill. The threads snap, one by one.

I grit my teeth and let go of the rope, kicking off the wall with all my strength. I lift and seize the rope higher up, closer to the window than before, but still not close enough.

The rope rips.

I plummet with a scream.

Henry seizes my wrist, so tight it already bruises.

I cry out as my arm wrenches painfully, but my shoulder stays in its socket. I brace my feet against the wall, climbing one step at a time, Henry alone keeping me from plummeting into the ash-filled courtyard.

Three agonizing steps. Then he grabs my shoulder with his other hand and hauls me inside.

We tumble to the floor. The mother cat leaps from my arms and limps around Thomas's ankles, giving me a silent, slit-eyed glare. Thomas grabs her and the wriggling bag, and then we all hurtle outside.

The collapsed apothecary blocks the entire street with fire. No one is around yet, save for someone screaming the scream of something destined for death: a person trapped inside a wagon, axle broken and the horse cut from its traces. "Maman!" Thomas cries, tearing his hand from mine and rushing to the wagon.

Louise's hands are tied. Her eyes widen at the sight of us.

I suck in a horrified breath. Whoever set fire to the shop tied up Louise outside to watch. "Who did this to you?"

Thomas tugs at Louise's bound hands, weeping. She glares at me. "The Societas Solis has many enemies. Someone has figured out I'm not what I seem. You've ruined our order's stronghold in Paris. I hope you're happy."

I set my foot on the broken wagon. "I think you did this to yourselves when you chose regicide."

"You saved my son." Louise's stare is suspicious, guarded, as if a good thing has never happened to her in her entire life. "Why?"

I know she's not asking why I saved an innocent life, but why did I take the time to do it. Why detour when so many more lives are at stake around us?

I lift my chin. "Because you were right about me. I don't have the heart to be like you."

Her mouth twists, taking in my soot-stained face, the daggers at my hips, and my king-husband at my side. "'Tis a pity. The order could've made you magnificent."

"She already is," Henry growls, going for his sword. I lay a warning hand on him, even as his words burrow deep and warm inside me.

Louise spies the movement and stills. "You mean to take your revenge, then?" she murmurs too low for Thomas to hear.

I frown, disgusted by the thought of more violence, of spilling more blood on the streets that already run red. Yes, Louise lied to me. She has betrayed me and Oncle both, but that's not a crime deserving of death.

"If you give us that, we'll let you go." I nod to the flask filled with divine light on her belt. "Tell the order you lost it in the fray. Give it to me, and you'll never see me again."

Louise laughs unkindly. "You think this can stop the massacre? The divine light can't be controlled or commanded. It has a mind of its own—"

I hold out my hand. "Give it to me if you wish to live."

She doesn't know about the undead king. The realization jolts through me. She thinks the massacre was human caused. And maybe it was, the spark of the undead king's violence encouraging human fear and greed to unimaginable actions.

Frowning, Louise nods. I undo the leather clasp binding the flask and fasten it to my belt. Then I slice through her bonds.

She moves to stand but I seize the front of her shift, leaning closer. "Remember this mercy next time you see my oncle."

She rubs her neck, Thomas pressed to her side with all his cats. "A dead man has no need of my mercy, but I'll humor your demand, Your Majesty." She bows, the gesture mocking. "The king's favor has made you reach too far. You're going to fail."

My fists clench. "I'd rather fail at something that feels right than succeed at something that feels wrong."

That's been the problem with the Societas Solis the entire time, hasn't it? I was good at my work, but it left me hollow inside, farther away from all the things that made life worth living.

More angry words ready themselves like arrows, but Henry puts an arm around my shoulders, pulling me away.

"All right. You saved a boy and a bag of cats, and I saved a baby, so I suppose we're even now," he murmurs, teasing and admonishing all at once. When I don't move, he presses his lips to my temple. "Let them go, love. The Societas Solis was never worth your time or effort."

I take in a long, shuddering breath and nod. I let my dream of working with them scatter like ash. Even the biggest monument can be destroyed with a single breath when it burns down to nothing, when there was never any substance to begin with.

We keep heading north, leaving the embracing mother and child limned by fire behind us.

CHAPTER FORTY-FOUR

THE AWFUL JOURNEY to the Saint-Denis Cathedral will haunt me forever.

Henry helps when he can, sending arrows hurtling with frightening accuracy into their targets, but it's not enough. Not nearly enough. When only three arrows remain, he stops shooting entirely. I lose a dagger when we scramble over the medieval city walls, earning a gash in my leg. It bleeds sluggishly as we limp on toward the Saint-Denis Cathedral and its royal necropolis.

Compared to the gore and chaos of Paris, the faubourg around the cathedral is quiet. If anyone remains in their home, they stay hidden behind locked doors and shuttered windows streaked bloody red in the setting sun.

My foot snags. Henry catches me right before my teeth bite the cobblestones.

"Enough," he says. Exhaustion has carved deep hollows in his cheeks, pressed dark shadows under his eyes.

We enter an empty house. Henry, worried it won't stay empty, insists we take their pillows and bed linens out through the window and onto the flat roof. The groan that escapes me when I finally sit down is near obscene. The water in Henry's waterskin tastes finer than champagne, the stale bread we found in the kitchen better than honey-soaked boar.

Henry sits with both knees bent. He doesn't remove his leather armor. He smiles, just barely. "You've been awake for an entire day. Did you realize that?"

I stare up at the sky, the stars peeking out in twos and threes. Silvery fish beneath the water's surface. "That . . . would explain some things."

A chunk of pilfered cheese replaces my view.

"Eat more," he commands.

For once, I don't argue with him.

The entire sky is dotted with stars when we're done. To the south, Paris lies dark and gleaming, a wolf curled in its den waiting to hunt. Here and there, orange blossoms burst along its flanks. I stare into the distant fires, brighter than anything else in that blood-soaked city.

How many dead have I seen today?

How many more people will die tonight while we rest?

"Jac." His murmur is a cloak thrown over my shoulders after a cold walk. "We must gather our strength. Destroying the king's heart is the best way to end the bloodshed."

He's right, but it does nothing to ease my guilt or banish the nasty things I've seen today. I close my eyes, easing into his side. "Tell me about Navarre, then."

"Navarre." He repeats the word softly, reverently. "The capital city, Pau, sits like a throne at the mountains' feet. You can see them in the distance year-round, snowcapped even in summer." He breathes in the scent of my hair, curling the end of my braid in his scarred fingers. "I think you'll love the mountains."

I smile up at him. "Would I, now?"

"Yes. They're all lush valleys and thick trees and endless waterfalls. You could ride for miles and never see a single soul."

I can almost see it. How the sun would spike over the jagged peaks, slanting into my eyes as Anémone picked her way along the clear stream to the roaring falls, the thrill of birdsong around us. In the beginning Henry would race ahead, eager to point out everything in case one single, lovely detail slipped past. Years later he would trail behind, perhaps showing little golden heads on thick-furred ponies each place where we first stepped, revealing how each moment knotted together to build a life vaster than I could ever imagine. My throat closes up. It feels too precious, too fragile to even think of surrounded by all this death and destruction.

"It sounds like a dream."

"It'll be our life," he says simply, pressing a kiss to the soft skin just before my ear.

"Can we marry in the mountains?" I can't stop thinking of the imaginary place where the waterfalls tumble from sky to earth beneath the stony peaks, the sun on my face.

He goes still. Then his hand travels along my thigh, taps the flask of the divine light pressed betwixt our hips. "I thought we were already married."

I turn so he can see my face, its serious lines and the steadfastness in my eyes. "I want to make the promise myself. As me and not Margot."

He draws in a soft, shuddering breath. "You would do this?"

"No priest. Just us and the sky," I say quickly, before he can get too carried away.

There are a thousand words for what we have, and if marriage is one of them, so be it. I don't care for the word, but the promise to love is older than any ceremony.

The world can call this bright golden thing betwixt us whatever it likes. I want forever unspooling before us like a gleaming road, him at my side, heading toward that unreachable horizon until one of us can travel no farther.

There's bravery in deeds and bravery in words. I've always been good at one and not the other.

I'm finally brave enough now to promise myself to him the way he's promised himself to me.

I feel his smile against my cheek. "Would you mind carrying this, then?"

He presses something small into my palm. A ruby ring. The very same one from his proposal. A lifetime has passed since then. I laugh at the sight of it now.

"Have you just been carrying this around? Waiting to propose again?"

He bends his leg, an elbow on his knee and his head upon his fist. "Of course not. I learned my lesson. I knew you'd want it back eventually." There is—to his credit—only the smallest amount of smugness in his voice.

I blush, despising every second of it. With good-natured grumbling, I slip his ring onto the chain where it joins Oncle's, right beside my heart.

"Good, because I'll only wear it if you *don't* propose."

414 | ERIN COTTER

His smug smile widens. "Behold, brave Jacqueline d'Argenson-Aunis. A woman who fears nothing but her feelings!"

I shove him and he laughs.

"I'll take first watch. You sleep." He gathers my head onto his lap, ignoring the cushions and linens we dragged outside.

And I do, dreaming of mountains and whispered promises.

We approach Saint-Denis Cathedral when the sky is still dark.

The gothic face rises from the other end of the plaza like a monster, all pointed spires and curved lines. Inside are the final resting places of the French kings and their queens. Somewhere inside there's a heart in a jar. *Does it beat?* I wonder. Jerk with the same strangeness that moves King Henry II's long-dead limbs?

I lower my head and push on, but Henry's hand stops me.

He's still so lovely, even beneath all the grime, even sleepless and rumpled. My throat aches with an unbearable tenderness.

"You are dearer to me than my own soul." He takes me by the chin, kissing me slowly. It has a horrible feeling of goodbye to it, settling in my chest like the lowest note of a church organ.

"I have no need yet of your farewells, Henry of Navarre."

He smiles, the expression not touching his eyes.

We check our weapons one last time and keep going. The cathedral façade is carved with scenes of the Last Judgment. Columns depicting solemn kings and queens of the Old Testament frame the double doors. They frown disapprovingly at our approach. I cross myself and murmur a prayer for forgiveness and fortune. I think we'll need both tonight.

Henry lays a gauntleted hand on the bronze doors.

They groan open, unlocked.

Moonlight feathers through the rose window overhead, illuminating the long aisle to the high altar, catching on rows of pews that disappear into a darkness so deep I can't see the walls. My heart races at the thought of some slick ambush predator tearing from the gloom.

Something gleams on the altar, balanced at the very edge of the moonlight. The canopic jar where the heart lies, just as the dying sorcerer promised.

We rush toward it, footsteps echoing wildly. Henry reaches it first. I rip off the lid, readying my dagger as Henry upends it.

Nothing.

The jar is empty.

My breath catches roughly. Cosimo said the heart would be here. He was dying. There was no reason to lie.

The moonlight disappears.

"Who looks for my lord's kingly heart?" The voice is something dredged from a lake bottom, weed-strangled, stubbornly resisting the pull to the surface. Gooseflesh bursts across my skin.

I twist but there's nothing. Except—near the great bronze doors, I squint, looking closer. A spot of shadow, darker than all the rest. The more I try to focus, the more it twists and wavers before me.

Henry nudges me, looking up.

Something . . . crawls over the rose window, sliding and dripping toward the floor. The moonlight returns bit by bit as the darkness grows under the window, shifting into something almost human shaped but blurred at the edges, as if the shadows tug on its shape, trying to pull the darkness back where it belongs. The darkness laughs. Each grotesque step toward us moves as if with an extra joint.

"Catherine de' Medici." Henry's face has gone ghost white.

I shake my head, yanking the rings out from under my armor. I grab Henry's hand, clasp the ring tightly betwixt us so he can see what I see. "No, something that wears her shape."

With a battle-hewn swiftness, Henry nocks an arrow to his bow and fires.

The shade wavers as the bolt rips through her shoulder. But the darkness re-forms, the arrow dropping from the flesh with a clatter. She walks again.

I pull Oncle's ring from my skin and see the Queen Mother again. Something isn't right about her eyes. There is a distant look to them, a fever sheen.

A disgusting, shriveled-looking brown item hangs around her neck. I swallow.

"She's wearing the heart."

"Well, we'll have to take it from her, then." Henry leaps forward, sword drawn.

"Wait!"

But it's too late. The king crashes into an invisible barrier and falls. When I clasp the ring once more, I see how the heart pulses, a red so deep it borders on black. My legs start to shake.

What dark promises has Catherine de' Medici made to creatures beyond our world to have such power?

And how are we supposed to fight it?

With a high keening wail, the shade bolts for Henry. He ducks and rolls away, arrows slipping from his quiver and rolling underneath the pews.

I dive toward the arrows as the thing that wears Catherine de' Medici's shape rounds on Henry again. I unscrew the cap on the ichor of the gods at my hip, slicking my palm with the oil before rubbing the arrowheads.

The shade whips around, sniffing. It screams and rushes me.

"Henry!" I toss one of the arrows to him.

The shade rears above me. Its fingers taper to long needle shadows.

An arrow *thunks* into its thigh.

The creature's blow goes wide. The pew beside me explodes into splinters.

The shade grabs its thigh and screams. The wound glows faintly. This time the darkness doesn't re-form. I scramble to join Henry on the high altar. With a rage-filled bellow, the shade rips the arrow out and snaps it in half. Each half whips toward Henry. One strikes his bow and sends it flying from his hand.

It's stronger than the undead assassin. The thought makes my skin go cold.

Sweat already rolls down Henry's face. He shakes his hair from his eyes and draws his sword.

"Hold that out," I say.

I uncap the ichor and tip some into the groove running along the sword's length. The gold gleams and coats the steel.

The shade stops. The too-wide gash of its mouth pulls in a sickening smile.

"I have seen the future. My sons will die, one by one, and then you'll take the crown that belongs to the Valois."

Henry slashes his blade with a flourish. He laughs savagely. "Why would I covet your son's crown when I wear my own better than he ever could?"

The shade snarls. One bloodied hand grips something at its chest. The heart.

I gasp at an explosion of brightness. The violet-red light sears itself into my eyes even behind closed lids. A deep note thrums, and I can't tell whether it's inside me or around me.

For a moment, there's no sound but our ragged breaths.

Then the dead explode from their tombs.

They pour from the mausoleums and ossuaries beyond the transept. Bones jutting from rotting flesh, clinking like hobnails on the floor. Unearthly screams shred the rotting remains of throats, leaving jaws gaping with too-long teeth. The kings and queens of France, tarnished crowns hanging low on putrid brows. Their empty eye sockets burn violet red. Henry's back thuds against mine.

We circle, his sword angled out, but there's no break in the wave of skeletal faces, no way out.

I only have time to wipe the divine light onto my dagger before they fall upon us.

We fight back-to-back, his gleaming sword cleaving a path through the soft, rotting bodies. My dagger doesn't have the reach. I fend off the ones that rush Henry's back, grimacing at how close they must come for me to strike.

We can't last long like this.

Over the whirling chaos, the shade stands in the aisle, a proud mother watching her children play.

"Use the last arrow. Shoot for the heart!" Henry pants.

I pull the final arrow from his quiver. The bow lies abandoned on the high altar behind us, a crowd of writhing dead between it and me.

Even though every bit of my body screams not to, even though it makes my very soul shudder, I stop fighting.

I go perfectly still.

The dead rush past me, clawing for Henry. I whimper as a wet, slimy arm scrapes against me.

Like the undead king, they only sense movement.

Henry leads them away from me until all is clear.

I leap onto the high altar and grab the bow.

The nave is filled with fallen dead, but still more whir on Henry. His battle bellow shakes the dust from the vaulted ceilings, each expert swing of his blade a lesson in elegance. France was wrong to say that the king of Navarre could not dance so many months ago. He knows the beat of battle.

But he has been dancing for too long. I see how his sword tip flags, how his hair hangs limp, how each breath heaves against his damp leather breastplate.

The shade sees it too. Its fingers lengthen once more into long needle spears.

It rushes forward.

The sea of dead part for it, a channel aiming right at my husband's unprotected back.

"HENRY!"

He looks up. The shade rears above him, suddenly lengthening like a shadow at twilight.

I draw the bow with a shuddering breath and let the final arrow fly.

My arrow buries itself where an eye should be. An unearthly scream tears from the shade. It doubles over, hands over its face, dripping violet-red light where the golden arrow smokes and smolders. Now Henry can grab the heart from its neck and crush it in his gauntleted hand. He can put an end to it all.

"JAC!"

I turn, too late. Something crashes into me. I fall on the stairs, on my wrist. Something in it crunches horridly.

One of the skeletons looms over me. A grinning long-dead queen, her royal gown rotted to pieces. A hand more bone than skin darts for my throat.

I feel the whoosh of a blade inches from my face. Hear the skeleton's unearthly shriek.

Her hand falls to my chest, severed from the wrist. The fingers twitch like spider legs, still inching toward my neck. I scream and hurl it away.

Over my shoulder the shade still cowers on its knees; the heart still hangs from its throat. "You didn't get the heart!"

Henry gives me his hand, grinning. "I swore I'd protect you, didn't I?"

He shudders suddenly. Wetness splatters my face.

The point of a sword gleams from Henry's chest, the tip inches from mine.

Something has stabbed him from behind.

He slumps to his knees, a dazed look in his eyes. Already his front is stained dark. A puddle spreads beneath him.

Green-grey eyes float above Henry. Meet mine with devastating familiarity.

Cosimo Ruggeri's assassin. The very same one I left buried in the rubble. Its leg is now bent and twisted. One of its arms is missing from the elbow down, the bone jagged and skin torn. It looks as though it pulled itself from the rubble with sheer strength, not caring if it left parts of itself behind. Didn't Cosimo tell me it was spelled to hunt the Navarrese king? And I left it, certain it was crushed beneath the stones, but still the wicked magic compelled it to carry out its only task.

Its face seems to grin for one horrible moment before it collapses.

The spell that kept it animated is needed no more. The king is dying.

A barely human sound rips from my chest. My hands flap uselessly over the sword. Everything I've ever learned about injuries vanishes when I reach for it. Leave the blade in or out? Put pressure on the wound to stop the bleeding or not? A tortured moan slips from me, as if I'm the one mortally injured.

Henry catches my hand. His fingers are slick, his grip weak. He shakes his head just once, the meaning clear.

Keep fighting.

And so I do.

With a terrible cry, I charge the shade. The skeleton kings and queens turn, too slow to stop me. My dagger is gone, the bow forgotten. The shade snarls and stabs with its claws. I roll beneath the blow, not away as it expects, but closer, into its guard.

I grab the pulsing heart with an ichor-stained hand and pull. The chain snaps as easily as a finger bone. The shade screams, outraged, but I am already gone, leaping from pew to pew back to the high altar, to Henry's sword still glowing with the divine light.

I move to stab the heart.

"No." Henry reaches out, teeth red and gritted against the tremendous pain. "Together."

Henry too weak to hold it, I settle the sword across his lap. We take the shriveled dead thing that was once the heart of a king and press it along the sword's glowing edge. It splits like a ripe plum.

For a moment, nothing.

And then, an eerie howl builds, something not meant for human ears, something from beyond our world. A phantom wind blasts through the nave. One by one the cathedral's great stained glass windows shatter. I throw myself over Henry.

The dead collapse one by one, jerking terribly, fighting the force that wrenches away their second life. An anguished cry comes from the shade that wears Catherine de' Medici's shape. Black wings rush from her before she collapses.

Then there's nothing but the sound of my own ragged panting.

I rise from Henry. He's curled on his side, eyes closed. Were it not for the horrid wetness of his chest, the dark hole I can't make myself look at, he would seem to only be sleeping.

I grasp his wrist, my fingers slick with blood.

A flutter, soft as the blink of an eyelash.

I gasp, hope a wild, thrashing thing. I loosen his leather armor frantically. I unlace his jerkin and rip his chemise, exposing the fatal wound.

I free the bottle of ichor with a shaking hand. It tumbles, striking the floor with a noise that stops my heart, but no, it's whole, it's safe, the glass untouched. Fully sobbing now, I pour the entire bottle of ichor into the gruesome pit of his chest.

The bitter smell of myrrh washes over us, a garden in fullest bloom. The golden oil fills the wound and overflows, spilling across the floor.

Gently, oh so gently, I smooth the hair from Henry's brow, take his head into my lap. I hold his hand and press a trembling kiss to it, praying to any god, anything that might listen. *Please don't take him from me.*

I stay absolutely still. Hoping against hope a miracle will find me if I don't move.

The early-morning light thickens and gathers before pouring through the empty rose window. A single second or an entire lifetime passes. I hear the bells in the churches beyond begin to ring once more.

His hand finally slips from mine. Cold, so heartbreakingly cold.

A scream punches out of my chest. I scream until my throat is raw and ripped, until I taste blood. Hot angry tears splash into the divine light dripping from Henry. There's no glow. It stays as dull and plain as oil, otherworldliness dimmed by death.

I throw the empty flask as hard as I can. It shatters.

I beat my fists on the floor. My scream becomes a roar.

Stupid, foolish king!

Why didn't he destroy the heart when he had the chance? Why did he choose me when I've told him not to a hundred times over?

"You never listen!" My shout fills the entire cathedral. The guilt follows a second later, shuts me up at once. What if his soul still lingered? What if the last thing he heard is me yelling at him in anger? The thought splits me wide open. I lay my head on his ruined chest and howl.

Surrounded by broken glass and the bones of the dead kings of France, I weep for the king of Navarre, my husband, for the life we were supposed to build together. I picture him riding through the mountains, the ones he never got to show me, his smile dearer to me than any glittering treasure.

Everything I fought for.

Gone, all gone.

Blackness spreads at the edge of my vision, nudging my side like a too-swift current, eager to drown.

I slip into the water gladly.

CHAPTER FORTY-FIVE

TIME GROWS MEANINGLESS. Years pass in the space between breaths, faces flashing before me. Oncle, dead. Margot, weeping. One face that looks curiously like my own, soft and rippling, as if underwater. My mother. I reach out for her, but she dissolves to nothing.

It all dissolves back to *him*.

Golden and laughing, beckoning me to follow, but I can barely take a single step.

When I finally get close enough to touch him, he fades away.

I shudder awake.

Everything aches, the pain worst in my broken wrist and radiating everywhere else. My body feels wrung of all moisture. It feels like I drowned at sea and was left abandoned on a sun-scalded shore. The light feels like needles. I turn away with a wince. I don't want to wake up yet.

But something has woken me.

My good hand reaches for a dagger that isn't there. The skeletons are still lifeless piles. The cathedral is still in ruins. Rosy dawn now creeps finger by finger through the empty windows.

Catherine de' Medici is missing.

I sit up higher, staring at the place where the Queen Mother had fallen. Where did she go? And why would she not end me on her way out?

Something caresses my leg. I jolt away, gasping.

The king's dead, shriveled heart, now almost cleaved in two.

It shudders, the movement slow and obscene.

I suck in a breath, the hair rising along the back of my neck. Outside, church bells still ring. I assume they herald the end of the massacre, that somewhere in Paris a once-dead king fell to his knees for the final time, and his supporters scattered at the frightful sight of what they had followed into battle.

But what if I'm wrong? What if the undead king still lives and Henry's sacrifice was in vain?

The thought hollows me out, all my grief rushing in to fill it. It can't have been in vain. If I leave this place and murderers still terrorize Paris, I will lie down and hope to join the dead. I don't have anything left to give. I just want to sleep.

A wonderstruck laugh shocks me all the way awake.

"The king is dead." Henry has pushed himself to a seated position. He looks at his hands, flexing them. He turns to me, astonishment in every line of his face. "Long live the king."

I stare at him. Then I grab his torn chemise and kiss him, heedless of the blood and filth.

"You're alive."

He takes my hand. Kisses my fingers one by one. "I know."

"You shouldn't be," I whisper.

He hesitates and presses a final kiss to the pulse in my wrist. "No, I shouldn't be."

My hand skims his cheek, down the column of his throat and to his chest.

To the beat beneath his skin.

He lifts a blood-drenched object. The undead king's heart. I watch it stir in sync with the movement beneath my hand.

Henry grimaces. He holds the shriveled organ with only the very tips of his fingers, as far away from himself as possible. "I think . . . the spell reversed. His life has become mine."

I take the heart from him. Only a thread holds the halves together. It would take so little to tear it. A sickening feeling swells in my throat. I was warned that the ichor of the gods, the divine light, worked in mysterious ways.

I didn't listen and poured every last drop into Henry.

Now, he is—is what? Neither dead nor alive, but something in between. Something once alive in him now living in this dead thing shuddering in my palm.

He cups my cheek, brushing away a tear I didn't feel falling. "Don't cry, love. You brought me back when I wasn't ready to go."

He stands, lithe as a cat, clearly no longer suffering how I'm suffering, and offers me his hand. I hesitate before taking it. "We don't know what you are. We don't know what I did or how long this lasts or—"

His laugh silences me. It sounds utterly out of place, a merry tune at a funeral. "I don't care how it works. I'm not second-guessing a second chance."

I shake my head. A hot, wild feeling claws at my chest. "No. You don't get to be cavalier about this. You died, Henry!

You died in my arms and left me alone." I wipe the tears away, hating how I can't make them stop, wondering if I ever can or if something in me has been irrevocably broken by everything I've seen and done. "You don't get to not care about how you're here, not when you put me through that!"

His smile fades, as if he finally realizes I lived through the worst moment of my life without him. "I promise we'll investigate it together. We'll find a way to make sure the magic stays." He pulls my resistant body against him, settles my head upon his chest. Something in me unclenches at the reassuring pulse beneath my ear.

He's alive. Against all laws of God and nature and man, he's alive.

"I never want to spend a single second in this world without you again," I breathe against his skin.

He strokes my hair gently. "You won't."

Even though we should leave, even though I know we've lingered here for far too long, I can't bring myself to move, to leave this place that brought me a miracle.

Henry presses his lips to my brow. "I always thought that if Eurydice had led Orpheus out from the underworld, they would've made it. Now I know it's true."

"Of course," I say. "Men never listen. Look what happened to you."

He kisses me again and pulls away. I offer him the still-beating heart with a flourish. He looks at it, smile fading. "I think it's best if you hold on to that, my love."

Henry insists on climbing the bell tower. When we step out

into the bloody dawn light, Paris spreads before us like a curl of paper. The rising sun reddens the city walls like a knife opening a throat. I know more red runs through the cobblestones where we can't see it. But there's a stillness to the city now. Like a wounded body waiting for the battlefield chirurgeon to do his work.

The massacre is over. We stopped it.

But I feel no joy, only exhausted relief. How many people lost their lives, and for what? What was the purpose of all the bloodletting except to poison peace between the people of France and Navarre? The Catholics and Huguenots? The rebuilding of trust shall be harder than everything else that's come before.

Henry turns to me, feeling the weight of it too. "Navarre needs a mighty queen to lead her through these stormy swells." His hand circles my waist, drawing me closer. His other rises to touch the ruby ring hanging on its chain. "Do you think you'll be up for the task?"

I flash a wry smile and lean into him, the fatigue hitting me all at once.

"As long as there's no magic, I think I can handle it."

We lace our hands together and descend toward the new world.

CHAPTER FORTY-SIX

NOT ALL OF Catherine de' Medici's prophecy came to pass.

While the Seine did run red, King Charles still sat upon the throne that bloody dawn. Or perhaps cowered behind it is more accurate, if the stories from his guards are true.

Catherine de' Medici claims to have stayed in her chambers, stuck in rapturous prayers and visions of victory. When asked about the day, even years later, the Queen Mother sticks to the same story, and I believe her. After all, I saw the darkness wear her shape, saw how it fled her body when we cleaved the undead king's heart. Perhaps she doesn't remember any of it.

And if she does, she's too cunning to ever admit it.

If anyone saw the body of King Henry II when he finally stopped his terrifying rampage, no one heard of it. The king's remains were never found. I suspect he fell to his knees and became dust when his body lost its thrall under the spell.

And if someone did see him and told the tale?

Who would ever believe them?

Magic isn't real, after all.

•   •   •

Other than Henry's life, my other mercy is this: Oncle's cell was found empty. Presumed dead in the melee, but I know better. If Oncle's body wasn't found, he must have escaped.

Apparently so does King Charles, who banishes me from the Palais du Louvre. Margot protests, hissing and spitting, but her brother silences her with a roar.

"She's the niece of a traitor and not fit to breathe the same air as me!"

I have no money of my own, all of it seized because of Oncle's crimes, and no more home, for the estate has gone to a distant male cousin I've never heard of. I leave the Louvre on foot, Anémone carrying saddlebags stuffed with the few things I have left.

I have nothing.

No home, no money, no reputation, no prospects. The door of courtly society and the Societas Solis—everything I've ever known—has been lost or taken. It's the dire future I always feared for myself.

And yet, I've never felt freer.

"Not everything," Henry assures me when he slips into my apartments the night before I leave. "You'll never lose me again."

"You'll only lose me if I'm dead," Margot adds loyally. "If that should happen, you have my permission to bring me back like my dear father. Just make sure you do it before I lose my looks."

Tensions between the French and the Navarrese court are taut enough to choke—each of them blaming the other for the bloodshed—and me being named a traitor has not helped matters at all. King Charles has forbidden the Navarrese entourage to leave, a hopeless effort to keep Henry from returning to Navarre and raising arms against France in the war everyone knows is inevitable.

The peace promised by Henry and Margot's royal marriage has fallen through spectacularly.

And until we know what happens next, until we understand the strange magic that lets Henry live, we all think it best for me to lie low until we can leave for Navarre. Margot is still publicly his queen, but Henry's court knows the truth.

He assures me it won't be long before we can share the news of our marriage with everyone. But when I listen to the unnatural beat of his heart, I wonder if it's better for the truth to stay hidden.

Paris is still in shambles. Battle and fire scar countless buildings' faces, and while life flickers in the windows of some, many more remain dark and vacant. Even weeks after the massacre, fishermen won't fish for fear of what else they might catch.

Almost everyone has lost something in the fray, but as I walk, I see neighbors restoring broken shutters, girls watching the children of the entire block as their parents rebuild collapsed stables. Shopkeepers throw open their doors (or what's left of them) to give food and wine to the hungry. Paris is a city of passion and practicality. Life must go on, whether the people in power like it or not.

I walk past them all, drawing no attention in my plain cloak.

I detour to the arrondissement where Louise's apothecary

stood and pull up Oncle's ring from beneath my bodice. It gleams slyly. I tilt it in the sunlight, feeling a phantom ache in my limbs. What would happen if I willed the ichor to summon the Societas Solis? Would I be welcomed as hero or hag?

I remove my glove and trace the golden center.

A thought rises, fragile as the first spring flowers thrusting up from the snow. My fingers still.

Would it help me find Oncle?

The gold fills my vision until it's all I can see.

A scream shatters my focus. I drop the ring and reach for my knife, but then the sound dissolves into bright, wild laughter. Children playing. Of course.

I drag an unsteady hand down my face and pick up the ring. Anémone nudges my back, and it slips from my fingers once more. I laugh. Clearly my horse knows better than I do.

"Oh, all right then." The chain snaps easily.

I throw it with all my might. A glittering wink across the broad blue sky, disappearing into the charred wood and ash where the Societas Solis lair once stood.

I stare at where it went and will my heart to slow.

It's gone.

Unless someone else finds it, turns it over curiously, wondering what it is. Unless I climb up there now and give the people of Paris a new reason to feel troubled. It would be so easy to get back. I could—

I stop the thought in its tracks.

I breathe in and out until the panicked feeling subsides, until it's an errant thought and no longer an itch in my limbs.

434 | ERIN COTTER

I lead Anémone onward. If Oncle wants to find me, he'll have to try some other way.

The ring's presence is a glare at my back, demanding I return.

I ignore it and keep walking.

Home becomes a tidy stone cottage in Faubourg Saint-Germain. Margot begged me to stay within city limits, but after the bloodbath of the St. Bartholomew's Day massacre, the great walls surrounding Paris no longer felt like a protection, but a trap.

Madame Dupont and Jehan wait for me inside. The stern housekeeper's shoulders soften. "We expected you sooner." Jehan nods, worried lines finally easing from his brow.

I think about the ring. Guilt sparks through me. "Sorry. Something kept me."

She nods curtly and gestures to the table. "Well, hurry up. Dinner won't eat itself."

There are only two chairs, one with a rickety leg, so Jehan volunteers to eat sitting upon a footstool. It's surprisingly nice to sit here with the two people who've known me the longest. It's almost enough for me to pretend that everything's the same as before.

When we're done, Madame Dupont whisks the plates away and rejoins with a suspiciously clinking canvas satchel.

"I salvaged these for you." Within is my jewelry, silver and rubies and gold. I run my fingers over the gems, touched by her forward thinking. They'll sell for a hefty sum if I need it.

Jehan scoffs, crossing his arms. "You deserve more than

this. You had nothing to do with our lord's plots. You shouldn't be selling your things for money!"

I try to placate him. "It's only until we head to Navarre—"

He smacks a hand on the table. "Gabriel would *not* approve!"

"Perhaps not," Madame Dupont says, practical as ever. "But the estate would've never gone to Jac, and a traitor's wealth is seized by the crown." She stands and looks to me. "The new lord of the d'Argenson-Aunis estate wrote and asked that all Gabriel's servants who wish to remain in service return to him. I'm going back. My sister's family lives close, and I want to spend the rest of my days with them. This has been quite enough adventure for me." Her mouth curves into a smile. "It's been an honor to know you, Jac."

There's a sudden lump in my throat. Madame Dupont has been with me for as long as I can remember. She near raised me. She was the person I ran to with skinned knees, who fed me broth when I was sick. I want to ask her to stay, offer to pay her double what Oncle did. But even if I could do that, something in her eyes stops me. An exhaustion that wasn't there before. She's grieving Oncle's loss as much as I am, the loss of our entire way of being. I swallow down the lump instead. "Of course. Travel well, and thank you for your service. I owe you so much."

She curtsies to me one last time.

Jehan bows as deeply to me as he would to Oncle.

"I want to stay in your service if you'll have me, mademoiselle."

Madame Dupont looks amused. "Do you care to arrange hair as one of your duties, Jehan?"

His ears go pink. "If Jac wills it," he says, "I'll do it."

Madame Dupont cackles, and Jehan's ears go ever redder. I take pity on him. "If you want to stay, you're more than welcome. But there might be less adventure than you imagine. I too have had quite enough of it to last me a while."

He bows again. "Thank you, mademoiselle."

I duck my head, hiding how my smile trembles, how much it means to me that I don't have to lose them both today. "You must call me Jac like everyone else. I'm no lady anymore."

He puts his hand on the pommel of his sword. "You'll always be my lady. I know what you did to end the massacre. I would choose to serve you again and again as long as I live." His eyes lift, watching me carefully, and I suddenly know he knows about the divine light, the ichor of the gods, even though Oncle was sworn to secrecy.

The realization—that Oncle told Jehan something he hid from me—would've once gutted me. Now I'm just glad to know that Oncle had someone to lean on even as the terrible weight of his vow slowly crushed him.

Jehan was always Oncle's man, through and through. I bite back a smile.

"I suppose a girl alone could use the help of a sworn guardsman," Madame Dupont admits.

I gesture to the rustic cottage, its splintering furniture and the flowers growing rogue beyond the windows. "Welcome to my kingdom, Jehan. I have dire need of your services here."

. . .

Jehan and I fall into a comfortable rhythm within Saint-Germain. We stroll through its famed markets and dutifully attend mass at the ancient abbey. If our neighbors think it disreputable that a woman lives alone with only a footman, no one says anything. The ruby gleaming on my left hand lets them craft their own stories, and I don't correct them. More than one woman was widowed in the massacre.

But God, how I miss Henry and Margot! The letters Jehan brings me aren't nearly enough. I don't miss the court and how it shrinks the vast world to the size of a single cramped ballroom, but I miss them, with a tender fierceness that makes my eyes well up whenever I dwell on it for too long.

Margot lasts only three weeks before she bursts into my cottage.

"Is this where Henry has been keeping you?" She spins in a circle, aghast, the circumference of her fine skirt brushing nearly every piece of furniture in the room. "Why, this isn't a place for a queen! I'll have words with Henry; he must fix this." She laughs and takes my hands. "I cannot wait for you to become the queen publicly and free me! No one trusts me at all. Some of Henry's advisors claim I put a spell on him to make him think you were his bride. Can you believe it?"

"After the things I've seen, I would believe it," I say with complete seriousness. "I've missed you, Margot, but you shouldn't be here. No one can know I'm still near the city."

She pouts prettily, even as a flush fills her cheeks. "I know, but I was worried about you. You never share anything with me in your letters."

That's because I can't. But I keep the words to myself. Instead I summon up a smile. I want it to be reassuring, but I know it's as limp as the radishes in our kitchen. Neither Jehan nor I can quite figure out how to cook yet.

"You might have to play queen for a little longer."

Her eyes narrow. "Why?"

I say nothing, but my smile turns sad.

She sighs, long and mighty. "You and Henry are planning something I'll hate, aren't you? That's why you won't tell me a thing. I might try to stop it."

"Perhaps," I say hedgingly.

Instead of wheedling an answer from me, Margot bursts into tears. She wraps me in an embrace tight with a feeling I can't lay a finger on. "As long as we are together, I don't care how it happens!"

I squeeze her back. "I want that too."

After she leaves, I realize what the feeling is.

It feels like a goodbye.

CHAPTER FORTY-SEVEN

WHEN CRIMSON AND gold paint the horizon and the roads grow littered with fallen leaves, I see Henry again.

He's finally been granted leave from Paris by the Valois family. Not that they frame it like that, of course.

I meet him at the very outskirts of Saint-Germain, where charming windmills whir alongside the Seine and drying laundry snaps in the brisk wind. With Margot's help, Henry managed to give his men the slip and come alone, his simple clothes all the disguise he needs. After all, who would ever expect to find a king in Saint-Germain?

I show him the ducks roosting beneath the willow tree. We sample all my favorite things from the marketplace. We talk about everything and nothing, the warm autumn sun burnishing it all with a hazy bronze glow.

His hand is always in mine, his arm around my waist, lips on my brow, as if I would disappear if we were to ever be apart for more than a moment.

My neighbors smile knowingly as they spot me leading him home, their delight that my husband lives, that I'm not alone after all, making my heart soar. One boy even gives a bawdy cheer and tosses flowers beneath our feet as his mother slams their window shut.

Henry laughs, sweeping me unexpectedly into his arms before carrying me over the threshold.

Jehan, bless his heart, has the good sense to spend his night somewhere else.

Afterward, we sprawl across the bed linens in the moonlight. Henry combs my hair with reverent fingers, and I relax into it, as supine as a cat, more content than I've ever felt in my life.

"I like this."

Henry kisses my neck. He knows I don't speak of what we have just done, but the entire day. The simple pleasure of two people in love, alone and together at last. "I never dreamed it could be easy," I say.

He pulls me closer, slotting me against him like I've always belonged there. His whisper makes me shiver. "When it's good, it's easy."

I feel the steady thud of his heartbeat. I turn, pressing my hand against his chest. The scar on his skin is grave and frightening, thick and spiderwebbed and red still, even weeks after the injury. If I had kept Oncle's ring (and perhaps I should've just for this), I wonder if I pressed it to my skin if I would see a faint glow in his scar.

Henry kisses my temple, but his eyes stick to the small strongbox on the cupboard beside the bed. If I focus, I can almost hear a thumping coming from within it.

"My life is tied to that immortal heart."

I trace the panes of his face, the strong line of his jaw. "I know."

I've done many experiments in Saint-Germain. I've held the undead heart beneath coursing water. I've brought it near fire and near deep cold. Each situation has caused Henry to gasp, his fist to his breastbone, sending advisors and courtiers crying and scrambling to his aid. Afterward they mutter darkly that this is the unholy work of his queen, Marguerite de Valois, who learned the ways of the occult from her mother's black-skirted lap.

Like all tantalizing lies, this one too has some truth to it.

My sweet king's immortal heart is too breakable for the world's roughness.

If something happens to the heart, then Henry will die.

I swallow hard, saying the words we haven't dared to put in writing, the thing I couldn't share with Margot, the truth we're putting off with every long glance and each lingering kiss.

"We can't stay together. If your enemies knew—" My voice breaks. I see his slack face, feel his blood cooling against my skin once more. "If even one of your enemies discovered what binds you to life—"

Henry crushes me to his chest. "I know. Oh God, I know!"

I force myself to keep talking, to say the things that must be said because he's already crying. "Leaving France is a must, of course. I thought about Spain, but the Inquisition gives me pause. Italy could work." My smile is a shield, lifted to hide how my heart is being torn asunder. "I wouldn't mind escaping winter." I need to go somewhere no one would think to look for me.

Henry scoffs, already shaking his head. "No. As long as I live, you'll never be alone and wanting."

I grit my teeth, hating how he's making this harder. "We both knew this was goodbye, Henry. Must you make it more painful?"

He stretches one long, lovely arm over me to pluck a folded notice from his discarded doublet. "You're not the only one capable of scheming and plotting."

"What's this?" I whisper, even though I can read the missive and its royal stamp quite clearly. A deed to a château near the Col d'Aubisque mountain pass deep in Navarre.

"I have had it made out to Jacqueline de Bourbon. Please forgive me for giving you my name. It seemed best given—" He hesitates.

"Given how I'm a traitor to the French crown?" I suggest dryly.

He smiles sharply, gaze darkening. "No. Given that you're my wife and what's mine is now yours."

His look steals the air from my lungs, leaving me with nothing but a soft "*oh*."

He draws me closer, my curves tucked against his muscled side. "As much as you'd like to, you're not exiling yourself, Jac. If keeping me alive means keeping me from you, then it's not a life I want to live."

I trace a finger along the parchment. Will I ever be able to look at him when he says and does things like this? Will he ever not make me feel like I could burst? "What's the château like?"

"It's built above a gorge. A narrow staircase carved into

the mountain leads to it. A strong swordswoman could defend it alone."

My smile grows. "Jehan will be so excited to teach me. He tires of plaiting hair."

Henry laughs. "There is a stable at the bottom of the stairs. I've ordered it rebuilt for you. Pau, the royal city, is only a half day's ride away."

"A half day's ride away," I whisper wonderingly.

"Aye." He strokes my hand, his thumb catching and lingering on my ruby ring. "The château is small, but there's more than enough room for us and Margot and all her dogs."

"And Margot's school." I prod him sharply. "You promised her! It's the least you can do if she must pretend to be your queen."

He lays a fist over his scarred chest. "You know I honor my promises. I told my builders to set up her school in your estate's village, but if it's châteaux you two want, then it's châteaux you'll get. The winters can't recommend themselves, but I hope everything else is to your liking."

I nod breathlessly. There is a swelling in my chest, burgeoning voices rising in a chorus. "And what of you?"

He shrugs carelessly. "What about me? I have armies to lead, but I'll be there as much as I can."

I glance again at the hidden strongbox. "But what if someone suspects?"

A single finger catches my chin, pulls me toward the devastating recklessness of his smile. "Then let them wonder. I'm never, ever letting you go. We can't be together how we imagined, but you will always be my queen." He kisses me, long and languorous, until my thoughts scatter and I nearly forget what we were talking about. "My heart belonged to you long before this."

"I'll keep it safe forever." I've never meant anything more.

"I know," he says. "I wouldn't have anyone else guarding it."

The darkness of his stare spreads. His hands reach hungrily for me. I fall into them gladly, feeling how his blood rushes, how mine answers.

The tenderhearted king. The princess with an eye for queens. The girl born from scandal.

There's never been a royal marriage quite like ours.

THERE IS NO doubt among the people of Aas: their mistress is strange.

'Tis strange how she refuses to answer to any name or title but Jac, how she strides around the village in trousers, followed by a pack of tiny white dogs, to check on the school herself. 'Tis strange how messengers scurry in and out of her estate at all hours of the day, none of them lingering in Aas for more than a night. She is strange because the queen of Navarre, Marguerite, lives with her for months, the women's laughter spilling from the château's high walls down the mountain gorge.

In the spring her oncle, a stern man who walks with a limp, comes to live with her. He doesn't take over managing the château as expected, but instead joins the newly opened school as its arms master. He shares both the position and a small house with the smiling manservant who came with their mistress and only answers questions about their lady's past with a mysterious wink.

But by far the strangest thing about their mistress is how often the king of Navarre visits her in their tiny village in the middle of nowhere.

The king calls upon her whenever he pleases. The morning, the dead of night, but always with few men at his side. He comes up the steps reverently, his face brighter than the sun itself. She always stands at the top of the great stone steps to greet him, her dark braid whipping in the wind.

Why does Good King Henry, scion of the kingdom, leader of armies, fall to his knees before their strange mistress at the edge of the earth? Men whisper he's the greatest warrior who ever lived. That he's impervious to the bolts and blades of France. That God himself cups the king in his hand, keeping him from harm to protect the Navarrese people from their enemies.

Perhaps their mistress is a witch. A sly sorceress whose powers protect the king. It's why he must come to their village so often, to beg her favor and lay offerings at her feet.

They say this with winks and nods, a murmured prayer, a sprinkling of salt on their windowsills to ward off the dark things in the shadows.

Perhaps she's a witch. And that would be all well and good.

After all, everyone knows there's some truth to every tale about magic.

ACKNOWLEDGMENTS

Everyone warned me that a sophomore book was a very tricky thing to write, and they were right! *A Traitorous Heart* would not be possible without the wildly talented people behind it.

My deepest gratitude goes to my editor, Nicole Ellul, for saying yes to a very weird book idea! Your boundless enthusiasm and keen editorial eye have transformed *A Traitorous Heart* from a first draft—so terrible that I cringed when I sent it to you—into a story that I'm very proud of. Please never stop telling your writers to put more romance on the page!

A million thank-yous go to the rest of the fabulous team over at Simon & Schuster: Jessica Egan, Krista Vossen, Hilary Zarycky, Kimberly Capriola, Sara Berko, Mitch Thorpe, Amy Lavigne, Kendra Levin, Justin Chanda, and Anne Zafian. This book would not exist without y'all, and I'm grateful I got to work with so many of you a second time!

I'm thankful for both agents who worked on this project: Hilary Harwell and Kari Sutherland. Hilary, I'm grateful to you for encouraging me to write about the things that interest me—even if it brings us to the French Wars of Religion! Kari, thank you for jumping into this project in medias res and making sure I had everything I needed as I finished it.

Thank you, Mona Finden, for creating the moody, opulent cover of my dreams! Jamie Pacton, thank you for your unbelievably kind blurb; I feel so lucky to have you in my corner. Carlie Sorosiak, thank you for not just asking, but demanding that you read an early draft to reassure me that the book was not in as bad of shape as I had feared! This intervention was sorely needed and much appreciated.

My writing community is truly the best, and I'm grateful to every person who told me everything would be fine during the Trying Times of this sophomore book. Thank you to Adrianna Cuevas, Catherine Bakewell, Matthew Hubbard, Pascale Lacelle, Rachel Lynn Solomon, and every other person who has gushed in my direct messages or let me gush in theirs.

Thank you to my friends who have had to hear an awful lot about this project. Please know that if I owe you a text, a call, or a meal, I'll make good on my promises soon! Special thanks goes to Alyssa Morris for helping me navigate the plunge into freelancing with practicality and grace.

Thank you to Andrew at Mondo Sports Therapy for quite literally getting me back on my feet. I told you that you'd end up in this book!

Thank you to my family for supporting me just as much in my wins as in my losses. To my parents, thank you for championing me in this new career, and in everything else, for my whole life.

Thank you to my animals: Tybalt, Hermione, and the entire parade of foster cats. I wouldn't go as far as to say you supported me while I was writing this book (if anything, there were many moments where y'all were active saboteurs to the process), but you did remind me to touch grass, which was more important.

Loren Cressler, you were right. Your dissertation *was* a fantastic book idea. Thanks for the inspiration, and for making sure I didn't accidentally starve/poison myself on deadline. You make my life incredibly full.

To all the booksellers and readers who have read or recommended my work: THANK YOU SO MUCH! My career would not exist without you, and there actually aren't enough thanks-yous in the world for me to express how much your support means to me. I really hope I didn't kill off your favorite character in this book.

AUTHOR NOTE

While Catherine de' Medici's prophecy does not come to pass in *A Traitorous Heart*, the Valois line did end shortly after the awful St. Bartholomew's Day massacre. King Charles IX died of consumption in 1575 and left the throne to his younger brother, Henry III. Henry III was assassinated in 1589 without an heir, and so the crown of France passed over to a distant cousin: Henry de Bourbon, the king of Navarre.

Henry IV was the first of the Bourbon kings, which would be the last royal family in France. The preserved heart of the last dauphin, Louis XVII, is currently interred in a crystal jar in the Saint-Denis Cathedral. DNA tests have proven that the boy is the son of Louis XVI and Marie Antoinette.